Praise for
THE LAUNCHING OF SCAEVA

'The Launching of Scaeva has a magnificent sense of place . . . . . . a fascinating story based on real events, intertwined with mythology . . . . . . This novel has the ingredients of a fantastic historical tale.'

' . . . . a thrilling historical novel. The life and journey of Scaeva is rich with superb detail and storytelling.'

Faber Academy Reviewer

About the Author

Roger Brook was born in London. After several years of doing not a lot, he settled into a career in IT spanning thirty-five years, which took him to several locations in Europe and the USA. The germ of an idea for a series of historical novels was in incubation for many years before he took early retirement from his final IT position as a software engineer with Rolls Royce. After a further five years of research, the first book of the series 'The Launching of Scaeva', was completed. He has two children and now lives in South Gloucestershire with his wife, Carol.

King of Kings

Book I

The Launching of Scaeva

Roger Brook

Basilica Books

A CIP catalogue record for this book is available from the British Library.

Paperback ISBN 978-1-0687807-1-4
Hardback ISBN 978-1-0687807-6-9

Copyediting and editorial advice: Erica, a druid
Maps: Michael Athanson
Portraits: Rachel James
Cover design: Philip Avery

First published in the United Kingdom in 2024 by Basilica Books

For information regarding further books in this series visit:
www.facebook.com/rogerbrookauthor

For Rosanna, Timothy, and Brianna

AUTHOR'S NOTE

Readers who wish to clarify the terminology of the
Roman Republic or would like to refer to a list of places
or characters mentioned in the text will find a glossary at
the end of this book followed by a dramatis personae of
all the characters who play an active part in the story.

FRONT COVER ILLUSTRATION

Adapted from an engraving by Edmund Evans in a book by James Doyle dated 1864 and entitled: 'A Chronicle of England BC 55 – AD 1485'. The description reads: 'The Standard Bearer of the Tenth Legion jumps from his ship and marches up the shores of England, leading the Roman invasion.'

The name of the standard-bearer is thought to be Marcus Cassius Scaeva. Who, as legend would have it, was also instrumental in Caesar's crossing of the Thames the following year. According to Suetonius, he was wounded in action at Dyrrhachium in 48 BC.

Much less is known of his namesake, Scaeva of the Trinovantes.

He appears only in, 'A History of the Kings of Britain', a book completed in 1136 by author Geoffrey of Monmouth. Scaeva is named as the son of a duke, given to Julius Ceasar as a hostage for security in a pact that would enable Caesar to gain possession of Britain. In return, the duke would have Caesar's assistance in subduing his warlike cousin, King Cassibellaun.

Scaeva is never mentioned again, by Monmouth or anyone else. This is his story …

PROLOGUE

The hermit had lived amongst the reed beds for as long as it had taken his beard to reach his waist. He had lived amongst people, and he had lived alone, and he knew what he preferred. People meant war and strife. In his ramshackle thatched hut, half stable for his horse and workshop, half living quarters for himself, he had almost everything he needed. What he couldn't provide for himself, he bartered for in the village market once a week, half a morning's ride away. Only he knew the route through the causeways in the marshes, so he never had visitors, until today.

Today, there was something almost imperceptible in the air that was different, disturbingly different. He turned from his workbench in the stable, where he made the baskets he sold at the market and stepped outside. The wind through the reeds from across the river smelt different. He ventured around the back of the stable and peered across the high stalks towards the river. Sea birds were circling something on the riverbank.

He picked his way towards the circling birds and there, caught in the reeds in shallow water, was a coracle. He approached the small craft apprehensively. There was an iron-bound wooden trunk in the middle and a body of a man lying on his side in a curve around the inside of the hull. It was motionless. The hermit broke off a long stalk, crept closer, and from a safe enough distance, prodded the man behind the ear. No movement. Wading into the water to reach the small round boat, he grabbed the rail around the rim and dragged it to the bank. The man was bound hand and foot, unconscious but still breathing. He was a big man, far too heavy for the hermit to drag out of the coracle, and the trunk looked heavy too, so he regained the bank and returned to the stable. He had a small horse-drawn cart he used to transport his baskets, so he harnessed the horse and led him back to the riverbank. Attaching the harness chain to the metal cleat on the rim of the small craft, he urged the horse to pull. It wasn't enough to get the load onto the bank without breaking the cleat under the strain, so he returned to the water, this time waist-deep, and pushed from behind. Once the coracle was on the bank, it slid easily over the flattened reeds back to the stable.

Rescuing the stranger was a natural human reaction, but what to do now? The first thing was to cut the ties that bound his wrists and ankles. There was blood where they had cut into his skin and the side of his face was blistered. The man had been in the boat for a long time. The hermit knew that druid priests used this method of exiling perpetrators of failed attempts to usurp power in a tribe. They would be cast into the jurisdiction of a river spirit to transport them far away. His river ran through the territories of many Belgic tribes before reaching his sanctuary close to the sea. He did wonder fleetingly if the contents of the trunk might give a clue to the stranger's identity, but those thoughts were instantly dismissed. The less the hermit knew about this man, the better. He didn't even need to know his name. The fact that he was both deaf and dumb was no hindrance to his weekly transactions in the village, and no complication to living his chosen solitary life, but this situation would be different. As a member of the human race, he felt obliged at the very least to give this man shelter, food, and water enough for him to recover and then send him on his way, but even that carried a risk.

The first thing the stranger was conscious of was the smell of hay and horses. He felt hungry and weak. Before he even opened his eyes, he was aware that his whole body ached. His wrists and ankles were sore, and one side of his face hurt. Something stiff around his neck had chaffed against his skin. He gingerly raised his hand from under the rank woollen blanket draped over him to the object around his neck. It was a leather strap, there was no buckle, but someone had fastened it at the back with rivets. His eyelids were so stuck together with dirt and dried sweat he needed his fingers to prise them apart. It took several seconds for them to focus. He was in a small stable; just one horse, just one cart, single axle, tipped on its back with the traces pointing up to the roof beams. In the corner were a workbench and a pile of reed and wicker baskets, some of them half-finished. He tried to prop himself up on his elbows, but he was too weak, and the weight of a heavy chain attached to the neck strap pulled him flat on his back again on the bed of straw he'd been lying in. A few moments later, a figure appeared silhouetted in the open doorway. The slender, long-bearded figure stepped inside the stable, knelt next to his captive, gently lifted his head, and, from a wooden pail, carefully ladled some water between his lips.

For the next two days, the hermit went about his business, making his baskets and fishing for carp amongst the reeds with a line, and eels with his bare hands on the muddy riverbank. Now that his captive was conscious, he fed him a plate of grilled carp or a bowl of stewed eels twice a day until he was strong enough to feed himself and help himself to water from the pail.

The hermit had been in a quandary about how he was going to release the stranger once he had recovered enough to leave. He couldn't just signal for him to go; the man might never find his way out of the marshes. He dared not drive him to the village in case he remembered the route and betrayed his location to anyone. He couldn't insist he departed the way he came, on the river in the coracle, so he kept the stranger tethered until he decided what to do.

After four days, the stranger was up on his feet and exploring the stable to the limit allowed by the chain, and that wasn't much. The hermit now had a plan of action. He would attach the end of the chain to the cart, blindfold the stranger, lead him out of the marshes to the outskirts of the village and there release him back into the community.

The following day, the horse plodded his usual trail through the causeways, but this time he went beyond the market, down to the fishing port on the coast. The stranger had been thinking about a future for himself across the sea in the land of the Britons. No one would know him there and he had heard a good living could be made as a mercenary. His only regret was that he would never see his son again, but probably his son was already dead. The stranger bartered a horse, cart, and a cargo of baskets for a one-way passage across the sea for himself and his precious chest.

Meanwhile, the hermit floated face down in the shallows amongst the reeds, sightless eyes wide open, the carp and eels staring back up at him.

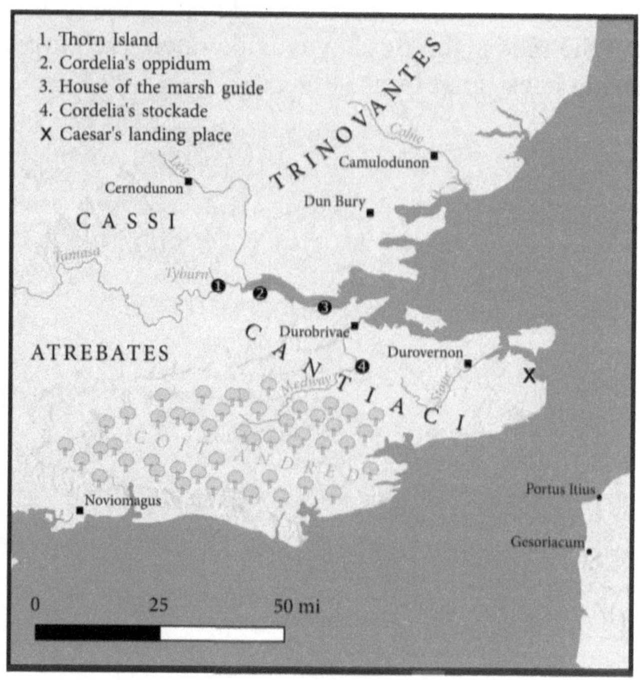

Southeastern Britain 55 BC

PART ONE

BRITANNIA

'By far the most civilised inhabitants are those living in Cantium—a purely maritime district—whose way of life differs little from the Gauls. Most of the tribes in the interior do not grow corn but live on milk and meat, and wear skins. All the Britons dye their bodies with woad, which produces a blue colour, and shave the whole of their bodies except the head and upper lip.'

Julius Caesar, Gallic Wars V.14

I

22nd August 55 BC
Cernodunon, the Stronghold of the Cassi

Heli knew he was dying. He focused his fading vision on the giant stag antlers and auroch horns of his ceremonial headdress, suspended above his bed below the smoke-blackened thatch of his sleeping chamber, until blackness was all that remained. His vision had now completely gone, and he stood at the veil between life and death, but he was still aware of the presence of his sons on either side of his bed. All his adult life he had naturally assumed that he would breathe his last impaled on a spear or hacked to pieces on a battlefield. He felt cheated of the glory. Stories of the bards, about old men who died in their beds, were less often repeated than those of men granted a glorious death by the gods. But he was spent and ready for the journey to the Otherworld, a happy resting place to await his new incarnation. Nennius, his younger son, knelt by the bed, held his father's hand, and passed his other palm across his eyes.

Seeing no reaction, he softly closed the lids but still whispered, 'Father, can you hear me?' Heli responded with a weak squeeze of his son's hand.

The elder son, Vellaunus, on noticing this last remaining sign of life, knelt at the other side of the bed.

'Hear this, father. You are a king, but I swear that I will be the high king, The Brehin. king of all the kings of Prydain before the end of my time here.' He paused, sensing his brother's tension, held his troubled gaze for a moment, then switched his eyes back to his father's motionless face. 'You named me "Overlord" and I will not follow you to the Happy Place until Ludd is avenged, until every other tribe bows to me, and I have driven the invaders back into the sea.'

Nennius was about to speak when they both detected the merest inclination of their father's head and then he was completely still. There was no longer even the slightest movement in his chest. Nennius' words caught in his throat, and with his own eyes now tight shut, to stem the unmanly tears welling up inside him, he gently folded his father's arms across his chest.

His brother rose slowly to his feet. 'It's done,' he said, and with a challenging glare at his younger brother, turned towards the opening of the curtained bedchamber within the large circular room. Speaking over his shoulder as he left, he rasped, 'I'll order Hirelglas to summon the assembly.' As Vellaunus strode outside, blinking in the strong sunlight, he caught sight of his nephew waiting with a group of tribesmen. 'Hirelglas, send out the riders. All regions. Heli is dead.'

Hirelglas had been awaiting the word. He knew what to do. He was a loose-limbed youth with a shock of uncut blonde hair, but still too immature to be bearded and was perpetually daubed in the blue battle insignia of the warriors. Blue-faced and, unlike the other tribesmen clothed in goatskin tunics and drab woollen trousers, totally naked, he idolised his uncle and spent many hours training with the chariots and war horses. Despite his youth, he had earned the respect of many of the older warriors, several of whom followed the young prince as he turned and made swiftly for the corrals of patient horses. He and his party of riders quickly mounted and set off at a gallop towards the open gates at the far end of the stronghold, and out through the woods.

King Heli and his tribe of Celtic Britons, the Cassi, had for many years been opposing the flow of migrants and merchants from the lands of the Belgae across the East Sea. In an attempt to form an alliance to hold back the invaders, Heli's eldest son Ludd had married his cousin Luna, a princess of the neighbouring tribe, the Trinovantes, but he was murdered and usurped by Luna's half-brother who was in league with Ludd's enemies. Ludd's young sons were saved from their parents' fate and brought back under the protection of King Heli, their grandfather. Since then, the Cassi and the Trinovantes had been at war. It was a war that the Trinovantes, reinforced by an ever-increasing flow of forces from the continent, with their modern weapons, were winning. The other Celtic tribes had long retreated far to the west, but Heli had stood firm in defence of his territory that stretched many miles southwards as far as the banks of the Tamasa. Forests and marshes protected his stronghold, a place of great natural strength, further fortified by double rows of ditches and high ramparts. From there, Heli's warriors and charioteers defended their ancient boundaries and kept his people insulated from the incoming tide of the outside world.

Nennius, unlike his warlike elder brother, accepted that the tide could not be held back forever. What's more, although he would never dare admit it, he understood the benefits that peaceful integration would bring. During the perpetual war with the Trinovantes, he had on occasion met with Trinovantian emissaries to arrange a mutual exchange of hostages during brief cessations of hostilities. During such missions, he had gained a glimpse of their way of life. He envied the clothes they wore, and the food they ate, although much of their imported fripperies he regarded as having no value. The ards they used had shares made of iron instead of the primitive stone shares of the Cassi. This prepared the soil for a more plentiful harvest of grain. He had seen the spinning devices their potters used to make an impressive array of perfectly smooth round vessels of varied shapes and sizes. The clayware of the Cassi was crude by comparison. Although the Cassi were expert bronze-workers, they reserved iron for their weapons and warcraft. He couldn't confront his more charismatic brother about these benefits to their way of life on his own. He would have to entreat the druids to order Vellaunus to make peace, but now was not the time.

Nennius pulled the pelt blanket up over his father's face, a death mask of resigned serenity. He then knelt beside his father's favourite hound, tenderly cradling its noble head in his hands, and looking meaningfully into its mournful eyes. Heli would need him on his journey. This was his way of saying goodbye. Then he turned, stood up slowly, and headed for the open doorway. The sun, low in the sky now, was in his eyes and it reminded him that the height of summer had passed, and the days were growing shorter.

Outside the large conical thatched and wattle-walled abode, the tribal council, dressed in assorted animal skins, had assembled behind Eneid, the High Priest and his party of druids and students. Eneid had been summoned to Cernodunon from his sanctuary deep within the sacred oak woods to perform the funeral rites of the tribal chieftain. His tall, bony hooded figure cast an even longer shadow. Nennius nodded to them and Eneid, carrying his ceremonial ash sapling, led his followers, each carrying a large stone to the doorway of Heli's residence. The men placed the stones in a triangular pile across the doorway as Eneid made his ritual incantation. From under his long goatskin cloak, he withdrew a small bronze jug filled from the spring of the water nymph, the contents of which he sprinkled over the stones. Heli would remain in the care of Caita, the sacred deity of Cernodunon, until his burial ceremony.

Heli's stronghold was sited around a natural spring in a large clearing hidden deep in a forest. A double row of earthen ramparts had been raised around the perimeter with a spiked palisade atop the innermost bank and a pair of double gates built one behind the other, across gaps in both banks to form an entrance. Spreading across and above the inner gates was a palisaded platform, allowing defenders to rain missiles down upon attackers. The spring rose from a pond in a small depression in the ground at one end of the interior. A simple wooden shrine to Caita, regularly garlanded with wildflowers in the summer and berries in the winter, stood beside it. The overflow from the pond fed a stream that divided a corner of the camp and flowed out through a gap in the earthworks into a marsh that further protected one side of the encampment.

In that private corner were sited the grand spacious living quarters of Heli and his sons. The sons of Ludd had lived with their grandfather since their rescue from

Camulodunon but would now be quartered with their uncles until the removal of the stones on the day of Heli's funeral. Across the narrow stream, forded in several places by simple arrays of planks, was an open area used for tribal gatherings, in the centre of which was a sacrificial stone used for offerings to the gods. The dwellings of other noble families of the tribe were spread around the rest of the perimeter. An assortment of animal pens, forges and workshops and the smaller mean roundhouses of carpenters, smiths, tanners and their families that worked in them were clustered behind the guardhouses at the gated end of the enclosure. Scattered around the encampment were drying frames for animal skins, and pits gradually being filled with discarded oddments of stone, bone, fragments of clay pottery and wood that were now broken, blunt, or unable to be put to any other use. Beside the guard houses were stables and corrals for the war horses.

Outside the entrance, a track led through the forest to the sacred grove of the druids where Heli's burial ceremony would be taking place. In the open common land beyond the woods, primitively cultivated fields of wheat had recently been harvested while cattle, sheep and goats grazed in enclosed pastures.

Such was the stronghold of Heli, now passed to Vellaunus. Similar tribal settlements and farmsteads of his clansmen were stationed in each of the regions throughout his territory, each region overseen by a thane, who had the authority to raise militia amongst the local menfolk in times of tribal conflict. The number of servants, warriors, and retainers he could muster was dependent upon his birth and fortune. Laws, religion, healing, learning, and justice were all administered by the druids, otherwise, the people were free to live their lives and work in the fields and forges, potteries, and workshops according to their skill. Copses of woodland still fringed the tops of hills, but the lower pastures were given over to grazing lands and primitive crop farming.

This was his tribal homeland. The villages and settlements across this area were his people and lived in peace under his protection. It was to this population that Hirelglas, young prince and nephew of Vellaunus and Nennius, was directing groups of horsemen to spread the news of Heli's passing and summon the Nobles and their attendants to the funeral. They would come to pay their respects to the old king and swear their allegiance to the new.

II

22nd August 55 BC
Near Camulodunon, the Citadel of the
Trinovantes

Scaeva squinted at the red ball of the sun as it set on the flat horizon. For the first time in his young life, he wondered, how and why did Lugh make his daily journey through the sky, and where did he go at night? Every morning, he reappeared on the opposite horizon over the East Sea at the mouth of his river. He had never questioned it before. His thoughts were disturbed by the excited shouts of his older brother Ebracus, who was a short distance away with their grandfather. He was being taught how to launch stones from a leather slingshot, and after weeks of trying, had brought down his first bird.

Scaeva was pleased for him, because although two years older, at twelve, Ebracus was behind his younger brother in most other respects. Ebracus was taller and heavier, but Scaeva ran faster and further and mastered skills more quickly. They both had inherited their grandfather's bright blue eyes. Their dark hair was cut into the same rough fringe but whereas Ebracus, whose eyes were narrow and set into a long bony face, was clearly his father's son, Scaeva whose eyes were round pools of misleading innocence, had the oval face and lightly freckled cheeks of his departed mother.

As Ebracus raced off to retrieve his prey, Scaeva chased after him, being careful not to catch up with him before his brother had reached the stricken creature. The plump, brown-feathered bird was still trying to scuttle along the ground and Ebracus hesitated, not sure what to do next.

Scaeva stepped in, picked up the bird by its neck and dispatched it with one slick twist. He smiled at his brother as he tossed him his prize. 'Come on, let's take it home.'

The boys both wore striped woven tunics that came down to mid-thigh over knee-length breeches. Their grandfather was similarly attired, but with breeches bound at the ankle into leather boots. He also wore a cloak fastened at the shoulder with a heavy brooch and carried a leather bag in which he kept assorted slings and a collection of smooth round pebbles.

They were about to race home when their grandfather waved his stick. 'Wait! You can't go back like that. Just wait for me.' When the old man caught up with them, he produced a belt and a large hook from his bag. He buckled the belt loosely around Ebracus' waist, forced the sharp end of the hook through the bird's mouth and hooked it on the belt. 'Now, what did I tell you? Never give up,' his grandfather said. 'Never, ever give up. You don't ever submit and say you can't beat it, or you won't amount to anything. Now you can go home like a real hunter.' They hadn't gone a hundred paces along the shallow sunken bridleway when something stirred in the shade beneath the low branches of a single tree in the pasture beside their path.

'Look, Grandfather,' cried Scaeva, eyes wide with excitement. 'Wild ponies. Can I capture one and take it home to ride?'

He then took off across the pasture without waiting for the plaintive reply, 'No, come back, they will not let you near them, and besides, it will be dark soon and I want you safely back home.'

Disturbed by Scaeva's sudden approach, the ponies took off into the lengthening shadows of the woods surrounding the pasture. Scaeva simply took no notice of his grandfather and was undeterred by the flight of the ponies. He turned and called to Ebracus, 'Come on, I need you to help me find them.'

Ebracus looked imploringly at his grandfather.

'Go on then,' said the old man with a resigned smile. 'But as his older brother, you must make sure he is home while it is still light.'

'Wait for me, Scaeva,' he shouted and hurried off in pursuit of the younger boy, who had already reached the shadows. Ebracus turned back to his grandfather for encouragement to continue his chase, but he had disappeared from view behind a thicket at a bend in the track. Just as his grandfather had predicted, the ponies had melted into the protection of the gathering darkness under the canopy of trees by the time Scaeva reached the woods. He turned to look back; Ebracus was picked out by the evening sunlight, making his sticking-out ears appear even pinker than usual. He was hesitating on the edge of the shadows. Then, hearing movement deeper in the woods, Scaeva identified the outline of one pony just a few yards away. He crouched down and approached the animal as silently as possible, but every step he took crunched on a dry twig or rustled some early-fallen leaves. To his amazement, the pony stood its ground, sideways on and holding his gaze.

He reached out and touched it gently on its forehead, then a husky female voice behind him made him start. 'Go on, you can do it.'

Scaeva turned in shock; a tall woman, fair hair loosely tied to one side of her face, stood between a mare and her foal. There had been no sound of their approach. 'Who are you and where did you come from?' demanded the boy, trying to cover his fluster and embarrassment at being taken by surprise so easily.

'My name is Epona. I've been watching you. You have an affinity with these creatures. Shall I show you how to gain their confidence?'

Scaeva needed no second bidding. His desire to mount the animal momentarily overcame his need to know where Epona had suddenly appeared from; questions could wait. Within a few minutes, he was astride the pony, gripping its mane with both hands, its short wiry hair prickling the inside of his calves.

A worried shout interrupted the lesson. 'Scaeva, where are you?' It was the voice of Ebracus, calling from the pasture in the failing light beyond the gloom of the woods. 'Come on out, it's getting dark.'

Scaeva turned to Epona. 'That's my brother. Can I ride it out, and will you come with me? Then you can tell us all about yourself.'

'Ride on,' she replied. 'You lead, and I will follow.'

Scaeva squeezed gently with his knees and guided the pony out towards the open pasture. They broke out from the cover of the shadows about fifty paces from where

Ebracus was still peering into the darkness. Epona, who had mounted the mare, followed with the foal by their side.

Ebracus caught the sound of the movement and came running towards them. 'You've got one!' he shouted excitedly.

'Yes, and it was all with the help of Epona,' Scaeva replied triumphantly.

Ebracus was by now reaching out to pat the pony on the shoulder. 'Who is Epona?'

'Epona? Why, she's right here,' answered Scaeva, glancing behind him. To his astonishment, Epona and her companions were gone, as silently as they had appeared. 'But they were here just a moment ago. They rode out of the copse with me. You must have seen them.'

'Them? She? They? What are you talking about? There's no one there. You came out of the woods on your own. I know it's getting dark, but I saw you plainly.'

Scaeva couldn't decide whether to pretend the story about Epona was just a joke or to insist that he wasn't imagining things, but he wondered if anyone would believe him. If he just laughed it off as a silly game, he could then claim the kudos for mounting and riding the wild pony all on his own. Standing by the truth would lead to difficult conversations with his elders. From the stories his grandfather had told him, spirits, and even the gods, aided chosen people they considered to be special in some way. But why should he be chosen? He didn't think there was anything special about himself, but the mysterious lady must have been a spirit of some kind because she appeared only to him and vanished as Ebracus approached. Sticking to his story was too complicated. It would be far easier to confess to making it all up.

'All right, I can't fool you, can I? I just made it up for a laugh, to see the look on your face,' replied Scaeva with as much dismissiveness as he could muster.

'Well, you saw the look on my face, and I hope you're satisfied. Come, we must get back. Grandfather will be so proud of you.' Then he added, not even trying to hide the admiration he had for his younger brother. 'And I can't wait to see His face!'

III

22nd August 55 BC
South coast of Britain, in the land of the Cantiaci

The sun had long sunk below the horizon and the prisoner was left in complete darkness to contemplate his precipitous fall from grace. That very morning, he was the proud King of the Atrebates, appointed by none other than the Great Caesar himself, but now Commius, despite his noble demeanour and famed diplomatic connections, was in chains, betrayed by his own allies.

His mission had been going according to plan. On arrival in Prydain, he'd been treated with the utmost respect by his hosts, who gratefully received his gifts. They were most appreciative of Commius' generosity. The matching sets of solid gold jewellery, provided by Caesar as a gift to the four rulers of the coastal tribes, were of exceptional quality in the eyes of the natives. The torcs were thick and gaudy, designed to appeal to a barbarian taste, but with the ends covered with granules of precious metal, and with fine filigrees, made using methods unknown to the Britons. The bracelets were plainer, but Carvillus displayed particular delight as he fingered the fine gold brooches with bow-shaped clips, and immediately adorned his cloak with one of them. His hosts had arranged a splendid feast in his honour. It embarrassed him that thirty hand-picked and fully armed Atrebatian horsemen from his own tribe had accompanied him as bodyguards in case of difficulties. His extravagant welcome, however, was a sham.

Two weeks earlier, Carvillus had arrived in Gaul at the head of a delegation of envoys from Britannia. He bore a message written in careful Latin on a scroll bearing the royal seal of Llyr, King of the Cantiaci, from his seat at Durovernon. The message offered to cease their support for the Belgic tribes still opposed to Caesar, give hostages, and submit to Rome. All this in the hope of peace and the gaining of some benefit from increased trade; a subject on which Caesar had made them generous promises. Commius knew of Carvillus as one of the sons-in-law of the old king, who, Carvillus explained, had sadly passed away only a few months before. Accompanying him was his son, Cingetorix, and an assortment of lesser nobles and attendants.

With the benefit of hindsight, Commius now considered he was far too willing to vouch for their integrity. Although the Gauls were renowned for their deviousness, the Britons, by comparison, were simple souls lacking in sophistication. He'd assumed that Caesar's invincibility and his preparations for an expedition to their island—relayed to them by merchants and traders—had prompted their initiative. Caesar's primary concern was the lateness of the time of year for a sea-borne military operation, but the ambassadors and the news of their voluntary subservience tilted Caesar's decision in favour of making the crossing.

The plan was that Commius would escort the party back to Cantium to prepare the ground for Caesar and his Legions. The delegation had denied the rumours that much gold was to be found; instead, there was a promise of pearls and bounty enough to make the expedition worthwhile. Had it all been a deception from the beginning, or did some major event during their absence cause their plans to be hastily changed on their arrival on home soil? If it had been a hoax, Commius begrudgingly applauded their ability to keep up the pretence throughout their time in Gaul and the journey back across the sea. Carvillus' wife Rigontia and her sister, Gonerila, must have known about the deception but were not the slightest bit embarrassed at the gifts Commius had bestowed upon them. It wasn't until the feasting was over and the heavy drinking got underway that Commius retired to his quarters, unaware of the inebriated state of his bodyguards. He had been paying more attention to a dark-eyed pubescent beauty and a blonde, buxom wench old enough to be the younger girl's mother, both of whom had supported him back towards his bedchamber. His feeling of intoxication had stemmed not only from the sweet mead but also from the glowing success of his mission. However, his anticipation of a delightful end to the day was shattered when four armed warriors appeared from out of the shadows and took the place of the women who had vanished, giggling into the night.

In the pitch darkness of the tiny, windowless hut that imprisoned him, the sounds of the night were amplified. The wind picked up through the trees and the first drops of heavy rain began to fall. A sudden damp chill in the air made him shiver. He laid down on the musty sacking that would be his bed for an unknowable number of nights to come. Despite his chained wrists, he pulled his cloak around his shoulders. He must have drifted in and out of troubled sleep for several hours until voices and movement outside jolted him awake. Straining his hearing in the darkness to catch what was being said, he knew enough of their language to understand most of the orders and shouts of the men. "The Romans are coming," was a phrase that had been used all over Gaul in recent years, and Commius was familiar enough with it whatever the language or dialect. The sound of chariots being rigged, and the snorting of the horses, was unmistakable. A large body of men was being prepared for battle.

As much as Commius tried, now that he was truly awake, he could not get back to sleep again. One question kept nagging at him. Would Caesar suspect he was part of the deception? It wasn't as if the pre-emptive surrender of the Cantiaci had lulled the Romans into a false sense of security. Caesar had assembled a fleet of eighty transport vessels to convey two entire legions, the Seventh and the battle-hardened Tenth, plus several other warships for his officers. Labienus, his chief *legate*, would follow with a further eighteen transports, bearing his cavalry and heavy equipment, more than enough to contain a betrayal should the situation arise.

Just before dawn, his captors stood side-by-side, gold brooches glinting in the firelight from the many braziers dotted around the encampment and surveyed the activity with quiet satisfaction. Their spies had informed them that Caesar's fleet would sail that night. Their sons, Cingetorix and Segovax had been dispatched with a small army to deal with the youngest daughter of the old king, who had succeeded him in his will. Carefully laid plans were coming together. Taximagulus sniffed at the chilly morning air and fingered his amulet of five bronze wheels, worn around his neck in homage to Taranis, the god of thunder. He sensed a storm brewing. It was predicted to be the most devastating autumn storm in living memory, enough to turn any shipping into driftwood.

He murmured to his brother Carvillus, 'Those fucking augurs had better be right.'

Dawn broke in a cold, grey drizzle; the long spell of soft balmy days had come abruptly to an end. Nennius woke with a shiver to find that the light patchwork of lambs-wool tufts that had served as a blanket throughout the summer months was wrapped around the hunched back of his wife. His eyes struggled to become accustomed to the darkness challenged only by the faint glow of embers from the fire pit in the middle of the room. The knock on the door which had originally disturbed his sleep sounded again, a little more urgently. The myriad of thoughts that were troubling him the night before were still racing through his mind, defying all efforts to marshal them into some semblance of order. He eased his legs over the side of the bed and reached for the rough woollen shift that lay across the bench by his bedside and pulled it over his head. Nennius reasoned that his early visitor would probably be a member of the priesthood, summoning him to the pre-burial ceremony for his father. He shuffled the ten or so paces to the door, pulled aside the heavy drapes and cracked it open. There, in the early dawn drizzle, stood the bedraggled figure of one of Eneid's students. The youth cut a sad comic figure with his spindly legs and bare feet sticking out from below his goatskin cloak and his student's short sapling wand poking through his dark mop of hair in line with his shoulders.

'Wait here,' said Nennius suppressing a smile. Leaving the door slightly ajar he returned to his dressing bench. As he felt for his belt, boots and cloak, his mind raced beyond the imminent ceremony to the troubling conversations to come with his brother over the future of the crop fields his father had been encouraged to nurture by the Chief Priest.

The druids were the glue that held ancient Celtic society together and transcended tribal rivalries. Their customs and religion were widespread throughout the continent, and they were consequently quite relaxed about the influx of Gallic and Belgic people into the coastal areas of Prydain. Several years earlier, Eneid had convinced King Heli of the benefits of rearing crops, much against the advice of Vellaunus, who maintained that training horses for pulling ploughs instead of chariots and turning warriors into farmers and millers were not in the future interests of his people. Besides that, he argued, unlike a herd of cattle or sheep, a field of crops could not be moved to safety if his territory came under attack.

Now that Vellaunus was about to take his father's place at the head of the tribe, Nennius had a fight on his hands, and as ever, was inwardly fearful of crossing his more powerful and charismatic sibling. The key problem was that the complete process took years of practice; sowing, reaping, storing, milling and finally baking the sparse grain into something edible was a learning curve that was always going to be too steep for Vellaunus to bear. Unlike Nennius and Eneid, who had both sampled the breads produced by their more advanced Trinovantian neighbours, Vellaunus had shunned anything from the bordering tribes and had tried only the first paltry attempts of his novice farmers and bakers before declaring that it gave him "the shits" and wanted no further part of it.

These were the thoughts inhabiting Nennius' mind as he dressed in the semi-darkness of his hut. He suddenly became aware of them and felt ashamed, as he should have been thinking of his father on the day he was to be buried. Returning swiftly to the door by the shaft of early dawn light shining through, he yanked it open by the handle and stepped over the ring ditch, now almost overflowing with rainwater, and ducked under the eaves of the thatch in one habitual reflex movement. He then followed the soggy student out into the still morning mist and took his place next to his elder brother to witness the ceremonial removal of the stones covering the doorway to Heli's quarters.

IV

23rd August 55 BC
ROME

Marcus sat on the cold stone bench outside the back door of the schoolhouse, waiting to be introduced to his new classmates. It wasn't the chill morning air that caused his knee to tremble and bounce unconsciously. It was the thought of being pitched into a room full of boys descended from the oldest and most aristocratic families in Rome. He'd been told none other than the stepson of last year's consul, Lucius Marcius Philippus, would be one of his classmates. His slave sat next to him still dutifully holding a lantern aloft, even though dawn was breaking. Marcus' bulging leather satchel, containing books and wax tablets, was balanced carefully on his knees. Marcus had just been deposited at the schoolhouse by the *paedagogus* employed to tutor him at home.

His father had given him a stern warning to stand up for himself and not to be bullied by the other boys. He was a wealthy man; self-made from humble plebian origins who had now achieved equestrian status. He could afford to live in Rome and send his second son to one of the best schools under the tutelage of the esteemed *grammarian* Orbilius Pupillus. Marcus needn't have worried too much about being the only pleb in the classroom. His backside was just getting over its numbness when two more figures appeared out of the lightening gloom. A man and a young boy.

'Budge-up,' said the man, who Marcus assumed to be the boy's father, indicating he wanted his son to take a place on the bench. 'Are you waiting for Orbilius?'

'Orbilius Pupillus? Yes, indeed we are,' answered Marcus politely, reluctantly surrendering his—only slightly warmed—spot on the bench. 'You speak as if he's familiar to you.'

'Yes, indeed he is,' answered the boy's father, mimicking Marcus, with a wink that said, *please don't take offence. I'm only having a little joke with you.* 'Old Orbilius and my father go back a long way.' As his son snuggled his bottom into the space Marcus had just vacated, the boy's father introduced him. 'This is Quintus, and I'm afraid I must leave him with you 'cos I'm late for work.' Then, turning to his son and handing him a single wax tablet and stylus, said, 'Now you make friends with this polite young man. Behave yourself with old Orbilius. I'll pick you up later and remember. Up the Reds!'

'Up the Reds,' responded Quintus, mirroring his father's air punch, but stopping rather self-consciously at shoulder height.

With that, his father turned and set off down the hill towards the forum, the early rising sunlight reflecting off his bald patch as he passed the gaps between the buildings.

'I'm Marcus Vipsanius,' ventured Marcus.

'Quintus Horatius,' replied the boy, following suit.

'What does your father do?' asked Marcus with a nod towards the jaunty figure who had now disappeared into the long, early morning shadows.

'He works at the auction house down by the forum,' replied Quintus, just as the door behind them opened and they were ushered into the still-dark interior of the building. Marcus' slave handed him his satchel, nodded deferentially, and withdrew, leaving the boys to follow the school-house slave along a corridor leading to a large oak panelled door. In the gloom of the flickering candlelight, Marcus could just make out some carvings on the panels and, by the garb of the figures, assumed they were scenes from Greek plays. The slave tapped on the door and opened it, ushering the boys into a large airy room with high ceilings. Leather-bound books on shelves covered the walls on either side. Two large windows with open shutters dominated the wall opposite the door, and blinding sunlight shone through, showing up dust particles in the air.

From behind a desk between the windows, the soft voice of a woman addressed them. 'Welcome to the *ludus grammaticus* of my husband Lucius Orbilius. Thank you Aphrodisius, we are expecting no more new pupils this morning.' The slave bowed and left the room. The woman arose and emerged from the deep shadows behind her desk to stand in front of the boys. She was middle-aged and pleasant-faced and she leant forward, bracing the palms of her hands against her knees to match their height.

'Now, how old are you and which one of you is Marcus and which is Quintus?'

'I'm Marcus, I will soon be nine.'

'And I'm Quintus, I will be ten come December,' replied the boys in the order they were asked.

'And you may address me as Matrona. So, Marcus, what do you have in your satchel?'

'Tablets and books,' replied Marcus brightly. 'The Homer, Pindar, and Sappho I've been learning with my *paedagogus*.'

'Well, there will be no singing or playing the lyre here young man so you can take the Sappho home with you. As for the others, I will keep them here as Orbilius will be giving you a reading list at the end of lessons. And you Quintus?'

'I just have my tablet.'

'That's all you will need for this morning, Quintus. Marcus, I noticed you have a number of tablets. Take your favourite one and leave the others in your satchel with your books and collect them from me before you go home. Now there is just one thing you both will need for later.' The Matrona returned to the dark side of her desk and opened the door of a tall cupboard behind her chair. She reached up to the top shelf and retrieved two small tablets, each with a ribbon attached to a stylus. A flurry of dust particles sprang up and floated around her in the bright sunlight as she removed them from the cupboard and handed one to each of the boys. Unlike other tablets they had seen, the wax was black, and a thin film of dust remained stuck to it. 'Take these also, you will need them for this afternoon's lesson in arithmetic with the calculator.'

Today was the first day with a *grammarian* for both boys, and Orbilius had a fearsome reputation. Marcus wondered if he could be such an ogre since he had such a kindly sweet-natured wife, whilst Quintus was regretting not paying more attention to basic arithmetic in elementary school.

'I must warn you before I take you through to the classroom; most of the boys here are the sons of senators and magistrates and are not kindly disposed to children of a lower rank. That is why I am starting you two together for your first day. However, joining us most recently is the stepson of last year's consul. Octavius is his name. He is the youngest and is said to be quite bright. He is also a well-behaved boy. Remember that Orbilius is a strict disciplinarian, so behave yourselves and you will come to no harm.'

Quintus, who had been feeling just a little queasy about his first day was now full of dread, whilst Marcus, who had relaxed in the company of the kindly matrona, stiffened again and set his jaw.

The Matrona led them through a door in the back corner of her office, into a bright corridor with a row of windows on the right, illuminating a row of busts of famous poets arranged, Quintus noticed, in alphabetical order along the left. As they proceeded along the corridor, the sound of the class repeating the passages of poetry the *grammarian* was reading out to them floated above the noises coming in from the street outside. There was no door at the far end of the corridor. It simply led into the side of a veranda, open to the street. Seated on a chair in the middle of the veranda, the omnipotent figure of Orbilius faced his pupils, perched behind their desks on three pairs of benches. Despite the daylight streaming into the room, each desk still had a lighted candle. Maps decorated the walls showing all the provinces of the Republic, with the rivers and cities marked, although some were blackened by the smoke of lamps.

As the stern, wrinkled face of Orbilius turned towards them, Marcus and Quintus looked away, scanning the faces of the boys on the benches. Which one was Octavius?

V

23rd August 55 BC
A stockade in the territory of the Cantiaci

The storm that was brewing during the night failed to materialise, and early morning shards of sunlight pierced the dark grey clouds like shining spears. Cingetorix and his cousin Segovax were mounted at the head of a long column of armed warriors. A beam of light picked out a watchtower, above which the banners of the late King Llyr hung limply in the motionless morning air. As they met the rising ground, the detail of the lower earthen ramparts came into view from out of the shadows. Felled trees laid close together blocked the entrances.

Segovax turned to Cingetorix. 'Do you see that? I think they might be expecting us.'

'Maybe so,' answered Cingetorix, 'but we must pretend we come in peace. We'll keep to the story agreed with our fathers, and she will come peacefully with us.'

As they came into hailing distance, a sentry on the watchtower called down to them and the sounds of raised voices and frenzied activity arose from inside the fortifications.

'Who are you and what do you want?' was the abrupt challenge from the tower.

Cingetorix, the youngest, and by far the most diplomatic of the two young nobles, replied. 'We are the queen's nephews. We have come to report that the Roman fleet has been sighted off the coast and we have come to take her into safekeeping.'

'Wait there,' was the order from the sentry as he disappeared behind the spiked log walls of the stockade. A dozen or more guards replaced him immediately. Some with slingshots at the ready, others holding javelins aloft.

'I can't be done with this,' sneered Segovax. 'We know there are no more than a hundred men to defend the queen. Why don't we just storm the walls, kill the virgin bitch and have done with it?'

Segovax had been most aggrieved at the contents of Llyr's will. His stepmother, Gonerila, was the eldest of the king's three daughters, but she and her sister Rigontia had been estranged from the old king in his later years. The sisters had married the two most powerful warlords in his realm, Segovax's father Taximagulus and his brother, Carvillus, which had meant Llyr had lost their allegiance too. Although he had occupied the seat of authority over all the tribes of the southeastern corner of Prydain, collectively known as the Cantiaci, the power had seeped away as his health and vigour declined. Just a handful of troops in his personal bodyguard had remained loyal. When Llyr died, not five months earlier, he had already nominated his youngest daughter, the twenty-one-year-old Cordelia as ruler. With her gone, Segovax would be heir to the entire kingdom of the Cantiaci after his parents.

'We cannot do that,' insisted Cingetorix. 'The Priestess Dianann still abides with them. It was under her auspices that Llyr's will was endorsed.'

Inside the stockade, the news of the queen's nephews and their armed escort had caused more anxiety than the sighting of the Romans. Brennus, the captain of the queen's bodyguard, received the message from the cloaked and helmeted sentry in the presence of Cordelia's chief advisor, Digueillus. They had been waiting outside the only habitable building in the enclosure for the emergence of the queen from her private quarters, in order to discuss, over breakfast, the rumours of an impending Roman invasion.

'So, the stories are true?' asked Brennus with a questioning look to the old counsellor. 'If so, we need to put the old bitterness aside and make our peace with the queen's sisters, then at least we can get back to Durovernon and leave this stinking place to the cattle it was intended for.' Then replying to the sentry, 'Tell them to wait their ground while the queen makes ready.' There was no doubting the bravery of Brennus or his devotion to the queen, but his ability to think things through was sparse.

'No wait,' cried Digueillus. 'How many in their escort?'

'Couldn't say,' replied the sentry. 'The end of the column was out of sight behind the woods in the bend of the valley.'

'By the spirits! There could be over a thousand. How were they armed?'

'Slings, axes and javelins mostly. Some were fully armed and bearing the sigils of Taximagulus, hard to tell how many.'

'Then they have come prepared for us to refuse their request and will not take no for an answer. I do not trust

Gonerila or the boy of that son of a lizard she married. They plan to take us by force if necessary. Yes, as Brennus has said, tell them to await the queen, we will alert her immediately, but you must summon the priestess to meet with us here. And one more thing, take down the king's banners and bring them to me.'

The sentry turned and hurried away, and the two men stepped inside the mean roundhouse. They had made it as comfortable as possible for Cordelia to inhabit since Digueillus had insisted she leave her capital for her own safety. A circular flag-stoned hearth covered the middle of the floor space, in the centre of which glowed the embers of a fire on a large iron grate. To one side was a kitchen area where two of the queen's personal servants were preparing breakfast from the leftovers of the previous evening's meal and setting it out on a low table surrounded by straw matting. Clearly, they had overheard the conversation with the sentry because they both hurried across the room and disappeared behind the curtain that enclosed the queen's bedchamber, upon a dais opposite the kitchen.

Brennus turned to Digueillus as they awaited Cordelia's attendance. 'Why do you strike the flags, do you mean to surrender?'

'Not by any means, but we cannot let them fall into the hands of our enemies. I have been pondering the Romans, and from what I have heard, I would rather seek a peaceful negotiation with Julius Caesar, than an alliance with people we mistrust, to oppose him.'

At that moment, the Priestess Dianann appeared at the open doorway, flanked by the two young deer that accompanied her everywhere she went. She had heard the commotion and was already on her way to attend the conference. She led her four-legged companions across to the kitchen and selected the choicest root vegetables from a basket.

Breaking the produce in half and offering the pieces to the fawns by her side, she succinctly acknowledged Digueillus' observation and prioritised the discussion. 'Since you are currently in no position to achieve that which you seek, and Gonerila's soldiers are at our gates I suggest your first duty is to ensure the queen's safety.'

Now it was the turn of Brennus to speak. 'We can hold the stockade while we raise a call to arms to the homesteads, but all our cattle are still in the fields, and we haven't gathered the harvests enough to withstand a siege for any great length of time.'

'I fear all the fighting men of the Cantiaci have already been conscripted into the armies of Taximagulus and Carvillus,' countered Digueillus. 'If we need to raise an army to protect our queen, we must get word to our allies amongst the Atrabates.'

'And why should I need our allies to protect me?' Cordelia appeared from behind the curtain. Her undressed hair fell in long curls over her shoulders. The two men present bowed respectfully as befitted their station, but Dianann, a member of the priesthood and not beholden to royalty, remained upright.

'Segovax and Cingetorix are at the gates with a column of armed warriors,' replied Digueillus. 'They are saying that the Roman fleet has been sighted and they are here to take you into their protection.'

Cordelia calmly stepped down from the dais and took her seat on the matting at one end of the low table. While sipping on milk and helping herself to some slices of boiled bacon, she said, 'Dianann has provided me with a potion to consume if ever I am taken into the care of my sisters, so I would rather entrust my fate to the Romans.' Her bodyguard grimaced at the thought of losing his queen in such a manner and he too took his place at the table, but the priestess, who had more to lose if the Romans prevailed, remained standing and impassive as she bit into a raw carrot.

The elderly counsellor bent down slowly to take his place on the matting opposite Brennus. The effort caused a groan to escape his lips. 'Then we must form an alliance with the tribes who might accept Rome. The Atrabates could increase their regular trade with Roman Gaul. The Trinovantes too, across the Dark River under the rule of Imanuentus, have considerable trading links with the Belgic tribes.'

'Crossing the Tamasa would be a risk,' warned Brennus. 'The Cassi still control much of the north bank around the fording points and Vellaunus is at war with everyone except Taximagulus.'

'True,' admitted Digueillus. 'But we can travel the Way of Lugh. The gods will protect us. I can escort the queen through the great forest of Coit Andred, to Noviomagus, while you can travel the opposite direction back to Durobrivae and thence to the marsh crossing at low tide and pass safely into the territory of the Trinovantes.'

At that moment, the sentry returned with the banners and reported that Segovax would wait no longer than mid-morning and that his troops were surrounding the stronghold carrying lit torches.

Dianann was the first to react. 'We must act now. We must take the concealed steps down to the river and abandon this place.'

The stockade was not built for people to inhabit. It had been hastily constructed many decades previously as a safe haven for cattle during the tribal wars before the supremacy of Lugios. One side was bound by a river and was naturally too steep to be assaulted. A single ditch and bank had been dug around the other three sides to create a rampart, topped with a palisade. The wide expanse within the enclosure was suitable for grazing, as natural springs fed a pond and a stream. Since Llyr's rift with his eldest daughters, and the loss of potency that came with his old age, Digueillus had considered the stockade to be a place of relative safety should the king be forced from his seat. Because he had envisaged a circumstance where the increasing power of Llyr's daughters and their belligerent husbands could lead to a situation such as the present, he had advised the excavation of a secret tunnel, down to the back of a cave at the foot of the hill on which the stockade was sited. Soldiers remaining loyal to the crown could be deployed to defend the perimeter, so as a last resort, the tunnel would serve as an escape route to the river below. This would provide access to any number of hiding places in the depths of the great forest that divided them from the Atrabates in the west.

No one questioned the priestess' decision. Guards were called in to move the fire grate to one side and lift the flag stone that concealed the entrance to the tunnel. The queen's servants in attendance, under direction from Digueillus, hastily cleared the table of the loaves, hens' eggs and sliced meats and started packing them into a hamper.

Brennus grabbed a torch from a basket by the hearth and ignited it with the embers in the grate. He was first to descend the iron ladder into the darkness. Cordelia was next, followed by Digueillus, who struggled with the hamper on his shoulder. Dianann followed them into the tunnel. She insisted the guard pass her two companions down to her before replacing the flagstone over the tunnel entrance. Brennus led the way down the curving stone staircase, lighting the bronze cressets fixed to the walls along the way. Cordelia hoisted the hem of her dress above her knees as she picked her way down the seemingly never-ending flight of steps into the darkness that retreated before them. Digueillus cursed under his burden as he occasionally slipped in the sections where water had run down the rock walls of the tunnel. Eventually, a dim light lit the sides of the tunnel as it emerged into the back of a deep cave.

As they picked their way across the rock-strewn floor, the silhouette of a rowing boat came into view against the low, wide cave entrance. Brennus lit the final cressets in the cave walls to give him enough light to check that the craft was sound, and the oars were shipped. Digueillus stowed their provisions aboard, and then the four of them pushed the boat over the smooth prepared rocks and crouched as they took it out of the low cave mouth and into the early morning dappled light of the thick woods at the foot of the hill. Trees had been removed to allow a curving slipway of undergrowth into an open meadow, sloping two hundred paces down to the riverbank. As they approached the clearing, they smelt the smoke from the burning watchtower, and the shouts of Segovax's men, further up the hill behind them, filled the air as they surrounded the stockade.

Brennus stopped at the edge of the woods and raised his hand for silence as he assessed their chances. Even if they made it to the river unseen, there was still nearly half a mile of open bankside before the river disappeared into the impenetrable forest downstream. They would be an easy target for the javelins of the soldiers, but there was no other way. The only decision was either to pick their way as quietly as possible and hope to escape detection or make a mad dash and hope for the best. One look at Digueillus, who was clearly suffering from his exertions, was enough to decide. Turning to the others, Brennus raised a finger to his lips for a continued silence as they slid the boat into the long grass of the open meadow. They were halfway to the bank when one of Dianann's deer disturbed a pair of partridges which flew, squawking into the air. Several of the soldiers turned, saw them, and raised the alarm.

'Run for the bank!' screamed Dianann. 'When you reach the woods, my mother will protect you.'

Brennus didn't hesitate or question the priestess. He bundled Cordelia and the old counsellor into the boat and heaved against it. The momentum set the boat sliding down the slope. Brennus raced behind it, head down, pushing with both hands on the stern, flattening the long grass on its way. As the first spears and javelins whistled past, the priestess let out an ear-piercing scream and rushed up the slope at the oncoming warriors, uprooting the long grass by the handful as she went. Each handful was thrown up into the air while she reached with her other hand into a sack beneath her cloak that she had been filling with leaves as they had passed through the woods. Up into the air went the leaves too. The warriors were stunned by the sight that suddenly confronted them. Each leaf appeared to them as a charioteer charging toward them. Each long blade of grass was a javelin hurled directly at them. They could hear the screams of their comrades as they fell or were trampled or skewered around them. The survivors threw down their weapons and fled back up the hill. Segovax, seeing the carnage, flew into a rage and drove his horse directly at the priestess. Ignoring the charioteers who passed him by, and the javelins, of which none had hit their mark, he raised his sword and struck the priestess with a blow that cut diagonally through her neck and cleaved through to her midriff as he galloped past. He pulled his mount to a halt and turned to face the scene. There was no sign of anyone else, alive or dead. Turning again towards the river, Dianann's deer were quietly grazing, and the boat carrying Cordelia and her companions was disappearing around a distant bend, into the deep woods and out of sight.

When he was sure they were out of sight and range of the enemy, Brennus, perspiring heavily after his exertions, shipped his oars and let the boat drift, while Cordelia nursed Digueillus' shins that were grazed when Brennus had pushed him over the gunwale. They had all seen what had happened to Dianann, and they owed their lives to her, but what had made the warriors turn and flee for their lives? They could only guess it was an act of sorcery. There was a silence between them while they gathered their own thoughts, but the surrounding air was filled with birdsong, the wind in the trees and the relaxing sound of the river bubbling through the woods.

Eventually, Digueillus answered the call of his grumbling stomach and suggested they had breakfast while they had the chance. Cordelia declared she had no appetite, so the men shared the fare between them. They had no plan other than to seek refuge in the forest and find their way through to the territory of the Atrabates. Digueillus was sure they would be offered asylum while they awaited the outcome of the contest between Taximagulus and the Romans. As the boat drifted towards a sunlit clearing on the further bank, something caught Brennus' eye, something moving in the trees beyond. Antlers on the head of a stag, perhaps? The clearing was as good a place as any to land the boat and explore the woods for a path or drove-way that might lead to a homestead where they could beg provisions and ask directions. The forest was known to be sparsely populated by people who had no interest in or use for the silver in the pouch that Digueillus always carried with him. They lived in small self-sufficient hamlets and spent their entire lives without being disturbed by the generations of kings and queens and the wars and tribulations they wreaked upon each other. They had fresh water and animals that they kept on the high pastures in summer and drove down into the woods for shelter throughout the winters. Brennus collected the oars and steered towards the bank. Stepping out into the shallows, he offered a hand to help his companions onto the lush green turf. It was the least he could do after the unceremonious way he had bullied them on board. In the centre of the clearing, there was a low stone slab that appeared to have served recently as an altar. Brennus went over to it, took a pinch of the remains of some burnt offerings, and held it to his nose. After a long sniff, he shook his head and released the particles into the breeze.

'I've no idea what that might have been, but before we reached the bank, I thought I saw something moving amongst the trees.'

'Well, it's not there now,' said Digueillus, squinting beyond the depths of bracken and nettle that surrounded the clearing.

'Over here!' called Cordelia, who had been exploring the perimeter of the thickets that enclosed them. 'There is a pathway here, recently trodden.'

The narrow track through the waist-high undergrowth soon led to a straight, wide, drove-way; one of many that crisscrossed the dense woodland. Brennus glanced to the left, and the head of a deer emerged from the undergrowth less than two hundred paces away.

'Look,' he cried. 'I thought I saw a deer earlier; I think there are two of them.'

In clear sight of the three companions, two deer emerged side-by-side from the forest, harnessed to a chariot. A tall woman stood in the chariot, holding the reins. She had long fair hair tumbling over her shoulders and down her back. She appeared to be staring at them, cocking her head as if to encourage them to follow her. The chariot turned out of the woods and along the drove-way ahead of them.

'She wants us to follow her,' Cordelia exclaimed.

'Come on then, let's hasten. We must speak with her,' added Digueillus as the trio set off in pursuit, the old counsellor hobbling along behind. They had closed the gap to within hailing distance when the chariot turned a corner at a point where two drove-ways intersected. Brennus sprinted on ahead, but when he reached the corner, the chariot and its mysterious driver were still two hundred paces distant. Brennus waited until Cordelia and the out-of-breath Digueillus caught up with him.

'What bewitchment is this that keeps her out of reach?' whispered Brennus.

'This is what Dianann must have meant,' gasped Digueillus, 'when she said her mother would protect us.' Cordelia looked blankly at Brennus and then questioningly at Digueillus. 'She claimed to be the daughter of Flidais, the goddess of the forest. That is why she always had two young deer in attendance. Flidais is said to be borne in a chariot pulled by two stags, but she rarely makes herself known to mortals.'

'So she is leading us to safety?' Cordelia guessed.

'Yes, we must keep sight of her,' said Digueillus, limping on in pain.

Brennus, recognising he was in difficulty, hoisted the old man's arm around his own shoulder and, with a strong arm around his waist, helped him along. For an hour, they continued following the chariot, never getting closer or further away than when they first saw it. Inexplicably, although the rain-softened ground bore the deep hoof prints of cattle, the wheels of the chariot left no trace. Eventually, they came to a place where the undergrowth on the forest floor was less dense; the chariot left the track and glided effortlessly and soundlessly between the trees and groves. A small herd of swine was close by, taking no notice of the mysterious chariot or its followers.

'These are domestic animals,' exclaimed Digueillus, 'not wild boar, but swine, hand-reared and put out to pannage. There must be a farmstead nearby.'

'And see here,' added Brennus, 'the birch has been coppiced and the hazel has been prepared for wattle.'

They detected the smoke from a settlement almost immediately. Workshops and birch-fenced animal pens came into view in a clearing leading to an area of open pasture. In the centre of the clearing stood a sacrificial stone, like the one on the riverbank. Of the goddess and the chariot, there was no sign. The barking of dogs and the honking of several sacred geese greeted them, causing the occupants of the buildings to come running out, armed with whatever blunt or sharp instrument came to hand. Two old men, a younger woman and a frightened youth confronted them. The sound of a crying baby came from one of the huts. The two dogs crouched and snarled in front of the line of four. These were working dogs, not the larger breeds that were trained to attack in battle. Cordelia and her companions must have made a strange, bedraggled sight to the residents. Clearly, they did not represent a threat. One of the older men put two fingers to his mouth and whistled a signal to the dogs who reluctantly stopped barking and slunk away. Just then, two men, clearly the most able-bodied of the community, alarmed by the sound of the dogs, galloped into the clearing from the pastures behind the settlement. For a few moments, the two groups of strangers confronted each other in shocked silence, until it became clear that neither was equipped to do any great deal of harm to the other.

One of the older men was the first to speak. He stepped forward, eyeing the interlopers with caution, still holding aloft the rusty sickle he had brandished when he came out of the hut.

'Who are you and what do you want with us?'

Before they made any answer, some homesteaders, emboldened to speak by their elder, joined the interrogation.

'How did you find us here?'

'Who sent you?'

The sickle carrier held up his other hand for silence from his family members. Digueillus, considering himself the natural spokesman of the party, took five tottering paces forward, halving the distance between the two groups. He drew a deep breath and tried to appear composed and authoritative despite his bloodied appearance.

'My name is Digueillus. I am the Counsellor-in-Chief to Queen Cordelia of the Cantiaci.'

'And I am the captain of the queen's bodyguard,' added Brennus, striding up to join the older man, in two minds about whether to keep his sword at his hip, or slide the scabbard around his back, so as not to antagonise or put fear into the minds of the simple folk whose help they would need. Both men turned inward to invite the queen to present herself between them.

'I am Cordelia, daughter of Llyr. My father bequeathed the kingdom of Cantiaci to me in his will, but it is contested by my sisters who sent arms against us this very morning and caused us to flee from our refuge on the edge of this forest.'

Due to the richness of their clothing and the dishevelled state in which the strangers presented themselves, not one of the forest dwellers had any doubt over the truthfulness of her statement, but the thought of them being pursued by armed men rang alarms.

'Were you followed?' was the next question. This from one of the men still mounted and peering anxiously down the drove-way behind them.

'We escaped on a small boat and came into the woods by way of the river. I'm certain no one followed us,' answered Brennus. 'All we need are horses and a guide through the forest to the Way of Lugh. Our queen needs to reach the citadel of Noviomagus to seek an alliance with the Atrabates, and I must ride north to make common cause with the Trinovantes.'

The two older men retreated a few steps and engaged in a whispered animated discussion, while the horsemen stood their ground, never taking their eyes off the trio, but occasionally taking nervous glances beyond them. By now, more of the family members had ventured outside the huts, or come into the clearing from the pasture, to ogle the strange spectacle that the queen and her companions presented. Even the baby had stopped crying as its mother bobbed it gently up and down under a brightly coloured shawl around her shoulder. She was standing by a doorway, surrounded by several other small children, some of them still carrying the baskets of eggs they had collected that morning. Of course, the forest dwellers were aware of the great highway and the outsiders that travelled it but preferred to keep their distance. Settlements had evolved throughout the woods, close enough to be known as neighbours, but not so close as to risk or encourage intrusion, even from their own kind.

It was again the sickle carrier who addressed them. 'We can spare neither horses nor men to act as guides to your destinations. The most we can do is offer you food and water to sustain you through your journey. We can lead you to the next settlement closer to Noviomagus, but there is no guarantee they can help you any more than we can.' Then, turning to address Brennus, the man continued. 'There is no other hirst between us and the villages to the north beyond the woods under the escarpments, so if you need to reach the Tamasa and the Trinovantes, you must go back the way you came from the river and journey on from there.'

The bluntness of the adjudication came as a shock to all three. Clearly, their status amongst the outsiders carried no weight with the people of the Coit Andred.

'But how can I find my way back?' blurted Brennus, struggling to suppress the anger rising inside him. 'We followed the Lady of the Woods all the way here from the sacrificial stone by the river. Her chariot left no marks in the bridleways. I cannot retrace my steps.'

Brennus' revelation of how they were led to the settlement immediately changed the attitude of the elders and their family members from defiance to consternation.

'A lady in a chariot?' questioned one. Brennus nodded.

'Pulled by two stags?' quavered another.

'The Priestess Dianann was the daughter of Flidais,' confirmed Digueillus. 'She gave her life to help us escape our enemies. She said her mother would take us under her protection in the woods.'

'Then why did you not make this plain?' implored the sickle carrier. 'If our mother goddess has aided you in your quest, by bringing you to us, then we must make sacrifices to her, to beg her forgiveness for not granting you the things you require.'

By late morning, the trio had been fed and refreshed. Digueillus had received a tea made from willow bark to ease his pain, and the young girl in the shawl had applied a poultice of comfrey to his bruised and swollen shins. They judged that the provision of horses and guides, along with the sacrifice of a goat, had appeased the Goddess of the Forest. Throughout their meal of ham and choice berries, washed down by a rough barley mead that Cordelia needed more than she had wanted, Digueillus' thoughts were troubling him deeply. The initial plan was for Brennus to undertake the more dangerous journey to the north, avoiding the Cassi, to engage with Imanuentus of the Trinovantes, while Digueillus escorted Cordelia through the forest to the south to seek asylum with the Atrabates. They readied their mounts and met with their guides and were just about to bid each other farewell and depart their separate ways when Digueillus could no longer contain his conscience.

'We cannot do it this way! It is I, not you Brennus, who must meet with Imanuentus.'

'But it is far too perilous a journey for you to undertake,' protested the younger man.

'The truth of the matter is that I am known to the king.' Digueillus had to spit the words out, knowing that his chances of reaching the Trinovantes were slim. He was not by nature a brave man, and his physical courage had never been put to the test, but he also knew he would be of little use to Cordelia, should she come into danger on her journey. 'I have met with him on many occasions whilst in the service of Llyr. You, on the other hand, are a stranger with no one to vouch for your status. You are the captain of the queen's personal guard. Your place is with her. Your duty is to protect her. It is you, not I, who should conduct her to safety with the Atrabates.'

Cordelia and Brennus exchanged glances. Neither of them could find fault in his reasoning, and their pained expressions said it all.

Digueillus leant across his mount and took the queen's wrist. He lifted it dutifully towards his lips and, as if for the last time, pressed them against the back of her hand and murmured, 'My Queen.' Turning to Brennus' guide, he then barked a terse, 'Lead on.'

Digueillus' companions watched in silence as he followed the guide across the clearing and out of sight into the woods. During the ride through the forest glades and bridleways, he was too deep in thought to make much in the way of conversation. It had been many years since his last visit to the stronghold of the Trinovantes. Since then, their perpetual war with the Cassi had been waged by means of raids and skirmishes in and around their disputed territory, beyond the far bank of the great dark river known as the Tamasa. Once he had crossed, it would be in the gift of the spirits to decide whether he arrived safely at Camulodunon, a day's further ride to the north, or was taken by the Cassi, who did not entertain strangers. There were but two crossing points; the ford at Thorn Island was the easiest, but the marshes below the chalk cliffs downstream nearer the estuary were the safest. At low tide, a man could wade across at the sacred island, but that crossing would more likely be in the territory held by the Cassi. The further east the crossing, the more likelihood there was of being met by the Trinovantes on the other side, but an experienced guide would be required to find the safe route through the marshes. Digueillus was more familiar with this crossing point. He knew where to find the services of a local guide and that would be his destination to be reached before nightfall. He was far too old to be spending the night beneath the boughs of trees in a bed of dry leaves, not that any dry leaves would be found. Another storm was brewing; it was in the air before the raindrops began to drum upon the canopy of the forest. Soon heavy drips were coming off the leaves and soaking his cloak and tunic.

By the time Digueillus reached the edge of the forest, sheets of rain were blowing in from the north, stinging his face. Although it was still only just after mid-day, the grey horizon, comprising a continuous escarpment in the distance, was barely visible.

His guide pointed the way. 'Follow this trail. It leads up through a fault in the chalk edge to the high plateau and the way to Durobrivae. By the time you reach it, the storm will have passed. I have never ventured beyond that point, but with a steady canter, you should reach the Tamasa before nightfall.'

'I have it,' replied Digueillus, although he doubted his ability to ride at that pace for any amount of time. His shins were still paining him. 'I know I can find my way once I reach the higher ground.'

'May the gods go with you.'

'And may you have their blessing,' replied Digueillus as he kicked his mount into a canter towards the distant horizon.

He was not kitted out for a long journey; he lacked boots and a riding cape. The forest folk could not provide him with those, since they had no need of them; but he reckoned there would be such items available from the marsh guide, who was accustomed to long-distance travellers passing through.

Riding into the teeth of the storm emphasised the indestructibility of the shape of his surroundings. The driving rain blurred all around him into a featureless obscurity of trees and soil. The barely visible chalk escarpment ahead appeared to be an ordinary specimen of any smooth-edged outcrop anywhere on earth, which might remain undisturbed on some future day of great upheaval when far grander natural monuments of rock and granite could be struck down. Digueillus' initial canter soon gave way to a trot that was easier on his mount, but only made a different set of his muscles ache. Despite having the means to pay, he resisted the desire to stop at a hamlet like a vagrant and seek shelter and alms. Instead, he chose to press on and reach the river in daylight. He knew that the marsh guide, an old acquaintance, would provide accommodation for the night. Fortunately for Digueillus, the forest guide's assessment of the weather proved accurate. By the time he met the rising ground at the foot of the escarpment, the storm had given way to a light drizzle, and breaks in the cloud cover threw light on the fathomless shade below it. The topmost branches of a row of beeches came into view and formed a line fringing the crest like a mane. His mount was young and nimble enough to make short work of the climb as the track twisted and turned, ascending the steep, narrow valley through the break in the edge of the plateau. As Digueillus came up out of the sparse woods to the high ground, the sun broke free of the last of the storm clouds. He dismounted to give his willing horse a rest and stood alone, seemingly on top of the world, and allowed his eyes to rest upon the view. The vast weald sprawled below him as far as the eye could see. A panoramic view of a landscape, now still as the grave, that had been writhing in the storm as he passed through it, gave him a deep sense of calm and gratification.

The sudden snorting of his horse broke his reverie. The instant remembrance of the hazards of his quest, and the urgency of his need to reach a place of shelter before nightfall came as a jolt to his consciousness. He turned back to his steed and had a mild panic. He had last mounted his horse several hours ago with the aid of a leg-up, but now, with no help available, and his aching muscles stiffened by just a few minutes' stillness, he struggled to remount. His frantic gymnastics while hoisting his leg only caused the horse to rotate away from him, making it even more difficult; pulling a muscle in his shoulder in the process as he heaved on the bridle. Calculating that he had a good three hours of daylight, and ignoring the new pain in his shoulder, he kicked his still frisky mount into a canter.

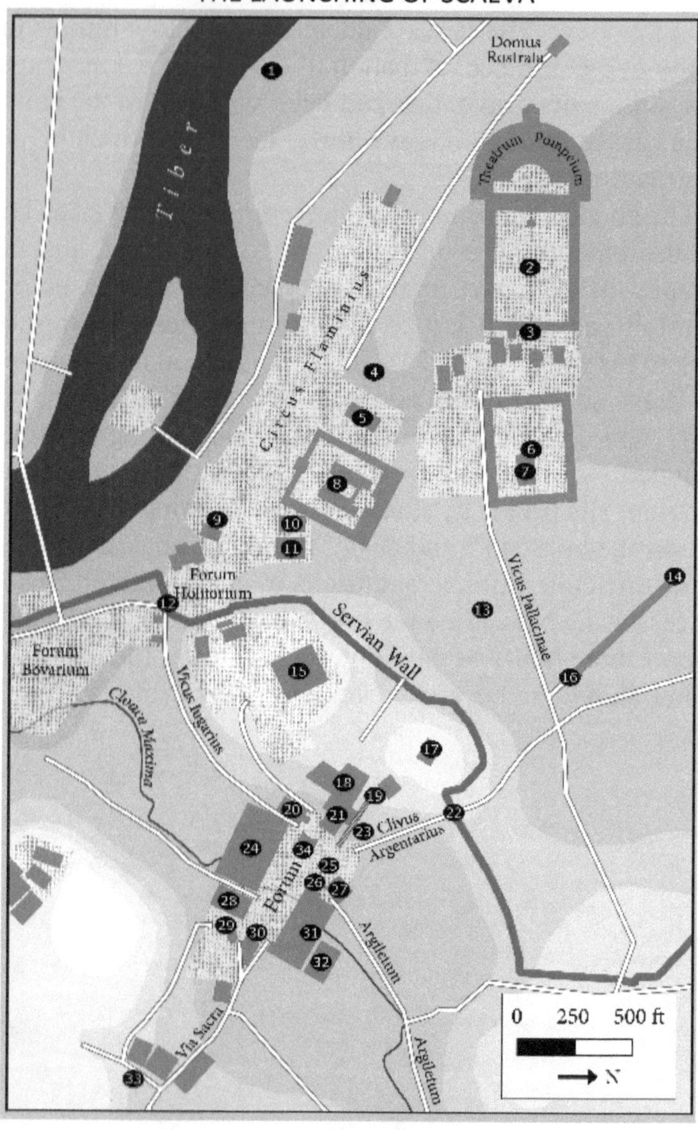

Domus Rostrata
Theatrum Pompeium
Tiber
Circus Flaminius
Forum Holitorium
Vicus Pallacinae
Forum Bovarium
Servian Wall
Cloaca Maxima
Vicus Iugarius
Clivus Argentarius
Forum
Argiletum
Argiletum
Via Sacra
0 250 500 ft
N

ROGER BROOK

Map Key Republican Rome
The Forum and The Field of Mars 55 BC

1	Navalia. Ship sheds of the war fleet
2	Porticus Pompeii. Recreational area adjoining the theatre
3	Curia Pompeii. Meeting place for the senate
4	Temple of Neptune
5	Temple of Hercules
6	Porticus Minucia Vetus.
7	Temple of Lares Permarini
8	Temples of Juno Regina and Jupiter Stator
9	Temple of Pietas
10	Temple of Apollo
11	Temple of Bellona
12	Porta Carmentalis
13	Balneae Pallacinae. Bathhouse
14	Altar of Mars
15	Temple of Jupiter Optimus Maximus Capitolinus
16	Porticus Aemilia
17	Temple of Juno Moneta
18	Tabularium
19	Auguraculum
20	Temple of Saturn
21	Temple of Concordia
22	Porta Fontinalis
23	Gradus of Moneta (steps)
24	Basilica Sempronia
25	Comitium. Civic assembly area
26	Temple of Janus
27	Curia Hostilia. Senate house
28	Temple of Castor and Pollux
29	Temple of Vesta
30	Regia. The headquarters of the Pontifex Maximus
31	Basilica Fulvia
32	Macellum. Food and fish market
33	Temple of Jupiter Stator
34	The Rostra

VI

23rd August 55 BC
ROME

Gaius Octavius Thurinus couldn't wait for the school day to end. His family had been invited to a special *convivium* at the home of the consul, Gnaeus Pompeius Magnus, in honour of his house guest King Ptolemy of Egypt. Octavius was looking forward to it and finding it difficult to concentrate on his lessons. Halfway through the afternoon class, the calculator picked boys out at random to answer questions about the lesson just delivered.

'Let the son of Philippus answer; If an *uncia* is deducted from a *quincunx*, what remains?'

Octavius panicked; he hated it when the calculator, who was older even than Orbilius, used examples of ancient coins, long out of circulation, to act as examples in his lessons. He knew that if one twelfth is taken away from five twelfths, only four twelfths remain, but he could not remember that the name of the coin—worth four twelfths of an *as*—was a *triens*.

The sudden appearance of the Matrona saved him from a black mark or a cuff around the ear. She interrupted the class to announce that Philippus had arrived and was asking permission to collect Octavius for a family celebration. Octavius stared at the Matrona in open-mouthed surprise. His stepfather was currently away from Rome, fulfilling his pro-consular duties as a governor. The Matrona hesitated a moment for Orbilius' nod of acknowledgement, before escorting Octavius through a door at the back of the classroom. It led into the dark passage and the entrance door, that was being held open by the school slave Aphrodisius. Through the open door, Octavius recognised, not his stepfather but his stepbrother, also named Lucius Marcius Philippus, waiting beside his father's sumptuous *lectica*. Eight liveried slaves stood beside it, two at each corner. Inside, sitting up from her reclining position and beaming at him, was his sister Octavia. Octavius bounded down the steps to the pavement and Philippus, who was in his mid-twenties and head of the household in his father's absence, motioned him inside. As he climbed aboard and stretched out on the divan, his older sister greeted him with a sigh of relief. Philippus, following on from Octavius, resumed his position opposite the children. He was fond of Octavia but could never think of anything to say that she might be interested in, and was as relieved as his stepsister, that Octavius was now the centre of attention. The lectica rose steadily to shoulder height and swayed forwards. Octavia, feeling more content now that she had her brother to converse with, inquired about his day at school.

'Oh, that little prig Lucius Pinarius was making an ass of himself as usual,' snorted Octavius. 'Two new boys started class today. During the break from lessons, Pinarius lost no time in digging it out of them. One is from an equestrian family, and the other, poor little sod, is the son of a freedman made good, who made the mistake of sending his son to school just because he could afford it. Lucius put them in their place, going on and on about his gens Pinarii going back as far as the kings.'

'Poor souls,' said Octavia with sympathy. 'Cousin Lucius can be quite pompous when the mood takes him. What were their names?'

'Didn't catch their names. One of them was a bit of a limp lettuce, the other one was alright though.' Then he paused in thought. 'Vipsanius, yes, Marcus Vipsanius; he's a pleb but he seemed like a solid enough chap.'

The children, since their move from their father's family home in the country, were now living in Rome in the house of their stepfather. They got on with their older stepbrother well enough but considered him stuffy. They secretly referred to him as Droopypus because of his stilted attempts to woo their Aunt Tertia at earlier family gatherings. His dark good looks, inherited from his father, belied his awkwardness in company with the opposite sex.

Octavius smiled cheekily up at him. 'Will Tertia be at the dinner party too, Philippus?' All it took was the mention of her name to make him blush, and Octavius wasn't disappointed.

'Yes, yes I think so,' said Philippus, reddening slightly. 'She's taking your grandmother I believe.'

Since Octavius' father had died when he was just three years old, his grandmother, Julia, had brought him up. She was known as Julia Minor to distinguish her from her older sister, also named Julia. This Julia was the grandmother of his upstart cousin, Lucius. The two Julias had a younger brother, naturally called Julius, and it was his daughter, also named Julia, who had recently married Pompeius

Magnus. Hence the family connection and the invitation to the dinner. A further connection was that Octavius' grandfather was also the cousin of Pompeius, but they could never socialise as much as the female cousins who were all close. Octavius' father served as governor of Macedonia and was returning to Rome to stand for election as consul but had died during the journey. His mother Atia, an extremely devout woman, remarried within a year. She was not obliged to wait the customary ten months before re-marrying because of her separation from her late husband. The match with Philippus, who had recently lost his wife and returned from serving as governor in Syria, was convenient for both families.

The lectica weaved its way through the bustling forum. It slowed as it passed by the ornamental fountain of Servilius, between the Temple of Saturn and the Basilica Sempronia. The bearers then jostled their way through the congested mass of pedestrians, porters, and street vendors of the Vicus Iugarius. As they skirted the bottom of the Capitoline Hill towards the Porta Carmentalis, a double gateway through the Servian wall, a familiar feeling of anxiety came over Octavius. He had visited the Domus Rostrata, home of Pompeius Magnus, many times since Magnus had married his mother, Atia's younger cousin Julia. The first time he made the journey, his stepfather told him that one should never exit the city via the right-hand archway, the Accursed Gate, of the Porta Carmentalis. It was seriously bad luck to do so. This is because corpses used to be transported from the city, through this gate, to their funeral pyres on the Campus Martius. Surely, thought Octavius, Droopypus would have known this and would have instructed his slaves to transport them through the arch on the left known as the Porta Triumphalis. This was the route into the city that Magnus' procession had taken when he celebrated his third triumph. Octavius was too young to remember that. It was before his father died, but his sister Octavia, who would have been the same age Octavius was now, did remember witnessing it. Pompeius Magnus, conqueror of the three continents in all the world, appeared God-like in his jewel-encrusted chariot, drawn by four horses. He wore the cloak that once belonged to Alexander the Great over his gilded purple tunic. Octavius remembered that on that first visit to the domus, he had meekly asked the great man if he could see Alexander's cloak.

Pompeius had smiled down at him. 'The one I wore in my latest triumph? Let me see, where is it now? I do believe I haven't laid eyes on it recently.' Then, patting Octavius on the head, he had added, 'I shall have to get a servant to find it for me, and then I shall send it to Philippus. After all, he has claimed that Alexander was one of his ancestors, so I think he should have it.'

Since then, Octavius never found the right moment to ask his stepfather if he had received it.

The sounds and shouts of the vendors in the vegetable market of the Forum Holitorium snapped Octavius out of his reverie. Oh no! He was so deep in his remembrances that he hadn't noticed whether the bearers had taken him through the Accursed Gate. They were already passing the three ancient temples in the forum and approaching the Temple of Pietas, outside which was the sad sight of unwanted young children and even newborn babies. These outcasts and orphans were left at the Columna Lactaria, to be nursed, fed, or taken in by benevolent passers-by; or just left to die. Panicking just a little, he craned his neck outside and looked back to see if he could tell which archway they might have passed through. Too late. The fluted columns of the temples dedicated to Apollo and Bellona now filled his vision. To take his mind off it, he turned on his tummy, chin resting in the palms of his hands, and counted the columns. He then pondered their classical lines and spacious precincts in sharp contrast to the crude dwellings on the opposite side of the road. This was one of the rougher areas of Rome, housing immigrants; Jews and Syrians spilling over from the poorer area across the Tiber inhabited by sailors and fishermen. Octavius yanked the curtains closed.

Their journey continued between the open expanse of the Circus Flaminius and the Porticus Metelli. Octavius pulled the curtains open again. He liked to inspect the row of twenty-five equestrian statues of the Companions of Alexander, cast in bronze, that lined the front of the porticus. As they left the crowds behind, the magnificent edifice that was the newly dedicated Theatre of Pompeius came into view in splendid isolation on the Campus Martius. No sooner had he forgotten his fright over the accursed gate than he had a new concern; he smelt smoke and that really unnerved him. Several columns of it appeared to rise above the theatre.

'Look, Octavia! Look, Philippus! The theatre is on fire!'

Octavia leaned across him in alarm to see out of his side and let out a shriek!

'Calm down the pair of you,' said Droopypus. 'Don't they teach you anything at that school of yours, you little pea-brain?' Philippus was still cross that Octavius teased him about Tertia.

'What do you mean?' demanded Octavius.

'Don't you even know what festival day it is?' Octavius looked puzzled. 'Does the seventh day before the *kalends* of *Septimus* mean anything to you?

Octavius was still a month away from his eighth birthday. To him, the many festivals of Rome just came and went. He couldn't think of anything to say.

'I think Philippus is reminding us that it is the festival of Vulcanalia today,' explained Octavia softly, realising what Philippus was driving at. 'The smoke must be coming from the bonfires people are lighting for their sacrifices in the Campus, beyond the theatre.'

'Only the same time every year since Titus Tatius,' mocked Philippus tartly.

'It's all right for you,' Octavius was sulking. 'I bet you can remember because you've celebrated it hundreds of times.' Philippus' face turned redder than it had when Tertia was mentioned.

'Octavius, don't you be so rude,' cried Octavia. She and her little brother enjoyed their private jokes about Philippus, but Octavius was now being disrespectful. 'Stop it now and apologise.'

Philippus' expression softened in anticipation and Octavius, accepting that he wasn't bantering with his classmates, offered a sincere apology.

Octavia gave him a stern look which said, *Don't even think about saying anything in front of Tertia at the dinner.*

They continued in silence past the temples of Neptune and Hercules into the tangle of temporary dwellings of construction workers who were erecting a vast rectangular porticus. It filled the space from behind the theatre almost up to the row of small ancient temples that faced the Porticus Minucia below the western slope of the Capitolium. Soon, the back wall of the theatre towered above them. As they followed the curve of the outer wall of the auditorium, Octavius' sullen mood evaporated. He loved to see the elaborate sculptures set against the piers in the arcade; they represented all the nations subdued by Pompeius Magnus, as far afield as Hispania, Africa, and Syria. He had first seen them earlier in the year when he and his family attended the wild animal displays, farces, and gladiatorial matches of the five-day inaugural ceremonies. The mid-point of the outer wall incorporated a temple dedicated to Venus Victrix. It towered above the cavea overlooking the auditorium. From here a wide tree-lined boulevard led towards the new domus of Pompeius; built near his theatre after his victorious return to Rome seven years earlier.

Octavius' attention was now drawn to the bonfires of the Vulcanalia; they were visible a safe distance from the theatre; in the middle of the grassy expanse of the Campus to the north. The smoke drifted away towards the heights of the Collis Hortorum, where several of the great families of Rome had built their villas and gardens on its southern slopes, overlooking the city. In the distance to the south, naval sheds stood on the banks of the Tiber housing warships from Pompeius' victory over the Pirates, several years before Octavius was born. It was the *rostrum,* the ramming beaks of those pirate ships Pompeius had captured, which gave his new house its name. Built into the open fronted *vestibulum,* no visitor could miss them, a spectacle that Octavius never tired of.

Julia welcomed her aunt and cousin into her home with open arms.

'You look wonderful,' cooed Aunt Julia as she hugged her niece, five months pregnant with her first child. Cousin Tertia beamed as she waited for her turn to embrace.

'Where are the rest of the family?' asked Julia. 'Are they coming?'

'Your uncle Marcus is suffering another bout of colic,' replied her aunt. 'And Atia has insisted it is the will of the gods that she should nurse him and make sure he takes his horseheal, rather than engage in "frivolous socialising" as she calls it. Uncle insisted that Atia is quite capable of looking after him and that I should still come and give you a big hug from him. I'm sure he was looking forward to the dinner, but he's in no fit state to enjoy the sort of fare your Gnaeus will be providing for the King of Egypt!'

'That is sad,' replied Julia, as she greeted her cousin with a kiss. 'Dear Gnaeus doesn't get to see much of his cousin these days. What about Atia's children? With Philippus being away, who is looking after them?'

'Oh, they are coming,' said Tertia brightly. 'Philippus' son is bringing Octavia and collecting Octavius from school on the way. They should be here soon.'

'Oh good,' cried Julia. 'His sister Marcia is here already with her new husband Hortensius. I'm sure they will enjoy catching up with each other.'

'I do hope so,' remarked Tertia, 'then I might escape the younger Philippus' attentions. He is such a dreadful bore. How is his sister Marcia, now that she has remarried?'

'Marcia, would you believe, is pregnant too!' exclaimed Julia.

The story of Marcia and Quintus Hortensius Hortalus had shocked Roman society the previous year. Deep into retirement now, Hortensius had been a leading statesman, unparalleled as an advocate in law and a cornerstone of the conservative senatorial aristocracy. He was, however, such a great admirer and friend of the younger conservative senator Cato that he wished to be related to him and so asked permission to marry Cato's daughter, who was already married and had children. Cato refused, not so much because his daughter was already married, but because there was a forty-year age difference. Hortensius then suggested that Cato divorce his own wife Marcia on the grounds that she had already borne him children. This, Cato was willing to do, on the condition that her father, Lucius Marcius Philippus senior, consented to the arrangement!

'Oh, I'm so happy for her,' beamed Aunt Julia. 'Being married to that miserly tippler Cato must have been horrible. I was so pleased that Philippus agreed to the match. She will be far happier with old Hortensius, at least he knows how to live.'

'And she'll be much closer to inheriting his fortune,' added Tertia, as the giggling trio passed into the *atrium* to join the other guests awaiting dinner.

VII

23rd August 55 BC
Near the banks of the Tamasa, in the land of the Cantiaci

Digueillus had lived most of his life amongst the Cantiaci and once out of the dense forest, knew the lie of the land. By the time he reached his destination, a hamlet on a plateau made by a low chalk cliff above the marshes, he was casting a long shadow. It had been years since his previous visit, and he was reminded of how the river resembled a lake at high tide when it flooded the marshlands protecting its southern approaches.

Smoke was escaping through the thatched roofs of a collection of round houses and workshops, assembled haphazardly around animal pens and a grain store on short stilts. A broken-down palisade was all that surrounded the hamlet, suggesting that the inhabitants felt safe from intruders, even from wild animals. There was also a high platform outside the boundary of the palisade that Digueillus didn't recall from his previous visits, the purpose of which was a mystery. His approach was announced by the barking of dogs tethered outside some buildings. The sound of the dogs brought a familiar figure out to greet him. The rotund shape and rolling gait of Bodelic, the marsh guide himself, came waddling out through a clucking brood of hens, waving his hands in a scissors motion above his head.

'Come back tomorrow,' he called out to the silhouette of the stray traveller. 'No more river crossing today. It'll be too dark for me to return.'

'Bodelic, I'm so glad to see you,' said Digueillus, ignoring the less than welcoming gesticulations of his old acquaintance. Despite its hoarseness, it was the voice, far more than the appearance of the nebulous mounted figure, backlit by the setting sun, that gave the marsh guide a clue to the stranger's identity.

'Digueillus? Can it be you? What has happened?' On all the occasions the two of them had met over the years, Digueillus had always been accompanied by a coterie of people on important business. Initially, as a younger member of court, and more recently as the chief ambassador of the Cantiaci, sometimes accompanied by Llyr himself. The bloodied, dishevelled and exhausted figure on the heavily sweating mare appeared ghost-like in comparison.

By the time the sun had set, Digueillus was sitting at Bodelic's fireplace, enjoying the hospitality of his simple, one-roomed abode. Cured game, hams and sides of other carcasses hung from rafters, gently twisting in the smoke that collected inside the pinnacle of the thatched roof. A selection of cold meats, fried eggs, and toasted bread had sated his hunger, and he took a long draught from his horn of mead. Bodelic, his wife and eldest of two daughters, sat cross-legged on the floor opposite. Between mouthfuls, Digueillus had recounted the momentous events of the day, only omitting the episode with Flidais, the lady of the woods. That would have elicited questions that Digueillus could not answer. During the telling of the story, the loud exclamations of Bodelic and his wife disturbed their younger daughter. She woke from her cot behind a drape by the wall and came to sit on her father's lap.

'If you're heading for Camulodunon tomorrow we will need an early start,' Bodelic was saying. 'You'll need some decent boots and a riding coat. I can furnish you with them for a fair price.'

'Thank you,' replied Digueillus. 'I was rather hoping you would.'

'Surely Imanuentus will look favourably on your plea. His father, Madawc, was King of the Trinovantes and the elder brother of Llyr, so Imanuentus was Llyr's nephew. Surely, he would want to come to the aid of Llyr's beloved daughter and appointed successor.'

Bodelic liked nothing more than to exhibit his intimate knowledge of events past and present on both sides of his river. Along with his father before him, he and his brother had been helping travellers across the Tamasa and through the marshes for four decades. With Digueillus, who was a captive audience, and someone who could attest to his knowledge, Bodelic warmed to his theme and continued.

'And after the king died, didn't Llyr wed Imanuentus' widowed mother Etain, and adopt him and his elder brother?'

'Indeed he did,' confirmed Digueillus, shaking his head sadly. 'That didn't end well. The year following the betrothal and the adoption, Etain died. Llyr remarried and had two daughters. He then made the mistake of passing over Imanuentus and his brother in favour of his own girls. Imanuentus eventually fulfilled his destiny as king of the Trinovantes by his own hand with no help from Llyr. In my dealings with him since, as Llyr's ambassador, I have detected a distinct lack of warmth towards the Cantiaci. My best hope is that I can persuade him that the Cantiaci under Cordelia will be a valuable ally in his war against the Cassi. Whereas, if his elder daughters' new spouses, Taximagulus and Carvillus prevail, Imanuentus will face a new enemy, for they are both creatures of Vellaunus.'

Since the conversation had moved on to politics, Bodelic's younger daughter returned to her cot and both his elder daughter, and his wife retired behind the curtains of their bedchambers.

Bodelic rose to poke the embers of the fire and add another log. 'If it was Segovax and Cingetorix that were sent to arrest Cordelia this morning, what of Gonerila and Rigontia's own sons, Margan and Cundag?'

'Don't even mention them,' sighed Digueillus, leaning back against a straw bale and nursing the last of his mead. His shins and shoulder were throbbing again. 'Since you are so well informed, I'm surprised you hadn't heard.'

Bodelic allowed the mild rebuke to pass. He was too eager to learn something new to take any offence, although none was intended.

He sat down again and leaned forward to speak in lower tones to his guest now that his family was sleeping. 'I've heard nothing of them these past few years. I do know that Llyr split his kingdom between his two elder daughters and their husbands while he was still alive. Then something must have happened because he went across to Gaul to reconcile with Cordelia, returning with her, and her husband, at the head of his army. Then I heard he had both his other two sons-in-law put to death when he reclaimed the crown. But I never heard what happened to the princes.'

'It's a long story,' murmured Digueillus, chin on his chest and eyelids beginning to droop. 'Suffice to say that after Diviciacus returned to Gaul with his army, the young fools acted like crows around carrion waiting for Llyr to die. They quarrelled constantly over who should succeed him; Margan was the son of Llyr's eldest daughter, though Cundag was his senior by three days. Cundag slew his cousin, and in a vain attempt to prove himself, led an army against the Cassi. Needless to say, Heli and Vellaunus made short work of him. Gonerila and Rigontia, their husbands and sons dead, quickly remarried, and that's why it was their stepsons, Segovax and Cingetorix, no doubt on orders from their fathers, who came to take Cordelia.'

Although Digueillus needed his bed, he had asked for no news of his host. Bodelic's brother and his family lived on the north bank of the river and acted as a guide for those travelling south.

Changing the subject out of politeness and hoping for a brief exchange of pleasantries before retiring for the night, he asked, 'And how is your brother? I expect we will see him tomorrow.'

The pained expression that descended over Bodelic's face foretold a calamity had occurred. First, the light went from his eyes, then even in the flickering firelight, the colour visibly drained from his cheeks. Finally, the corners of his mouth turned down to form a tragic mask. 'We won't be seeing Boden tomorrow,' said Bodelic in a hushed voice, as if not wanting his wife and children to be reminded of something terrible. 'He and his family were taken by wolves last winter.'

The shocking revelation jolted Digueillus upright. His previously drooping eyes shot wide open. 'I'm so sorry. I had no idea.'

'Since the Trinovantes have been at war with the Cassi, the local thanes, even as far south as the Tamasa, have been conscripting most of the able-bodied men into the army of Imanuentus. There have been too few left to organise the wolf hunts that kept their numbers down. Here, on the Cantiaci side of the river, the hunts are regular, and the wolves keep away from us.' Digueillus fleetingly recalled the broken-down palisade around the hamlet. 'But don't you worry. You should have no fear of them on your journey, my friend. In daylight, in the warmer months, they rarely emerge from the woods.'

Digueillus was alarmed rather than reassured by his host's remark, but he let it pass. 'Has anyone taken Boden's place to continue working in tandem with you, bringing travellers across from the north?'

As soon as the question was asked, Digueillus felt ashamed he should so swiftly be thinking of his own return journey instead of showing greater sympathy, but if Bodelic was affronted, he didn't show it.

'There are many around these parts that know the marshes, but none will take his place. Not that I blame them. I built a high platform with a store of faggots and a cresset atop a pole. Anyone wishing to cross from the north takes a faggot to light it. When I see it alight, I light the cresset on this side to let them know I'm coming to collect them. I charge double but no one has complained so far.' Then, standing and rubbing his face as if to restore his usual affable expression, he added, 'You'll need to leave at dawn with a hearty breakfast inside you, so I'll keep you from your bed no longer.'

He turned away to join his wife in their curtained chamber, leaving Digueillus to settle down on his makeshift bed for the night—a pile of wolf skins. Thankfully, he fell quickly into a dreamless sleep.

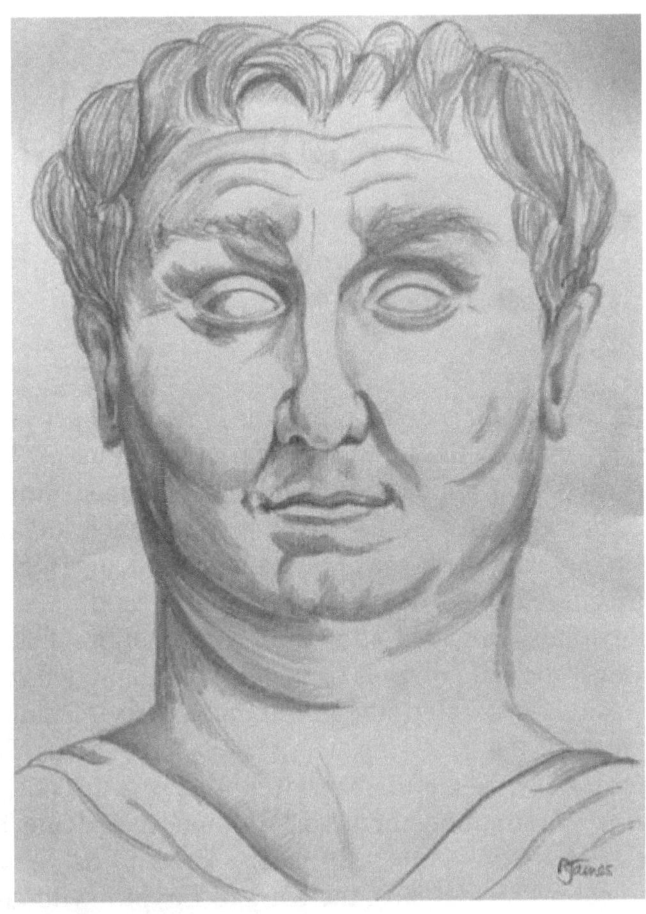

Gnaeus Pompeius Magnus

VIII

23rd August 55 BC
ROME The Domus Rostrata

At the far side of a marble *impluvium* set into the mosaic floor stood a life-sized statue of Venus, patron goddess of Pompeius Magnus. Sitting by the water feature on a flat white marble bench inlaid with green malachite fish, was Marcia with the King of Egypt's fourteen-year-old daughter Cleopatra and her tutor Philostratos, engaged in polite conversation. Clustered amongst the tall columns of the Corinthian-styled *atrium*, exquisitely decorated silver drinking vessels in hand, were the men of the gathering. Hortensius and Marcus Tullius Cicero, old rivals at the bar but now best of friends, were noisily entertaining their host Pompeius and his house guest Auletes—more formally known as Ptolemy Philopater Philadelphos, the King of Egypt—with tales of their legal skirmishes of the past.

'I should never have defended that scoundrel Verres,' Hortensius was saying, 'I'd been *summo canis* for so long … thought an acquittal was a formality.'

'My dear Dionysia,' replied Cicero using the nickname Hortensius had acquired because of his foppishness and extravagant gestures in front of a jury, which had caused him to be compared with a notorious dancing girl, famous in Rome's theatres, 'you will forgive me for suggesting that the main reason those scoundrels—your word not mine—you made a habit of defending, were always acquitted, was because, as governors accused of plundering their provinces, they could afford to buy any magistrate or tribunal assembled to judge them.'

The crescendo with which Cicero ended his comment prompted peals of laughter from Auletes and their host, and frowns of disapproval from the women trying to have a quiet conversation.

'Perhaps there's some truth in that,' admitted Hortensius, with an exaggerated toss of his head and flick of his hand.

'So why was Verres found guilty?' enquired Auletes.

'Go on, be honest,' urged Cicero.

'The reason Verres was found guilty,' continued Hortensius in a mock fit of pique, 'in spite of the massive bribes—and I know you are dying for me to admit this— is because it was you, Cicero, who was conducting the prosecution!'

'By Hercules, there's definitely some truth in that,' quipped Cicero, mimicking Hortensius' head and hand movements amongst more peals of laughter and backslapping.

'The boys seem to be enjoying themselves,' said Julia to her relatives, as she came into the *atrium*, motioning to a waiting slave to add a little more water to the wine amphorae. No sooner had they joined Marcia and Cleopatra than the janitor announced more guests had arrived. This time it was her absent cousin Atia's children; Octavia and Octavius, who came running through the *vestibulum* to give Julia a hug and exclaim about the size of her bump, whilst their stepbrother Philippus kept a respectful distance and a slightly more formal greeting.

'Can I look at the *rostrum*?' pleaded Octavius, who was secretly a little overawed at the prospect of being presented to the King of Egypt.

'Yes,' replied Julia indulgently, 'but do not be long, we have other guests here. Philippus, lovely to see you, come through, your sister Marcia is here. You must have a lot to catch up on.'

Although fabulously wealthy and able to spend lavishly on public works to his greater glory, Gnaeus Pompeius Magnus, whose lack of patrician breeding was often mocked by his enemies, had no need of a palace on the Palatine hill, as preferred by others of the senatorial ranks, including Cicero. Pompeius' new domus, built outside the city walls in the Campus Martius with no restrictions on size, was still only a little larger than the modest family home he still owned in the city. The Domus Rostrata was indeed the house of a rich man, but Pompeius was not self-indulgent in a fondness for sensuous luxury. The fundamental difference between the two houses was the frontage. In the city, the house built by his father, on the Carinae at the foot of the Esquiline Hill, was a typical domus; neighbours on either side and tabernae, leased to local artisans or shopkeepers, flanking a narrow *vestibulum* facing out onto the street. Conversely, the *vestibulum* of the Domus Rostrata spread across the entire width of the front of the building. No tabernae, no neighbours. No street even. Open across the front, the *rostrum* of captured pirate ships formed the back and both sides, curved ramming beaks supporting the roof beams. It was the inscriptions on the marble plinths in which each of the *rostrum* was set that Octavius was keen to inspect. For his campaign against the pirates, Pompeius had been given extraordinary powers by the "Lex Gabinia", a law proposed and passed by the tribune, Aulus Gabinius, one of his supporters. He was authorised to recruit twenty-five lieutenants, each with fleets of ships, enough to scour every corner of Our Sea, from the Pillars of Hercules in the west to the Propontis in the east. They completed the mission to capture or destroy every pirate ship in existence, in just three months. Although this was comparatively recent history, it was one of the first things Octavius had learned at school. Carved on the marble plinths of each of the *rostrum* were the names of Pompeius' Lieutenants and their assigned areas. Sicily was assigned to Plotius Varus; Thrace, to Publius Piso; The Peloponnese, to Lucius Sisenna, and so on around the walls. Hundreds of ships were captured or surrendered, but just one for each lieutenant had been chosen to display the naval might of Rome.

Octavius had vague memories of visiting Julia with his sister and mother at the other house. Back then, he had known Pompeius only as the fat, jolly man Julia had married. But now, he couldn't remember when it dawned upon him that the fat jolly man and Pompeius the Great were one and the same person.

He was only halfway through the inscriptions when the voice of his grandmother came from inside.

'Octavius. Don't keep us waiting for you!'

He shouldn't have needed to be summoned. Walking sheepishly through to join the others unaccompanied was an intimidating experience. All conversation stopped, and all eyes were on him as he entered the *atrium*. His first thought was, *where is the king?* Four men, comprising Pompeius and Cicero, who he recognised, and two older men that he didn't, were standing together at the far end of the *impluvium* by the statue of Venus. All were dressed in splendid tunicas as befitting the occasion of an informal private dinner. His family, who had already made their introductions, stood with an exotic-looking, but skinny, young woman, who Octavius guessed was Cleopatra. Her neatly braided jet-black hair formed a wide circle on the back of her head, but unlike Roman women, her lips were painted a deep red beneath a curved beak of a nose. Philippus, forever awkward in the company of women, even his sister, was standing beside the only other male in the group, who, in a plain white toga, did not look at all royal. Octavius had been primed in the correct way of greeting, to prepare for this moment. A kiss on the lips was appropriate for both men and women of equal status, so Octavius was expecting Cleopatra to offer a hand or a cheek. Her choice was her right cheek. Octavius leant forward to comply, with a respectful peck, catching a whiff of the sweet perfume she wore to cover the odour of the cosmetic preparations that masked the blotches on her cheeks and forehead.

Julia took him by the hand. 'Come and meet the king.' As she led a clearly nervous Octavius towards the group of four men, Auletes, wishing to put the boy at his ease, strode forward offering his right hand.

'Octavius, young man. I've heard so much about you.'

Taking the soft manicured hand in his own right, Octavius blurted, 'And I you sir,' to hoots of laughter from the other three men and Auletes himself, which rather took Octavius aback.

Although he felt he might be the butt of a joke he didn't understand, Octavius decided that he rather liked Auletes. He probably had been quite a handsome chap in his younger days, despite a rather fleshy lower lip. Octavius was a little disappointed that he looked nothing like the exotic king of his imagination, but his open show of friendliness to one so young and insignificant, in front of all the family members, put the boy at ease amongst the exalted company. Any further embarrassment on his part was spared as the janitor announced that the final three invited guests had arrived. Pompeius immediately declared he would go through to the *vestibulum* to greet them personally.

'I was unaware there was anyone else to arrive,' murmured Cicero to Hortensius. 'Certainly, they must be highly honoured guests for Pompeius to rush off like that to greet them personally.'

'I was beginning to wonder when dinner was being served,' replied Hortensius stuffily. 'My stomach thinks my throat has been cut.'

Octavius was merely glad he hadn't been the last to arrive. When Pompeius re-appeared with his three guests, two men and a woman, none of whom Octavius recognised, the atmosphere in the *atrium* changed dramatically. His family members all expressed surprise, although Julia's glimmer of a smile betrayed the probability that she had been expecting them. Auletes' countenance was inscrutable. Cleopatra's was equally unreadable, but the expression on the face of Cicero was black as thunder. If looks could kill, then any one or all three of the guests following Pompeius in from the *vestibulum* would have dropped dead upon the mosaic floor. The older man was dressed flamboyantly, a pure white ankle-length tunica, twin gold hoops around the hem and short sleeves, with brightly coloured vela scarves worn over his shoulder and carried across his arm in the style of a toga. Octavius had seen nothing like it. His hair was curled in ringlets below a purple and gold braided headband, and he appeared to have rouge on his high cheekbones. The younger man, whose shorter curls and good looks had not escaped Cleopatra, wore a short tunica with a bright red cloak across one shoulder. The woman, who Octavius took to be the older man's wife, was bedecked by more jewellery than Octavius had ever seen on just one woman. From the diadem at her brow to the gold anklet at her feet, all the rings, earrings, bracelets, brooches and necklaces appeared to be precious stones set in gold. Were they a troupe of entertainers? Not likely, judging by Pompeius' effusive welcome. As Octavius had surmised, the only introductions necessary were to the members of his own family. The older man was Aulus Gabinius, a name that Octavius had heard of but couldn't quite place. The lady, a well-preserved woman, was his wife, Lollia, and the younger man was introduced as Marcus Antonius.

Pompeius then clapped his hands three times, signalling that the food should be served, and with the lovely Julia on his arm, led his guests out of the *atrium* through the beautifully landscaped *peristylium* to the lavishly decorated *triclinium* at the far end, where a deep brick-lined aquarium had been sunk into the ground. This would be a treat for Octavius because, on previous visits, he had only eaten in the smaller family dining room at the *atrium* end of the internal garden. Cleopatra had joined Auletes and the three newly arrived guests at the head of the procession along the colonnaded walkway, followed by Octavius and his family. Following them was his stepbrother and the plain-clad guest, who Octavius had learned was Cleopatra's mentor. Philippus was still engaging him, under sparsely hidden sufferance, in an academic conversation about something or other. This left Cicero and Hortensius lingering at the rear, conversing in hushed tones.

Cicero barely contained his rage. 'What in the name of Pollux is that band of brigands and harlots doing here? Something is afoot.' During his tenure as consul, Cicero had made powerful enemies. Apart from ordering the execution of Antonius' stepfather on charges of conspiracy and accusing Antonius himself of having homosexual relationships, Cicero had implied in a letter that Gabinius pimped his wife to powerful politicians in order to further his own career.

'I've no idea,' whispered Hortensius. 'I didn't even know Auletes was back in Rome until I received the invitation from Pompeius a few days ago.'

'Nor I. I'll wager there is unfinished business between Pompeius, Auletes and Gabinius and they are using this *convivium* as a masquerade to cover their vile business. The fact that no *adventus* was arranged, to celebrate the arrival of one so exalted, raised my suspicions immediately.'

'Then why were we invited?'

'To give the gathering a coating of respectability no doubt, and we can't speak out in front of Julia's family for fear of being accused of misconstruing their intentions.'

'Well, I did wonder that my family connections were scant. Being married to Marcia, whose father is married to Julia's aunt, hardly puts me high on the list of invitees. So, you think Pompeius' explanation for Auletes' return to Rome is a sham?'

'Given Auletes' love of all things Greek, an invitation to attend the opening of Pompeius' new theatre, now that Auletes is safely returned to the throne in Alexandria, doesn't sound unreasonable; especially when you consider the lengths he went to, supporting him during his exile here in Italy.'

'Yes, I recall he entertained Auletes and his daughter at his villa in the Alban hills for a year or more until the senate finally refused to grant military support for a return to Egypt.'

'And the next thing we know is,' Cicero added testily, 'Auletes shuffles off to Ephesus, ostensibly to spend the rest of his exile making sacrifices at the Temple of Artemis; then Gabinius, faster than you can cook asparagus, quits his province in Syria, marches his army into Egypt and Auletes is re-instated after all!'

'So, what is Antonius' part in all this?'

'The worthless braggart fled to Greece to escape his creditors. I heard he went on to join the military staff of Gabinius in Syria as a cavalry officer. No doubt their shared tastes and lascivious appetites created a bond of depravity between them.'

'I don't know how you keep up with all this, Cicero. Makes me glad I retired from politics to concentrate on my fish farm. Listen, you have a garden and a library, so you have everything you need.'

'Hmm, yes I know,' murmured Cicero. 'I should remember that and be content.' The arrival of Gabinius had put Cicero in a quandary. He had been delighted to receive the invitation from Pompeius and viewed it as an opportunity not only to cement his relationship with the great man but also to make a good impression on Auletes, who was newly restored to his throne. He felt he had to challenge Gabinius for leaving his post in Syria, but he knew from bitter experience that it did not pay to cross wealthy men in positions of power and influence— especially over the street gangs of Rome. His own exile and escape from a baying mob, during the consulship of Gabinius just three years earlier, were seared into his memory. 'But someone has to speak up when provinces are being trafficked, and the honour of Rome is being bought and sold.'

'Yes, but there is a time and a place,' retorted Hortensius under his breath. 'Don't you go spoiling my dinner. I will not back you up this time; the last time I spoke in your favour nearly got me lynched.'

'Then I shall have no need of an emetic tonight,' concluded Cicero, as he and Hortensius entered the sumptuous *triclinium* and viewed the cornucopia laid before them, 'in order to enjoy this veritable feast of delights.'

Being the youngest, Octavius waited until everyone else had taken their places. Some reclined amongst luxurious cushions, scattered on a broad "U" shaped couch. The couch was indeed fit for a king, Octavius thought; decorated with inlaid ivory and supported on ivory sculpted legs resembling the heads of lions, it surrounded, on three sides, a matching table. Two plainer couches, and another table —for the less exalted guests—had been brought from the smaller family *triclinium*. A sumptuous selection of *gustatio,* displayed on silverware engraved with floral images and designs, adorned the tables to stimulate even the most jaded of appetites. Smoothly sculpted bowls and dishes of brightly coloured agate, spectacularly mirrored in the shining silverware, were laid out for each guest, with a selection of silver spoons, some with pointed handles, such as the cochlear, for shellfish, tiny quail's eggs, and snails, none of which Octavius was yet ready to try.

He was admiring the vivid scenes of feasting and dancing painted on the walls, and the marble sculpted figures set in alcoves around the room when he suddenly realised that everyone was now waiting for him to take his place at the table. They had left a space for him on the end of one of the less ornate couches. He hurriedly took up his position. The serving slaves, all in matching tunics and with garlanded hair, filed past him between the pillars at the open end of the room and began serving the guests their chosen dishes. Octavius wondered if, with his mother absent, he would be allowed to have fish sauce with everything.

Reclining next to him was his sister Octavia. She found herself fascinated by the Egyptian Princess, one year her senior, on the couch opposite and was trying hard not to stare at her too much. On her right was Cicero, busily availing himself of the fare set before them, in animated conversation with Hortensius about his fish breeding activities, and real estate prices on the Palatine. He had resolved to take the older man's advice and not let the late arrivals spoil his dinner. He was determined not to look across the table for fear of catching the eye of Antonius, who appeared slightly inebriated when he arrived and was now sprawled languidly next to Cleopatra. Philostratos, on the end of that couch and quite happy to be ignored by everyone after suffering Philippus' stilted conversation, was quietly contemplating the range of reactions their host might have to the announcement that Auletes would be making later in the evening.

Hortensius, because of his age, was the only one not reclining. He was seated in a chair between the fixed and moveable couches, Cicero on one side and his new wife Marcia on the other. Marcia didn't mind her husband's attention being exclusively taken by his old friend, as it allowed her an opportunity to catch up with her brother, lounging uncomfortably next to her. She had seen so little of him since her marriage the previous year. Philippus had been looking forward to the *convivium* with mixed feelings; any opportunity to see Tertia filled his heart with joy and dread in equal measure. An additional agitation was the presence of his young stepbrother. Could Octavius be trusted not to embarrass him again? One thing he had no qualms about was his delight at the prospect of becoming an uncle. He was only too pleased to have Marcia to talk to, as she was the only person in the room he was comfortable with; despite her having half an ear on the girlie conversation going on between Julia and the delectable Tertia, reclining on the ornate couch across the head of the tables.

Octavius reached for his *calix* and raised it to his lips with both handles. He took a sip of his thoroughly watered wine and carefully replaced the drinking vessel on the table. He then drizzled the last of his favourite *garum*, from a small, sealed amphora, over his half of a goose's egg he was sharing with his sister. Before he had taken a mouthful, the house slaves began to lay the tables for the second course. One of them, carrying a small net on the end of a rod, approached the aquarium just beyond the colonnade at the foot of Octavius' couch. He carefully lifted out a shiny fish with a long barb below its lip. Pompeius raised a hand to get everyone's attention.

'If I am to serve red mullet to a connoisseur such as Hortensius, it has to be the best!'

'Magnus, I am honoured,' replied Hortensius as the fish writhed in the net. 'The *mullus barbatus* is a very delicate creature. I should know, I feed mine by hand in my breeding pond at Baculo. They are most intolerant of captivity. For how long has this fine specimen been in your aquarium?'

'I had it brought fresh from Puteoli this morning.'

'Excellent!' exclaimed Hortensius. 'I always send to Puteoli myself when I wish to dine upon one.'

'And at five thousand *sesterces* a plate, I'll wager that Hortensius' mullets are better fed than he is,' quipped Cicero.

'No expense spared for my honoured guests,' added the beaming host with a sweeping gesture of his arm.

Octavius had never eaten red mullet before, but he recalled his stepfather having one brought into his aquarium for a special occasion during the year of his consulship. Octavia had explained to him that when the fish is taken out of water, its scales change to vivid shades of red and blue as it dies. It is then grilled and served to guests as a delicacy. When the fish's most violent contortions had abated, a second servant deftly lifted it out of the net by its tail, laid it upon a gold inlay dish, and placed it in the centre of the top table where the guests admired the display. Octavius estimated it could not have weighed over two pounds, so there wouldn't be much to share between the sixteen guests around the tables. The mullet expired and was taken away to be grilled and served. The slaves returned with meats, shellfish, and vegetables. Octavius avoided the lobster. He was not adept at extracting the meat from the shell and was too hungry to waste time on it when his favourite, honeyed rabbit, was within easy reach. It was one of the few things he didn't adorn with fish sauce.

On these occasions, he liked to listen in on adult conversation. The loudest voices were coming from the top table. Pompeius, his bulk taking up half the couch and squeezing Julia uncomplainingly up against her cousin, was having an animated discussion with Auletes.

Octavius nudged his sister and said, 'What's Pompeius talking to Auletes about? Your Greek is better than mine. Are they talking about his new theatre?'

'Oh yes, I think so,' said Octavia, pretending she had been taking notice. Instead, she had been far more preoccupied with the body language between Cleopatra, the handsome young man next to her, and the middle-aged woman, under the weight of her jewels, leaning across from the other couch. She found it far more arresting than their actual conversation, but quickly realised that she should turn her attention to her brother before they noticed her interest.

Greek was the first language of the Ptolemy dynasty and since Auletes and Pompeius were discussing the Greek tragedies recently performed at the theatre, it was natural they should converse in that language. 'Auletes is telling Pompeius how much he enjoyed the plays and ceremonies at the opening of the theatre.'

'My favourite bit was the Elephant hunt,' said Octavius, chewing on his rabbit.

'Don't speak with your mouth full,' whispered his sister.

'Mother isn't here and besides, no one else is taking any notice,' complained Octavius, daring his older sister to make a scene. He spread out his arm to show that everyone else had concluded their private conversations and had tuned in to the discussion between Pompeius and Auletes.

At that moment, the *mullus barbatus* was served on individual dishes, each with a slice of emmer loaf, to widespread expressions of approval. Octavius reached for the last miniature amphorae of *garum*, broke the seal and drowned his portion of fish in the salty sauce, despite the disapproving look from Cicero and even Philostratos, sitting opposite.

Cleopatra's tutor was enjoying his meal and feeling more relaxed in the company, now that there was a general topic of conversation he was qualified to contribute to.

He asked, 'And do you think, Auletes, that the Roman playwrights and actors did justice to the Greek tragedians?'

'I'm no expert on the tragedies my dear Philostratos, so I'm not one to make judgement. As I was explaining to Magnus just now, I am unashamed to say that my preference is for the comedies of Aristophanes.'

'I do hope that you didn't look upon Aesopus' performance too badly for losing his voice in mid-sentence,' said Pompeius apologetically. 'He really should never have come out of retirement for the role.'

'In his time, he was the greatest tragic actor on the Roman stage,' interjected Cicero, eager to contribute and repair Aesopus' reputation. 'Did you know that both he and the dear departed Roscius Gallus used to regularly attend court cases where my dear friend Hortensius was due to speak, so perfecting their art, learned from the sumptuousness and grandeur of his delivery at the bar?'

'Oh, my dear sweet modest husband,' cried Marcia. 'You never told me that.'

'Stop embarrassing me the pair of you,' retorted Hortensius. 'Why don't you make reply to the question Philostratos raised?'

'Since you ask, I hailed Accius' Clytemnestra as a triumph, although a little overdone in the staging. Of course, having met Accius himself in my younger days, I'll wager he never felt the need for six hundred mules to dress the stage for the entry of Agamemnon.'

Ignoring Cicero's outrageous namedropping, Gabinius remarked dryly, 'You are forgetting that this is Rome, and the *pleb*s need something to gawp at.'

Cicero lowered his voice in an aside to Hortensius that was calculated to be heard across the table. 'I suspect that Gabinius would make the perfect *Leno* to Antonius' *Miles Gloriosus* in any comedy for gawping *pleb*s.' Cicero's barb did find a mark across the table, but not the target he had intended. Lollia sat upright and stared at Cicero, aghast.

Gabinius, ignoring the implication that he pimped out his wife, shamelessly hinted that he was paid to restore Auletes, by replying, 'You forget again Cicero, that the *Leno* always acts legally and is paid in full for his services.'

Antonius, who either hadn't heard Cicero alluding to him as another stock character in Roman comedies—the arrogant braggart soldier—or simply chose to ignore it, rose unsteadily to his feet. He raised his hand, spilling some wine in the process, and prepared to make an announcement. Julia glanced anxiously at her husband, as did Aunt Julia at her grandchildren for fear of what was coming next. It hadn't escaped their attention that the calix had hardly left his hand all evening.

'Enough of this talk of the Greek tragedies!' declared Antonius. Then, turning to address Auletes at the far end of the couch next to him, continued, 'Auletes, the guest of honour, has already intimated his preference for comedy. Few of you will know that before joining Gabinius in Syria, I studied in Athens and consequently know much of Aristophanes by heart. So, my dear friend Auletes, do you have a favourite play or verse? If you have your instrument perhaps you can accompany me?'

Auletes beamed. 'Sadly, I didn't think to bring it with me, but anything from the Frogs would lighten the mood.'

Cicero was furious and to no small degree envious that Antonius was displaying his easy familiarity with Auletes for all to see. Without further introduction, Antonius put down his *calix*. He reached rudely across Lollia, grabbed one of Gabinius' brightly coloured vela scarves, draped it around his shoulders and held one end across his face like a veil. Upon demonstrating that he was playing a female character, Antonius proceeded to sing in a humorous falsetto voice.

'*Last night as we revelled from twilight to dawn,*
My clothes and my sandals to ribbons were torn.
It's the fault of the god, but perhaps his defence is …'

At this point, Auletes joined in with a roar of laughter:

'*That it raises a laugh and cuts down the expenses.*'

Gabinius, recognising what was coming next, filled in with the chorus to encourage his young protégé with the next verse:

'*Lacchos, lacchos, dance on and we'll follow.*'

Antonius needed no encouragement as he threw off the veil, fixed his gaze on Tertia and continued, this time in his own voice:

'*A girl I did spy as we sported and played,*
A really remarkably pretty young maid,
She winked and she giggled, but what I liked best …'

Again, but from his position on the couch, not realising the object of Antonius' delivery, Auletes joined in raucously with the last line:

'*Was the little pink titty that peeped from her vest.*'

Julia's silent stare at Pompeius said it all. *I warned you this might happen.*

Philippus boiled with impotent rage at the rudeness offered to the object of his affections. Tertia merely lowered her eyelids and blushed faintly, while Cleopatra, although embarrassed at her father's impropriety, remained inscrutable as ever. Lollia simply felt old.

But it was Aunt Julia who took action and stood, sounding two sharp claps of her hands, obviously not in this case as a show of applause.

'I think it's past my grandchildren's bedtime.' Turning to Pompeius, she added, 'Thank you Gnaeus for your invitation and kind hospitality. Come now Octavia, come now Octavius, thank Gnaeus and Julia, it's time to go.'

'But grandmother,' wailed Octavius, 'we haven't had dessert yet.'

'You can have a pear when we get home. Come on Tertia, you are coming with us.'

'In that case I will escort you,' added Philippus, dabbing the corners of his mouth with a napkin and getting hurriedly to his feet.

Hortensius, sensing that the evening was over, also prepared to leave with Marcia helping him up from his chair.

He whispered to Cicero, 'What was that you said recently about us living in the era of leisure with dignity?' and then to his host, 'Thank you Magnus, thank you Julia. Marcia and I are most grateful for your invitation, but an old man needs his bed. The *mullus* was delicious.' And with a nod to three of the guests opposite added, 'Auletes, Cleopatra, Philostratos, it was a pleasure to meet with your acquaintance.'

Pompeius smiled as he acknowledged the expressions of thanks, but was angry at the behaviour of Antonius, and disappointed that Auletes and Gabinius joined in so readily with his antics. He had known of Antonius by reputation only and would not have given an invitation but for the entreaties of Auletes, who had praised the young cavalry officer for his part in restoring him to the throne. Despite his disappointment at the abrupt end of the social side of the evening, Pompeius had accomplished his goal in hosting the occasion. Before Julia's family completed their farewells, Philostratos caught Auletes' eye.

Auletes was replying to Hortensius. 'The pleasure was all mine, my dear Hortensius and congratulations to you and your charming wife on your forthcoming family event.' Then, noticing Philostratos' questioning glance, raised an arm to attract everyone's attention. 'Before you all leave, I have an important announcement to make.' Beckoning Cleopatra and Philostratos to his side and turning to face Pompeius, he reached inside his tunic for a roll of parchment, released the silk cord and unrolled the scroll. After clearing his throat, he continued in his Egyptian, Greek accented Latin. 'My dearest friends, Gnaeus and Julia, I wish to give thanks for all you have done for me and my daughter. No amount of gold can be enough to reward you for your unwavering support. So, as a token of my gratitude, I offer you and your forthcoming family the services of Philostratos. He has mentored and educated my dear daughter to the highest degree. Now she is of age, and has no further need of his guidance, she will be ready to rule my kingdom with wisdom and learning when the time comes.'

Auletes' prepared speech transformed the mood. Suddenly everyone was smiling, except for Cleopatra, whose expression gave no clue as to whether she had prior knowledge of the announcement or not.

As his *lectica* swayed gently through the quiet streets back to his lavish home on the Palatine, Hortensius sat deep in thought.

Shaking his head, he said to Marcia. 'Cicero's greatest asset is his tongue. It can also be his worst enemy. If he does not learn to control it, it will be the death of him.'

Also heading back to the city on their own transport were Julia and her youngest daughter, Tertia. Julia was fretting not only about the effect Antonius' behaviour had on her daughter, but also on her grandchildren. She needn't have worried about Tertia, who was sitting quietly, contemplating the relative merits of her unfulfilled suitors. Although the stilted Philippus would be the better match, she tingled at the thought of a private encounter with the recklessly handsome young man she had met for the first time that evening. When the two women spoke, it was only to agree that, thanks to the will of the gods, Atia had not been present to witness events.

A short distance behind and following at an easy pace were the eight *lecticarii* of Philippus, bearing him aloft with his young charges on board. Their journey home was completed in silence.

Back at the Domus Rostrata, Philostratos sat on the side of his bed in a small chamber that would be his retreat for the foreseeable future. He was contemplating the beginning of a new life and reflecting on the past. His old life began in the same year as his master, sixty-two years ago. Born the son of an Egyptian soldier, it was soon apparent that he was not cut out for a life in the military. His father fought in the successful army of Ptolemy the Benefactor during the civil war supporting of the Egyptians, against his sister, who had the support of the Greek population of Alexandria. Ptolemy's victory marked the start of a period when native Egyptians were appointed and promoted to positions of power and influence. His father was recruited into the palace guard, where he met and married the daughter of a Greek member of the Royal Court. The following year, Philostratos was born.

In the year that The Benefactor's son, Alexander, had his mother murdered so he could marry his niece and make her his co-regent, Philostratos was sixteen years of age. Having shown more aptitude as a scholar than a soldier, he was put to work in the temple of Serapis. The temple was, at that time, being used as an overflow repository of scrolls and other documents for which there was no space in the Great Library. Any works written in languages other than Greek or Egyptian came to him to make copies of, catalogue, and file in the vast array of dusty shelves and pigeonholes. Many of these items were confiscated from the ships that docked in the harbour.

As the years rolled by, the Ptolemaic dynasty fought itself almost to the point of extinction. Philostratos was in his mid-thirties when Auletes, despite accusations of illegitimacy, was summoned back to Alexandria from abroad to be proclaimed King of Egypt. Once he had married his cousin, Tryphaeana, and made her his co-regent, things began to change. With no dynastic or external wars to fight, Auletes had time to seek better relations with the ancient priesthood in Memphis. He adopted a positive relationship with Rome in case he ever needed their support to secure his position. More importantly for Philostratos, the king developed a hedonistic interest in ancient Greek culture and literature. By the time Philostratos was in his mid-forties, the most accomplished linguist and one of the foremost academics in the library, Auletes dismissed the head librarian and appointed Philostratos in his place. The hapless incumbent had merely been an acolyte of the king's predecessor, knowing nothing of the contents of the library and caring even less. Ultimately, he incurred Auletes' wrath by being unable to locate the original manuscripts of the plays of Aeschylus, Euripides and Sophocles. These treasured items of antiquity had been secured in Alexandria for nearly two hundred years since the Athenians were tricked into lending them to a previous king of Egypt to be copied, only to find that it was the copies that were sent back to them. It was a sign of the growing stature of the Alexandrians over the Athenians that they had never been retrieved. With his extensive knowledge of the library and its filing systems, Philostratos quickly discovered the documents and presented them to Auletes on the eve of the birth of his second daughter, Cleopatra. Locating those fabled documents and holding them in his hands had given Philostratos the greatest thrill of his life. Auletes was ecstatic. He pronounced himself with the epithet "New Dionysus" and was so grateful to Philostratos that five years later, when Cleopatra began her education, the king revived the ancient custom of appointing the head librarian as a tutor in the royal household. Cleopatra proved to be an able student.

Throughout those five intervening years, Auletes sent Philostratos in the wake of Alexander the Great to learn to speak the languages and dialects of the people who previously formed his empire. During his enforced long absences from Egypt in his younger days, Auletes developed the concept that communicating with people in their own language solved disputes amicably without resorting to war. He consequently wanted the finest education for his daughter, backed by Roman military might, if necessary, as the best guarantee for the continuance of his dynasty.

Unfortunately, his courtship of the Romans did not come cheap. His enormous bribes were causing him to raise taxes. Then when the Romans took control of Cyprus, Auletes took no action and his younger brother, the King of Cyprus, committed suicide. The mood of the people turned against him. Philostratos, who by this time was declining in health, discovered that Auletes' eldest daughter, Berenice, was plotting with his wife to incite the mob, by disclosing Auletes' levels of debt and blaming him for his brother's suicide. That night three years ago was still fresh in his memory. Together with Auletes and Cleopatra, he slipped out of the palace and down to the port under cover of darkness. Having disguised themselves, Auletes bribed a captain bound for Puteoli to take them on board. The long voyage was uneventful, but two months at sea proved a tonic for him.

On their arrival in Italy, they were met by agents of Pompeius who escorted them directly to his luxurious villa in the Alban hills twenty miles short of Rome. Philostratos was disappointed not to see the famous city, but the convalescence in the cooler climate, from the summer through to the autumn of the following year, restored his constitution. During their long sojourn at Pompeius' villa, Auletes failed to win the backing of the senate to restore him to the throne, and Philostratos resigned himself to living out his days in exile with his master in Ephesus.

What he had not prepared himself for was a continuation of the journey eastwards into Syria for an assignation with Gabinius, followed by a long haul in the company of his army, back through the deserts of Judea, to the stifling heat and dust of Alexandria. That last leg of the journey that brought him full circle was horrendous. Life with the army when he was in his teen years was arduous enough, in his sixties it nearly killed him.

Fortunately for Philostratos, although Auletes was restored to the throne and his rebellious daughter put to death, he was not destined to remain in a climate that was so detrimental to his health. The coffers of the Alexandrian treasury were empty, so Auletes was obliged to make one final trip to Rome to raise funds to pay Gabinius for his troubles. Philostratos pleaded with Auletes to be allowed to accompany him on the journey in order to restore his health. Auletes was magnanimous in response. Recognising the devoted service and loyalty Philostratos had shown to both him and his precious daughter, who was now of an age to have completed her studies, he said he would take him to Rome and seek a suitable position for him with Pompeius Magnus so that he might live out his days in a kinder climate.

Throughout the day, Philostratos had been in a quiet state of anxiety about how Auletes would broach the subject and what Magnus' response would be. Now, at last, he could sleep peacefully. Pompeius had been delighted with Auletes' offer. He declared that since Julia was with child, it would be some years before a mentor would be required, but he would be honoured to admit such an eminent scholar to his service and would find amenable duties for him to attend to in the meantime.

With Pompeius' soothing words the last thing on his mind as he fell asleep, the voice of his new master echoed faintly from across the *atrium*.

'I'm glad this wretched business is finally at an end. How did you leave things in Alexandria? I understand the mob there are notoriously difficult to control.' In company with Pompeius in his *tablinum*, the other men of the gathering, apart from Philippus and Hortensius, had retired to discuss the events that brought Auletes back to Rome.

Although the question was aimed at Auletes, it was Gabinius who answered. 'I left two thousand auxiliary legionaries and enough Gallic and German cavalry to keep them quiet. After destroying Archelaus' army, the palace guard surrendered. I had the city scoured for potential troublemakers …' Gabinius set down his *calix* on the table, belched, and casually began to peel a peach with his knife, '… displayed what's left of two hundred of them on poles around the city.'

'Did you say Archelaus?' queried Pompeius in some consternation. 'Not the Archelaus who I appointed High Priest of Comana?'

'The same,' admitted Gabinius casually. 'What of it?'

'What of it?' repeated Pompeius in disbelief. 'I made him a client king of Rome. How did he come to command an Egyptian army in opposition to you?'

'Initially he approached me in Syria offering to join with my preparations against the Parthians. We made an agreement, but then he got word that Berenice desired to marry a prince of royal descent to become her co-regent in Alexandria. The little shit obviously fancied himself as Pharaoh.'

'Don't be too hard on him Gabinius,' ventured Antonius. 'His family are royalty. I knew some of them quite well. Understandably, he needed to make a good match.'

'He wouldn't have lasted long anyway,' added Auletes bitterly. 'Married to the serpent of my loins. That she-devil poisoned my dear Tryphaeana, her own mother, and I heard there was a suitor prior to Archelaus. Someone, poor soul, from the Seleucid royal house in Syria. She found his conduct not to her taste, so she had him strangled. It gave me the greatest pleasure to slit her throat personally.'

'Perhaps in hindsight, he shouldn't have replaced the gold coffin of Alexander the Great with one of glass and melted down the original gold casket for his own coinage,' mused Antonius with a sardonic grin.

Cicero, who had been listening to the revelations with great interest, shivered at Auletes' terrible disclosure. He thought to himself it was a good thing that Cleopatra retired to her room earlier and had not witnessed her father's confession that he murdered her sister. He had approached the evening with happy anticipation of cementing his friendship with Pompeius and creating a positive relationship with Auletes, but his mood had changed. The arrival of Gabinius and Antonius, together with Auletes' companionable rapport with them, had stunned him. He still suspected that his invitation to the Domus Rostrata that evening had been for the purpose of giving the event an air of respectability, but he was feeling uneasy about the reasons behind his invitation into the private office of the host to witness a de-briefing after the other guests had left.

'But what of Archelaus?' said Pompeius returning to his original question to Gabinius. 'Why did you let him break his agreement with you?'

'Simple,' replied Gabinius, 'he bribed me. Of course, that was before Auletes caught up with me and delivered my new orders as I was crossing the Euphrates.'

'Orders?' questioned Pompeius archly. 'No no no. Not orders. I merely gave my blessing for you to assist our friend Auletes and negotiate compensation for your trouble and expenses.'

Gabinius nodded his acceptance of Pompeius' definition and continued. 'I perfectly understood that Crassus was desirous to replace me in Syria, presumably because he fancied a crack at the Parthians himself. It all worked out rather well. With Archelaus and his army now supporting Berenice in Alexandria, I charged Auletes a higher price for dislodging her.'

'You never told me Archelaus bribed you as well,' uttered Auletes, aghast. 'I would never have gone to ten thousand talents if I'd have known that.'

'Ten thousand talents?' exclaimed Pompeius in surprise. 'That's nearly a year's revenue from the whole of Egypt. You drove a hard bargain Gabinius. But of course, you calculated that Rabirius would have to lend any amount to Auletes in order to restore him to the throne; otherwise, he could not afford to repay his previous loans.' Then, turning to Auletes, he asked, 'How did you convince Rabirius that he will get his money back?'

'I offered to put him in charge of taxation in Alexandria. He can stay in the post for as long as it takes for the debt to be repaid with interest.'

'Auletes agreed the contracts with Rabirius this morning,' added Gabinius. 'I met Rabirius at the baths this afternoon to confirm how I am to receive the money once he has raised it from his investors. That is why I was a little late this evening, for which, Magnus, you have my apologies.'

'Under the circumstances,' replied Pompeius, with a degree of smug satisfaction, 'apologies accepted.'

'Of course, it wouldn't do,' chimed Cicero, 'for the three of you to be seen in Rome doing business together, all in one place. Once this gets out, the *optimates* in the senate, Cato in particular, will deduce there is no smoke without fire, and one or more of you will have to answer charges of corruption.'

'And that is exactly why we are in need of the most venerable advocate in Rome,' said Pompeius in a flourish.

'You don't mean me?' gasped Cicero, who was beginning to regret accepting the dinner invitation. 'I couldn't possibly defend the existence of a Roman army of occupation in Egypt. Cato claimed that the Sibylline books forbade the king's restoration by armed force, and the senate has agreed with him.'

'A Roman army of occupation in Egypt?' scoffed Gabinius. 'There is no such thing. Archelaus was defeated by a Jewish army under Antipater, on the orders of Hyrcanus the High Priest of Judea. The soldiers terrorising Alexandria are nothing but a horde of mercenaries. Who in the senate is there to testify otherwise? If anyone can be found to testify, I will claim that the Egyptians were encouraging pirates to damage Roman trade. There, that is your answer. Will I have to conduct my own defence?'

'I still maintain you acted rashly,' countered Cicero. 'I wrote several times to Lentulus in Cyprus, urging him with all his military resources to oblige the inhabitants of Egypt to accept their king. Then, when the population has been subdued, Auletes would be reinstated in a peaceful manner. By acting in this fashion, Rome would have abided with, what Cato and his zealots insist is, the word of the Sibyl. We all know that is merely a political contrivance designed to disappoint the expectations of Pompeius' faction. And another thing, if it weren't for that statue of Jupiter in the Alban hills being struck by lightning, no one would have consulted the Sibylline books in the first place.'

'Spoken like a true lawyer,' sneered Gabinius. 'Splitting hairs may suffice to sway a jury in Rome but it wasn't enough to move Lentulus in Cyprus.'

'It would seem that the law falls silent in times of war,' retorted Cicero, settling back in his chair, arms folded.

Gabinius responded angrily, stabbing his finger. 'We have the result we desired, and the result justifies the deed.'

'But as some poet or another says, ill-gotten gains come quickly to an end.' Cicero could have bitten off his own tongue when he realised, too late, that his last comment could equally be seen as an attack on Auletes, the one man on whom Cicero most wanted to make a good impression.

The last word on the subject came from Auletes himself, whose stern expression betrayed the softness of his words. 'My dear Cicero, I am at pains to remind you, but if you hadn't blocked Caesar and Crassus' initial proposal to annex Egypt ten years ago, I wouldn't have ruined my finances by bribing Roman politicians to support me.'

The following pause was a sign that all five of the men present considered the subject of Auletes' restoration closed. Cicero, although feeling chastised, smirked internally, knowing that when Auletes had left Rome for Ephesus, he was so strapped for cash that he sold his state sedan and all its attendants to Cicero's good friend Anicius for a bargain price.

It was Pompeius who broke the silence. 'Talking of Caesar, have you received any word from Gallia, Cicero, regarding his latest exploits?'

'Nothing from Caesar since his most recent dispatches as announced by the senate, confirming that he had bridged the Rhenus to intimidate the Germanic tribes and was intending to march west in order to mop up the remaining tribes of Belgica before the winter sets in.'

'I wonder,' mused Pompeius, 'if he's still harbouring ambitions to invade Britannia? It was two years ago that he claimed Gallia was pacified and he was ordering the construction of the necessary galleys to invade, on the pretext that attacks from that quarter would threaten unrest.'

'Britannia!' exclaimed Auletes. 'That mysterious island on the edge of the world. What kind of warriors might he encounter there?'

Gaius Julius Caesar

IX

23rd August 55 BC
South coast of Britain, in the land of the Cantiaci

Caesar rubbed his eyes and tried to focus on the sparsely drawn maps spread across the table before him. Their clarity was not improved by the flickering light from the oil lamps inside his tented headquarters. Outside, it was still daylight, but swirling storm clouds were racing across a darkening sky. The heavy downpours during the day had abated to a grey drizzle. Sodden legionaries of the Seventh, under the direction of the *architecti*, swung into their well-practised task of digging the *fossa* and the *agger*, the ditch and ramparts of a marching camp, big enough to house two legions, their auxiliaries and cavalry. Every man aboard Caesar's invasion fleet, no matter what his rank and status, knew his duties once the landing was accomplished. They chose a site next to a stream emptying onto the eastern end of the landing beach for the assembly of their castrum. The officer *metatores* had flagged the ground to identify the rectangular boundaries, using his sighting devices and measuring rods. The Tenth Legion, directed by their centurions and *optiones*, had formed defensive battle formations to protect the construction site and its occupants. Outside Caesar's headquarters, the first tent to be erected, auxiliaries were lighting braziers and erecting row upon row of smaller tents for the soldiers in the areas geometrically designated for each legion. Looking up from the table, he met the gazes of the five men opposite him. His quaestor, Gaius Antistius Vetus, and his two *legati* Quintus Laberius Durus and Lucilius Racilius, flanked by the chief centurion of the Tenth Legion and his *optio*, all wore the same serious expression. Antistius and Racilius had served the republic as tribunes in Rome the previous year and had only joined his staff at the beginning of the summer campaigns. Caesar had nominated Antistius as his quaestor because Caesar himself had served as quaestor to Antistius' father while on military service in Spain many years earlier. The only other man present was Faberius, Caesar's chief secretary, whose task was to diarise the day-to-day events, facilitating Caesar's reports back to Rome.

'Gentlemen,' said Caesar, breaking the silence and stabbing his finger at a point on the coast, 'according to these maps we have beached here. The stream isn't marked, but neither is there much else from which to determine our exact position. We appear to have no choice but to dig in here and await the arrival of Labienus.' Dropping his gaze back to the table, he exhaled heavily and asked, 'What are our losses today?'

The *optio* handed Durus a tablet. Durus opened it from its twine hinges, and blinking in the flickering light, declared that they had lost twenty-four men, with another thirty-seven wounded, but only five of them seriously. Durus was ranked a military tribune, deputising for general Titus Atius Labienus, erstwhile commander of the Tenth. A broad stripe on his tunic denoted his standing as a *laticlavius*, a senatorial officer, second in command of a legion.

Much earlier that morning, just after midnight, Caesar had set sail for Britannia with two legions tightly packed into eighty transports, accompanied by warships conveying his *legati* and junior officers. His main port of departure had lacked the facilities and space sufficient for his entire army to sail together, so Labienus, his most senior *legate*, had taken the cavalry, extra baggage and heavy equipment to a smaller port further along the coast where another eighteen transport vessels had been waiting to depart. On sighting the coast of Britannia, Caesar had waited several hours at anchor, before the huge white cliffs, for Labienus' fleet to join them. Uncountable numbers of armed natives watched them from the clifftops. When the wind and tide turned in his favour, he waited no more. He sailed eastwards along the coast for several miles in search of a suitable landing site, only to find that the Britons had tracked his progress on land. Hordes of native horsemen opposed him on the beach, with others in pairs, a driver and a spearman, riding in two-wheeled chariots. Half-naked, blue-painted warriors joined them on foot, screaming abuse and banging their weapons in deafening unison on their circular brass shields.

The first wave of transports ground to a halt on the gently sloping pebble beach. Because of their deep hulls, they were well short of the shoreline, leaving a worrying drop into an unknown depth of water for the legionnaires to negotiate.

This was not how they had practised their disembarkation during the previous weeks. For a while, there was a standoff. The natives could not attack the

Romans until they came ashore, and the legionnaires baulked at leaping into the waves in full armour. The standard-bearer of the Tenth broke the stalemate. After praying to the gods, he barged his way to the gunwale of his transport and leapt into the sea, carrying the Eagle of the legion with him. At first, only the bravest of his comrades dared to follow. Scores of others, emboldened by the example set to them, and at the exhortations of their officers, followed suit and leapt into the swell. Once the legionnaires were up to their necks in the water, the natives rushed into the shallows to engage them with a rain of javelins and slingshot.

'Only twenty-four dead? I had feared worse than that, but that is still twenty-four too many,' mused Caesar. Then turning to the centurion he added, 'Crastinus, if it were not for the actions of your *aquilifer*, we might not have got ashore at all. What's his name?'

Gaius Crastinus, *Primus Pilus* Centurion of the Tenth Legion, straightened his back and visibly, even in the gloom, flushed with pride at the recognition of the bravery of one of his men.

'His name is Marcus Cassius. When he leapt overboard, I had intended to have him disciplined, if he survived, for endangering the Eagle; but his actions, and the fury in which he fought the Britons surrounding him, inspired the men into their landing formations to protect their standard.'

'Landing formations?' Antistius raised a quizzical eyebrow. 'Yes, we practised landing formations in the weeks before we set sail, but never in the conditions we faced today. The men were out of their depth and under fire. Only by the will of the gods did they reach the shore in enough numbers to put the natives to flight.'

'You don't know the Tenth, Antistius,' said Caesar. 'They have had the valour to overcome worse predicaments than this. However, before we attempt anything like it again, we must use vessels more suitable for beach landings in these conditions. Crastinus, this Marcus Cassius you speak of, I've yet to meet him. For how long has he been your *aquilifer*?'

'He joined the Tenth from the auxiliaries following our victory over the Nervii two years ago,' replied Crastinus, 'It was he who found and returned the Eagle that was lost in battle after the bearer and several centurions were killed.'

Caesar needed no reminding of that engagement. During his expedition against the Belgic tribes, he learned that the Nervian army was assembled not ten miles from his camp on the far side of the river Sabis. After sending his cavalry ahead, he led his army comprising his six most experienced legions, followed by their baggage and two new legions guarding the rear. Arriving at the top of a hill with a gentle slope down to the shallow river, he instructed his soldiers to construct a camp. Meanwhile, his cavalry crossed the river to engage with enemy horsemen on the far side, who retreated up to a similar wooded hilltop opposite. As Caesar's baggage came into view, the massed armies of the Nervii, Atrebates and Viromandui poured out of the woods, put Caesar's cavalry to flight, crossed the river and raced up the hill. The soldiers were still constructing their camp and had no time to prepare for battle. If ever there was a time to panic, this was it, but Caesar does not panic.

He recalled the thoughts that were racing through his mind. He needed to do everything at once but had no time to do anything. Give the signal to go to arms, recall men from their work on the camp and those that had gone further afield in search of material for the ramparts. Form up in battle formation and sound the *cornu* to go into action. He only had time for giving the minimal essential orders, then directed the Ninth and Twelfth against the Atrebates.

Meanwhile, the Eighth and Eleventh had driven the Viromandui back to the river, but this left the full force of the Nervii against the Seventh and the Tenth. They were still constructing the camp and suffered heavy losses. Caesar, having given orders to his *legati*, took up his shield and sword. He fought side by side with his soldiers, urging the legions with help from his military tribunes to join the two legions in a defensive formation. The Twelfth saved the day. After driving the Atrebates from the field, they returned to attack the Nervii from the rear. This coincided with his two reserve legions arriving on the scene and turning the tide. Eventually, his cavalry reformed and, trying to make up for their earlier lack of resolve, scoured the battlefield for any enemy left alive. The warriors of the Nervii were surrounded and destroyed. Row after row of them had climbed atop the corpses of their fallen comrades to hurl their javelins and stand, bare-chested, as the Roman *pila* rained down upon them as if it were a sacred place to die. It was a show of courage that Caesar would never forget.

Caesar had paused momentarily in his remembrance.

'Joined from the auxiliaries? So, he is not a Roman citizen?'

'I don't know the full story of his background General, but I'm thankful he joined our side,' replied Crastinus. 'By returning the Eagle he single-handedly saved the legion from disgrace and *decimation*. The troops hailed him and entreated him to join them, saying the post of *aquilifer* should be held open for him. Since then, he has completed his training and taken charge of the Eagle.'

Caesar considered for a moment and said, 'On that day the Tenth lost nearly all their centurions. None of the fourth cohort survived. The legion is still how many short, four?'

'Five short,' interjected Durus. 'We lost Sextus Sempronius in action this morning.'

'Sempronius gone too? I must speak with his brother.' Gaius Julius Caesar was like no other Roman General. Caesar knew by name, face and reputation every centurion in his army and whether they had siblings under arms. 'This Marcus Cassius is a born leader, Crastinus. Whether he is a Roman citizen or not, I will have him prepare for his own century when we return to Gallia. Have him report directly to me tomorrow, I need to know more about him.'

Returning to business, Caesar concluded. 'Racilius, we will need foraging parties organised for first light, and an inventory of the supplies we managed to bring up from the beach. But right now, we need a team of auxiliaries with an armed escort, detailed to build three bonfires on the higher ground across the stream before we lose what daylight remains. Have them set one hundred paces apart. Labienus must have been delayed, not to have joined our fleet during the voyage, he will be expecting a signal to locate our position. You can take care of that.'

Lucilius Racilius saluted, turned smartly, and left the tent followed by the chief centurion and his *optio*. They had unpacked only the most rudimentary folding furniture in their haste to erect a shelter. Caesar reached behind him for a chair and sat down thoughtfully, motioning for Durus and Antistius to do the same.

Antistius asked, 'What do you make of the Britons' tactics on the beach today? Do you think they will surrender, or re-group with re-enforcements?'

Caesar considered for a moment. 'Since I first set foot in Gallia, never have I seen such a disorganised rabble take to the field. But their fearlessness brings to mind the Nervii at the Sabis two campaigns ago. Their chariots are a concern, that mode of warfare has not been seen on the continent in living memory and our soldiers were not prepared. They could cause us trouble out in the open but will be of little use to the Britons once we have completed our defences.'

Durus chipped in. 'This was not the kind of welcome their envoys had promised.'

Caesar acknowledged the young tribune's comment with a nod. 'My information is that there are other warlords in the area; Taximagulus and Segovax, who have a good number of men between them. Perhaps they never agreed to send envoys in the first place and rejected Commius and his companions.' Caesar rubbed his eyes again. 'Until Labienus arrives with our cavalry and more supplies, we will have to remain vigilant. Double the watches and then I suggest you get some sleep.'

Antistius and Durus stood to salute, turned on their heels, and left the tent. Caesar nodded to his secretary, who did likewise and, for the first time in that momentous day,

Caesar found himself alone with his mildly troubled thoughts. All things considered; it had not gone too badly. He had triumphed through more serious situations than he had encountered on the beach. Looking on the positive side, the great unknown was now a reality, and he stood on the soil of that mysterious land beyond the sea at the furthest point of the known world. A frisson of excitement ran through him as he prepared for his cot, and he allowed himself to dwell upon the prospect of the bounty, and the glory that would surely be his from such a conquest. As he turned in his camp bed, one last thought conspired to give him a troubled night. Where was Commius?

* * *

The morning broke with a bright red sky in the east under dark and threatening clouds. Marcus Cassius, a bull of a man, stood to attention before his general, who was seated across the other side of a table, still covered with maps from the night before. Julius Caesar, who despite everything he had to attend to, still made opportunities to build a strong rapport with his foot-soldiers. They knew it, and they loved him for it.

'Relax trooper, stand at ease. Your valour on the beach yesterday did not go unnoticed. I wanted to meet you in person, to get to know you.' He pointed at the stack of folding chairs in the corner of the tent. The huge aquilifer took one, shook it open, and gingerly lowered his frame into it. Caesar continued, 'Marcus Cassius, that's a good Roman name but by the look of you, you are not of Roman stock. Where are you from?'

The average Roman soldier was shorter than the Gauls they fought against and those that had joined them as auxiliaries, but Marcus stood head and shoulders above them all. In action, his furious, single-handed assault on the enemy had created a beachhead for his comrades, but in person, a natural timidity sat at odds with his formidable frame.

'Belgae, originally from the Viromandui,' said the giant, in little more than a hoarse whisper.

'Belgae, that's about as far from Roman civilisation as you can get.' Caesar nodded and paused, to allow a response that wasn't forthcoming. 'And the Viromandui, one of the bravest tribes west of the Rhenus. The gods must have been smiling on us both, to spare you from my legions.' Caesar looked him up and down approvingly, to put the soldier at ease, but concluded he would only be drawn into a conversation if asked a direct question. 'Crastinus has told me you were given the name of Marcus Cassius in honour of the *aquilifer* of the Tenth who preceded you, so by what name were you known before you joined the legion?'

Marcus answered, this time with a note of pride in his voice. 'I was known as Scaeva. I am now Marcus Cassius Scaeva.'

'And you said you were from the Viromandui originally, so were you a member of another tribe?'

The sudden appearance of Durus at the open flap of Caesar's tent saved Marcus from the pain of having to talk about his distant past.

'General, the Britons have come asking for peace. Commius is here with their envoys. They wish to make terms.'

That the predicted storm did not materialise, allowing the Roman fleet to arrive intact, caused great consternation amongst the Britons. Carvillus, who had previously visited Caesar under the guise of a peace mission to encourage him to make the crossing, had argued most strongly that they should abandon all efforts to confront him. But Taximagulus, by far the most hawkish of the two, had insisted he would attack the Romans at the shoreline, and force them back into the waves.

The heavy swell on the morning of the landings encouraged the Britons as they sighted the Roman approach from the towering clifftops. Taximagulus counted the ships and assessed their strength as the fleet stood at anchor until the middle of the afternoon. A triumphant smile danced across his face, confident in the overwhelming might of his warriors and chariots to repel the invaders. When the Romans finally weighed anchor and sailed eastwards in search of a suitable landing point, Taximagulus gave the order for his armies to follow on land. As soon as the troop transports turned towards the shore, the charioteers and horsemen halted to allow the foot-soldiers to join them. When the first of the Romans leapt into the sea, the Britons, in their chariots, with their cavalry and with thousands of blue-painted warriors, swooped down onto the beach.

The transports with their deep hulls forced the Romans, in heavy armour, to disembark into a swell, unable to use their weapons. For a while, it looked as if Taximagulus' strategy would triumph. What the Britons were not prepared for were Caesar's huge warships being rowed hard from behind the transports and crashing onto the beach on the warrior's right flank. The unfamiliar mechanical motion of the oars and the sight and sound of the ramming beaks as they smashed into the shingle unnerved the defenders. But it was the devastation wrought by the ballistae, launching volleys of heavy javelins and large stones from the high platforms on the decks that made the Britons freeze in terror. The missiles hit with such force that chariots were smashed and overturned. His warriors reeled from the onslaught.

Taximagulus, from his vantage point behind the beach, saw the giant Roman carry the eagle standard and emerge from the waves, followed by streams of his comrades. Soon, troops storming ashore from smaller craft launched from the warships reinforced them. His warriors rushed in a chaotic mass to confront the invaders in the shallows, rendering their slingers impotent for fear of hitting their own comrades. Their wild fury was met by a systematic fury of equal intensity. The Romans made their defensive formations on the beach; the Britons failed to break them and faltered. When the *cornu* sounded the signal to charge, the Britons, depleted by the deadly artillery missiles against which they had no defence, fled. They clambered aboard the remaining chariots and scattered back over the ridge of dunes and out of sight. The only saving grace was that the Romans, with no cavalry of their own, could not give chase, and so, although suffering heavy losses, the bulk of Taximagulus' army survived.

Later that evening, Taximagulus returned to his stronghold. Because of its location near the coast, it was being used to coordinate opposition to the Roman landings. Not long after dusk, Carvillus and their sons joined him. Cingetorix and Segovax were still at odds over their failure to capture Cordelia earlier that day. The four of them sat around the fire grate on hay bales covered with wolf skins. The thanes and local chieftains of the chastened Cantiaci stood around the stone-floored council chamber in the shadows of the flickering firelight; several of them with bloodstains discolouring blue-painted faces and torsos. But the priests that usually oversaw such tribal meetings had melted away to their secret sacred groves, for fear of the Romans close by.

Cingetorix, and particularly Carvillus, sat stony-faced, glaring at Taximagulus, silently demanding contrition, challenging him to be the first to speak, until Carvillus could hold his tongue no longer.

'Drive the invaders back into the waves—you said. Teach the Roman curs a lesson they would never forget—you said. Wasn't it obvious to you, that when the gods allowed Caesar to land unharmed, we should make sacrifices and look to the druids for guidance?'

Taximagulus' hubris was such that even though he lost a battle, he would not lose face. Ignoring the accusing stares of his brother and nephew, he ordered Commius to be released and brought to the assembly.

It was Commius who, after having the situation explained to him, proposed a course of action. Release him immediately and he would pretend to Caesar it was the common people and the local tribesmen who had imprisoned him. Not knowing of the invitation from Carvillus, they had organised themselves and attacked Caesar on the beach. If Carvillus and Cingetorix had been at fault, it was only in failing to communicate to the people the welcome that should have been afforded to the honoured Roman guests, and for that, they were truly sorry.

And that is precisely the explanation that Commius, flanked by Carvillus, his son and a group of bloodied warriors, offered to Caesar in his campaign tent the following morning. The contingent of Britons gaped in awe at the sight of the *castrum*, complete with high watch towers in pairs on either side of the gates set in each of the palisaded walls, that had sprung up from the depths of the earth overnight as if summoned by the Romans' mighty gods.

Commius was a master at keeping a foot in both camps. He was born in Brittania to a noble family of Atrebatian descent. A generation before, his branch of that Belgic tribe migrated and formed alliances with peaceful traders who were separated from the Cantiaci in the east by the vast, dense woodland of the Coit Andred. He had always favoured maintaining ties with his Belgic cousins and eventually settled there to hone his diplomatic skills amongst the warring tribes. He had viewed Caesar's arrival after his conquest of Gaul as an opportunity to increase regular trade in woven fabrics, furs, and fine bronze-decorated weaponry. Caesar, having previously formed a triple alliance with Pompeius Magnus and Marcus Licinius Crassus back in Rome, recognised the usefulness of influential allies and both he and Commius had cultivated a mutually beneficial relationship. Caesar appointed him King of the Atrebates just two years earlier when his tribe suffered defeat and their neighbours, the Nervii, were nearly exterminated. Since then, Commius had proved himself to be loyal and courageous, of good judgement and, most importantly on this mission, respected in Britain.

For this reason, he invented a story that maintained his reputation with Caesar as a man of influence with the kings of the Cantiaci and demonstrated to those most recalcitrant amongst them he was also a man of influence with Julius Caesar. It would be foolish to cross him again.

After apologising profusely for not adequately communicating their plan to the local population, Carvillus and Cingetorix assured Caesar they would punish those responsible for the attack on the beach. Commius had assured the Britons that if Caesar's defeated enemies showed contrition, he would treat them with generosity. This he did. Having reprimanded them for the unprovoked attack, especially after sending peace envoys to him whilst on the continent, he demanded hostages to insure against future aggression. Not knowing how long it would take for Labienus' fleet to arrive with further provisions, he also demanded a daily supply of corn from the surrounding fields. Carvillus and Cingetorix led their miserable scapegoats away, leaving Caesar with Durus and Commius; Scaeva having been dismissed from the tent as soon as Durus had arrived with his message.

Commius was the first to speak, hoping to lead the topic of conversation away from any discussion of the excuses made by the Britons.

'I have to say, Caesar, I was treated with respect. Apart from being imprisoned, that is. I was unharmed and so was my escort.'

Caesar was adamant. 'I do not trust them. There are four kings of the Cantiaci. Where are the other two? Are they using these two cretins as puppets?' Commius was momentarily fearful that Caesar was directing his questions at him but was relieved when Caesar continued on a different tack. 'I'll be happier when the storms abate and Labienus arrives with the cavalry and the rest of our baggage. We are sitting here like stunned mullets. Commius my friend, I have a new mission for you. I want you to pass my good intentions on to the tribes to the north of the river they call Tamasa. They may have already heard of the surrender of their countrymen and should be less likely to cause trouble.' Looking Commius up and down, he added an afterthought. 'You may want to clean yourself up first.'

That last comment set Commius' mind buzzing. Was his somewhat dishevelled appearance at odds with his claim that he had been treated with respect? Did Caesar suspect his story was a fabrication? He contented himself that Caesar was still entrusting him to ambassadorial duties. After a rather apologetic salute, he left the tent and went in search of the camp commander to track down the trunks containing the wardrobe and personal effects he foresaw he would need once reunited with Caesar in Britannia. He knew the tribes to the north had been in a state of war for as long as anyone could remember, so he would have to tread carefully. Of Heli and the Cassi, he knew very little. His preference was to start with the Trinovantes, so if he were to seek an audience with the legendary King Imanuentus, he was going to have to look the part.

Imanuentus: King of the Trinovantes

X

25th August 55 BC
Near Cernodunon, the Stronghold of the Cassi

Following the removal of the stones, there had been nothing further to witness whilst Eneid prepared Heli's body for his last journey. A site was chosen amongst the sacred oak groves and the burial pit dug. Posts were set into the four corners of the pit to support the platform on which the body of the king would be carried in a torch-lit procession from his earthly dwelling to the consecrated place of new beginnings. Carpenters had been at work on the great sacrificial cage through the constant drizzle since early dawn, and it was now complete.

The giant effigy of a man built from wicker imprisoned terrified victims taken from the adjoining lands of the Trinovantes in recent raids, for the purpose of providing Heli with a human sacrifice, sufficient to alert the gods to his impending arrival. The burial pit was provisioned with all Heli would require for his journey; his shield, spear and sword bent out of shape as a symbol of death, ready for him in the afterlife. His corpse and that of his favourite hound would be left on the platform as carrion for the birds whose flight paths, flock shapes and behavioural patterns transmitted the will of the gods to the druid priests to interpret. Once picked clean, the bones would be laid in the pit in a final burial ceremony.

Throughout the day, the chief nobles of the Cassi and their entourages had been arriving and were now joined by Vellaunus and his closest family. They were in private celebration of Heli's life, anticipating his final journey to the Happy Place. When Eneid considered the sun, obscured by the overcast sky, had set below the horizon, he signalled for the funeral procession to begin.

Vellaunus, along with his brother Nennius and their brother Ludd's two grown sons, Androgeus and Tenvantius, hoisted the platform on which lay the body of the dead king onto their shoulders. Behind them, his sisters, Aurgania and Aryanyot accompanied by their sons Caradoc and Hirelglas. Other nobles and thanes stood amongst the tribesmen and women who lined the route, carrying torches and beating their elk-skinned drums in time to the incantations of the blue-robed bards. They followed the procession, retelling the stories that glorified the life and victories of Heli, first-born of Lugios, the Shining One.

Ahead of the platform, Eneid led the column, accompanied by his highest-ranking priests, including his brother Dwynrid, who presided over the religious rites and dispensed justice, learning and arbitration across the lands of the Trinovantes.

As the procession passed the torchbearers lining the route, they and the tribespeople around them fell in behind the bards. On arrival at the burial site, women priests danced in a frenzy around the edge of the pit to awaken the spirits. Their ululations and the drumbeats drowned out the wailing of the prisoners as they begged for mercy.

Digueillus calmly observed the spectacle lit up before him by hundreds of flaming torches. He closed his eyes and took himself back to the beginning of the previous day when he had crossed the marshes of the Tamasa soon after dawn, wearing his new leather riding boots and coat. He had bidden farewell to Bodelic and told him to look out for his signal on the evening of the following day. His fine horse was fed and rested, and he himself felt much refreshed by his deep sleep and hearty breakfast. Hope and confidence replaced the dread and fear that gripped him on the commencement of his epic journey. After Stopping only at Dun Bury encampment for refreshments, his destination came into view by late afternoon. Deep ditches and high earthworks topped by palisades and towers guarded Camulodunon, named in honour of Camulus, the God of War. It always occurred to him whenever he entered that citadel that the walls built by Ludd to guard against attack from Belgic mercenaries were now protecting Imanuentus from the revenge of Ludd's own kinfolk.

His reception in the council chamber of Imanuentus had been as formal as ever and the king listened to his story of the previous day's events with cold impartiality. From the news of Caesar's fleet being sighted, through the attempt at Cordelia's abduction, and the fugitives' encounter with the folk of the Coit Andred, his countenance had remained impassive. Unlike his son, Prince Mandubracus, seated at the king's right hand, whose expression of intense interest had replaced his usual bored malevolent scowl.

'This is all very interesting to note, but what has any of this to do with me?' said the king.

Digueillus was taken aback. He was expecting a more sympathetic response. Perhaps it was too much to hope that Imanuentus would make an immediate offer of assistance without further explanation.

'Your uncle Llyr had always been your faithful ally. Unfortunately, his faith in the love his elder daughters had for him was misplaced. As you may well be aware, he found it necessary to flee to the protection of—'

'Yes, I am well aware of my uncle's misfortunes,' interrupted Imanuentus. 'And although the fair Cordelia cannot be blamed for his treatment of me while he was my adoptive father, I have no intention of taking sides within the realms of the Cantiaci. Certainly not while I need every able-bodied man armed and ready to keep Vellaunus and his Cassi hordes away from my land.'

Digueillus now bitterly regretted not pushing his argument further. If he had done so, would he now be returning to Cordelia with an army, thus escaping the fate that had befallen him? The sickly-sweet stench of burning flesh filled his nostrils. As the heat from the flames began to scorch the soles of his feet, his agonised screams became indistinguishable from those of the other wretched captives below him, bound inside the frame of the cage.

* * *

On the morning after Heli's funeral, the information regarding the sighting of the Roman fleet, extracted from Digueillus during the time between his capture and his incarceration, was confirmed by messengers from the southern priesthoods, bringing news of Taximagulus' surrender to Caesar. The high priest

Eneid and his brother Dwynrid received the dispatch, whilst still within the stronghold of Vellaunus, with a degree of anxiety. Although it was known that the Romans were tolerant of religions other than their own, and it was customary for them to accommodate the deities of the nations they subdued, they did not countenance human sacrifice. Consequently, many of the druid communities across the continent had been hunted down and mercilessly eradicated.

Eneid and his brother joined immediately with Vellaunus, Nennius and their nephews in conference around the sacrificial stone in the centre of the stockade. The chief priest wore a sparse headdress comprising a narrow brass band around his head and a similar strip of the same metal joined to it across the top. It was customary for the simple crown to be worn when addressing tribal chieftains on matters of grave urgency.

He was first to speak. 'I have just received word from the brethren amongst the Cantiaci that the southern tribes have surrendered to a Roman invasion fleet under the command of Julius Caesar.'

Both Vellaunus and his brother had heard of the testimony garnered from one of the newly captured victims of the previous night's ceremony, so Eneid's announcement came as no surprise.

'This has come at a bad time,' said Vellaunus. 'Taximagulus told me of his plans to lure the Romans into a trap, but I had no idea the fool had put it into operation. I sent word to him to wait until I had dealt with the Trinovantes before taking such a risk.'

'There is no time for you to settle your scores with Imanuentus,' declared Dwynrid in a tone that forbade dissent, even from a king. 'The Cassi and the Trinovantes must unite. I have this morning sent a bird to Camulodunon carrying a decree bidding Imanuentus to cease all hostilities against the Cassi with immediate effect, on pain of being barred henceforth from all religious rites and festivals.'

'And I am applying the same constraint upon you, Vellaunus,' added Eneid, before the king could utter a word. The druids rarely interfered with inter-tribal matters but kept the authority to stop a war if they chose to.

Vellaunus was stunned into silence, but this was the chance Nennius had been waiting for, and with the highest members of the priesthood present to support him, he summoned the courage to openly speak his mind to his brother.

'This is the opportunity we must take in order to end the bloodshed. Ludd died attempting to bring peace between the tribes by marrying his cousin. What better way to honour him, than by completing what he set out to do?'

'You have spoken well Nennius,' said Eneid. 'We have had to make our decisions swiftly. There is no time to lose. Imanuentus has been ordered to send his entire army to occupy the southern approaches of the Tamasa while we build a defensive barrier in the river.'

Vellaunus' moment of protestation had already passed. He shot a glance at the impassive faces of Androgeus and Tenvantius. He would counsel their opinion later, in private.

Dwynrid continued setting out the plan. 'You, Vellaunus, will assemble your army on this side of the Tamasa and both tribes will send teams of carpenters and labourers to work on the construction of the defences.'

'At what point on the river should we choose to defend?' asked Nennius. Vellaunus and the sons of Ludd remained sullenly silent.

'There are but two,' answered Eneid. 'The spirits of the marshes will swallow any army that attempts to cross near the mouth. The Romans will follow the ancient high road through the lands of the Cantiaci to the first fording point, when the tide is low, at the sacred Island of Thorns. We will need a thousand men from the Cassi to build a dam upstream at the flood plains, while another thousand bury two rows of sharpened stakes into the drained riverbed. One row visible along the bank and the second beneath the water level at the deepest part. When the defences are complete, the Trinovantes can return through gaps in the barriers that are known only to us, and the dam can be removed allowing the river to flow and cover the spikes.'

'And the spirits of the sacred island will ensure our victory over the Romans,' concluded Nennius, who was happier than at any time since the death of his father. 'Allow me to escort you both back to your sanctuary and we can speak more of the benefits of peace between the tribes'.

Nennius and the druid brothers departed and Vellaunus was left at the sacrificial stone with the sons of Ludd. He placed his right hand on the stone. 'Mark my words. I have sworn an oath on my father's shadow. Imanuentus will die. Your father will be avenged, and you both will inherit your birthrights.'

Meanwhile, at Camulodunon, the followers of Dwynrid had received his bird and conveyed the directive it carried, along with its attendant threats, to Imanuentus. The threat of instant ex-communication was the most powerful weapon of persuasion that the druids possessed. Imanuentus, knowing that Vellaunus had received the same ultimatum, complied without demur. Immediately, he dispatched Mandubracus at the head of two thousand charioteers and cavalry to defend the ford at the sacred Island of Thorns, with twice as many foot-soldiers following behind. Thousands more under the command of local thanes joined the columns heading south.

Later that same day, Commius and his escort of thirty horsemen, being unaware of the existence of guides through the marshes near the estuary, approached the Thorn Island ford. He planned to cross the Tamasa at that point and bluff his way past the Cassi into the territory of the Trinovantes to meet with Imanuentus. He was therefore surprised to find the Trinovantes taking up defensive positions to the south of the great river.

Of all the diplomatic skills he employed to further his ambitions, his versatility with languages was the most useful. Not only could he communicate easily with the tribes of Gaul and Belgae, but also spoke almost perfect Latin. Now, back in the land of his birth, Commius reverted to his natural Atrebatian dialect of Brythonic, and was accepted anywhere among the Cymric Celts of Prydain as a native.

By the time of Commius' arrival on the scene, fires had been lit and the air in the vast camp was filled with the heavy aroma of roasting meat. The teams of drivers and spearmen in the camp were making themselves comfortable after their long trip, preparing their bivouacs in the fading daylight by the side of their gaudily decorated chariots and grazing horses.

His authoritative appearance at the head of his detachment of cavalry carried him through the advanced guard and ranks of charioteers until a challenge came from a local commander, who blocked his way and demanded he lay down his arms and state his business.

Courageous as ever, Commius dismounted, handed his sword to the commander as requested, and left his own tribesmen behind to barter trinkets and horse tackle with the British warriors.

Campfire conversations halted, and heads turned, following the progression of their commander leading the impressive stranger through the camp into the presence of the prince.

Mandubracus himself was gnawing double-fisted on a rack of pork ribs as they approached. Commius raised his right hand, open-palmed in the commonly accepted signal that he was unarmed and seeking a peaceful discourse, and then caught a tantalizing whiff of roasted fat, as the prince casually waved a greasy palm in response.

Gestorix, the commander, made formal introductions. 'Mandubracus, this is Commius of the Atrebates. He has heard the news of the surrender of the Cantiaci to the Romans and has come to speak with Imanuentus.'

Eyeing up the handsome features and noble garb of his visitor, Mandubracus tossed the bones of his meal onto the small fire pit beside him—causing a shower of spitting sparks—and wiped the grease from his chin and moustache on his sleeve.

'Imanuentus is in Camulodunon' he growled. 'Anything you wish to say to my father, you can say to me.'

Commius feared the warring tribes to the north of the Tamasa had already joined forces to oppose Caesar, in which case his mission would be nigh impossible, but he could not be sure. This was the moment he had to be extremely careful, not to reveal the true reasons for his assignment, or who had sent him. He would first have to weigh up the prince's likely response to Caesar's proposition.

He opened with a casual comment and hoped Mandubracus would give him an insight. 'I had not expected to find the Trinovantes on this side of the Tamasa.'

Mandubracus, not the most communicative of individuals, suppressed his instinct to give an abrupt and unhelpful answer. A thought had been germinating since he learned from Digueillus that Caesar's fleet had been sighted. He shared with his father a deep hatred of Vellaunus and the Cassi but did not share his father's blind obsequiousness to the druids. He cared not a jot for Dwynrid and his followers. Once the threat of the Romans was rebuffed by an alliance with the Cassi, the civil war would resume. He was certain of it because it would be he, Mandubracus, who resumed it. However, an alliance with Caesar would break the bloody stalemate between the tribes and leave the Trinovantes triumphant. Too bad if the priests were hunted down by the Romans and exterminated. He knew of the Atrebates, their capital, Noviomagus, and where their territory lay.

He had also heard the name Commius, but knew nothing of him, only that he was in front of him now and clearly fishing for something.

'Gestorix tells me you have heard of the surrender of the Cantiaci to the Romans. So, you are here to see which way the wind is blowing, are you not?'

Commius was taken aback by Mandubracus' bluntness and ability to read his intentions but was on safe ground as long as the prince did not suspect he had come directly from Caesar. He had been captured and held hostage once already and did not care to repeat the experience.

'Mandubracus, I know which way the wind blows. My kinsmen, the Atrabates of Belgae, accepted terms with Caesar after being defeated in battle two summers ago. Their neighbours, the Nervii, the most powerful tribe of all, fought on and were destroyed. Now the Romans are here, on our soil. The Cantiaci opposed just a small expeditionary force and were swept aside. My kinsmen have learned to live at peace with Rome and their way of life is respected. It would be foolish to oppose first and be forced into terms later. Together, we can make more favourable terms if we still have our armies intact behind us.'

Although an alliance with Caesar would suit Mandubracus perfectly, Commius' proposal was not exactly what he had in mind. He also knew that his father and the druids, and probably Vellaunus too, would fight to the death rather than accept life under Rome, and that is exactly what he told Commius.

Then he added his own thoughts, 'While my father is king, I must obey him, so if you are looking for an alliance of tribes to approach Caesar peacefully, you have come to the wrong place; you should have stayed at home. Queen Cordelia of the Cantiaci is on her way to Noviomagus to seek protection after her own family tried to take her prisoner. It is said she would favour an alliance with Caesar if it meant returning her to her throne.'

Commius was shocked by the revelation. Since the news of Llyr's death and the invitation to Caesar from Carvillus, he hadn't given a thought to the whereabouts of Llyr's youngest daughter. He knew of her history but assumed she had returned to the continent with her husband, after Diviciacus had restored her father, Llyr, to his seat as King of the Cantiaci. It had been many years since Commius had met with his closest kinfolk, the Atrabates of Prydain. Noviomagus was his family home. He knew his family to be traders rather than warriors. They would welcome Cordelia and give her shelter but could not restore her to her seat unless persuaded to join cause with the Romans. The possibilities flitted through his mind like the sparks from the campfires around him. He kept his composure and hoped that Mandubracus was not still reading his thoughts.

'This is news to me. How did you come by this information?'

'An ambassador from Cordelia came to us at Camulodunon the day after Caesar's fleet was sighted,' said Mandubracus matter-of-factly. 'He appealed to Imanuentus for aid but was turned away.'

Keeping up the pretext that he had travelled to the Tamasa from his homeland in Prydain, Commius replied, 'Then I will return home tomorrow at first light, to seek an audience with the deposed Queen of the Cantiaci.'

'Be our guests,' offered Mandubracus with uncustomary geniality, then to his commander, who had been listening attentively to the conversation. 'Gestorix, see that our friend and his escort have food and drink.'

As the pair turned and made their way back through the camp, a rare expression came across the face of Mandubracus. It was a smile of satisfaction.

Later that evening, Gestorix returned to Mandubracus after entertaining Commius and his men.

The prince enquired, 'So, were there any loose tongues amongst them?'

'There were. One or two let it be known they were grateful for the genuine hospitality, because the last time they were invited to eat, they were overpowered and held captive.'

'Held captive by who?'

'The Cantiaci. Out of the earshot of Commius, they told me they had escorted him to Prydain as an ambassador from none other than Caesar himself. They were released when Taximagulus surrendered.'

'I knew it. I knew he was hiding something. Good work my friend. Tonight, we have gained an important ally. We must be careful how we use him.'

XI

27ᵗʰ August 55 BC
South coast of Britain, in the land of the Cantiaci

The bonfires had been burning for four days and it was no longer a secret from the natives that Caesar was waiting for the rest of his fleet to arrive. Although local thanes visited to pledge their allegiance, and provide corn supplies and labour for the camp, the promised number of hostages had not been sent and there was no further dialogue with the tribal leaders. Locals tasked with supplying the Romans with corn had now returned to their farmsteads and were seen no great distance from the *castrum* at work in their fields.

A feeling of uneasy peace enveloped the encampment, and the sentries were kept on full alert. Perhaps it was because Durus was deputising for Labienus that Caesar gave him the responsibility of keeping bonfires alight.

It was during his daily inspection of the stores of logs and faggots keeping dry under canvas shelters that the glimmer of a ship's light twinkled momentarily through the incessant grey drizzle. Coastal visibility had been limited ever since they landed. No sooner had he glimpsed it, than several more appeared. Within the next few minutes, he counted all eighteen of Labienus' transports out at sea, beyond the eighty of the first landing riding at anchor. The warships were hauled up the beach to the rear of the camp below his vantage point. The wind had been picking up throughout the day and a tremendous gust fanned the flames of his bonfires almost to extinction. Then came the rain, first in heavy droplets, then in sheets, then torrents. Surely Labienus must have seen his signal and pinpointed the position, but Durus couldn't be sure. He ordered the auxiliaries tending the bonfires to light more faggots under the cover of the shelters, but the sudden gale ripped at the canvas covers until they broke free in a frenzied dance and tumbled away towards the beach. Durus looked on helplessly. The deluge extinguished two of the three fires. Now, with his saturated cloak clinging to his body and acting like a sail, almost taking him off his feet, he gritted his teeth and stared out to sea. The lights were still there but appeared no closer to the shore. If anything, they were moving further along the coast, driven before the north-easterly gale that took hold of them. He stared after them in disbelief until the last light disappeared from view into the storm.

Lowering his gaze into the nearer distance, an even more harrowing sight took his breath away; several of the transports had smashed against each other after breaking free of their anchors in the storm. Each massive wave tossed their wreckage further up the beach. Others lost their masts and sails but were still afloat. The beached warships used as temporary grain stores were tipped on their sides by the high tide and were now waterlogged; the supplies, gathered by the foraging parties, ruined.

Durus had kept his head in desperate situations before. Two years earlier he had seen action at the Battle of the Sabis, where he had fought sword-in-hand, side-by-side with Caesar himself, against the massed tribes of the

Nervii, Atrabates and Viromandui. but this was quite a different plight. Labienus commanded the Tenth on that occasion, but now he was gone, blown away.

It was Labienus who had sponsored him into the role of military tribune as a favour to Durus' father. He was a wealthy man of the Equestrian rank, who owned land and vineyards that enabled him to finance much of Labienus' fortifications of their hometown of Cingulum when young Quintus was just twelve years old. The peaceful view from his father's vineyard on the slopes of the Apennines, across the rolling hills of Picenum to the Mare Superum, was a world away from the nightmare view of the sea before him now. Under the clear blue sky of home, the mountains of Illyricum were visible on the distant horizon. Since his arrival in the—once mythical—land of the Britons, the sky had only been shades of grey.

The despair in the Roman camp that greeted the effects of the storm was felt in equal and opposite measures amongst the Britons. The seer, who predicted the storm at the conjunction of a full moon occurring near the autumn equinox, and foresaw the wreckage of the Roman fleet, was vindicated. The atmosphere in the council chamber was full of jubilation.

Taximagulus was exultant. 'I say we attack the camp at dawn, while they are still in disarray.'

The cheers that met this announcement were stilled by his brother Carvillus, as ever the cautious one, who raised both arms to quell the tumult.

'That would be a grave mistake. They were in disarray on the beach, but they still made unbreakable formations we could not penetrate.' The sudden silence in the room showed he had everyone's attention, so he continued. 'To attack them in their own fortress would be futile. Our chariots would have destroyed them on the beach had they not made their defensive positions, so they will be useless trying to breach their ditches and ramparts now.'

'I say we attack now with our brave soldiers while we can catch them off their guard,' cried Segovax, supporting his father's initiative.

'Yes, catch them off their guard, but out in the open where we can use our chariots against them effectively,' was the immediate riposte from Carvillus.

'And how do you propose to force them from their camp?' growled Taximagulus.

All eyes were on Carvillus now. This was his chance to present his plans without further interruption.

'Their bellies will force them out. Our farmers, under the direction of the local thanes, have been delivering corn to their camp. The Romans kept it inside their warships on the beach, while they completed the construction of their grain stores. We now know, from our people inside the camp who have slipped away under cover of darkness, that those vessels are now overturned and flooded, and the grain is ruined. All the local fields have been harvested and the Romans will now have to search further afield, or they will starve.

'This is when we will strike, but we must bide our time and not give them any reason to suspect our intentions. That is when we catch them off their guard. Out in the open, with their arms laid down, cutting the corn; then they will be at the mercy of our charioteers.'

'What say you Taximagulus?' crowed Cingetorix, full of admiration for his father's plan.

His uncle pulled at his moustache and exchanged a thoughtful nod with Segovax before deciding, as if it were his own idea.

'We have waited a long time for this moment since the storm and the wrecking of the Roman fleet were foreseen during the festival of Beltane. We have made plans and sent our envoys to Caesar, led by my good brother, to persuade him to make the voyage across the sea into our hands. Now he is helpless, and we have him where we want him, we should not spoil our chance of destroying him by acting in haste.'

XII

28th August 55 BC
The banks of the Tamasa, at the Island of Thorns

Scaeva was thrilled when Gestorix had invited him to ride in his chariot, for the dash to the great dark river. Scaeva's uncle was much more of a father to him than his real father ever was. Ebracus, the first-born, had always been the favourite. Gestorix had deposited Scaeva, out of harm's way, just before crossing the river to join his army on the southern bank. The young boy was left to wander at will amongst the muscular sweating tribesmen of the Cassi, most of whom still wore clothes made from an assortment of animal skins. He stood and watched them hauling huge logs and sawing them into stakes, then sharpening one end with axes, ready to be positioned in a row and driven into the middle of the riverbed. Because of a dam built several miles upstream, the mighty river had all but disappeared. At low tide only a few feet of water now trickled through the mud in the watercourse.

No one had taken any notice of him until a familiar, mop-haired, stick-thin figure approached from out of the throng of burly workmen and called to him. 'I've been talking to your brother.'

'What about?'

'About the wild pony you captured.'

'What of it?'

'You told him a story. A story about your encounter with Epona.'

'I just made that up for a laugh.'

'That's what Ebracus told me. But you should not make a joke of such things. You have been taught the spirits only make themselves known to the chosen. That's one of the first things you learn at your sittings in the sacred groves, and you have been attending all summer.'

'Well, what about Lugh? He makes himself known to us. We can watch his journey across the sky every day.'

'That's different.'

'What's different about it?'

'Questions, Scaeva. Questions. You ask too many,' replied the older boy in the customary superior tone he reserved for when he didn't know the answer. Caspar was a few years older than Scaeva's brother Ebracus and had been training for the priesthood since he was eight.

'You started it, asking questions,' retorted the younger boy.

'I don't ask, young Scaeva. When I speak to you, I tell, and I am telling you now, the word druid means "The Truth." The Truth against the world, so don't go telling lies about the spirits.'

'Then tell me where Lugh goes at nighttime.'

'Pay attention to your instructor during your lessons and you will find out.' Caspar enjoyed teasing Scaeva. He made a casual sport out of their encounters because the younger boy always rose to the bait.

Like most boys and girls of his age, three mornings each week, Scaeva attended the college run by the druids where he learned the three main principles of wisdom: obedience to the laws of the gods, concern for the common good, and courage in the face of the accidents of life. This moral philosophy was taught alongside an appreciation of the natural world and respect for the sacred entities that inhabited it. Although not the most attentive student, he enjoyed his lessons; but unlike Caspar, he had no intention of remaining beyond the minimum term to be inducted into the higher mysteries.

Scaeva fought back the urge to blurt out that the story about Epona was true, but was concerned, because he did not know what being chosen actually meant, and no one would believe him anyway, so he changed the subject. 'My uncle Gestorix brought me here to watch the defences being built in the Tamasa. I didn't expect to find you here though.'

'I'm here with my mentor,' ventured Caspar freely, 'and he's here to witness our stand against the Romans. History will be made right here, Scaeva, and my mentor will be the first to tell the story that will be re-told until the end of time. No doubt you will listen to it with your grandchildren, and you will tell them you were there to witness the glorious victory over Rome.'

Scaeva had never known Caspar to be so animated or so forthcoming. 'But I thought you were studying with the priesthood to become a druid?'

'That comes later. The first twelve years are spent mainly with the bards, learning the stories and the poems. We learn the newer ones first, but it takes many years to go all the way back to our earliest ancestors. I have just learnt the englyn to Heli, the old King of the Cassi. He has recently returned to the Happy Place. His son Vellaunus would have continued the war against your people had the Romans not arrived in our midst.'

'I do know that much,' said Scaeva. 'Uncle Gestorix has told me about that. The war between the tribes is over.'

He shivered at the thought of being at war with these savage-looking people. He had never seen the Cassi up close before. A team of them, ankle-deep in mud, were taking turns pounding the wooden stakes into the riverbed with their massive iron hammers. A second team was following them, hewing the top ends of the logs into sharp points with their axes. Scanning the activity upstream, a second row of huge spikes was being driven into the nearside bank at the same angle as the shorter stakes in the middle of the riverbed. Beyond them, through the drifting smoke from sacrificial offerings, the sacred Island of Thorns was no longer an island. The stream that had surrounded it had also been dammed and scores of Cassi workmen were being escorted in and out of its dense woods by women priestesses wailing their incantations to the spirits.

'What's going on over there?' said Scaeva, pointing towards the smoke.

'The spirits have given their permission to use the beech from the sacred island to form our defences. The priesthood is there to ensure that no sacred trees are touched, and to offer thanks to the spirits in sacrifices.'

'Aren't the oak and the ash sacred trees?' offered Scaeva, trying to display what little knowledge he had of such things.

Caspar stared at him in exaggerated shock and surprise. 'I can't believe that you've actually learned something useful.'

As usual, any respite from Caspar's teasing was short-lived. Scaeva struggled to think of something he knew that Caspar didn't. For just a moment, he considered boasting that his encounter with Epona was true, but he'd already decided it was for the best to keep that to himself, and he had lied about it once already. Then he thought of the stories his uncle had told him. 'I wager you don't know what my uncle keeps in a chest.'

'Why should I care?' came Caspar's lofty reply.

Scaeva told him anyway because Caspar's one weakness was his squeamishness. 'It is the head of one of his grandfather's enemies. It's embalmed in cedar oil and it's older than he is, but its eyes are open,' and with extra relish, he added, 'and it stares up at you like it's still alive.'

Caspar pulled a grimace. 'That doesn't surprise me. I've heard that he nails the heads of his own battle victims to his door'.

'They're not all battle victims,' said Scaeva. 'He told me that some of them are human sacrifices from his homeland. They have druids there too. The high priests cut their hearts out while they are still alive and watch the blood pump. No doubt, in time you will be taught how to do it.'

Caspar kept his composure but some of the colour drained from his face. 'I have plenty of time to prepare for that, but I cannot waste time with you all day. I need to rejoin my mentor.' With that, he turned sharply and strode off, trying to keep out of the way of the busy tribesmen. A wide grin grew across Scaeva's face, and he felt a glow of satisfaction. He had a trump card if Caspar got too far above himself again.

XIII

2nd September 55 BC
South coast of Britain, in the land of the Cantiaci

Four days and nights of feverish activity had transformed the scene on the beach. Under the direction of Titus Sillius, an experienced auxiliary officer of equestrian rank, the Romans salvaged everything they could from the most severely damaged vessels. Rigging, timber, bronze and iron fittings had all been stripped from the wrecks. Barrels of nails, sails, spars, and other items of naval equipment, to replace that which was damaged beyond repair, had been brought from the continent on commandeered merchant vessels.

Sillius had campaigned two years previously with the Seventh Legion under Publius Crassus against the sea-going tribes of Armorica. He was central to the building of the Roman fleet that defeated the Veneti, the strongest of the naval powers on the Atlantic coast. Consequently, all the maritime tribes in that part of Gaul were now subjected to Roman rule. That winter, because of a scarcity of food in the region, Crassus had sent officers, including Sillius, amongst the settled tribes to negotiate grain supplies. The Veneti, who were still aggrieved that the hostages they gave to the Romans on their surrender had not been returned to them, detained Sillius, despite their cordial relations with him personally, and demanded their hostages back. Other tribes in the area followed suit and kept Crassus' envoys as prisoners. The situation remained unresolved throughout the winter until Caesar himself returned from his province at the beginning of the new campaigning season. This eventually resulted in the Veneti, and their neighbours being crushed for a second time. Although Sillius and his fellow officers were left unharmed, the rebellious tribal leaders were all executed and many of the people sold into slavery. Sillius spent his time in captivity honing his knowledge of the construction of ocean-going vessels, which stood him in good stead as overseer of the repairs to Caesar's stricken fleet on this beach in Britannia.

The legionnaires were not known for their shipwright skills, but enough of them had been involved with the building of the fleet during the summer for them to be effective in making the necessary rude repairs. Now, the last few vessels to be renovated stood as massive hulks between their wedges in the shingle as legionnaires and the most skilled of the engineering auxiliaries scrambled up and down the netting, attending to the final snagging. All but twelve ships were repaired and declared seaworthy enough for the return home—whenever the gods decreed that might be.

Sillius and Durus surveyed the scene. Sillius nodded with quiet satisfaction, but Durus' thoughts had sped back to the day of departure when offerings were made to those same gods to ensure a successful crossing. In all his young life, Durus had, until that day, never set foot on board any kind of floating vessel. As a boy, he used to gaze across the Mare Superum, that innocuous-looking expanse of water, to the distant mountains. He had paddled and frolicked in the warm surf on the beaches until a sudden swell lifted him momentarily out of his depth. He panicked and gulped mouthfuls of seawater before his desperately kicking feet grounded again in the soft sand. A common experience for many, but it left him with an inert fear of drowning. A fear that he struggled to suppress in the days leading up to their embarkation.

So, the moment he had been secretly dreading finally arrived. Dark clouds scudded across the face of the moon, creating an eerie glow on the rigging and masts of the assembled fleet. He marched down the dock and across the gangplank of the massive bireme in the company of the other officers with no outward sign of fear, but his stomach was in knots at the thought of what was to be endured. The gentle rise and fall of the deck under his feet was uncomfortable, but the morale-boosting banter of the other officers had initially put him at ease.

Once the anchor was weighed and the oarsmen had manoeuvred the craft out of the shelter of the port, the stiff westerly wind snapped the huge single square sail taut. The ship almost leapt into the fearsome foam-flecked waves and the all-enveloping blackness beyond. Their course was east along the coast before the steady wind, but the captains tacked to the north to reach their destination. This caused the bow to pitch and yaw through the waves, with the icy sea crashing over the gunwales and soaking the high spirits out of the high-ranking Romans on board; many of whom had fallen silent, emptying their stomachs into the bilges. After a seemingly never-ending starless night of clinging to any sodden handhold in reach, a faded pink dawn lit the sky on their starboard side. Evidence at least that they were travelling in the right direction; but all around, nothing was in sight but the heaving, grey-green deep. A cry came down from the lookouts atop the masthead, and shortly afterwards Durus caught his first sight of the mythical land of the Britons. As the bow rose and fell through the crashing white foam and the horizon bobbed in and out of view, the towering white cliffs caught his eye in the early morning light and a terrifying thought flashed through his mind. Could the stories be true? That the land behind those stupendous masses of natural bulwarks was inhabited by giants? Those thoughts were soon banished by the comforting sight of the other ships in the fleet, confidently powering undaunted through the swell, towards their destination. The oncoming daylight and the sight of dry land restored his spirits. He would be ready to do his duty.

Sillius turned to the young tribune. 'Have the merchants brought any word of Labienus? They've been going back and forth for three days now.'

Durus, who was privy to the General's briefings, was jolted out of his thoughts by the question.

He shook his head. 'Nothing. Not a word officially, but the story is that his fleet was badly scattered by the storm. The tides took the transports back to Gallia, separated by many miles of coastline. It could take a *nundinae* or more for them to re-group, so I will have to keep the bonfires burning for many days to come. Did you salvage any corn from the hulls of the warships?'

'Not much,' said Sillius. 'What we saved will last us a few days if we are careful. We lost nearly everything the natives harvested in the local area. Since the storm, they've stopped bringing in supplies.'

'That's what worries me,' said Durus. 'They will be aware that our cavalry and much of our baggage and heavy equipment has failed to reach us and we are vulnerable. The Seventh is sending out cohorts every day on foraging missions. They are bringing in all they can find, but they're having to travel further afield each day.'

'Yes, I know,' said Sillius with a wry smile. 'My comrade in captivity, Quintus Velanius, is leading them. He told me last night it was safer to forage in the company of four cohorts of armed legionnaires than to be sent in pairs to approach the natives to negotiate a grain supply. We've both been there, done that and got the tabard!'

The sweet smell of the rain-drenched wheat came to Velanius on the wind before he sighted the unharvested fields beyond the rising ground ahead. His scouts had led him fully seven miles inland from camp. Beads of sweat trickled down the small of his back under his *cuirass* and tunic. It wasn't from the exertion of the march; seven miles was nothing to Quintus Velanius, nor to the columns of infantry stretched out in marching formation behind him. It was the silent, abandoned hamlets, newly harvested cornfields, and empty grain stores they had passed that filled him with a sense of foreboding.

As he breasted the rise through two rows of pine trees, a field of wheat, tall stemmed, ripe-eared, and ready for harvesting, lay before him at the bottom of the slope on the other side. It was surrounded on three sides by thick forest and was so obviously a perfect spot for the ambush that— he could feel in his bones—had been coming for the past three days. The recent heavy shower that sweetened the aroma of the wheat on the breeze was the first rain since the storm that devastated Caesar's fleet, at anchor on the night of the full moon. The well-drained ground had dried, and the broken stalks of recently harvested wheat fields crunched beneath the hob-nailed, leather-soled *caligae* of four cohorts, two and a half thousand battle-hardened common soldiers, the *milites gregarii* of the Seventh Legion. There was not a man among them who wasn't aware of the danger; it only heightened their sense of readiness for a sudden attack. There was not a man among them who was afraid. There was not a man among them who hadn't killed uncounted numbers of Gauls and Belgic alike, and if the Britons dared to show their blue-painted faces, they would undoubtedly suffer the same fate.

One of those men was Lucius Casca, an olive-skinned veteran of many bloody campaigns, who had followed Caesar out from Rome three years earlier when the General embarked upon his conquest of Gaul. He had marched and fought every inch of the way from the Alpes to the Rhenus, and then to the very edge of the known world, and beyond. He was not one for collecting battle souvenirs, but he was intrigued by the stories of the mythical Britons that circulated around their coastal encampment prior to their embarkation. There was nothing worth taking from the bodies of the dead natives left on the beach, but he had satchelled a bronze decoration from the wreck of one of their chariots. This item, small enough to fit in the palm of his hand, was a beautifully fashioned fox's head, crowned with oak leaves. He had it in mind, as he eyed the rolling open landscape and the wooded horizons around him, that if the Britons dared to attack again, he might start a collection.

Casca was brought up amongst the slum tenements of Suburra. Due to the military reforms of Marius, a career in the army had been opened to the landless poor, with the promise of land of their own to farm on retirement. Casca signed up for his twenty-five years of service at the tender age of eighteen. The dictator Sulla had recently died, and Rome had enjoyed several years of relative peace until Spartacus' slave revolt. That was when Casca first saw action. Now he had just two more campaigning seasons before he would retire with his savings, and his trophies, to his promised plot of land.

Unlike the seasoned professionals behind him, this was only Velanius' second campaigning season. He had spent his first as a hostage prisoner of the Veneti in Armorica the previous year, along with fellow staff officer Titus Sillius. Although Velanius had complete confidence in his centurions, should he have cause to call them into action, he'd grown more anxious with each passing mile away from the camp. As he stood amongst the lines of trees on the low ridge, he surveyed the tranquil scene around him. Down the slope ahead of him was the field of wheat, discovered by his scouts, bordered on three sides by broad-leafed forest. Behind him was the wide flat valley of harvested fields he had passed through. The rolling hills on either side were topped with distant wooded fringes. If there were to be an ambush, it would come from the forest around the wheatfield. The ground behind them was far too open. Infantry would be seen a mile away and would carry no element of surprise. The trunks of the rows of trees along the ridge looked close enough together to protect them from a sudden attack by chariots. He gave the order to send scouts into the woods around the perimeter of the wheat fields, and for the centurions of three of the four cohorts to adopt defensive positions.

Casca's cohort, along with the legionary auxiliaries, was assigned to the harvesting and baling of the wheat and loading it onto the many ox-drawn carts now stationed around the fields. He was disgruntled that he should be assigned to a menial rather than a military task, but cheerfully joked with his comrades that they had drawn the short straw. It was warm work in their full marching armour.

By mid-afternoon, when the anticipated ambush had not materialised, several of his comrades defied the orders of the *optiones* and unlaced and discarded their chain mail shirts. A faint rumbling made Casca straighten up and peer back up the slope through the line of trees to where a cloud of dust was drifting up in the distance. He wasn't sure whether it was a sound he heard or a vibration in the ground beneath his feet. Velanius, from his position on the ridge amongst the pines, had a direct line of sight to the rapidly advancing wave of chariots surging along the wide valley towards him. Too numerous to count against the dust cloud in their wake; hundreds more poured out of woods on either side to join them. He ordered the cohort in the field to gather the wheat-laden carts, collect their arms, and line up in battle formation behind the trees. But he hesitated on how to deploy the other three cohorts around the edge. As the chief centurions of each cohort stood before him, poised for action but awaiting his command, the low droning sound of Celtic carnyx horns reached their ears from all sides. His scouts came racing out of the forest, shouting their warnings, followed by volleys of spears, two of which found their mark and grounded the screaming legionnaires.

Velanius stood open-mouthed for a moment, then screamed, 'Agmen formate!'

Even though a defensive square would lead to them being surrounded and unable to establish a front line against the enemy, the centurions leapt off in all directions, shouting orders to their *optiones*. Casca collected his *scutum* and *pilum*, and ran to take his place in the formation, taking shape behind the trees, as the auxiliaries were left to drive the wagons into position. Along the edges of the field, the other cohorts had already locked shields against the hail of slingshot being loosed against them from the unseen Britons in the shelter of the thick forest. Under bellowed directions from their *optiones*, the lines of legionnaires were backing away from the forest edge, forming additional rows behind as their front lines contracted. The manoeuvre was completed in textbook fashion by the well-drilled soldiers, without further casualty; but there was a limit to this kind of retreat before the standards became confused with each other, causing a lack of cohesion and discipline amongst the ranks.

Casca's century, forming the front row of the cohort facing the pines, was instructed to attack any chariots that squeezed through the tree-lined ridge less than a hundred paces before them. First, they would loose their *pila* at anything that came through the trees, then attack in skirmishing groups on orders from their *optio*.

And so they waited in formation, with the dust cloud getting closer by the second beyond the rows of trees. The sound of thundering hooves melded with the screams of abuse being hurled with accompanying slingshot from the woods all around them. Suddenly, waving javelins and the heads of horses appeared between the rows of trees on the short horizon. In a flash, scores of chariots shot through the gaps between the pines at full speed with such precision that there couldn't have been a thumb's width between the spinning wheels and the tree trunks. Unlike the engagement on the beach where the shiny wet pebbles and shifting shingle had made them appear ungainly and difficult to control, the firm even ground allowed these archaic war machines to be used to terrifying effect on an enemy trapped in the open, that had no tactics to oppose them. Each was manned by a driver and a spearman, throwing javelins from an onboard quiver. The chargers were driven full tilt at the Roman front line, which shrank back against the rows behind; then at the last moment, pulled abruptly to one side, causing the chariots to scythe like a pendulum, skittling the front row and allowing the following spear man a clear shot through the gap. The legionnaires hurled their *pila* at the fast-moving targets with little effect until one driver was hit. His horses, now out of control and maddened by the noise of battle, leapt the front row of soldiers. The men at the front ducked the flying hooves instinctively but were mown down by the heavy spinning wheels that followed. The spearman was quickly dispatched, but the crazed and wounded horses thrashed around amongst the ranks, causing mayhem.

Once the line was breached, other chariots poured through the gap into the open space behind, exposing the backs of the ranks facing the slingshot from the forest. This threw the legionnaires into confusion and, at that moment, a second signal from the carnyces sent thousands of tribesmen armed with swords and bronze-bossed shields pouring out of the woods to clash with the soldiers in the front rows. Once the javelins of the spearmen were exhausted, they leapt naked out of their chariots to engage the Roman lines from the rear with their long swords. Even though the troopers trained daily at their skirmishing posts to prepare for such encounters, they soon began to tire. The Britons, when pressed, were relieved by their charioteers skilfully driving their war machines close enough for their comrades to leap aboard allowing fresh warriors to take their place.

Casca, having avoided being mown down when the chariots first crashed through the lines, found himself in the thick of the melee. He discarded his *scutum* as an encumbrance with the enemy all around him. He found himself in single combat with a naked, blue-painted Briton who nimbly evaded every thrust he made with his short *gladius*. Out of nowhere, a chariot thundered straight at him from behind his adversary. In the blink of an eye, the Briton spun around and leapt into the air between the chargers, grabbing on to their harnesses as he did so. Casca dived to his right, avoiding the hooves, but the wheel of the chariot took his left leg as it shot past. Casca screamed in agony as he writhed on the ground, clutching at his shattered knee. The Briton, meanwhile, skipped along the harness pole of the rig, joined his comrade in the cockpit and resumed hurling a fresh set of javelins at any shiny-helmeted target that presented itself.

Casca regained consciousness to the haunting sound of male voices in harmony. Their native language, unpronounceable to him, transformed into something you could almost touch; a mixture of deep velvet and smooth, shining leather. He was immobilised, not only by the injury to his leg but by the weight of two dead comrades, fallen across him, pinning him to the ground. Within his field of vision, he saw native warriors traversing the battlefield, carrying away their slain comrades and accompanying their harpers with mournful songs. The sound of footsteps nearby came closer, so he dropped his head to the ground and held his breath. A native warrior, a bare-chested, blue-painted woman, moved amongst the dead bodies as if searching for something. She carried a long knife. As the figure came towards him, he shut his eyes and dared not to breathe at all. The warrior now stood above him and bent down. She pressed a cold steel blade against his neck. He offered his final silent prayer to Jupiter, as the Briton flicked her wrist and sliced the blade through the leather chinstrap of his helmet. Casca didn't know whether to thank his gods or curse them, as the Briton wandered away with her trophy.

Cordelia: Queen of the Cantiaci

XIV

2nd September 55 BC
South coast of Britain, in the land of the Cantiaci

Caesar returned to camp to find a message from Labienus awaiting his attention. He collected it from the communications tent erected next to his headquarters in the *principia*. Antistius, Caesar's quaestor, handed it to him. He had been assigned duties, including the setting up of communications with the continent. Antistius was seated in his customary position in front of racks of pigeon-holed shelving, most of which were empty. The message had arrived during the past hour on the pinnace that was now being used for vital communications with his Chief of Staff, until such time as both were on the same side of the Oceanus Britannicus.

Eight hours earlier, his sentries sighted a cloud of dust in the distance to the north. It was in the same direction that Velanius had set off with four cohorts of the Seventh, soon after dawn that morning, to gather much-needed grain supplies. Guessing what might be occurring, Caesar had acted speedily. The soldiers most readily available were the cohorts on guard duty. He ordered them to arm themselves fully and follow him immediately, leaving orders for them to be replaced at their posts and for Racilius to follow with the rest of the legion in all haste.

After a forced march of an hour and a half, he reached the wheel-churned fields and breasted the rise in the ground through a row of tall trees. His worst fears had not prepared him for the scene of devastation that greeted him. A body count confirmed the likelihood that none had escaped or been taken prisoner. It was not possible to cremate them. It would have taken too long to build pyres, and there was insufficient fuel available. A pile of smouldering blackened corpses was not a fitting end for soldiers of Republican Rome. To keep up morale in the legion, so each common soldier knew he would not be left to rot on some foreign field, Caesar ordered their burial in a communal trench. If Roman soldiers were known for one thing besides fighting, it was digging. Not a single Briton had been left on the battlefield and Caesar concluded, correctly, that the natives would afford the Romans the dignity of burying their dead.

As the relief column put their backs into the grim task, it occurred to him that the corn supplies in the camp stores would last longer, with two and a half thousand fewer mouths to feed. Pragmatic as he was, Caesar's own thoughts revolted him. Out of the four cohorts, just one trooper, with a smashed leg, had been found alive amongst the bodies. He was brought back to camp, unconscious, and despite being unable to afford it, he was now in the care of the *medicus* at Caesar's personal expense. The body of Velanius was recovered from the battlefield to be buried outside the gates of the *castrum* in the morning.

Of the five men that now stood before him in his tented *praetorium*, only Durus and Crastinus of the Tenth had not witnessed the calamity that had befallen Velanius' foraging party. The other three men standing were Racilius, Marcus Cocceius Priscus, the Chief Centurion of the Seventh, who accompanied Caesar on his fruitless rescue mission, and Sillius, who was brought to tears at the sight of the body of his dear friend. Velanius' remarks to him just two evenings prior, that he felt safer foraging with a legion for protection, than he did negotiating for grain with a presumably friendly tribe, would haunt him for years to come. The only other man present, seated at his desk, was the ever-present Faberius.

It had been six days since the storm scattered Labienus' transports and this was only the second official word from him. The first had arrived with the first consignment of nails and equipment Caesar ordered to cobble his storm-damaged fleet together again. That message had confirmed his fears that Labienus' transports had been blown back to the continent and spread over a wide area of coastline, but at least none were lost at sea.

He toyed for a moment with the leather cylinder containing this latest missive from Labienus, turning it slowly around with his fingers as he composed himself to prepare for further bad news. Caesar slowly and deliberately pressed his thumbnail through the seal and prised the cap from the body of the container, then inserted two fingers and drew out the small scroll of papyrus from inside. It was short, typical of his second-in-command. No frills or preambles, simply hard facts. It was written in Labienus' own tight hand, not dictated to a secretary. He lowered his eyes and scanned the page:

I SEPT. M. LICINIO ET GN. POMPEIO CONSVLIBVS

T. LABIENVS AD G. IVLIVM CAESAREM

THE LAUNCHING OF SCAEVA

CONFIRMO NVLLAS NAVES IN TEMPESTATE PERDITAS ESSE.

OMNES TAMEN COPIAE MACHINAEQVE IN STEGA MARE AMISSAE SVNT.

NECESSE ERIT NOBIS NOVEM DIES CLASSEM PARARE ET SVPPLERE.

VENTIQVE FLVMINA FORTRES MAIOREM MORAM EFFICIENT.

SI EXPEDITIONEM RELINQVERE VIS, OCTO NAVES VACVAE STATIM MITTI POSSVNT.

A rising clamour coming from outside the tent made Caesar look up, and at that moment, the tent flap was flung open and Crastinus's *optio* appeared in a barely disguised state of excitement. 'Pardon the intrusion Caesar, but Commius has returned, with a guest.'

Although Commius offered no verbal clue about the significance of his return, or the identity of his companion, his triumphant demeanour as he led his faithful mounted escort along the Via Praetoria was not lost on those who witnessed it.

Caesar had taken in the content of Labienus' message with merely a glance. He deftly slipped the scroll inside his tunic. To his assembled officers, he said, 'This can wait,' then to the *optio*. 'Show him in.'

Durus, Crastinus and the others with their backs to the entrance turned and stepped back to form a row on either side of Caesar, as the King of the Atrabates swept into the centre of the assembly with a small, hooded figure beside him.

'Caesar, may I present to you, Queen Cordelia of the Cantiaci.' And with that, Commius respectfully untied the hooded cloak from under his companion's chin, and in a graceful sweep of his arm, draped it over his knee as he knelt before her. That flowing movement was conducted with such reverence that the assembled Romans had to fight a compulsion to do likewise. So much so that Durus was halfway down before he realised his fellow officers were maintaining their upright stance.

To them, an unknown beautiful young woman stood before them, but to Caesar, it was as if the gods had returned to him, his first love; his dearly departed first wife whom he had married when just seventeen years of age. The same name, Cornelia, or had Commius said Cordelia? No matter. It was the same delicate upturned nose between perfectly sculpted cheekbones; and the mouth, downturned at the corners in an expression of defiance, to form a perfect cupid's bow above a small, rounded chin. It took him back to his teen years in an instant. The same long, deep auburn-coloured hair, shaken free from the hood of her cloak to tumble across her slim shoulders. And the same light, bright blue eyes, intensely holding his gaze, that captured his heart and held it ever since the first day they'd met; even though she had now been dead for more than ten years.

It was an arranged marriage between two patrician families, both of whom were on the *populares* side of the Roman political divide. Then Sulla seized power for the *optimates* faction in a civil war and became Dictator. Caesar, both nephew and now son-in-law of two of Sulla's greatest enemies, was targeted. He was ordered to divorce his new wife, and Cornelia was stripped of her dowry and inheritances. Caesar's love for Cornelia was so great that he refused to divorce her and consequently fled for his life into exile. He returned to Rome after Sulla died and Cornelia bore him his only child, Julia.

Pretending to ignore the embarrassing tottering of the young officer, Cordelia gave a haughty tilt of her chin because not one of the Romans opposite her followed Commius' extravagant example. She did not know how she would be received by the Romans, but the dropped jaws on the faces opposite were disappointing. Caesar himself looked as if he had seen a ghost. It was clearly incumbent upon him to make reply, but there were no stock greetings for a Roman general to make to a foreign queen, and besides, he had never heard of her. She sensed his hesitancy and seized the initiative by offering him the back of her right hand. A kiss on the lips was a formal greeting between men or women of equal status in Rome; but, out of respect, Caesar complied with what in Roman culture would be considered an act of obeisance. He took her hand in his own right and brushed his lips against it, using the moment to collect his scattered thoughts. One of Caesar's greatest assets was his ability to keep his composure. Vital in the heat of a battle and quite useful on a variety of other occasions.

Silently cursing Commius for springing the introduction upon him at such an inopportune moment, he simply introduced the five other men present and said, 'We were about to eat. Will you join us?'

Caesar's *praetorium* was paved with the mosaic squares and marble veneer always included in his baggage for the purpose of receiving important guests. It was customary for Caesar and his officers to have their meals in the mess tent with the rankers. But on this occasion, he ordered a table for five to be set up where they stood and, because of the status of their guest, the last remaining amphorae of wine to be opened. Sillius and the two centurions were dismissed while Commius, Cordelia, and the three remaining Romans took their places at the table; Caesar, flanked by his two officers, sat facing the new arrivals.

As they were taking their seats, Durus whispered to the more experienced officer, 'What do you think was in the message from Labienus?'

Under his breath, Racilius replied, 'We'll find out when Julius needs us to know.'

Caesar was the first to speak, adopting the common Gallic that he presumed would be understood by the beautiful young woman seated opposite. 'My dear Commius, you never cease to surprise me. Perhaps you could begin by recounting your adventures since our last meeting.'

The Romans then set about dipping their hard bread in the third-grade olive oil set before them, whilst Cordelia, ignoring the bread, picked at the roast hare and sipped her watered wine with a disdainful expression. She'd been better catered for by the forest people.

After first taking an alternate bite of bread and hare leg, followed by a gulp of wine, Commius began his tale between mouthfuls. 'As you know, Caesar, I was intending to slip across the Tamasa without attracting the attention of the Cassi and make my way to Camulodunon, but I was surprised to find the Trinovantian army encamped this side of the river. I was planning to address Imanuentus in his citadel, as an ambassador of Rome, and offer assistance against his sworn enemy, but instead, I was shown into the presence of his boorish son Mandubracus in a camp on the riverbank. I suspected that the warring tribes had already come together to oppose us.'

'As usual,' interjected Caesar, 'you survived to tell the tale. What did you say to him?'

'Naturally, I had to think on my feet. I had been forced to surrender my sword and leave the protection of my escort to be allowed to meet with him. Just one slip-of-the-tongue and I would find myself a prisoner again, or worse.'

Durus and Racilius caught each other's glances at Commius' customary dramatics. Cordelia delicately chewed on her joint of meat, trying to disguise her boredom. She had heard the tale before, and probably more than once, but Caesar, accommodating as ever to his trusted envoy gesticulated, bread roll in hand, for him to continue.

'Since I can still pass myself off as a native Briton, I introduced myself to his commander merely as Commius of the Atrebates so as not to arouse suspicion, and he led me through their camp to meet with him. The man is brighter than he looks. He knew immediately that I was there to take soundings on their willingness to accept a treaty with Rome, but he wasn't bright enough to suspect that I came as your envoy Caesar. Just as well because, having already heard of our arrival and the surrender of the Cantiaci, their druids demanded his tribe make peace with the Cassi, join forces to oppose us, and prevent us from crossing the Tamasa. Clearly, he took me at face value, assuming I came from Noviomagus because he then volunteered the information that Cordelia had escaped capture from her own family and was seeking asylum with the Atrebates. He actually told me to go home.'

'So would you say he has no plans to come south in support of Taximagulus?'

'I don't know. He does what his father tells him. What I would say is that I detected no personal animosity from him to the notion of a treaty with Rome and he said nothing to deter me, as an envoy from the Atrebates, to do just that.'

Caesar glanced at his *legati* sitting on either side of him. 'Are you following this?' he asked.

Although Caesar himself had been in Gallia long enough to be quite fluent, neither of them were there for more than two years and they may not have picked up on everything Commius said, speaking as he was with his mouth full. A nod of consent from either side, and Caesar continued, this time directing his question to the queen and, for the first time since that first moment, looking deeply into her eyes.

'And I assume you had reached Noviomagus by the time Commius arrived?'

When she spoke, in perfect high Gallic, her voice betrayed a vulnerability that hitherto had been disguised by her regal demeanour.

'Yes, I had. Under the protection and guidance of the spirits, I was accompanied on my journey by my personal bodyguard. We were awaiting the arrival of my chief counsellor, Digueillus. He had gone on a quest to bring Imanuentus to our aid. Imanuentus was my late father's adopted son. But then Commius arrived, having met with the Trinovantes himself and we now fear for my counsellor's life.'

Noticing Caesar's slightly quizzical expression, Commius stepped in. 'When I met Mandubracus, he told me that an envoy from Cordelia had approached him in Camulodunon the previous day, seeking assistance, but

Imanuentus turned him down. We assume he would have returned empty-handed to Noviomagus, but I saw no sign of him on the road. A lone traveller?' Commius shrugged his shoulders. 'Anything could have happened.'

'I'm just trying to piece things together,' said Caesar, raising an open palm in a plea for Commius to pause, while he assembled the back-story in his own mind.

'Cordelia, I assume you are the daughter of the recently departed King Llyr? And that your own family recently tried to imprison you? Would that have anything to do with Taximagulus?'

'He is my brother-in-law. He and his brother Carvillus are married to my two elder sisters. They have been undermining my authority ever since my father died. They sent their sons to take me into their, so-called protection on the morning your ships were sighted.'

'But you managed to escape to seek asylum with the Atrebates. How have you been received?'

'They have treated me well. They are peaceful people. The day following my arrival we learned of Taximagulus' surrender to the Romans. We were waiting for Digueillus to join us before making an approach to you personally when word came from Gaul that your second fleet had been driven away by the storm.'

Having sated his initial hunger and thirst, Commius took up the story. 'It was soon after that when I arrived at Noviomagus. I knew you were waiting on supplies and heavy baggage, but also, Labienus' cavalry would be vital to your mission here. I guessed Taximagulus would be looking to take advantage of the situation so I persuaded the elders it would be in their interests to send supplies with as large a mounted escort as they can muster. We left

Brennus, Cordelia's Captain, to help organise a relief column.'

'That is timely news indeed,' said Caesar. 'Taximagulus has today resumed hostilities. We lost a foraging party comprising of four cohorts, and I've just had word from Labienus that the best he can do in the short term is send empty transports in case we need to get out quickly. How soon before the column arrives, and with how many cavalry?'

'Not less than two days. According to my cousin Granovus, who commands their military, he can gather about two thousand horsemen on the way from Noviomagus, enrolling the men they need as they pass through the lands of the local thanes.'

Caesar sat back for a moment in consideration of the news from Commius, then turned again to the queen. 'So, Cordelia, now that you are here, what do you propose?'

Cordelia drew a deep breath. 'The people of the Cantiaci still hold allegiance to my father, and therefore to me, his declared successor. Taximagulus and his brother are nothing but warlords and bullies with more in common with the Cassi than the Cantiaci. They have no nobility. If I can seek refuge with you, and fly my father's sigil from your watchtower, it will be a symbol to all the people. They will turn away from my evil sisters and their worthless husbands, just as they did three summers past when my husband led his army across the sea to re-instate my father on his seat at Durovernon.'

The mention of a husband raised all manner of questions in Caesar's mind, but he swiftly concluded they could be saved for another time. There was so much he didn't know about this strange country and its people.

Commius, never silent for long, chipped in, 'And when they see two thousand of my mounted kinsmen, with many on foot to follow no doubt, the game will be up for Taximagulus and his renegades. As for Vellaunus and Imanuentus, I wager they intend only to defend what they hold beyond the Tamasa.'

This was all beginning to make sense to the general. It answered his nagging question. Why did such a relatively small force oppose him on the beach? Especially when a deliberate trap was set for him. And again, if a huge force representative of the coming together of many tribes—the like of which he'd seen on the continent—was allied against him, why did the Britons only strike in an ambush against a foraging party, out in the open? It rang true that only part of a divided tribe was in opposition.

'And if all goes to plan and you are returned to Durovernon, what's in it for me.'

'I will ensure the promises made to you by Carvillus earlier this year are honoured,' replied the queen.

'And what do you know of those?'

'I gave my father's royal seal of approval to the document. This was just after my father died, before I suspected any plots against me or deceit towards you.'

'Faberius, my secretary still has the original. But it carries no weight for as long as Carvillus and his brother wield any power.' Caesar leant forward, elbows on the table, and massaged his temples with the forefingers of each hand. It had been a long and harrowing day. 'We shall hoist Llyr's banners for all to see at first light, but we must await the cavalry and the supplies before we can take any initiative. I suggest we all get a good night's sleep.'

Ever since Cordelia's arrival, a night spent sleeping was the furthest thing from Caesar's thoughts. He had ordered the three Spanish slaves he always kept in attendance to procure an extra cot and prepare two hot baths in his tented private quarters. The steaming baths had created a warm, moist atmosphere inside the tent. Beside them was a bench covered with fresh linen sheets and an array of decorated shiny metal flasks, each about the size and shape of a pear. A set of curved bronze strigils had been laid beside a pile of small linen towels. Apart from these items, the interior did not differ from that of the rank-and-file soldiers. After two days on horseback, Cordelia was in no mood to decline her first opportunity to engage with the exotic Roman habit of bathing. Since her designs on that god of war in human form, whose tent she had just entered, were both personal and intimate as well as military, she discarded her travelling clothes without demure or invitation and made to dip a toe in the steaming water to test the temperature, but Caesar called on her to wait.

'It's far too hot. The bench first.'

The flasks and strigils aroused her curiosity, but she turned to face her host with a nervous smile. Obediently, she climbed atop the bench, laid flat on her stomach and gathered her hair on one side, allowing it to drop over her shoulder almost to the floor. The soft yellow glow of oil lamps lent a light golden hue to her, faintly glistening skin, milk-white against the sheet.

With her face deliberately turned away from him, she asked innocently, 'Now Julius, what are you going to do to me?'

Caesar, who had lost no time disrobing himself, made a tantalising reply. 'Just pay attention, it will be your turn next.'

He stepped up to the bench, removed the stoppers from the flasks, held each one to his nose and selected the fragranced oil most suited to his mood. He then let a few droplets fall onto each of her shoulders and drizzled a thin line of oil along her spine, the sensation of which made her shiver with a hitherto unknown pleasure. Spreading the oil across her back and shoulders, he massaged it gently into her body with the palms of his hands. On reaching her buttocks, he poured a few more drops into his palms and applied it to each of the perfectly proportioned orbs, then, enjoying their firmness, squeezed with a hand on each, gently at first, and then clenching his fingers into fists and kneading them with his knuckles so she felt the hardness of the bench pressing against her pubis. The sensation caused her inadvertently to part her legs a little as her tutor shifted his attention to her thighs. Maddeningly, he ignored the hint of an invitation and concentrated on the backs of her legs and finally her calves and the soles of her feet, which relaxed her so much that the build-up of sexual tension in her body simply melted away. After wiping the oil from his hands on a towel, he selected the strigil shaped most suitably for scraping the oil from the flatter areas of her back and set to work, wiping the implement on the towel as he went.

Not only was Caesar fastidious in his own personal hygiene, even whilst campaigning, but no woman could ever share his bed unless she had been through the same scrupulous preparations as himself. When he had finished, he kissed her lightly on the back of her neck, a signal for her to turn over onto her back, which she did without shame or apparent surprise at Caesar's own nakedness. He repeated the process, stroking the oil into her arms and torso, carefully working it around and in between her breasts without his deft fingers encountering her nipples or disturbing her tight auburn curls. He used a greater selection of strigils to cater for the deeper contours on the front of her body and, when he had finished, wiped his hands on a cloth and held them out towards her. Taking them for support, she sat up, swivelled slowly off the bench, and stood in front of him, looking up into his eyes.

'Now it's your turn,' he whispered.

'No Julius,' she said softly, 'it's your turn.'

Caesar took his position on the bench slowly and deliberately, dressing himself between his own legs for comfort on the hard surface. Cordelia selected her preferred scented oil and worked it into his back and shoulders in the same manner he had done to her. This time passing over his buttocks more lightly and caressing each of his upper thighs with both hands, taking care not to touch him privately with the tips of her fingers. When he turned over, she contemplated the only naked male physique she had ever encountered apart from her husband, and what a difference there was. Diviciacus was an old man by the time she became his bride. Still powerful and vigorous in demeanour, but a spent force for purposes of virility. He was a giant bear of a man, a full head of wild grey hair and fleshy features above a hairy mass of a torso on relatively spindly legs. In his time, he was a man of great power and influence amongst his neighbouring tribes on the continent. In the southeastern corner of Prydain as well, it was his coinage that was used widely amongst the Cantiaci and beyond.

The Roman stretched out naked before her was a different species by comparison. His thinning hair and gaunt features belied the tight, muscular body. She lowered her gaze from his hairless chest and flat stomach to appraise the heavy, gradually swelling penis. She considered it complemented by the thickness and muscularity of his calves, which resulted from marching many hundreds of miles on foot with his men. Just one of the many singularities which made them love him. She replenished the oil in her palms from the flask and massaged his chest, arms, and stomach. Once she had scraped his torso clean of the oil, she re-positioned herself, facing away from him and allowing her hair to fall across his lower body as she rubbed the oil into his hips and upper thighs. That which Caesar had carefully tucked away to the south was edging its way around the compass and was now pointing west under Cordelia's incredulous gaze. By the time she had finished, it was straining to reach his navel. Caesar raised his head and shoulders off the bench by supporting himself on his elbows. Although it was the queen who had been at work, his expression was one of self-satisfaction.

'It is now time for the bath,' he said. 'The water should be a good temperature.'

Cordelia wiped her hands, laid her strigil on the bench, and stepped carefully into one of the—still lightly steaming—baths. She turned to face him and raised her hands behind her head, accentuating the pertness of her breasts, and gathered her hair atop her head. Keeping her back upright, she slowly lowered herself down into the tub by bending her knees and keeping her balance on the balls of her feet, until she could lean back against the high end of the bath and let her hair tumble down behind it. The entire movement was carried out with such grace and poise that the surface of the bathwater hardly rippled. As her back slid gently down the smooth surface and her bottom found the floor, she slid a little further forward and settled her shoulders just beneath the surface of the rising steam. Without the space to stretch her legs out in front of her, she lifted her feet out of the water and draped her slender calves over the low end of the bath, which fitted snugly under the backs of her knees. Caesar dismounted the bench and stepped into the bath beside hers; then bending over, grasped the sides of the tub with his hands. He took his full weight on his arms, tensed his stomach muscles and swung his legs straight out in front of him, gradually lowering himself—biceps bulging—into the hot water. For a moment, they both luxuriated in identical poses as their muscles relaxed, facing each other like the twins of Gemini. Knowing that they had all night before them, Caesar was content to finish any business before pleasure.

'So, what was it that you were saying about your husband coming to your father's rescue?'

'It's a long story. I was married when I was just fourteen years of age, to Diviciacus, who was once the most powerful king in Gaul. He was king of a Belgic tribe, the Suessiones.'

'Diviciacus? I have heard talk of him. The Suessiones were ruled more recently though by Galba. He led an alliance of Belgic tribes against me at my camp on the Axona, near Bibrax. I routed them of course. My troops killed as many of them as daylight allowed.'

Although Cordelia had no particular attachment to the tribe she had been married into, she still bridled at Caesar's arrogance. 'Then it's fortunate for you that Diviciacus was at that time in Prydain, with me. He has destroyed armies from Rome before, and no doubt would have done so again had he not come to my father's aid.'

Caesar was puzzled by this revelation. No Roman army before his own had ventured so far to the north as to have entered the territory of the Belgae, and he told her so.

'When he was a younger man,' she retorted, 'he defeated a Roman army under your consul, Cassius Longinus, who was himself killed in the fighting.'

Caesar thought for a moment and then nodded slowly, 'Yes, of course, the battle of Burdigala. That was before I was born. I know of it because a relative of mine was also slain there. My father-in-law's grandfather. He had also been consul. And you say that your husband, Diviciacus of the Suessiones was the victor?'

'He was known as Divico back then. He's told me the story many times.' retorted Cordelia, becoming more irked.'

'To impress his gullible young bride no doubt,' replied Caesar with a wry grin. 'Longinus was indeed defeated by Divico. Divico of the Tigurini, one of the tribes of the Helvetii. It occurred in the territory of the Allobroges, just this side of the Alpes. I suspect your dear husband, not satisfied with his own accomplishments, has embellished them with those of his namesake.'

Cordelia's expression hardened as she boiled inside. During her life, she had suffered ignominy, but she would not be made a fool of. 'And why should I believe the word of someone who I have just met.'

Her change of mood did not give him the slightest doubt regarding the outcome of their private encounter. He was enjoying the sport of their conversation. He had long recognised the ability to delay gratification was a major determiner of how successful an individual would become in every aspect of their life. Caesar was a master of the art, so he warmed to his theme.

'By divine providence, I had the opportunity of avenging the death of my relative. It was the threat to Rome, instigated by the movement of the Helvetii, that caused me to intervene in Gallia at the outset. They were marauding through territories friendly toward Rome when I caught them as they were crossing the Saône on primitive rafts. Their rearguard just happened to consist of the Tigurini. I killed large numbers of them before they scattered into the woods. It took me just a day to build a bridge to enable me to pursue the rest. They sent ambassadors, headed by none other than Divico himself. Divico of the Tigurini, not the Suessiones. Do you know what he had the audacity to say to me?'

In spite of herself, Cordelia's interest had been piqued. 'Go on,' she said,

'He told me the Helvetii would accept a peaceable agreement, but if I persisted in making war against them, I would do well to remember what had happened to Longinus all those years ago. He dismissed my routing of the Tigurini by saying I had made a surprise attack on them. And then he made the mistake of warning me that his tribe had learned from their ancestors how to fight like brave men; and the very place where we stood, on my bridge, would become famous in future ages as the scene of a Roman disaster and the destruction of yet another Roman army.'

'I'm sure my Diviciacus would have responded in a similar fashion,' said Cordelia, still defiantly defending her husband. 'How did you make reply to that?'

'I told him I resented the misfortune my ancestor suffered, all the more because it was undeserved. They were caught off their guard and the attack on them was unprovoked. I then warned him, there was a reason he had escaped retribution, and had been allowed to boast so arrogantly, for such a surprisingly long time, of such an undeserved victory.'

'And what reason was that?' asked the queen, no longer attempting to disguise her interest.

'I informed him that when the gods intend to make a man pay for his crimes, they allow him to enjoy moments of success and a long period of impunity, so he feels his reverse of fortune, when it eventually comes, more keenly. I demanded hostages and a guarantee that his kinsmen would return home and recompense the tribes allied to Rome for the injury he had done to them. To that, he defiantly replied that it was the traditional custom of the Helvetii to demand hostages of others, but never to give them, and then he took his leave. Needless to say, he paid for his arrogance. By the time I'd finished with him and his wretched tribe, they were back where they came from, with nothing to eat but his words. But enough of me, you still haven't told me about Diviciacus and your father.'

'As I was saying, before you interrupted and started talking about yourself,' replied the queen, feigning indignance and flicking her bathwater at him, 'it's a long story.' Cordelia shifted herself backwards a little and lifted her feet into the warm water of the bath. She clasped her hands around her shins and rested her cheek upon her bent knees to face him. A rueful expression replaced the moment of playfulness. 'I had fallen out of favour with my father at the time he divided his kingdom between my two elder sisters and their husbands. My punishment for offending him was that he refused to provide me with a dowry. Diviciacus, who knew me as a child and was an ally of my father, heard of my plight and was rich enough not to care about the dowry. He sent ambassadors to my father's court asking for my hand. I was returned with them to Gaul and spent the next three years as a plaything to amuse him.' Noticing Caesar's sudden look of consternation, she quickly added, 'I was not mistreated.'

'Why did you fall out of favour with your father?'

'That's no longer important. But having bestowed his authority on my sisters, he found his court and even his own liberty reduced by them, to such a degree that he came to Gaul to reconcile himself with me. My husband was so moved to see his old friend in such reduced circumstances, that he led his army back to Prydain and reinstated my father at Durovernon. My sisters were merely disinherited, but their husbands were put to death.' Given the sudden look of surprise on Caesar's face, Cordelia hastily explained, 'Diviciacus ruled jointly with my father just over a year before returning to Gaul with his army. The following year my sisters married Taximagulus and his brother. With Diviciacus gone they must have seen father's frailty as an opportunity to topple him again. After being disinherited by my father, they were keen to regain their status. They began to offer bribes and threats to local thanes, infiltrated his court and plotted against him.'

'So, when your father died,' added Caesar, 'Carvillus and his brother hatched a plot to lure me into a trap?'

'So it would seem, but at that time I had no reason to suspect their duplicity. When they came to me with their plans for offering peace with Rome, I was happy to apply my father's seal to the treaty they had drawn up. Soon after that, my chief advisor began to suspect a plot against me. Digueillus and Brennus were the only two I trusted. For my own safety, Digueillus advised me to seek refuge at a fortified stockade on the edge of the great forest. Brennus hand-picked a hundred men, whose loyalty to me was beyond reproach, to act as my bodyguard. The sons of Taximagulus and Carvillus came for me with a large body of men on the morning your ships were sighted.'

'Thus, you made your escape to the protection of the Atrebates,' said Caesar, concluding her story for her. 'A fascinating tale.' Caesar shifted and stretched his limbs before easing himself out of the now tepid water. Offering her his hand for support, he said, 'I think that brings us up to date. It's time for bed.'

She took his hand and noticed as she stood that his swelling was somewhat reduced; she allowed him to gently towel off the moisture from her body before rigorously applying the remaining towels to his own. Now that the business of the day was concluded, he led her to his cot and laid her down. Caesar found the musky odour of her *mons veneris* intoxicating as he prepared her for his conquest. He had known camp followers just the same way as any of his soldiers and bedded harlots and virgins alike, but with Cordelia, he was seventeen again.

Julius Caesar and Divico parley after the battle at the Saône in 58 BC. Historic painting of the 19th century by Karl Jauslin.

XV

September 55 BC
Cernodunon, the Stronghold of the Cassi

The news of the Romans' flight back to Gaul was greeted with joy and celebration amongst the tribes north of the Tamasa. The real circumstances of their departure were known there only by a few and spoken of by fewer. Taximagulus boasted of driving Caesar himself back into the waves in hand-to-hand combat. The bards of the Cassi would re-tell the story with their own Nennius in the leading role in further embellishments of their own imaginings. In time, Caesar would tell an entirely different version, but it was Carvillus who knew the truth and kept his counsel. Caesar was gone, and that was all that mattered.

Word of the failed attempt to capture Cordelia and the manner of her escape had filtered through to the population and divided loyalties amongst the Cantiaci. When Llyr's sigil was sighted fluttering above Caesar's *castrum*, and Cordelia openly displayed herself from the watchtowers, Taximagulus declared she had betrayed them and gone over to the enemy, but many remained loyal to the queen. The druids called for an all-out assault on the Roman camp, but only the henchmen of Taximagulus and Carvillus came to the muster. When the attack came, the

Romans came out of their fortress to fight in full battle formation and easily repelled the Britons. This time, they were pursued and routed by thousands of Atrebatian cavalry, led by Brennus and loyal to Commius. Taximagulus and the remnants of his army retreated a safe distance and regrouped.

It was left to Lugotorix, a nobleman of the Cantiaci, to surrender on behalf of the errant tribes, escort Cordelia back to her rightful seat at Durovernon and send the required hostages to Caesar. Despite Cordelia's heartfelt pleas to her new lover to stay the winter, he made haste back to Gaul before the autumn equinox, after which no sane man would put to sea in that part of the world with a large fleet of ships.

Taximagulus argued long and hard with his brother that to protect the honour of their family, they must give out a different version to their allies amongst the Cassi. The priesthood amongst the Cantiaci agreed and sent a bird to Eneid with news of Caesar's return to Gaul, with no mention of the part played by Cordelia or the Atrebates.

Now that the Atrebatian horsemen had returned to their homeland and Commius had gone with Caesar back to Gaul with his entire force, Cordelia was back on her throne but protected only by those thanes who were still loyal to her and Lugotorix. She was no more secure than she had been before the arrival of the Romans, and Caesar had made no promises of a return.

Taximagulus and his men were given a hero's welcome when they crossed the Tamasa. He would be guest of honour at the celebration feast to be held in Cernodunon, the capital of Vellaunus, on the night of the first full moon of the equinox. Eneid sent invitations, not only to

Imanuentus of the Trinovantes, to cement the new peace between the major tribes, but also to the smaller tribes; the Bibroci and Ancalites to the west and the Cenimagni and Segontiaci to the north. Nobles and their kinsmen, their thanes and chieftains, all were summoned to attend a day of sacrificial thanksgiving to the gods, and a night of feasting and drinking, as was their custom on such momentous occasions.

The master bakers of Camulodunon drew from their bursting grain stores to provide wagonloads of bread, sent in convoys across the now peaceful border. Freshly brewed local ales from every direction were prepared in barrels and sent by ox-drawn carts. Members of the priesthood of each local community came with their drovers and cattle to perform solemn sacrifices to their tutelary gods, who had given them the glorious victory. That which was not part of the burnt offerings was butchered and prepared for the feasting. Hundreds of wild boar were hunted and innumerable game birds trapped, killed, and plucked in the days leading up to the great feast. What was judged to be the finest specimen from each of the attendant communities was presented to Eneid at his sacrificial slab in a clearing between his oak groves. There he performed the ritual slaying and offered thanks to the spirits that had protected them from the monster of Rome.

Once Eneid had completed his incantations in front of all the hundreds of assembled guests, they fell in behind Vellaunus. He escorted Taximagulus at the head of the column, ascending the leaf-strewn bridleways through the autumn-tinged woods to his stronghold where the feasting and drinking were to take place.

The two of them were sufficiently ahead to enable a conversation without being overheard.

'I see the king of the Treenos has taken the bait,' said Taximagulus. 'Do you plan to kill him yourself or allow your nephews the opportunity to avenge their father's death?'

Vellaunus was already sufficiently irked that his subordinate was nominated by the druids as the guest of honour. His adulation based on the story he gave out regarding Caesar's retreat boosted his natural arrogance to the point of hubris, but Vellaunus let it pass.

'I have sworn an oath on my father's shadow. Imanuentus will die, and by my hand. His time is well-nigh, but I must bide my time further. Mandubracus is a hot-headed fool. Ply him with enough mead tonight and he will attempt something that breaks the truce, I swear it. It will be the Trinovantes that make the first move, not the Cassi. Then I will have his father here at my mercy.'

Behind the leading figures of the Cassi and their allies amongst the Cantiaci came the contingent from the Trinovantes. Riding three abreast ahead of their colourful bannermen were Imanuentus flanked by Mandubracus and Gestorix.

'I don't like this one bit,' snarled Mandubracus to his father, looking around and shifting uncomfortably on his mount. 'We could walk right into a trap. We know Taximagulus and his brother are close as flies around shit with Vellaunus. The Bibroci and the other tribes dare not cross him. He could slit our throats, and no one would so much as raise a sword in our defence. Our bannermen are hugely outnumbered.'

'Keep your voice down,' said the king, not even looking at his son. 'Eneid, Dwynrid and all the high priesthood will be in attendance. Even Vellaunus would not dare to defy their edict.'

'Well I would,' muttered Mandubracus to himself, then in reply to Imanuentus. 'Now that the threat from Rome has passed, this forced truce will not endure. We now know the location of his stronghold. I will note their fortifications for when the time comes to strike.'

'Over my dead body,' hissed the king, putting an end to the discussion.

They rode on through the open double gates of the outer ramparts and were met by a pungent mixture of odours. Due to the location of many of the buildings around the perimeter, sheltered from the wind by the trees surrounding the encampment, the rank smell of damp, rotting thatch was the first to assault their senses. They continued through the main gates, under the bridged palisade and into the main street between the guardhouses.

'What a shit heap,' said Mandubracus, surveying his surroundings, not caring who was within earshot.

The encampment was certainly many generations older than Camulodunon. They passed only one new structure; a solitary half-empty grain store, hastily assembled. The sun was setting behind the thinning trees on the western side of the palisaded banks before the aroma of roasting meat relieved them, but only until they reached the stables and dismounted. Two young men who, by their gold torcs and armlets, appeared to be nobles of the Cassi, came to meet them. It was their task to escort the nobility of the visiting tribes to their places at the feast.

Androgeus and Tenvantius were in no doubt as to the identity of their guests. For the first time in their lives, they were face-to-face with the man who, when they were mere children, usurped and murdered their parents. Imanuentus still cut an imposing figure. His helmet was lavishly decorated with two bronze crescent-shaped openwork crests, depicting boars entwined with serpents, and trimmed with red boar-bristle plumage. Long white hair hung down to his shoulders, and cold watery-blue eyes stared out of deep sockets below a high forehead. For a man of his age, he still displayed a vigorous demeanour. A deep blood-red cloak was fastened at his shoulder with a gold brooch, and under his tunic, despite his faith that the word of the druids would forestall any violence, he wore a coat of chain mail. He carried his sword at the hip. Mandubracus and his companion, who was unknown to the princes, had taken similar protective precautions, and both carried their swords in scabbards slung across their backs on a shoulder strap. Besides his sword, Mandubracus also carried, on a strap across his other shoulder, his most prized possession, a giant silver-rimmed auroch drinking horn; a gift from Gestorix, he always carried on such occasions. The two brothers carried out their assignment dutifully and with a calm dignity that belied their innermost feelings, giving no sign of them to their erstwhile sworn enemies.

The open ground in the centre of the stronghold was prepared for the feast with dozens of long, low tables, each one surrounded by hay bales and piles of straw and ferns for the comfort of the guests. Countless fires were lit for the hog-roast spits and black iron cauldrons of water, hanging from tripods for the boiled beef and hams.

Benches stacked with loaves and wagonloads of beer and mead in barrels were positioned amongst the tables.

Androgeus led Imanuentus and Mandubracus into the presence of the host and the other honoured guests, while Tenvantius led Gestorix, the bannermen, armour carriers and spear holders to their places at the feasting tables. Imanuentus removed his helmet and tucked it in the crook of his arm before ducking under the eaves of the sparsely furnished roundhouse that served as the council chamber of the Cassi. Following Androgeus inside, he and Mandubracus came face-to-face with Vellaunus, Taximagulus and their respective families. For the benefit only of the high priest and his brother, Vellaunus stepped forward, grabbed Imanuentus' cheeks with both hands, and kissed him firmly on the mouth, as was the custom. He then repeated the formal welcome with the similarly unflinching Mandubracus. Nennius, standing next to his nephew Hirelglas, was the only one present with even the faintest of smiles. The malign silence that followed was mercifully cut short by the arrival of the chieftains and nobles of the minor tribes. Vellaunus welcomed the new guests in the same manner, as well as a hearty greeting for each one. With the official welcoming completed, Eneid and Dwynrid led the high-ranking party back outside the chamber.

An attendant of Vellaunus was at hand bearing the ceremonial headdress of his late father; the antlered head of a great stag, set with the horns of an auroch that curved around from either side. This was the crown of Cernunnos, the god of all wild things, to whom the stronghold of the Cassi was dedicated. He handed it to Nennius, who placed it on his brother's head with great solemnity and symmetry so that the tips of his brother's moustache almost met with the tips of the horns on either side. Face to face and eyes locked beneath the open mouth of the great stag, Nennius was quietly confident that his brother would not risk the wrath of the druids by breaking the truce between the tribes; while Vellaunus was equally confident that he wouldn't have to. Headdress in place, the brothers led the royal procession to their places at the table of nobles where sheepskins had been laid, across the bales and ferns, for the additional comfort of their most honoured guests.

The spit and cauldron fires and braziers burned more brightly since the setting of the sun. Drumbeats accompanied their progress through the crowded cheering tables of thirsty tribesmen, and the harvest moon rose, casting its soft light across the flickering shadows.

In advance of the tribal leaders' arrival at their table, the armour carrier of each of them had taken up a position behind their allotted place, bearing their mighty bronze-clad rectangular shields. The most magnificent of them all was the gold-trimmed shield of Imanuentus. Red glass studs, flashing like the eyes of devils in the firelight from the braziers, were set into the heads of serpents, wound around the protruding bronze boar's head boss. At the head of the table stood the mighty shield of Vellaunus with its crossed battle-axe emblem. To the right, that of his guest of honour, Taximagulus, the Wolf's head. Next to Taximagulus was his brother Carvillus, the Eagle and their two sons, Segovax, the Fox and Cingetorix, the Trident. Then came the dazzling Boar and Serpents of Imanuentus and the Bull of his son, Prince Mandubracus. To the left of Vellaunus was his own family. Brother Nennius the Stag, nephews—both of them the sons of Ludd—Androgeus the

Falcon and Tenvantius the Leaping Deer, and finally the Chariot Wheels of Hirelglas, son of Aryanrot, sister of Vellaunus.

The others around the table were Carantus and Dagolitus of the Bibroci, Cerdo and Katumaros of the Ancalites, Aculia and Urus of the Segontiaci and Candurotus and Garomaros of the Cenimagni. The raucous cheering of the tribesmen continued until the ruling elite had all taken their places and Eneid, standing on a raised platform illuminated by a semi-circle of flaming torches behind him, held his hands aloft for silence.

'Men of Prydain. We are gathered here to celebrate the defeat of the yellow dog of Rome.' Another almighty cheer went up from the assembly, and Eneid raised his arms again for peace. 'He was driven back into the waves by none other than our honoured guest, Taximagulus of the Cantiaci.'

'Taximagulus, Taximagulus, Taximagulus,' roared the tribesmen, many of whom were on their feet already. As Taximagulus stood to receive the accolade, Androgeus and Tenvantius who had heard the rumours of the failed attempt at the kidnap of Cordelia, and were sitting opposite Carvillus, nudged each other and studied the resigned expression on his face. It was apparent the conquering hero's own brother was not impressed.

Even their sons sat with nothing but smug expressions on their faces as the chanting died down and Eneid continued. 'Men of Prydain. We all mourn the recent passing of King Heli, first born of Lugios, the Shining One. We are gathered here together as guests of his son Vellaunus, now King of the Cassi, who henceforth will be known as Cassivellaunus, King of Kings!'

Again, a chant went up. 'Cassivellaunus King of Kings, Cassivellaunus King of Kings, Cassivellaunus …'

Carantus of the Bibroci and the chieftains of the other minor tribes around the table were on their feet too, joining in and chanting his name, while Imanuentus and Mandubracus stared in disbelief at Eneid for his crassness, whether deliberate or accidental. They caught the eye of Dwynrid, who was standing to one side of the Chief Druid, along with other ranking members of their sect. The flickering torchlight disfigured his expression; did he approve of the title his brother had just bestowed on their avowed enemy?

Eneid waited for the chanting to abate, and for the third time addressed the exultant warriors. 'Men of Prydain. I have one last announcement. All the appropriate sacrifices have been made to the gods for our victory. They are now smiling upon us. Let the feasting begin!'

And at that, another roar filled the night air as teams of young boys ran amongst the tables bearing platters of meat, bread and jugs of foaming beer and mead to fill the drinking horns of the guests. It was the custom for all young nobles come of age to attend such feasts, but the younger youths amongst the tribes acted as servants. Women and slaves were barred from these celebrations, and so it was that Hirelglas took his place amongst his elders for the first time. His younger cousin, Caradoc, son of Aurgania, the second sister of Cassivellaunus, was amongst the throng of young boys from all the invited tribes, performing their customary duty, expecting one day to be taking their own places at the tables. The choicest cuts of meat had been delivered to Cassivellaunus' table and the drinking horns of all the guests had been filled and refilled. Taximagulus and his brother leant shoulder to shoulder, conversing in hushed tones. Cassivellaunus leant the other way to converse with Nennius.

Nennius said, 'You have Carantus and the other tribes well trained.'

'They know their place and have remained loyal,' Cassivellaunus replied coldly. 'They are merely immigrant vassal tribes and latecomers at that. Permanent guests, but guests nonetheless who will be righteously educated as to their lowly position in the ancient Brythonic pecking order of Prydain should they be foolish enough to refuse their orders. The same goes for Taximagulus. But the Trinovantes; they were always going to be a problem. Our brother's diplomatic approach cost him his life, but tonight, by the gods, we shall have our revenge.'

'You dare not raise your arm against Imanuentus. Eneid means what he said. He will carry out his threat on the first sign of aggression,' replied Nennius, suddenly full of earnestness.

'Exactly, and when that oaf Mandubracus has drowned what little sense he has in ale, he will easily be provoked to reach for his sword and take that first action, then we will have them. Both of them.'

There are three ways a man can be affected by an excess of strong drink. One is to become overly convivial to the point of raucousness, another is to become angry to the point of violence, and the third is to become mournful and morose before falling into a stupor. Cassivellaunus was soon to learn, much to his chagrin, that Mandubracus was of the third kind.

The noise level of the voices around the tables was increasing as the traditional games began amongst the tribesmen. Trials of strength and wrestling matches were being joined by champions and challengers alike, followed by the usual heated exchanges over who had eventually won. This was because there were never any rules agreed upon beforehand, and victory was usually signalled only by a submission. The drinking horns were still being topped up, although the food had been cleared away to make room for the bouts. All swords and other weapons were laid behind the straw bales, out of reach.

Androgeus, increasingly irritated by the smugness of the princes of the Cantiaci sitting opposite, was sufficiently loose enough in the tongue to be the first to start a dispute. 'Prince Segovax, there is no need to merely bask in the glory of the heroic deeds of your father, so remind us all of your own triumph, the capture of Queen Cordelia!'

'I don't know what you're talking about. You're drunk,' came the tart reply.

'Oh, come now,' said Tenvantius, 'put your modesty aside. Or perhaps you, Prince Cingetorix, can give us the story? Or perhaps that story is not true? Perhaps you two incompetent clots let her escape into the protection of the Atrebates?'

'Take that back,' roared Cingetorix, climbing unsteadily to his feet.

Imanuentus, seated next to him, was aware of the story of Cordelia's escape, but had kept his counsel throughout. It was a mystery to him that Androgeus and his brother knew of the attempt to capture her. Only Mandubracus had been with Imanuentus in the meeting with Digueillus and was privy to that information. The lamentable figure of his son now lay flat on his back next to him, snoring peacefully, with his folded arms clasping his precious drinking horn to his chest. Could he have said something privately to the sons of Ludd, intending to undermine the claims of Taximagulus and his family? He had not been at ease with the company he found himself in from the beginning of the evening, so took advantage of the angry exchange between the young princes as an excuse to take his leave. He leant back and whispered instructions to his armourers and spear carriers behind him. They quickly hoisted the sleeping Mandubracus to his feet, collected his sword, and, between them, dragged him away into the shadows. Imanuentus raised an arm and stood to interrupt the volleys of verbal abuse, now being thrown across the table and being enjoyed by the other guests as good sport.

Deliberately ignoring the new grand prefix to the name of his sworn enemy, he turned to Cassivellaunus and declared, 'Vellaunus, my good host, my son and I give thanks for your hospitality; but have no wish to take sides in a dispute, about which we have no side to take. So, we must take our leave.' And without waiting for a reply, lifted his ornate helmet from the sheepskin beside him, then turned and joined his bodyguards, who had responded swiftly to the whistled instructions of the armourer.

They fell smartly into formation and escorted Imanuentus back to the stables, where Gestorix was waiting with a revived Mandubracus, whose hair and moustache were now dripping with water.

'Gestorix, it's a full moon and the road back to Camulodunon will be well lit. I've not stayed a moment longer in the company of these creatures than I had to. Give word to our bannermen of my departure. They can stay or leave as they wish. But I want you to stay and look after our boy servants. Come home with them on the bread wagons in the morning.'

Gestorix helped Mandubracus mount his horse, then stood and watched the party head towards the gates of the stronghold, before turning back towards the raucous scenes amongst the hay bales and beer wagons.

Back at the feast, Cassivellaunus was furious. His plan had fallen apart in front of his eyes. The war of words between his nephews and the princes of the Cantiaci had been supplanted as entertainment by a wrestling match between Dagolitus and Urus, both of whom were stripped to the waist. As they locked together in an effort to attain a winning hold, they crashed through the circle of bales and knocked a serving boy off his feet. The boy cannoned into Caradoc, who was bringing his cousin Hirelglas a refill of mead.

'Look what that fat oaf has done,' screamed Hirelglas, who was clearly drunk. He tottered to his feet and wavered. Then, recognising the style of tunic and breeches the boy was wearing, he added, 'the Treeno pig, the one with the big ears. He needs to be taught a lesson.'

Caradoc was taken aback. It was not the other boy's fault, but so as not to lose face in front of his older cousin, gave the boy a perfunctory shove in the chest and warned him to watch his step.

'Not like that, like this!' Hirelglas flew at the younger boy, knocking him off his feet again. He squatted down hard on his back and twisted his arm, as he had seen the other wrestlers do. 'Submit, submit, give in,' yelled Hirelglas, as he twisted the boy's arm harder.

'No, I won't,' squealed the boy in genuine pain.

'Submit damn you,' screamed the older boy in a drunken frenzy as he put all his weight into twisting the boy's arm further up behind his back.

'No no no,' cried the boy sobbing in agony.

Gestorix, hearing Ebracus' squeals, ran to the scene just in time to witness Scaeva hurl himself at Hirelglas, knocking him off his brother's back and rolling over with him in the straw. As the unevenly matched pair struggled to their feet, Hirelglas gathered a handful of dirt and threw it in Scaeva's face, then followed up with a hard punch on the nose which drew blood. Scaeva went down, temporarily blinded and on his hands and knees. A vicious kick from Hirelglas sent him sprawling into the hay bales behind Nennius and his nephews. As Hirelglas bent down to grab the smaller boy by the neck, Scaeva's hand touched against the handle of Nennius' sword. Grabbing hold of it, he used every ounce of strength in his arm to jerk it free of its scabbard, and in one sweeping movement, swung it blindly through the air at his assailant. It caught Hirelglas in the side of his neck in its upward swing and sliced clean through, sending his head rotating through the air, spraying blood all over the sword's owner and landing with a dull thud in the lap of Cassivellaunus, King of the Cassi, the tribe that hates with a passion. Cassivellaunus was indeed well named.

Cassivellaunus: King of the Cassi

XVI

September 55 BC
Near Camulodunon, the Citadel of the Trinovantes

Scaeva was regaining consciousness. He lay face down on a hard surface; a flat stone raised from the ground. His arms were spreadeagled and lashed by the wrist to short wooden stakes set into the edges of the slab. Eyes still tight shut against the throbbing in his head and the shrill chirping and squawking of caged birds nearby, he felt sick. He was having trouble breathing because dried blood had blocked one of his nostrils. In the background, he was conscious of the soothing sound of water flowing over stones, and then came the sound of human voices, getting closer, speaking in the ancient language of the druids. He was aware of activity, several people busying themselves silently around him. Before he opened his eyes, he guessed the voices belonged to Dwynrid and his brother, the chief druid, whose name he couldn't remember.

'The vate has consulted with the spirits and they have revealed the boy's future,' Dwynrid was saying. 'He will die when he comes face to face with the King of Kings.'

'So Cassivellaunus will have his revenge,' confirmed the chief druid.

'Not immediately. Four other deaths are prophesied to occur before that happens, so he must be patient. The gods have spoken to the vate through the voices of the dead, and their prophecies will come to pass at a time of their choosing, so after I have performed the necessary rites, we must deliver the boy back to his family and let events take their course.'

'I fear that Cassivellaunus' first priority will be to avenge the killing of his brother, Ludd. He has a case that the truce that bound the tribes together against the threat of Caesar has been broken by the actions of the boy.'

'So, you think he will act against Imanuentus?' asked Dwynrid.

'He is determined to do so. Last night I had it out of him. He had hoped Mandubracus might make some rash action under the influence of his ale that would justify a retaliation, but that plan came to nought, and he lost his opportunity. His spies have informed him of Imanuentus' habitual movements beyond the walls of his citadel and he plans to strike imminently. Now that the threat from Rome has abated, I see no reason to keep him bound. The truce is over.'

Scaeva opened his eyes. The soreness reminded him immediately of the events of the previous night, or at least some of them. He shut his eyes tight again and squeezed the lids together to make them water. After the boy had thrown dirt in his face and kicked him to the ground, everything was a blur. He remembered seeing the boy's head turning through the air in an arc, as if in slow motion; and the blood pulsating out of the neck of the body, spraying over the hay bales. Gestorix was there with his sword drawn. There was a terrible commotion with everyone shouting. The last thing he remembered was a hand clamped over his mouth and nose, holding a pungent-smelling cloth. Then he must have passed out.

On opening his eyes a second time, the early morning light was sufficient for him to recognise his surroundings. He was in a clearing enclosed on three sides by a low cliff face of red-coloured rocks and gravel. He'd come across the distinctive rock formations once before when exploring during a break from his morning classes. Caspar had caught him and warned him to stay away because it was the private and sacred location of the crypt that housed the heads of long-dead druids, mummified to preserve their wisdom. It was also the sanctuary of the vate, and no living person outside the highest members of the priesthood may look upon him for fear of diluting his powers of divination. It was difficult to raise his head to see all around, but the lower branches of the trees, within reach, were hung with wicker cages that contained pairs of the noisy birds, all competing for the loudest call. Suspended above them were the putrefying remains of sacrificial victims; some human, others unidentifiable animals, hung on lines tied between the higher branches. In the ground surrounding him atop circles of poles were the sculls of sheep and goats, all of whom had, no doubt, taken their place before him on the slab. Several of the priesthood, or their followers, were now active to his right, making scraping, squeaking, rattling sounds as if iron rods were being laid on a wooden rack, but he could not move his head around to see what they were doing. Then came the busy crackling sound of a fire being lit. It was Dwynrid who addressed him in Brythonic.

'Are you awake?'

Scaeva affected a nodding movement which scuffed his right cheek against the slab and grunted an affirmative. The druid was dressed knee to elbow in a tight-fitting costume of brown wool that stressed his scrawny physique; it was ribbed to resemble the bark of an oak. On his head, he wore a similarly ribbed woollen cap.

'Count yourself lucky to be alive young man. If Gestorix had not protected you until we had been summoned to deal with the situation, Cassivellaunus would have had your head as surely as you took the head of his nephew.'

'I didn't know it was his nephew.'

'That is of no consequence. You took a life in times of peace, so you have been brought to this sacred place for your future to be determined and justice to be served. The spirits have been consulted and I must administer the measures that ensure you will carry their solemn prophecies with you until they are fulfilled.'

Dwynrid drew a long dagger from a scabbard on his belt, hooked the tip under Scaeva's tunic at the back of his neck, and then ran it down his back, slitting the garment open cleanly. Then one of his students came to his side bearing a shallow bowl of jelly-like substance. Dwynrid held the tips of his fingers together, scooped a handful of jelly out of the bowl, and applied the foul-smelling preparation to Scaeva's back and shoulders. The cold sliminess of it sent a shiver through him. Dwynrid continued until the bowl was emptied, and Scaeva's back was smothered from his neck to the belt around his trousers.

'What are you doing? What is that horrible stuff,' asked Scaeva with a grimace.

'Without this preparation, the shock a boy of your age would receive from the pain you are about to experience would probably kill you.'

'Whaaat!' screamed Scaeva, as sheer terror swiftly sprung from a feeling of mere foreboding. 'What are you gonna do? It wasn't my fault. He threw dirt in my eyes. I couldn't see what I was doing. He was hurting my brother.'

As the torrent of excuses and justifications spewed forth, he writhed on the slab and yanked his wrists against their bonds, all to no avail. He discovered his ankles were similarly bound.

'As I said before, that is of no consequence. Count yourself fortunate, boy. You will survive this, and the pain will eventually subside. The spirits unveiled what is in store for you. They prophesied the death of four others close to you. Your own death will not occur until the fifth prophecy is fulfilled. That moment, the moment of your death, will be when you come face to face with the King of Kings. Until then, you will live under the protection of Epona, but I expect you know that much already.'

Scaeva's mind, already in a state of blind panic, raced to comprehend the enormity of what had just been revealed to him. There was no time to make sense of it before Dwynrid began his ritual incantations to the spirits in the ancient tongue and the first red hot iron touched against him on the lower right side of his back. Before he caught the whiff of his own burning flesh in his nostrils, his ears were filled with the sound of his own screams. Again and again, the agony inflicted by the glowing irons seared through him as the first prophecy was branded in runes across his back. As each row of symbols seared into his flesh, the pain, terrible as it was, was no worse than the first. By the time the fifth and final prophecy was indelibly imprinted between his shoulders, he was delirious, and the druid fell silent. Scaeva's throat was too raw to scream anymore. His pain vented in garbled gasps until, at last, it was over, and he lapsed back into blissful unconsciousness.

XVII

September 55 BC
Near Camulodunon, the Citadel of the Trinovantes

The sickly smell of seared flesh in his nostrils had been replaced by the pungent odour of curdled milk. This was the first thing Scaeva was aware of as he came round. He was face down again, but this time, on a straw-filled palliasse in a candle-lit hut. Kneeling beside him was one of Dwynrid's students, a girl with long straight brown hair hanging down over her otherwise naked breasts. By the flickering light, her torso and cheeks were adorned with swirling blue painted symbols. Geometric black tattoos lined her forehead, the meaning of which, although of some significance in the priesthood, was lost on him. The odour was emitting from a thick white paste she was applying carefully to his back with a smooth softwood spatula. His whole body ached, but that was nature's way of dissipating the throbbing pain from his back, which was being eased by the treatment he was receiving.

Too weak to even speak, he closed his eyes and allowed his head to sink into the forgiving mattress. He wanted to sleep, but only a few moments later, or so it seemed, someone else came into the room and stood over him. The girl had gone. Was she just a dream?

'So, it was you raising the dead with your squeals yesterday,' Scaeva recognised the voice. It was Caspar. The older boy continued. 'And I hope that stench isn't your feet, Scaeva.'

'What the fuck do you want, Caspar? And no, it is not my feet. It's the stuff the girl was putting on my back.'

'Yes, of course, I know that. It is a poultice made from the root of the valerian plant. It helps you sleep and should ease your pain. I could tell you a few things about the girl too, but I think you're too young to understand.'

'Go away Caspar. I just want to be left alone.'

'Yes, I will go away, but I'm taking you with me. Dwynrid, in his wisdom, has chosen me to escort you home to Camulodunon. He has inspected his handiwork and declared you well enough to leave. Of course, it will be painful for several days, but you will survive. Until the Fifth Prophecy,' he added with a smirk, before continuing. 'Come on, up on your feet before you stiffen up completely.'

There was no point in resisting. Scaeva took hold of the hand Caspar offered in support and pulled himself to his feet. He clung onto the older boy's shoulder and took his first few steps towards the still-open doorway. On stepping outside, he recognised the quiet sleepy homestead as the one he had passed through before while exploring, just before Caspar had caught him and turned him back. His tunic was still ripped open and even a gentle breeze caressing his raw back made him wince. Soon they were passing through the groves of his morning classes, now deserted in the mid-afternoon. All the questions that had been buzzing in his brain, before the agony of the first red hot rune blotted them out, now came back to him.

'What has happened to me, Caspar?' he implored, hoping the other boy would take pity on him and not tease as he usually did. 'What do the runes mean?'

'Didn't Dwynrid tell you what has been foretold?'

'Only the final prophecy. There were four others. He said they foretold the death of people close to me.'

Caspar stopped and stepped behind Scaeva to open the flaps of his torn shirt. 'Yes, you are correct. That is what they say.'

'Then who are they? The four people. When will it happen?'

'If Dwynrid hasn't told you, it is not my place to do so,' replied Caspar in his usual superior tone. Scaeva suspected Caspar didn't have the first idea what they meant, and it was customary for him to taunt instead of admitting he didn't know. He guessed lessons in the reading of runes may not be taught until after a student had completed their training as a Bard, and Caspar was still several years away from that. He did seem to have some knowledge of herbal remedies though, and when Caspar did know something of interest, he often bragged about it.

'Well, maybe you can tell me, what was that brown slimy stuff he smeared on my back?'

'I can't tell you what it was because that is secret,' said Caspar. He continued in a schoolmasterly manner, 'But I can tell you it prevents the skin from blistering and causes the scar tissue to take its dark brown colour for the sake of clarity of the runes. If administered with sufficient skill and learning, the scars will not fade until after each prophecy it foretold has been fulfilled.' Then, in a more accusing tone, he added, 'But since your recklessness at the feast has caused the truce between the tribes to be broken, I don't suppose it will be long before the runes start to disappear.'

'What do you mean, the truce is over? I swear, I didn't know the boy was Vellaunus' nephew.'

'He's known as Cassivellaunus now,' corrected Caspar. 'You were drugged and taken out of harm's way when he started swearing dire oaths, so it really shouldn't have been necessary to disturb the vate to determine your fate. You are just small fry on his list of deaths to avenge. Fortunately for Imanuentus and Mandubracus, they had already left the feast before the fighting broke out, as they will surely be his first priority.'

Scaeva knew that before he was born, a long-standing feud between Imanuentus and Vellaunus was the reason for the war between the tribes, but no one had ever spoken of it in his presence. He was feeling all out of questions anyway, but despite that, he tried one more time.

'Caspar, why do Vellaunus, sorry, Cassivellaunus and Imanuentus hate each other so?'

Finally, Caspar resorted to his stock reply, 'Questions, Scaeva, questions. You ask too many.'

The boys continued their journey in silence. As they neared Camulodunon, a cloud of dust rose above the trees around a bend in the track before them. The sound of galloping hooves getting closer caused them both to halt and step aside from the bridleway. Within moments, a body of warriors, most of them wearing the animal skins favoured by the Cassi, and led by the unmistakable figure of Cassivellaunus, thundered past without affording them so much as a glance.

'Was that who I think it is?' gasped Scaeva in a state of shock.

The look of consternation on the face of the older boy said it all. 'Follow me,' shouted Caspar as he raced down the track in the direction from which the riders had come.

Scaeva forgot his pains and raced after him until they came to the familiar place near the woods where he had encountered Epona. In the middle of the pasture stood the tree where Scaeva first saw the ponies, but this time there were no ponies. Hanging from the low branches of the tree were two bodies: an adult and a child. The adult had been hung by the neck and run through the chest with a spear. Caspar was the first on the scene, staring in horror at the lifeless body of Imanuentus. He was already feeling faint at the sight of the blood when Scaeva, full of dread, came and stood beside him and looked mournfully up at the face of his grandfather. His dear brother Ebracus, hung by his neck beside him. Throat slit and gaping. Still oozing blood over the golden torc that identified him as his father's heir. Two birds were hooked into his belt. The bodies were suspended by ropes slung over the lower branches and anchored in the ground by a wooden stake. After all he had been through since the night of the feast, Scaeva had not cried a single tear. But now, try as he may, he could not stem the tears welling up behind his eyes until they trickled, causing glistening rivulets in the grime, down both his cheeks.

Caspar just had to get away. 'Come on, we must get you home and break this news. They will send someone to collect the bodies.'

'No wait,' Scaeva cuffed away the tears with his sleeve. 'We can't just leave them here; we have to take them with us.' As he spoke, there was a movement in the shadows of the trees on the edge of the wood. He pointed. 'Look there. Two horses are coming out of the woods. Can you see? A mare and her foal by the look of it.'

Caspar stared in disbelief. Was this the doing of Epona, or was it something else? Caspar knew that apart from the healing effect on humans, the valerian root had a calming effect on horses, but surely, they couldn't have detected the concoction smeared over Scaeva's back at that distance.

'Caspar, you're not going to faint on me, are you? Untie the ropes from those stakes and when I get the horses in position, you can lower them down.'

Caspar did as he was told and before long, both bodies were draped over the backs of the gentle creatures. Scaeva gently eased the open-ended torc from around his brother's neck and wiped the blood from it on his tunic. One grim task remained, to remove the spear that was still sticking out through his grandfather's back. Scaeva grasped it with both hands, just below the head, and heaved it out, all the way through, with a hideous slurping sound. Caspar almost retched. Scaeva turned on him and took aim with the spear, then hurled the dripping weapon at the tree just behind him. It flew inches from Caspar's ear and buried its head in the trunk with a thud; the bloody shaft still quivering with the force spraying droplets of blood across the grass.

'Caspar, I'm going to ask you one last time. You must know, otherwise you wouldn't have said my grandfather was Cassivellaunus' first priority. Why did he want to kill him? I deserve to know, and this has nothing to do with what happened at the feast.'

Caspar swallowed hard and tried to regain his composure. 'You're right. There is little point in keeping it from you anymore because everyone will talk about it when we get back. Let's get away from here, I'll explain on the way.'

The two boys turned back to the track that led to the great citadel of Camulodunon. The horses, with their grisly burdens, followed obediently behind.

'Everyone knows how you and your brother idolised your grandfather. The time he spent with you, doting on you, taking you out hunting every day. He wasn't always like that. Look at how your father turned out, a nasty piece of work if ever there was one. Don't ever tell him I said that, but you know it's true.'

Scaeva did know it. Mandubracus was cold and what little fatherly interest he had was saved for Ebracus, his first born. It was always Gestorix, the man Scaeva knew as their uncle, that treated him like a son.

'So, is that why no one told me what he was like before? They didn't want to spoil my image of him?'

'Yes, I suppose so. I'm way too young myself to know of it, but I learned the stories from the Bards. You probably know the story yourself but didn't realise who it was referring to. It's the one about the sons of Lugios.'

'Yes, I've heard it. I can remember the first two lines:
The sons of Lugios made their peace,
When Ludd, the fair Luna wed ...
But I don't know any more of it by heart.'

'That's the one,' said Caspar, nodding his confirmation. 'Do you remember a character named Manan, the half-brother of Luna? He murdered his own brother, Malin, because he wouldn't join his plot to kill Ludd and usurp his throne?'

'Well, sort of, I get confused about that because it has a bit that goes:

When Manan slew Silver Hand ...

But what does any of that have to do with my grandfather?'

'Manan,' said Caspar, emphasising the name, 'was your grandfather. He insisted people henceforth used his formal name, Imanuentus, when he took the throne of the Trinovantes and made a pact with the tribes from Belgica to join forces against the Cassi.'

'Then who was Silver Hand?' asked Scaeva as he began to work out the answer for himself.

'Ludd lost his left hand fighting against the Belgae,' explained Caspar. 'Craftsmen fashioned him a new hand made of silver. It enabled him to hold a shield or the reins of a horse, keeping his sword arm free. And Ludd, as you may have now guessed, was the older brother of Cassivellaunus.'

'And now Cassivellaunus has his revenge,' mused Scaeva, almost to himself. Then he added, 'Do you think the Bards will tell Grandfather's story too?'

'I'm certain they will,' said Caspar in a more positive tone. 'If I have learned correctly, Imanuentus was treated harshly as a younger man. There is a side to the story that he took what was rightfully his.'

'Then tell me of it,' pleaded Scaeva.

'It's a long story, but I will try to make it brief. Imanuentus was the son of the Brehin of Prydain, Madawc of the Trinovantes. He was one of the sons of Lugios, the Shining One. But when Madawc died, your grandfather was too young to rule, so his uncle Blad took the throne. Imanuentus' mother was furious. She wanted her sons to become kings, as was their right, so she married Blad's younger brother Llyr, who was King of the Cantiaci, and he adopted her two boys as his own, naming them as his heirs. Then she plotted to murder Blad so that her sons would rule over two kingdoms. Do you follow it so far?'

'Yes, I think so,' said Scaeva, concentrating hard.

Caspar continued. 'At first, it seemed as if her plans had succeeded. Blad was still childless when he was poisoned, but before your grandfather returned to Camulodunon to be rightfully crowned King of the Trinovantes, Ludd, first born of Heli of the Cassi, stepped in to marry your grandfather's elder half-sister Luna, and succeeded Blad as king. He did it to unite the Cassi and the Trinovantes against the invading Belgic tribes. So Imanuentus was foiled not once, but twice. Then things went from bad to worse.'

'But surely, wouldn't he still inherit the throne of the Cantiaci from Llyr?' reasoned Scaeva.

'Unfortunately not,' replied Caspar. 'Because his mother died. Llyr remarried and had three daughters of his own, so he disinherited both his stepsons.'

'So why did grandfather kill his own brother?'

'I already told you that bit. He planned secretly to make common cause with the Belgae and then use his kinship with Luna to gain entry to the royal household at Camulodunon and murder Ludd and his entire family. His brother, Malin, did not have the stomach for it and threatened to reveal his plans. And the rest, you now know.'

'Did he kill them all?'

'No, Ludd's two young sons were saved and sent to safety with their grandfather Heli. Their names were Androgeus and Tenvantius. You probably saw them at the feast sharing a table with Cassivellaunus. They were sitting next to your grandfather.'

XVIII

September 55 BC
Camulodunon, the Citadel of the Trinovantes

'If Dwynrid has harmed the boy, I'll gladly kill him.'
'And risk eternal damnation from the gods?' said
Mandubracus. Gestorix paced up and down the
raised platform behind a crenellated palisade, still in a state
of agitation following the events at the feast.

Below and before him were the vast system of dykes,
ditches, and ramparts that gave Camulodunon such a visual
impact of being impregnable against any known threat.
Behind him, the citadel, complete with its markets, shrines,
and compounds set aside for farming, industry and
commerce, spread back to the confluence of the two steep-
sided river valleys that protected its northern and southerly
approaches. This was no mere hillfort or stockade. Because
of the influence of Belgic immigrants, Camulodunon was
redolent of the oppida found extensively across Gaul and
Belgae.

'What do I care? I have survived eternal damnation
from my own people. Mandubracus, it's been nearly two
full days now since the night of the feast. What is Dwynrid
doing?' Gestorix turned to stare out across the flat
landscape towards the setting sun. Far below him on the
main road from the citadel, the steady stream of workers,

merchants, and herders were leaving for the day, heading home to their farms and families, scattered across the territory of the Trinovantes. Some in wagons or on horseback, but most of them on foot, carrying goods or the tools of their trade.

'We have to wait,' said Mandubracus. 'The vate can take four days or more. You told me yourself that Dwynrid would send him home when judgement has been made.'

'Yes, but there was no guarantee that he would still be alive. He is your own son Mandubracus. How can you be so calm? Imanuentus even took Ebracus for his afternoon hunting practice as if nothing had happened to Scaeva. The pair of you weren't even there when he needed you most.'

'As I recall,' replied Mandubracus coldly, 'the king's last instruction to you was to look after the boys.'

Gestorix was not going to take that, even from his superior. He snapped back. 'If you can remember that, then you were more sober than you looked.'

The two men glared at each other. In all the years they had been friends, this was the first time they had had a serious dispute. Gestorix had arrived with a boatload of mercenaries from Belgae many years before and had proved his worth as a warrior and a leader of men in the continuing war against the Cassi. Mandubracus' wife had died during the birth of his second son and was so distraught he couldn't bear even to give the infant a name. Gestorix, who had been banished from his own tribe for reasons which he never spoke about, suggested his own lost son's name for the boy. Taking pity on the child because of his father's indifference, he treated him as his own.

The silent standoff between the men was broken by sounds of a commotion in the distance. A crowd had gathered on the road from the citadel. Many of those who had been on their way home had now turned about and were following in the wake of two figures, each leading a horse with what looked like a body draped across its back. As the figures drew closer, several of the onlookers were running ahead, back towards the city gates, frantic, shouting something as they came. Before the figures were close enough for either Gestorix or Mandubracus to recognise, they heard clearly what the runners were shouting.

'The king is dead; the king is dead.'

'Slain by Cassivellaunus.'

Mandubracus froze. At that moment, he realised that the smaller of the two bodies could only be Ebracus. A moment later, both men identified the figures leading the horses as Scaeva and one of Dwynrid's pupils, the tall one with the blonde hair. Despite the shock at the news of the king's death, Gestorix's relief at Scaeva's safe return was matched in equal and opposite proportions by Mandubracus' grief at the sudden loss of his father and his first-born son. Mandubracus leapt down from the platform behind the palisade and ran to the guardhouse at the main gate, shouting orders that the bodies of the king and his son be taken immediately for preparation for their burial; that the two boys should be escorted directly to the king's council chamber; and that the throng following the boys should be sent home and not allowed back into the citadel until morning, when announcements regarding the tragedy would be made. Despite the shock and grief, his overriding thoughts were that with his father dead, he could now run things his own way.

Mandubracus' instructions were carried out to the last letter. In the chamber, flickering bronze oil lamps had been lit against the onset of dusk. Soon the four of them stood facing each other in the roundhouse where Imanuentus himself had enacted his murderous intentions against the previous incumbents all those years ago.

'Gestorix has briefed me on what happened at the feast after your grandfather and I left.' Mandubracus paused as if having difficulty with what he had to say next. 'I'm proud of you for coming to your brother's aid,' then almost as an afterthought added, 'fearlessly, and without thought for your own safety.'

This was the kindest thing Scaeva could remember his father ever saying to him. He presented his father with his elder brother's torc, daring to hope it would be returned to him as his new heir, but his hopes were shattered. Mandubracus took it without a word. Feeling humiliated, Scaeva was lost for words, but Mandubracus, bereft, as ever, of emotion, continued in a more urgent tone.

'But now we need to know what passed between you and the druid, and then what happened to your grandfather. Take your time boy.'

Scaeva swallowed his disappointment. He'd had plenty of time to think about relating his terrifying encounter with the druid, but his shocking discovery on the way home had shot his thoughts to fragments.

Gestorix prompted him gently. 'Vellaunus wanted your head. You appear unharmed. What judgement did the vate reveal?'

The question allowed Scaeva to provide an answer without having to form a sentence. Turning his back to his questioners, he slid his soiled tunic off his shoulders and allowed it to drop around his waist. The hideous state of his back drew gasps of horror from the men opposite. The five rows of symbols were imprinted across his back in clearly defined dark brown images, each surrounded with angry wheals of pink swollen flesh.

'By all the gods, what does this mean?'

Caspar froze as he realised Mandubracus was directing the question at him. 'I don't know, I swear it,' cried Caspar in alarm. 'I haven't learned the runes yet, not for years will I do so.'

Scaeva was quick to grab the opportunity to exact his revenge on the older boy for taunting him earlier about the meaning of the runes. 'Yes you do know what they mean,' rasped Scaeva accusingly. 'You said you wouldn't tell me because if the druid didn't, it wasn't your place to do so.'

Mandubracus gave a nod to Gestorix, who reached out, grabbed Caspar by the shoulder and pulled him on his back across the table, pinning him down. Then he moved swiftly to the other side, yanked down the older boy's trousers and grasped his penis with one hand whilst drawing his knife with the other.

'Tell me, tell me you little prick or I'll cut your cock off and stuff it down your throat.'

Caspar was horrified! He couldn't believe it, but the firmness of the prince's grip was giving him an erection. The image of Dwynrid's comely painted student, naked as he remembered her, flashed into his mind as the sharpness of the blade drew a thin red line of blood along the base of his throbbing member. 'No no no no no. Don't do it. I can't read them. I don't know what they mean, I swear it. I swear it by all the gods.' Caspar was sobbing so much that his whole body was shaking.

Scaeva just smiled with satisfaction and said, 'You can let him go, father. He doesn't know. He was just having his sport at my expense earlier, and now I've had mine at his expense, so we're even.'

For the second time in the space of a few days, Mandubracus was impressed by his youngest son. It pleased him that not only was he fearless in defence of his brother, but also that he could cause terror to be instilled in the mildest of adversaries, for nothing more than his own amusement. His hard-heartedness towards his second son, ten years in consolidation, had softened in a matter of moments.

'They are prophecies, father, five of them. The vate consulted the spirits to determine what would become of me. He told me I will die when I come face to face with the King of Kings.'

'No,' cried Mandubracus, 'this cannot be. If that is your fate, then Vellaunus would have taken you on the night of the feast. He had every opportunity.'

'But that is only the fifth. There are four others, each prophesying the death of people close to me. Dwynrid would not divulge their names, but I fear if Ebracus and grandfather are the first two to die, then you and Gestorix could be next.'

Caspar, who had been released and had hitched up his trews, was recovered enough to interject. 'But don't forget, Scaeva, the ointment that Dwynrid smeared on your back before he used the irons. I don't know what it is, I swear I don't. I said it was a secret because I wanted you to think

I knew but wouldn't tell, but I don't know. It's a secret from me too, but I was being honest when I told you of its purpose.' Then, trembling, and crossing both hands over his private parts, he said to Mandubracus. 'I wouldn't lie to you Lord; I swear I would never.'

Scaeva thought for a moment. 'Was it something about preventing blistering?'

'Yes, but more than that,' said Caspar. 'If it is applied correctly, and I mean the right mixture at the right thickness and with the right exhortations to the spirits, then the runes for each prophecy will fade and disappear as they are fulfilled.'

So that's what Dwynrid was mumbling, thought Scaeva.

'Well, have they faded?' snapped Mandubracus. 'Turn around boy.'

The first two rows of runes were every bit as clear and new as the rest. The prince glared at the student.

Caspar froze. 'I don't know how long after the event it takes effect.'

'That was a worthless piece of information if ever I heard,' bellowed Mandubracus, banging his fist on the table. Caspar shuddered in anticipation of further wrath from the prince, but Gestorix moved the conversation on.

'So, what happened to Ebracus and the king?'

Scaeva took up the story. 'We were on our way home from the sanctuary when a company of horsemen, Cassi, led by none other than Cassivellaunus himself, passed us at great speed in the opposite direction. It was just before the one-tree pasture. When we arrived at the pasture, there were two figures hung from the branches.'

'He must have had prior knowledge about the king's movements,' said Gestorix. 'He has his agents amongst us.'

'But it could be anyone,' replied Mandubracus. 'It is no secret that Imanuentus took his grandsons hunting in the afternoon. For our own sakes, we must act quickly and tell no one.' Then, as he called the guards from duty outside the door, he turned to Caspar and said, 'What's your name boy, and when was the last time you ate?'

'Caspar, Lord, and not since I left the sanctuary.'

When the guards entered the chamber, the prince gave them their orders. 'Take this boy Caspar, feed him well and lock him up for the night. In the morning, send him back to the priesthood.'

As soon as Caspar had been escorted from the room, Mandubracus suddenly became animated. 'I have a plan. But first, my son, you must eat too.'

Scaeva was given a change of clothes. Then he related the details of his ordeal over a plate of his favourite honey roast ham and a beaker of milk before his father outlined his plan of action.

'When I heard from Queen Cordelia's ambassador that the Romans were coming, it made me think that an alliance with Caesar would enable us to defeat the Cassi and put an end to Vellaunus. Of course, the Romans would destroy the priesthood too, but I can live with that, no bad thing in my opinion, but the king would never allow it, so I kept my own counsel. Then Commius turned up, sniffing for a treaty on Caesar's behalf, although he pretended otherwise. Now with Imanuentus gone, I am king, and I intend to thwart the prophecy and defeat Vellaunus with one bold move.'

Gestorix had known Mandubracus for many years and knew him to be the most cold-hearted of individuals, but he was still mildly shocked at the callousness on display; not only from the prince but also from his son, neither of whom showed any signs of distress at the brutal killing of their closest family.

'But Caesar has returned to Gaul. You do not know if he plans to return to Prydain.'

'Then we go to Gaul and make him an offer,' Mandubracus was emphatic.

'But how do we find him? We have no credentials. He will not know us.'

'But Commius does,' answered the prince. 'Commius is the key.'

'But even if you can locate Commius and make your offer to Caesar,' argued Gestorix, 'he will not return until Beltane, Alban Eilir at the earliest. Your son could be dead by then.'

'Not if we take him with us and offer him as a hostage to keep our side of the bargain.'

Scaeva's eyebrows shot up in surprise. 'You can't mean that,' he almost choked on his milk.

'Think about it,' said his father. 'What safer place for you than with Caesar in Gaul? It will guarantee your safety from Vellaunus until the Romans return and join with us to sweep Vellaunus away for all time.'

'The plan has its merits,' conceded Gestorix. 'I can warn our thanes and bannermen that Vellaunus may plan further offensives. I will also leave orders for them to bring in all the corn and cattle behind our defences here at

Camulodunon. There is plenty of space. Those too far to the south can muster at Dun Bury. But Mandubracus, how do we locate Commius? Did he return to his tribes in Belgae or retire to Noviomagus?'

'Queen Cordelia can tell us that. So, our first destination must be Durovernon. Rumours were circulating before the feast that Commius and Cordelia had brought the Atrebates to aid the Romans in defeating Taximagulus. Then Caesar reinstated her at her father's old seat before taking his army back across the sea. That would have left Taximagulus free to claim his victory and establish his version of events before the truth came out.'

'True, I'll wager he is capable of that,' said Gestorix. 'If Caesar does have a plan to return, the queen will surely have knowledge of that also.'

'Agreed,' said Mandubracus, 'if such a plan exists, we need to be part of it. We have much to discuss with Cordelia before we meet with the Roman. Tomorrow, we leave at dawn to cross the Tamasa before dusk.'

As with the Gauls, the custom amongst the Britons was that children were not permitted to approach their fathers in public until they were old enough to bear arms. Although it was regarded as inappropriate for a son who is still a boy to stand in sight of his father in a public place, Mandubracus was determined to lead his son to safety and would give short shrift to anyone who offered so much as a look disapproval.

Mandubracus

XIX

September 55 BC
Oceanus Britannicus, approaching the port of Gesoriacum

Five hours after putting out to sea, the coast of Gaul appeared above the horizon with the rise and fall of the ship's bow. At this, the oarsmen, visibly lifted in spirit, put their backs into finishing the job. Unable to hoist the sail because of the direction of the prevailing winds, the ship's master confidently steered the vessel towards the harbour-side buildings and jetties of Gesoriacum; so familiar to him, although they were not yet discernible to the three passengers.

Scaeva, who had watched with increasing trepidation the huge white cliffs of his homeland shrink in the distance, mulled over the events since he had left home with his father and uncle. Two things were troubling him. Why had he not seen the marsh guide and his family on the morning following their crossing of the Tamasa? The previous evening, the jovial fellow crossed in response to the lighted signal post and escorted the three of them safely back to the other side of the river. There was an awkward moment when he asked if they had heard the rumours that the king had been slain, but that apart, he had been most genial, introducing his family and offering them food and a berth in a barn for the night. And secondly, why was his father so angry after his audience with the queen earlier that afternoon?

Mandubracus too, was deep in his own thoughts. The meeting with Cordelia did not go as well as he had hoped. In hindsight, he was considering whether she held him and his father responsible in some way for the disappearance of her counsellor. There was also the fact that his father had refused to come to her aid. The only information she imparted was that Commius had returned with Caesar to the continent. Of Caesar's intentions to return to Prydain, she had appeared bitter and tight-lipped.

Gestorix, who had witnessed many scenes of brutality in his lifetime, and committed a few himself, was still not convinced that it was necessary for Mandubracus to butcher the marsh guide and his family in case any of them recognised who they were and betrayed their movements. He was also feeling anxious about journeying to the vicinity of his homeland, after so many years away, after vowing never to return.

The sighting of land quickly dispersed Scaeva's unease, which was now overtaken with a spirit of adventure he had not experienced since his first explorations down river from his home to the shores of the East Sea with Uncle Gestorix. The same Gestorix, who was now sitting next to Mandubracus, both of them stern-faced on the benches at the rear of the boat.

It was still over an hour before the ship pulled alongside the jetty in one of the few empty spaces against the long wooden structure. The oarsmen fixed their oars vertically in the iron rowlocks, enabling the boat to be tied up. Scaeva leapt onto the boards and overbalanced, breaking his fall at the cost of a palm-full of seagull droppings. Unused to a long sea crossing, he had temporarily lost control of his legs.

His father and Gestorix settled payment with the ship's master and thanked him for a safe journey before joining Scaeva on the messy platform. The sun momentarily peeped from behind the grey clouds behind them, creating deep shadows in the grassy windswept dunes along the beach. In the other direction, scores of larger vessels gently rose and fell at anchor on the high tide; the sun picking out details on the top rigging around the single sails, tied up in gently billowing bunches beneath the spars. These were the ships that had carried the Romans back to Gaul less than ten days before.

'It's no use asking anyone around here,' Gestorix was saying to Mandubracus. 'If we need to find Commius we'd be better off enquiring at the Roman camp. Alas with you being so obviously a Briton …' Gestorix was referring to the undisguisable tattoos that adorned the forehead, cheeks and chin of the prince, '…and seeing as Caesar just had his arse kicked by your countrymen, it would be better if I went on my own. At least I can talk to them without raising suspicion.'

Mandubracus had already attracted the attention of two Morini fishermen, despite having his face and torso scrubbed clean of blue dye. He simply scowled at them, and they returned their attention to mending their nets. A small group of urchins, probably younger than Scaeva, loitered at the end of the jetty, eyeing them momentarily to assess the weight of the prince's purse. They looked away sheepishly when Gestorix, tapping the hilt of his sword, made it clear he had guessed their purpose.

Mandubracus considered Gestorix's comments for a moment. 'Yes, I agree, but let's find a safe place to wait for you.'

They left the jetty, squeezed between the overflowing fish stalls, and had to dodge between the ox-drawn carts that rumbled along the cobbles. The odd trio left the   busy quayside; up a lane between some two-storey wharves packed with bales, barrels, and crates on one side, and a row of brothels on the other.

This led out to the wide main thoroughfare through the port. On the corner stood an inn, The Old Wolf's Head. Mandubracus suggested he and Scaeva wait there and secure refreshments and provisions, while Gestorix went in search of information as to the whereabouts of Commius. Gestorix grunted his approval and set off along the wide stone-paved roadway that could only have led to the Roman camp.

Although it wasn't a bright afternoon, it still took a moment or two for their eyes to become accustomed to the dark interior of the Inn. This was another new experience for Scaeva, who was still marvelling at the sheer scale of the buildings around the port, with high windows and tiled roofs. Mandubracus picked his way between the crowded tables to order their provisions. Years of co-operation with the influx of tribes from the continent had given him sufficient mastery of the common Gaulish language, quite similar to his own, to make himself understood; but there was no need to speak because the innkeeper, despite the gloom, immediately recognised him as a Briton.

'What have we here?' he declared in a voice loud enough to catch everyone's attention. 'A Briton! Have you come to make sure Caesar has fucked off back to Rome?'

A brief silence was followed by such an uproar that Scaeva was afraid his father was being attacked. Quite the contrary, the Gauls were clamouring around Mandubracus and slapping him on the back. When the commotion abated, a feast was prepared for the foreign hero and his son, whilst the innkeeper explained why their hatred of the Romans was still so raw. On Caesar's return from Britannia to Gaul, two of his transports had been blown off course and beached further along the coast. As the soldiers from the two ships were returning to camp, a group of Morini militia ambushed and attacked them, but the soldiers hung on until the Romans sent reinforcements to rescue them. The following day, Caesar sent Labienus to exact revenge, killing a great number of Morini, and burning their crops and houses.

Gestorix crested the rising ground from the port and stopped to take in the view across the flat plain beyond. For the first time in his life, he beheld a vast Roman military camp; one of many, no doubt, left in the wake of Caesar's advance. The sight of the rows of thousands of tents in perfect alignment behind a high barricade sent a mild shiver down his spine. He grimaced at the thought of the gamble he had taken all those years ago that cost him his home and his family. What had it all been for? The whole of Belgae, from the Narrow Sea to the banks of the Rhenus, was now under the heel of the Roman invaders. He drew a breath and continued down the other side of the hill. As he approached the main gates, a sentry came out from behind the barrier and addressed him with a simple sentence in a heavily accented version of the language that was common in the region.

'What the fuck do you want Gaul?'

'I have an urgent message for Commius, King of the Atrebates.'

'Piss off. He's not here.'

Gestorix was not expecting such an aggressive tone, but pressed his enquiry nonetheless. 'This is important. Surely your commander will know where I can find him?'

At this, the sentry drew his *gladius*. 'I said bugger off.'

Three of his comrades emerged from the guardhouse at the side of the gate, all reaching for their weapons. One of these legionnaires was the standard-bearer of the Tenth, Marcus Cassius Scaeva, who had distinguished himself on the beach during Caesar's landing in Britannia. While still inside the guardhouse, the voice from outside was distantly familiar. Now, as Marcus sized up the stranger standing just the other side of the barrier, something disquieting stirred deep in the back of his mind. The dark eyes and thin face disturbed his memory. The long, greying hair, unlike the local Morini, was pulled away from his face and tied at the back of his head, where it hung freely to his collar.

Gestorix was genuinely taken aback by the drawn weapons and the challenging glares of the guards, all except one, the tallest of them, who stared at him as if looking at a ghost. Gestorix momentarily met his gaze and merely shrugged. The Morini had been settled under Caesar for more than a year, so he was puzzled by the level of antagonism from the invaders. Of course, he was unaware of the recent events that caused the sentries to bristle with anger at his presence. Gestorix turned and sprinted back up the slope. Marcus stared after him, controlling an urge to give chase. Glancing over his shoulder and seeing that he wasn't being pursued, Gestorix slowed to a trot and then a walk until he crested the hill again. The earlier cloud covering had given way to a few streaks of high cirrus and the setting sun turned the sky and the sea, now calm as a millpond, the most glorious shades of pink and orange. He took a last look over his shoulder at the camp, now lit with countless braziers in the gathering gloom. One of the sentries was still watching him. Gestorix shrugged, waved defiantly, and set off back along the road to the port to rejoin his comrades.

The enigmatic figure disappeared over the hilltop, leaving Marcus to reflect on the other memorable events of his day.

After the usual muster parade and roll call, Crastinus, his centurion, delivered the orders for the day. Marcus was excused from roster duties and told to report immediately to the office of the camp commander. His centurion had given him no sign of the reason, but having to report to Rufus wasn't something to celebrate. He tried to remember anything he might have done recently to bring himself to the attention of the praetor. Since his return from Britannia, his duties in between watches, like most of the legionnaires, had been involved with the construction of permanent buildings to see them through the coming winter. He strode along the Via Principalis past row upon row of perfectly aligned tents and was hailed by a group of workmen constructing wooden huts to replace the temporary summer accommodation. He recognised them immediately as auxiliaries he had known well before joining the Tenth. His mind was still on his imminent interview with Rufus and hoped that his rather curt nod of recognition didn't make them think he had got above himself. He reached the *principia,* the large square parade ground in the centre of the camp, passing the grain store and guardhouse that were nearing completion. On the opposite side of the square were the offices and quarters of the camp commander, Publius Sulpicius Rufus, and his staff. He made his way across the busy expanse, avoiding the slow-moving carts full of timber and the muddy areas caused by the recent storms. He flushed with pride, as he always did when he passed the Legionary Standards, including the eagle of the Tenth, his eagle, on display outside the office of the praetor.

As Marcus mounted the three steps in front of the open entrance door, the two sentries on the veranda easily recognised him and stood aside. This was Marcus' first time in the *praetorium.* The orderly behind a single desk in the centre of the lobby looked up, asked his name, and told him to wait while he slipped through the door behind him. A few moments later, he returned to his desk and pointed to a bench under the window, where Marcus should wait.

He must have stewed for half an hour, watching the comings and goings of officers and staff carrying orders or boxes of scrolls between the *praetorium* and the business and communications tent next to it. When the door behind the orderly finally opened, it wasn't Rufus who stepped out, but the General himself. Caesar had been finalising last-minute instructions for the winter duration with Rufus and Labienus prior to his departure. Unlike the last time they met, he was wearing an embossed silver *cuirass* adorned with his red sash of imperium looped and knotted at a sloping angle between his chest and waist. From his shoulders hung a scarlet cloak.

'Marcus, good to see you again and apologies for keeping you waiting, as I'm sure you had other things to attend to.' Marcus was so taken aback by the casual geniality of the great man that for a moment he thought there was another Marcus in the room. Before he could think of a reply, Caesar continued. 'My secretary, Faberius, reminded me this morning that you and I had unfinished business. Come, we can talk outside.'

'Do you mean from back in Britannia?' Marcus was dismayed; he avoided talking about his distant past and was relieved when the surrender of the Britons interrupted their last conversation. He followed Caesar out onto the veranda, where the two sentries saluted sharply.

'Yes, that's correct,' said Caesar as he descended the steps in front of Marcus' Eagle, and pointing up at it said, 'I've been wanting to hear the story of how you managed to return this to the Tenth.'

Marcus was not a natural storyteller, but this was a tale he was happy to relate. He began with how he was marching with the auxiliaries towards the rear of the infantry column in the campaign against the Belgae. Many Gauls, including some of the Belgae who had surrendered to Caesar, were marching with them. Marcus had overheard some of them plotting to slip away at night and pass information to the Nervii regarding Caesar's progress and column formation. As Caesar listened with great interest, it occurred to Marcus that the entire camp could see how much attention the General was paying him. He proudly continued with his story, right through to the end where he had returned to camp with the re-captured eagle and the heads of eight Belgae warriors strung around his neck by their hair.

'And what did you do with the heads?' asked Caesar.

'The head of the best fighter, I preserved in cedar oil, as is the custom of my father and his father before him. Labienus allowed it, just the one, provided I kept it out of sight in my kit. The others, I would have nailed to my doorpost, but he would never allow any Legionnaire to do that, and besides, I didn't have a doorpost until now. My century is starting work on our winter quarters today'.

'Then I'd better let you get back to that,' Caesar replied, slapping him on the shoulder. 'You must tell me about your father and his customs next time we meet, but Commius awaits, he is a genial fellow but does get tetchy if kept waiting, and I'll have his company all the way to Samarobriva.'

During the telling of the story, the *principia* filled with columns of Aeduan cavalry from their quarter of the camp. The Aedui were held in special esteem by Caesar for their long-standing record of unbroken loyalty to both him and Rome. The tribe was well known to educated Romans as 'The People of the Hearth.' Today they were forming his bodyguard, four hundred of them, to escort him to the garrison at Samarobriva for final briefings with his officers. Then he would return to Gallia Cisalpina for the winter and attend on his duties as governor of the province.

Caesar turned and strode purposefully towards the head of the mounted column that had formed across the *principia,* pointing along the Via Praetoria towards the main gate. Standing there was the unmistakable figure of King Commius—all long blonde flowing locks— dismounted and arms akimbo, waiting with Caesar's horse. Next to him was the mounted figure of Quintus Laberius

Durus, who had deputised for Labienus as *legate* of the Tenth while in Britannia.

The sharp hollow notes of the *buccina* sounding the end of his watch broke Marcus from his reverie. He could not remember the last time he had spoken about his father. It was a long time since he had even thought of him. There was a face he could remember but no longer picture. A voice he would recognise but couldn't hear. With a last look at the empty horizon, he turned back towards the gates.

Now that their esteemed visitors had been sufficiently fed and watered, or in the case of the senior, wined and dined, the innkeeper asked the purpose of their expedition.

'We're here to parley with Commius,' said Mandubracus flatly.

'Commius! That Roman-arse-licking jackal,' exclaimed the innkeeper. 'He pissed off to Samarobriva with Caesar just this morning. What do you want with him?'

Although Mandubracus had had his fill of the hospitality offered, he wasn't sufficiently inebriated to blurt out the real reason for his being there. If the Gauls had any inkling that he wanted Commius to help broker a deal with Caesar, he wouldn't have got out alive. He instinctively played his trump card, intimidation. Rising slowly from his seat, he leaned across the table, so his face was inches from that of the innkeeper.

Then he said, in a tone that brooked no further questioning. 'That's my fucking business!'

If Mandubracus intended his remark to show that his intentions towards Commius were less than cordial, he succeeded. 'I need three horses. I have good coinage. I'll pay for them, and the rest of the food.' He signalled to Scaeva to gather up as much of the bread and joints of meat he could pack into the leather valise around his shoulder.

'I won't take your silver,' said the innkeeper, only slightly affronted by Mandubracus' lack of gratitude for the free meal and bonhomie. 'The dinner is on the house, but I can't sell you any horses. The Romans commandeered almost every animal for miles around. They only let me keep mine for my wagons so I can keep the inn provisioned.'

Although the innkeeper displayed no grudge for Mandubracus' behaviour, the mood in the room had changed. At that moment, Gestorix appeared at the front door.

'We've got what we came for. We leave now,' barked Mandubracus without explanation as he took Gestorix's arm and spun him around. Scaeva followed them out into the darkened street. No one followed them. 'We need to get to Samarobriva.'

'That's a long way from here,' replied Gestorix. 'I got nothing from the camp. What's going on?'

Mandubracus relayed to Gestorix the events at the inn, and added, 'Don't worry, we've got you some food, but we'll need horses.'

'Leave that to me,' said Scaeva with excitement, borne out of finally seeing an opportunity to play a part in the day's proceedings. 'Go out to the end of the street, well out of sight of the inn, and I'll meet you there.'

Scaeva tossed his pouch of food to Gestorix and disappeared around the side of the inn to where he hoped to find the stables. He slipped easily and silently between the bars of the corral. The sounds and the smell of the horses led him through the darkness to the stable door, which was partly ajar. Just then, the clouds parted, and moonlight flooded the stable yard, pouring beams of soft light through the high windows into the interior of the stable. There was a collection of carts and wagons and four stalls, three of which were occupied. Scaeva was in his element. He quickly located bridles, fitted them, and led the three horses silently out of the stable to the corral gate. It was secured with a heavy iron lock and chain. Quickly mounting the smallest of the three, he kicked his steed into a gallop and leapt the fence at the far end of the corral. Obediently, the other two horses followed. The sound of the horses escaping drew a chorus of shouts and threats from the innkeeper and his guests, who poured out from The Old Wolf's Head in pursuit, but Scaeva had the only three horses in town. Watching in amazement from the shadows further along the street were Mandubracus and Gestorix, who rushed to meet the boy. As Scaeva and the two spare mounts drew level, the men grabbed the bridles, swung onto the backs of the other two horses, and made off along the wide drover's lane, clearing the port and leaving the cursing Gauls far behind.

The trio hadn't gone far before they felt safe from pursuit. Gestorix was first to slow up and pull his mount to a halt.

'How did you know the two other horses would follow you like that?'

Scaeva was taken aback by the question. He instinctively knew they would, but he still hadn't admitted the truth to anyone, despite Ebracus having mentioned his encounter with Epona to Caspar.

'I don't know really,' he lied. 'I just hoped they would. They're herd animals, aren't they?'

'You must have been sure they would follow, otherwise you wouldn't have bothered to fit the bridles,' Gestorix countered. 'And another thing, those horses you led back to the citadel carrying the bodies of your brother and the king. They wore no tack and had never even been shod.'

Scaeva was still nervous about trying to explain his meeting with the goddess, and he wasn't a confident liar, so he told as much of the truth as he dared and hoped that satisfied his elders.

'They just came out of the forest; I swear by the spirits. Dwynrid said something to me about Epona. He said I would live under her protection until the fifth prophecy is fulfilled.'

'So why didn't you mention this before?' Gestorix wasn't giving up.

'I just forgot.' at least Scaeva could rely on the simple truth again. 'What with everything else that has happened.'

Gestorix exchanged glances with Mandubracus, who gave a nod of satisfaction.

'It bodes well enough.' Then he changed the subject. 'So where are we? Are we even heading in the right direction?'

Gestorix craned his neck and stared up into the clear, crisp night sky, searching for the most recognisable constellation in the heavens.

'Yes, we're heading south,' he confirmed. 'Samarobriva is in Ambiani territory, and I think they are south of here.'

'You think so,' echoed Mandubracus scornfully. 'Is that the best you can do? You told me you could be helpful if you came along. You've been useless so far. I found out where Commius is. I got us food; my son got the horses.'

'Then why don't you go back and ask your friendly host at the inn how to get there,' retorted Gestorix.

'And why don't you go back and ask your new friends at the Roman camp!'

'Father, Uncle,' pleaded Scaeva, 'please stop arguing.' Scaeva was accustomed to their fiery relationship, and it had stood the test of time. 'I feel Epona is with us. She will protect and guide us.'

Mandubracus considered for a moment remembering the way the spare mounts had followed Scaeva over the corral fence. 'All right then, south it is.'

'Yes, I remember now,' said Gestorix, 'there is a bridge there over the Som. If we keep going until we meet the river, we can follow the bankside all the way.'

'Let's go then,' agreed Mandubracus, and the three of them set off at a light canter along the broad moonlit track. Samarobriva was under thirty leagues from Gestorix's tribal homeland, but he didn't give that away. Other than sharing the contents of his private trunk with Scaeva, he had never spoken of his life before coming to Britannia, and he would not start now.

After six hours of trotting, walking, and resting to save their mounts, passing a few silent hamlets, and crossing many smaller rivers and streams, they finally arrived at the banks of a major river. The far side was clearly visible in the still moonlit night.

'This must be it,' bleated Scaeva, who was now beginning to feel tired and sore. The events of the past twenty-four hours were taking their toll on the young boy. 'Which way do we go? And how much further?'

'Judging by the width of the river the bridge must be upstream, it's too wide here,' said Gestorix. 'And as I don't know how far it is, I suggest we rest up here for a while and water the horses. Get some rest Scaeva, you look done in.'

The trio dismounted, led their horses to the riverbank, and filled their water skins. There was now a distinct chill in the air. The clear sky hinted at the first frost of the season.

'I couldn't sleep in the open, it's too bloody cold even to sit still for long,' grunted Mandubracus. 'I say we keep going.'

'But if I can get the horses to lie down,' ventured Scaeva, 'we can lay beside them for warmth, and we'll all feel better rested to continue the journey. I can make them feel safe enough and they will only need a couple of hours.'

Gestorix looked at Mandubracus. 'The boy has a point. He has a way with them, no doubt.'

Mandubracus nodded in agreement. 'We are going to need all our wits about us tomorrow. Come on lad, settle these horses down and may all the spirits hail Epona.'

Scaeva draped his travelling cloak on the ground and laid on his side next to his steed. Reaching over his shoulders, he eased his top clothes up his back until his tortured flesh was cooled by the chill of the night air.

It was gone midnight when Caesar dismissed the last of his secretaries, each with a missive, to prepare for dispatch to Rome first thing the following morning. These dispatches were part of Caesar's continued correspondence with Rome informing the senate of the progress of his military expansion beyond the Alps. Each dispatch to the senate would be in the form of traditional waxed wooden tablets, customary for when a general would report a victory. The courier service he had developed with his agent in Rome during his conquest of Gallia was vital to his persuading the senate to allow him the funding to raise new legions as required. The dispatches to private individuals were always in the form of a letter.

One letter was addressed to Crassus, Caesar's closest political ally and financier. He had last seen Crassus at Lucca the previous year, during his winter attendance on the assizes and other duties of his governorship of Gallia Cisalpina. Caesar had called a conference, primarily to cement his unofficial partnership with fellow Triumvirs, Crassus, and Caesar's son-in-law Pompeius Magnus. Events in Rome had been undermining the relationship between Crassus and Pompeius, and they were both beginning to feel uncomfortable with the wealth and charisma Caesar had been amassing in Gallia. The result of the meeting was to everyone's advantage. Crassus and Pompeius would both stand for the consulship in the current year, scaring away all opposition. They could then ensure Caesar a further five years in Gallia, and themselves a lucrative governorship of their own as proconsuls once they had completed their consular year. Crassus had chosen Syria, for which he was currently preparing to leave Rome. Pompeius would keep Hispania in absentia, leaving him free to attend to his projects in the Capital.

The letter to Pompeius had the same details regarding the reconnaissance mission to Britannia, but also personal enquiries into his health and that of his wife, Caesar's daughter Julia, who was pregnant with their first child. Their marriage had been arranged to seal a political bond between the two men. Pompeius, who was much older, had been married three times before, all for political reasons. Nonetheless, they were a devoted couple. Pompeius had delegated his province and command of his armies to his *legati* in Hispania, allowing him to travel pleasurably about Italy with his beautiful young wife. Pompeius showed great charm in personal relationships and had remained devoutly faithful to her.

Two other identical letters were addressed to the two consuls elect, due to take up their duties in January. One was Lucius Domitius Ahenobarbus, a declared enemy of Caesar who had threatened to deprive him of his province the previous year but had baulked at challenging Crassus and Pompeius for consulship then. The other was Appius Claudius Pulcher, who was related to Pompeius and would ensure Domitius didn't cause the triumvirs any trouble.

The last letter was addressed to Marcus Tullius Cicero. Cicero, a brilliant lawyer, an ex-consul himself, was a man that Caesar had always considered useful and had initially invited him to become a fourth member of their coterie. Cicero had declined the offer. He had recently been allowed to return to Rome from exile, having made enemies of powerful violent men and was in no hurry to repeat his mistakes. Consequently, although he was eager to curry favour with both Caesar and Pompeius, he fought shy of supporting an arrangement designed to undermine the constitution and principles of the Republic.

Caesar had been at pains while dictating the letters not to overplay his exploits in Britannia. Since he was still undecided whether to return with a larger force the next year, he did not want to encourage false expectations back in the senate. The tides and winds around the coast had taken him by surprise, not to mention the ferocity and tactics of the defenders, so if a second attempt were to be made, he would make it earlier in the year and with a much larger force.

Then there was Cordelia. For word of his affair to be included in the bawdy marching songs of his soldiers was one thing, but for news of it to spread to Rome would be quite another. Sexual conquest was considered manly, but to indulge in any excess would be seen as having lost control of one's desires, an unmanly attribute. His reputation at home as a sexual predator was the subject of gossip, having already seduced several women of nobility, including the ex-wives of both his fellow triumvirs. Best to make no mention of Cordelia at all. To do so would invite an unhelpful mix of questions and accusations. Their all-too-brief encounter had left its mark on him. He suppressed thoughts about her during the business of the day, but late at night, as he undressed and pulled on his nightshirt, he allowed her face into his mind's eye. Remembrances of the sweet innocence of her surrender to his lovemaking and her passionate responses took him into a deep sleep as soon as his head touched the pillow.

XX

Six Months Later
ROME

Pompeius and Crassus viewed proceedings from the elevated position of the colonnades at the top of the steps of the Temple of Saturn. Below them, on the curved wooden platform of the Rostra, the animated figure of Cicero held the rapt attention of the crowds. They had thronged to the forum to hail the return of the god Caesar with the goddess Cordelia, Queen of the Britons, descended from none other than Brutus of Troy. Cicero announced that the senate had decreed a new dynasty will rule Rome, a dynasty that is prophesied will rule the world from Rome for a thousand years.

'Who would have believed,' said Crassus to Pompeius, 'that Cicero would ever be so public an advocate of Caesar.' As he spoke, the doors of the senate-house opened. Beyond the Rostra on the far side of the Comitium, a procession formed. Despite his new status as a god, Caesar kept tradition by being preceded by twenty-four *lictor*s in pairs, each with their *fasces lictoriae* shouldered with the axe heads of the *fasces* glinting in the sunlight.

'The advocate for a god,' replied Pompeius. But on counting the *lictors* in the procession and noticing the axe heads, added, 'although I perceive Caesar is being his usual modest self and merely regarding himself as a dictator.'

As the crowd at the Capitolium end of the forum caught sight of the senate doors opening, a great cheer went up. Caesar was now in clear sight with the noticeably pregnant queen by his side. The couple descended the steps of the Curia Hostilia and crossed the open circular space of the Comitium. The cheer turned into a deafening roar as it rippled through the forum to the Via Sacra, where Caesar's triumphal procession was awaiting his arrival on the Rostra. His column of *lictors* made their way through the crowd to the foot of the Rostra where they lined both sets of stairs, forming a guard of honour for Caesar and Cordelia to ascend.

As they reached the floor of the Rostra, Cicero cried out, 'Citizens of Rome, I give you Caesar and Cordelia.'

The vast crowd erupted. 'Hail Caesar. Hail Cordelia.'

Cicero genuflected back to the steps of the Rostra. Caesar watched him descend backwards down the steps in such a comical fashion he couldn't help smiling. Then he turned to face Cordelia, her beauty made him catch his breath. Voluptuous auburn locks were dressed high on her head in the style of a true Roman patrician lady, but with ringlets curling down to her shoulders. Her pure white gold-trimmed gown in the style of a Greek goddess befitting a daughter of Brutus. An emerald-green sash matched the stones in her necklace, glittering in the sunshine as she turned this way and that, acknowledging the adoration of the massed throng before them.

Something made Caesar glance up to his right. High on the temple steps, standing amongst the Doric columns, were two figures who he instantly recognised despite the bright sunlight in his eyes making him squint. His fellow Triumvirs, Pompeius, and Crassus, were observing proceedings from a vantage point. Time had flown by; Caesar felt as though it was only yesterday, he was writing to them from Samarobriva of his exploits in Britannia. But what was Crassus doing there in Rome? Surely, he should be in Syria. Caesar doubted Crassus would make the journey back purely to witness Caesar's triumph, especially when that was the one thing Crassus wanted most for himself. Something that even his money couldn't buy.

The triumphal procession had now begun, led by a legionary standard-bearer. Even at a distance, Caesar recognised him. It was the standard-bearer of the Tenth. That giant of a man who had saved the day on the beach on the first day of Caesar's attempted invasion of Britannia, yet try as he may, Caesar could not recall his name.

Following the standard-bearer, passing in front of the Tabernae Novae, came a single column of chariots brought home from Britannia, painted white and decorated with gold leaf. Spectators were clambering out of the windows of the ancient and dilapidated upper storey of the Basilica Aemilia and clambering across the wooden roofs of the shops to get a better view. Each chariot was drawn by a pair of white horses, followed by a wagon with an iron cage in which the chained driver and spearman, naked and covered in blue woad, shrieked, and screamed at the crowd causing many of them to cower back in alarm.

The Temple of Janus stuck out like an island in the sea of bodies in the forum. A tiny shrine compared to architectural giants that now adorned the Capital. Caesar could remember playing there as a boy. A small stone-faced rectangular building with a decorated upper tier, open roof, and huge doors on the open arches at either end. It housed a bust of Janus, the two-faced god of boundaries, beginnings, and endings, mounted on a plinth. The bust faced both ways out of the two sets of double doors that were always open. Tradition held that the doors were kept open at times of war and only closed when Rome was at peace. As a child, Caesar had never known them to be closed, but they were now, with a garland of flowers hung across them. This meant the wars Caesar had fought in Gallia were finally over. It also explained why Crassus was back in Rome if he had defeated the Parthians and returned from Syria.

Now the standard of the Tenth, which had momentarily disappeared behind the temple, came back into view and was much closer, but a young boy had taken the place of the standard-bearer. A young boy dressed in the woollen tunic and braccae of the Britons,

Just then, some movement and jostling in the crowd below them caught his eye. Someone was moving determinedly towards the steps to the Rostra. It was Domitius, and he appeared to be hiding something in the folds of his toga. The *lictors* made no attempt to prevent him from mounting the steps and when he reached the platform, he withdrew the object he had been concealing and appeared to offer it to Cordelia. At first, Caesar thought it was a strigil, then realised with alarm that it was a dagger.

Caesar glanced sideways at his wife, but she had not noticed the danger they suddenly found themselves in. Turning quickly to face the would-be assailant, Caesar discovered it was not Domitius after all, but Appius Claudius Pulcher, and it wasn't a knife in his hand, it was a scroll.

Pulcher unrolled the piece of parchment and read. 'Caesar, you have a visitor.'

Caesar was totally confounded. Yes, it was Pulcher, but the voice wasn't. It was far deeper and gruffer, and he recognised it immediately. It was the voice of his *legate* from the campaign in Gallia, Quintus Titurius Sabinus. Caesar blinked in the sunlight that was now streaming through the window of his quarters in Samarobriva. A face was in front of his eyes, the face of Sabinus repeating, but with more urgency,

'Caesar, you have a visitor.'

Gestorix

XXI

September 55 BC
Near Samarobriva, in the land of the Ambiani

Gestorix was the first to wake. It was still dark. Sensing he was awake, the horse he had been clinging to for warmth got carefully to its feet and snorted. The other horses stirred, waking Scaeva and Mandubracus, who trudged to the riverbank, knelt, and splashed his face with the icy water. A light frost covered the grass and Scaeva slapped his arms around himself and stamped his feet to warm himself.

By this time, Gestorix had located Scaeva's satchel and passed round the remains of the bread they were given from the inn the previous evening.

'Let's move on,' he said, through a mouthful of crust. 'We'll soon be having a proper breakfast in Samarobriva.'

The three took to their refreshed mounts and set off along the riverside track at a fast trot. Before long, the sky lightened ahead of them and within another hour the high-walled oppidum, silhouetted against the sunrise, appeared on the horizon. As they approached the city along the riverside track, past a cemetery, they joined the end of a slow-moving queue of traffic on the main road. Wagonloads of goods of all kinds were heading towards the gates. As they passed through, they were greeted by the stench of the tanneries and the sound of hammers on anvils in the smoke-bellowing forges in the industrial quarter of the citadel. They followed the traders down the narrow lanes between hard brick buildings to the marketplace, where breakfast was sure to be available. The sight of Mandubracus in their midst drew one or two second glances from the native Ambiani residents, but a third was always discouraged by a practised scowl from the Briton.

Sounds and smells from the town centre were in the air before they turned the final corner that opened into a broad thoroughfare packed with animal pens and dotted with smoking braziers. The wagons from the queue at the town gates were being unloaded, and all manner of goods from workshops and produce from the fields were being arranged on trestle tables around the perimeter. They tied their horses to a post.

The aroma of freshly baked bread led Gestorix and Scaeva to the bakery, while Mandubracus bargained with street vendors for something to warm them. In the bakery, next to the racks of warm loaves, were shelves stacked with other produce, including blocks of butter and jars of honey. Scaeva pointed eagerly and the shopkeeper obligingly split his baton with a knife and ladled a generous spoonful of honey on one side and cut a thick slab of butter for the other. Gestorix settled with a few coins, and they went outside to find Mandubracus, who had claimed benches at an empty trestle table laid with three bowls of steaming porridge and a plate of hot chestnuts. The two men used their daggers to chop the nuts into their porridge while Scaeva drizzled in the excess honey from his baton.

Before they had finished their meal, two men sat down facing each other at the opposite end of the bench. By their clothes and general demeanour, they didn't look like traders or local peasants and were talking in hushed tones, sipping from steaming cups of liquid. They appeared to take no notice of the three foreigners until one of them looked across from their private conversation and casually asked them what had brought them to Samarobriva. Gestorix hesitated because he detected the question was more than an attempt at polite conversation, which made him unsure how much he should disclose of their true business there. He also noted there were bigger spaces at other tables.

'We have come from Britannia,' he ventured. The eyes of both men flickered at Mandubracus, and they nodded slowly. 'We have an urgent message for Commius and were told we would find him here in Samarobriva.'

The two men couldn't help but exchange glances before the senior of them cleared his throat and asked, 'And who are you?'

'What business is that of yours,' grunted Mandubracus, using his own colloquialisms and fixing the questioner with a stare that said in any language, *don't mess with me.*

'Calm down,' said Gestorix, raising his hands immediately in a diplomatic gesture. Then to the two strangers, 'Please excuse my friend.'

But the Briton continued. 'Something tells me you wouldn't have asked who we were unless you knew where Commius was.'

Gestorix shot a look across to Mandubracus that said, *leave it. I will deal with this.*

The older man drew a breath and replied, 'That is very astute of you, my friend. Allow me to speak plainly. We are in the employ of Commius and have just come from Britannia with news of, shall we say, developments. Yes, we do know where he is. In fact, we were with him in his office earlier this morning,' and with a defiant look at Mandubracus he added, 'and you can keep your temper my friend, one shout from me and half the garrison will be on your back.'

Before Mandubracus responded to the challenge in his usual manner, Gestorix immediately grabbed him by the arms to prevent him from reaching for his dagger. 'For fuck's sake man, remember why we are here. Leave this to me.'

Mandubracus, who was halfway to his feet, relaxed back onto the bench with a sullen nod.

'And why exactly are you here?' continued the older man, unmoved by Mandubracus' malevolent glare.

'As I said,' replied Gestorix, turning from Mandubracus and settling back on the bench. 'We are here to speak with Commius. Please excuse my comrade. His father and son were murdered recently and his second son here with us is in great danger.'

At that revelation, a look of total surprise took both men. Now it was the younger man who put the question. 'Has this anything to do with Imanuentus?'

Gestorix's eyes narrowed. 'What have you heard about Imanuentus?'

'Just a rumour before we left Britannia that Imanuentus had been slain,' the man replied. 'But we had brought news of a different nature.'

Gestorix considered for a moment, then said, 'I think it is time we introduced ourselves. My colleague is Mandubracus, son of Imanuentus, and the boy here is his son Scaeva. My name is Gestorix, a friend of the family, so to speak.' With the introductions over, he continued. 'Commius met with Mandubracus when he was in Britannia with Caesar. We have come to continue the conversation in light of recent events.'

'Yes, we know about that meeting,' said the older man. 'So I think you'd better come with us. By the way, I'm Teuto and my friend here is Perrus.'

As one, the five rose from the table and reclaimed their tethered horses. Teuto and Perrus led the Britons out of the marketplace through a maze of thatched roundhouses of all sizes, more like those at home, thought Scaeva, bringing up the rear.

Gestorix remarked to Teuto, 'If you and Perrus are spies for Commius you made it pretty obvious you didn't sit at our table by chance, and then make polite conversation.'

'Think yourself lucky we sat there at all,' Teuto replied. 'You would never have been allowed into the garrison.'

Soon the winding lanes led out through the rear gates of the oppidum and crossed a shallow ditch mostly full of debris. A short distance away, the newly completed winter quarters of Caesar's army bristled atop a perfectly regular rampart, protected by a deep ditch running into the marshes between the fort and the river. It had been constructed on the site of his old marching camp. Not on a scale to match the massive earthworks of Scaeva's hometown, but equally impregnable. The timber walls of horizontal logs set between stanchions were no mere palisade. The double gates were overlooked by a pair of lofty watchtowers, with more towers halfway along each wall and at the far corners.

Teuto answered the challenge from the sentry in the gate tower. 'Teuto and Perrus, again. These three have important news from Britannia for Commius.'

Scaeva peered up at the tall towers on either side of the gate and got his first sight of Roman soldiers. Looking down at them from the watchtower, the helmeted figures were certainly not the giants that Scaeva had imagined them to be. How did they dare to come from across the sea and challenge his countrymen with their fearsome swords and chariots? After a few moments, a gate was pulled open from the inside. Teuto spoke briefly to the guard and the party of five passed through into the interior.

A wide straight thoroughfare between rows of wooden buildings with slanting roofs, similar to those Scaeva had seen back at the port, led to a busy rectangular space in the centre of the fort, where they dismounted outside a two-storey building with a balcony at half-height running from end to end. Their hosts hurried them up two flights of steps at the end of the building and onto the balcony. They followed Teuto along the balcony to a door, where he told them to wait with Perrus before he gave a single knock and went straight in. Scaeva had a clear view across the central square to the stables and the grain stores where hundreds of sacks were being unloaded from queues of wagons. Immediately below him were rows of decorated poles. Some displayed a row of silver discs, some were topped with golden eagles, others with red banners embroidered with emblems and with gold tassels fluttering in the breeze.

Scaeva took them to be the tribal banners of the Romans, which, in a way, they were.

Beyond the banners were more puny soldiers sweating in red tunics over heavy mail shirts, carrying large rectangular shields that were too big for some of them. Some had short swords, others had long spears. They were shuffling back and forth in close formation, performing staccato movements with their weapons under the direction of their commanders. Others were blowing long notes on their curved carnyces, which wound around the shoulder of the player. Scaeva wondered what they were all doing. He concluded they must be performing a ritual dance in honour of their mighty gods of war. How else could they have been victorious against the massed tribes of Gaul? Just then, the door opened and Teuto called the group into a small antechamber. One wall was covered in square pigeonholes containing rolled scrolls of parchment and other paraphernalia, the use of which Scaeva couldn't fathom.

An orderly behind a small desk looked up and invited them to be seated. There were only two chairs. All five chose to remain standing. A door opposite the pigeon-holed wall opened and in strode Commius dressed in a red tunic under a gleaming *cuirass* complete with *pteruges* and *greaves*, but the long flowing freshly combed locks testified this was no Roman. Gone were the leather strapped leggings and jewellery bedecked cloak of a Celtic king that he had sported for his meeting with Mandubracus. Commius had only been told that his agents had returned with three messengers from Britannia, so when his eyes fell upon Mandubracus and Gestorix, he recognised them immediately and guessed that the rumour about Imanuentus was true. 'My dear friend Mandubracus, a pleasure to meet with you again, but under such sad circumstances I hear.'

Bullshit, you gilded cockroach, thought the Briton. Mandubracus didn't care much for Commius and his diplomatic niceties; except for Gestorix, Mandubracus didn't care much for anyone, even his close family.

However, he needed Commius to endorse his plan before presenting it to Caesar. 'Commius, it is true my father is dead and that is why I'm here. We need to speak with you privately,' and noticing Commius' questioning looks at the boy continued. 'This is my son Scaeva, and my friend Gestorix I'm sure you remember.'

Commius nodded and gestured the three of them through to his private quarters, signalling to Teuto and Perrus to wait in the antechamber. The room was sparsely furnished, and by the light from the high windows on both sides, Scaeva noted a cot, and a table in the corner with a basin and water jug; clothes and cloaks hung on hooks on the wall behind the door. Commius took his seat behind a desk cluttered with piles of parchments and scrolls.

He spoke first. 'I assume since you are now King of the Trinovantes, you wish to continue the conversation we started at the banks of the Tamasa.'

Gestorix figured he had done all the talking required to get this far so he should leave the story to Mandubracus and trust he wouldn't get angry and compromise their plan.

'Yes,' replied Mandubracus, 'but there is more. Before my father was slain, a prophecy was made that my younger son would die when brought face to face with the King of Kings.'

'And by that did they mean Vellaunus?' interrupted Commius.

'Who else could it be? Since his father Heli died, he now styles himself Cassivellaunus, Vellaunus of the Cassi. He murdered Imanuentus and is bent on further conquest of all the old Cymric kingdoms. The warlords of the Cantiaci would still bow to him, and so would the Bibroci and a few other of the smaller tribes. Only the Trinovantes have the will and the means to resist.'

Gestorix nodded with satisfaction at the way Mandubracus had summarised the events following Caesar's departure from Prydain, keeping to the points most essential to their mission.

Commius had opened a drawer in his desk, taken out a wax tablet and stylus and was now taking notes. 'Go on,' he said.

'So, I am here to take up your offer. If Caesar returns during the long days and reaches the Tamasa, the Trinovantes will join forces with him to defeat Cassivellaunus. Then I, and my son after me, will hold all of Prydain for Rome. I have brought my son Scaeva to serve two purposes. Firstly, to keep him safe until Cassivellaunus is defeated but also as a surety to Caesar that I will keep my side of the bargain.'

Commius completed his jottings in the wax and got to his feet. 'I need to bring all this to Caesar's attention immediately. You can wait with my attendant.' He led them back into the antechamber where Teuto and Perrus now occupied the two available seats, then went out to the long balcony and into the next door, which was the office of the garrison commander, Quintus Titurius Sabinus. Sabinus was one of Caesar's most highly trusted *legati*.

The previous year, he had gained a significant victory over three Gaulish tribes under Viridovix. Commius found Sabinus at his desk, with an orderly by his side, busy signing requisitions.

'Don't you ever knock? Commius,' said Sabinus without looking up.

'My humble apologies, Sabinus,' replied Commius, now conversing in Latin in the unerringly polite manner he reserved for the garrison commander. He knew that Sabinus considered him far too close to Caesar than any Gaulish king should be, but Commius had earned Caesar's confidence and respect, so he purposely disregarded Sabinus' abrasiveness because the Roman found it irksome. 'I urgently require an audience with Caesar. There have been significant developments in Britannia deserving of his attention.'

Most unusually, Caesar had not yet emerged from his private quarters. Not wishing to betray this to Commius, Sabinus simply replied that Caesar was not currently available and Commius should return later in the morning.

'May I suggest then that you at least advise him of my request, and the reason for it, so he might make his own decision.'

Sabinus, in uniformity with the other *legati*, considered his general trusted and indulged the renegade far too much for his own good, but grudgingly accepted that he had come through for them in Britannia. He also secretly enjoyed the understated banter with Commius, although he personally disliked him, but not enough to allow that dislike to interfere with his duty. Sabinus laid down his reed pen and stood up. 'I'll see what I can do.'

And with that, he went through a door behind his desk into a corridor that led past his own private quarters to Caesar's. Putting an ear to the door, he could discern no movement inside. He tapped the door gently with his knuckle. Nothing. A louder knock. Still nothing. He opened the door slowly. The room was still in darkness, so he went over to the window and opened the shutters. The bright morning sunlight lit upon the sleeping figure of Caesar, in his cot.

'Caesar, Commius is here to see you,' said Sabinus in a hoarse whisper, then more loudly, 'You have a visitor,' and louder still, 'Caesar, you have a visitor.'

Caesar awoke with a start and blinked in the sunlight, the sunlight streaming through the window of his quarters in Samarobriva. A face was in front of his eyes, the face of Sabinus.

'Caesar are you well?' asked Sabinus, voice full of concern.

Caesar covered his face with his hands and rubbed his eyes. 'Yes, yes. A dream. An all too real dream. What hour is it?'

'We have the second hour since dawn,' replied Sabinus. It was customary for Caesar, like his soldiers, to wake at cockcrow and be ready to start their day by dawn. It was not Sabinus' prerogative to question why Caesar was still asleep, so he stood to attention and simply delivered his message. 'Commius has news of developments in Britannia and needs to speak with you urgently.'

Commius was just thinking that Sabinus was a long time delivering his message when he reappeared at the door.

'Caesar will be with you directly,' is all he said to Commius before resuming his administrative duties.

A short while later, having splashed his face with cold water, dressed and combed his thinning and receding hair forward, Caesar himself appeared. Commius stood and saluted.

'Commius, my friend. Sabinus here tells me you have news of developments in Britannia.' Sabinus was irritated by the geniality Caesar always showed to the Gaul, but he tried to ignore it. Commius had used his waiting time wisely, considering how best to break the two items of news from his agents and the fact that Mandubracus himself was here to confirm one of them.

'Caesar, this very morning my informants have brung me two items of interest from Britannia. One has since been confirmed, the other remains unsubstantiated.'

'Go on,' Caesar was used to Commius' use of antecedents when reporting intelligence, and he rarely lost an opportunity to display his mastery of Latin, although, as in this case, his grammar was not always perfect.

'They have brought news that Cordelia is with child. Your child. And not only that but there is a prophecy that the child will rule all the world from Rome and create a dynasty of a thousand years.'

The exact same words from Caesar's dream, announced by Cicero on the Rostra, being repeated to him in reality by Commius, made the blood drain from Caesar's face, but in the early morning shadows, neither Commius nor Sabinus noticed.

'And you barged in here this morning with that load of bollocks,' said Sabinus with a sneer.

'My dear Sabinus,' responded Commius politely as ever. 'This prophecy is apparently from the same seer who foresaw the great storm in the Oceanus Britannicus, and the wrecking of our transports, with such clarity, that Carvillus and Cingetorix made the journey here to invite Caesar to launch an expedition. But even so, I did not consider it urgent enough to bring up ahead of our scheduled daily briefing, until my agents returned a second time within the hour with further developments.'

With his mind distracted by Commius' unintentionally shocking revelation, Caesar struggled to comprehend the exchange between his two officers but recovered his composure enough to respond. 'And what news did they bring this time?'

'Confirmation of what they reported initially as only a rumour, that Imanuentus, King of the Trinovantes had been slain. Confirmation from none other than his son, Mandubracus, whom my informants discovered here in the marketplace shortly after they left my office.'

Caesar was taken aback. 'Mandubracius is here?'

Commius was used to Caesar's unwitting habit of Romanising the names of foreigners, so he let the mispronunciation pass. Commius himself had been known as Commus all his life before he came to Caesar's attention. When Caesar had appointed him 'Commius, King of the Belgic Atrebates' after conquering that tribe two years beforehand, the change of name had stuck. Commius had since adopted a policy that had served him well; when with the Romans, be like the Romans.

'Yes, and he has brought his son and a travelling companion. They are currently waiting in the anteroom for an audience with you.' Commius then relayed

Mandubracus' story to Caesar about the prophecy of the druids and his request that Caesar take his son into protection.

Caesar took a moment to consider these latest revelations before replying. 'Then bring them in.' He was content to hold children of leading citizens as hostages. He had invited the Remi to do so two years earlier in a campaign in which Sabinus had distinguished himself.

Scaeva was relieved when Commius returned to the anteroom. Throughout his time away, which had seemed an age, no one had said a word, not Teuto, not Perrus, not even Gestorix. They all found the mundane activities of the orderly at his desk, or the contents of the pigeonholes, or even the floor in front of them, of great interest. Commius led the trio along the balcony, above where the soldiers were still drilling, and into the garrison commander's office where Caesar was now seated behind the desk with Sabinus standing by his side.

Commius spoke first, reverting to the common language of the Gauls which, because of the influx of migrants around Camulodunon, and its similarity to Brythonic, was understood by everyone present in the room. 'Caesar, Sabinus, meet Mandubracus, King of the Trinovantes.' then a nod to Mandubracus to complete the introductions.

'Gestorix, my most trusted commander and friend, and my son Scaeva.'

The sight of the boy and the announcement of his name hit Caesar like a mental thunderbolt. There, standing before him, dressed in a woollen tunic and braccae, was the boy of his dream. The boy carrying the standard of the Tenth through the crowds in the forum, and his name was

Scaeva. Yes, that was also the name of the Legionnaire *aquilifer*. Scaeva. Marcus Cassius Scaeva. For a moment, Caesar wasn't sure if he was still dreaming. One of those dreams where you dream you wake up but are still actually asleep.

Scaeva froze as Caesar stared at him, before shifting his eyes back to the boy's father as he assembled his thoughts. 'Mandubracius, Commius has explained your proposal to me, and I understand your reasons for being here, but tell me, how did your father die?'

Before Mandubracus could speak, Scaeva, who had felt overawed in Caesar's presence, suddenly blurted out, 'He was murdered. Cassivellaunus did it. He killed my brother too. Slit his throat he did, and he ran Grandfather through the chest with a spear and strung them up by the neck from a tree!'

'And you saw this?' asked Caesar, impressed with the spirit the boy had just shown.

'We found them. Me and Caspar. We found them in the one-tree pasture just after it happened. We know it was Cassivellaunus because he rode right past us with his men. Then we found two horses, a mare, and her foal, to carry the bodies home.'

'What do you mean, you found some horses?' asked Caesar, intrigued by the boy.

Now that Scaeva had overcome his nerves and was more at ease and encouraged by the great man's easy interaction with him, his desire to make an impression eclipsed his reticence about admitting too much to his father and Gestorix. 'Wild ones, grazing near the woods. Epona sent them.'

'Epona, I've heard of her. She's the Goddess of horses that the Gauls make sacrifices to.'

'And her spirit lives within the boy,' interjected Gestorix, who was eager for an opportunity to join in the conversation with the great Roman general.

'Is that a fact?' remarked Caesar with some scepticism.

'How do you think we found the horses to travel here from the port?' answered Gestorix boldly, warming to his theme. 'Especially when the Romans have commandeered all the animals for miles around.'

'Then the boy has a useful talent,' replied Caesar in a tone that signalled that part of the conversation was over.

During the conversation, Caesar had been assessing the impact of the morning's intelligence on his decision whether to mount a second invasion the following summer. He had hastily restored Cordelia's dominion over the troublesome warlords of Cantium before he left, but doubted how long that would hold once his ships had sailed for Gallia. On its own, the news regarding her pregnancy and the prophecy that went with it wouldn't have carried much weight, because a child could not become a citizen of Rome unless both his parents were. So, in the cold light of day, the decision of the senate in Caesar's dream, so gleefully announced by Cicero to the adoring crowds, was unlikely to become a reality. Caesar was also of the opinion, like most scholars in Rome, that dreams were not prophetic, merely the product of your own emotions and experiences. But this dream was already coming true. He dreamt Cordelia was pregnant, now he hears she is. He dreamt of the standard-bearer of the Tenth turning into a small boy, and there was the same boy standing before him with the same name. He dreamt that the doors of the

Temple were closed, signifying wars were over, and here was Mandubracius with his offer to help him conquer Britannia. And what was the significance of Cordelia being the daughter of this Brutus of Troy? Was this some ancient Trojan Royal line that the senate would decide qualifies for Roman Citizenship? Whatever the truth of that, Mandubracius and his offer were real, and that was the deciding factor.

'So Mandubracius, you need my help to seek revenge on Cassivellaunus for your father's death and, in return, you will bring the Trinovantes to my side against the other tribes. And in the meantime, I will keep your boy out of harm's way?'.

A simple nod from Mandubracus, who also ignored the mispronunciation of his name, and the deal was done. Caesar instructed Commius to draw up a treaty, then ordered an escort and safe passage back to the port for Mandubracus and Gestorix and for them to be safely ensconced on board a ship bound for Britannia. He then dismissed the four of them back to the anteroom, leaving him alone with Sabinus. With so many unpredictable factors at play, Caesar considered taking his own auspices, but privately doubted the flights of the birds in the skies above Samarobriva would prove any more accurate than his own gut feeling.

Turning to the garrison commander, he said, 'Sabinus my friend, Caesar has made his decision.' Caesar habitually wrote of himself in the third person and occasionally reverted to it in conversation, especially when making speeches. 'We are returning to Britannia next year to finish the job we started. We will need to raise a much bigger force and design and build ships more suited to the task.'

'And start earlier in the season,' added Sabinus.

'Agreed, schedule the initial planning for our staff meeting this afternoon. I need to leave within two days to return to my official duties before the mountain passes close for the winter, but first Caesar needs his breakfast. I think I will take the boy with me and show him around the garrison. He intrigues me.'

Something stirred in Caesar's memory. There was a soothsayer in Rome who, on the occasion of the foaling of Caesar's horse on his own land, had declared that the foal foretold the domination of the world for its master. There was something physically remarkable about the animal, for its hooves were cloven to resemble toes. He had named the foal Genitor, reared the horse himself and was the first to mount it. To this day, the creature had allowed none other than Caesar on its back.

'Meet me at the stables in one hour,' he said to Sabinus before leaving the office to collect Scaeva from the anteroom.

During Scaeva's long and exciting journey, the purpose of it had slipped to the back of his mind and he'd given little thought to what might become of him. It had all been a big adventure and now, with Caesar giving the order for the men to be escorted home, the reality was almost too much to bear. The parting from his father and his uncle had been sudden, brutal, and bittersweet. After a manly hug from Gestorix, he stood before his father. Never one to show emotions other than anger, he reached inside his tunic and withdrew Ebracus' golden torc, engraved on the open ends with the bull's head sigil of Mandubracus of the Trinovantes. He carefully fitted it around the neck of his son and heir. Whatever his feelings were, he could not voice them, but his expression of pride was unmistakable. He merely tousled his son's hair, and without a word, turned and left the room. That silent gesture meant everything. But the tragedy was, no sooner had his father truly recognised him, than he was gone. And gone for an unknowable length of time.

An hour later, the young boy's sadness was overtaken by a new sense of wonder and excitement. He had shared a second breakfast of the day—hot wheat pancakes, with none other than Julius Caesar himself—and enjoyed a guided tour of a world Scaeva never knew existed, namely a fully manned Roman garrison. Caesar was a master at putting lesser mortals at their ease in his company. He did so with his private soldiers, and so it was with Scaeva. Caesar actually found the lad quite entertaining. Over breakfast, he had been regaled with the story of his journey to Samarobriva. There was also something else about the young Briton, the way he peppered his stories with phrases from a Belgic tongue that Caesar struggled to understand. They came from his uncle Gestorix, the distinguished-looking Gaul with hair tied at the back of his head, who had accompanied him and his father to Samarobriva. Except he wasn't from Gaul. Scaeva explained his uncle was originally from Belgae, from a tribe called the Viromandui. Now, where had Caesar heard talk of that tribe during the past month? It had come up in conversation recently. Like many things about this bright young lad, it puzzled him.

By the time the garrison tour ended, the *principia* was empty of soldiers, and they joined Sabinus at the stables, where Caesar led them to the stall where his horse was berthed.

'Sabinus, I want you to witness this.' And then, turning to Scaeva, Caesar said, 'Your uncle mentioned that the spirit of Epona lives within you.' Scaeva nodded, a shade cautiously, clearly Caesar had a test in store for him. 'I want you to show me what you can do with horses, particularly my horse. I give you fair warning, he doesn't take kindly to strangers.'

'Was he broken in from the wild?' asked Scaeva.

'No,' Caesar replied, 'I bred him and raised him from my stables at home. Why do you ask?'

'Well, it makes a difference,' replied Scaeva, trying to affect an air of authority way beyond his years or status. 'If a horse has never been part of a wild herd, there are some things he won't respond to, certain behaviours he won't recognise. May I approach him?'

Caesar raised an eyebrow in surprised appreciation of the young boy's reply. 'Be my guest,' he said, before turning to Sabinus with a grin. 'He will get his head bitten off if he gets too close.'

Sabinus simply replied with an amused smirk.

Scaeva bowed his head, kept his eyes fixed on the floor of the stable, and moved sideways, crablike, towards the horse with his left arm outstretched, offering just the back of his hand. The animal turned its head from the manger where it was feeding to face him and eyed the boy with curiosity. Casually, the boy drew his right hand out of a pocket in his tunic and passed it across his mouth.

As Scaeva drew closer, the horse stiffened, raised its head and stamped its front hooves; then it snorted and sniffed at the back of Scaeva's outstretched hand.

'Interesting,' mused Caesar, 'did you notice him put something in his mouth just then?'

'Couldn't be sure, but so far so good,' replied Sabinus, both men watched with mild amusement that soon turned into genuine interest.

Scaeva was now close enough to turn and face the horse. He tilted his head backwards and blew gently up into the horse's nostrils. His left hand reached above the horse's nose, with the index finger scratching down between his nostrils in deliberate but gentle strokes. A few seconds later, he slipped his hand to the side of the horse's head, and out of sight of his audience, then slid a finger into the horse's mouth behind his back teeth and stroked his tongue. The steed immediately lowered his head to allow the young boy to press his forehead down against the beast's nostrils; skilfully releasing and reapplying pressure—imperceptibly to anyone watching—each time the horse gave way.

'The old bastard is enjoying this,' said Sabinus.

Caesar didn't reply, but a faint look of consternation showed around the corners of his mouth. His horse, his special horse, was being wooed in front of his eyes. It was clear that Genitor had accepted the boy into his personal space, allowing Scaeva to reach up with his right hand and knead in between the withers with his knuckles. Scaeva then removed his hand and turned his back on the horse, facing his audience for the first time and scanning their faces for signs of approval as he waited for the horse's expected reaction. The jaws of both men dropped in unison as the beast nudged the boy forcefully between the shoulder blades, as if asking the boy to continue his massage, before resting his chin on Scaeva's left shoulder. Scaeva stepped three slow paces towards the Romans, and to their disbelief, the horse followed. The boy turned to the left and increased his pace; the horse went with him. He then spun back and ran to the space in the middle of the stable and the horse never left his side. Scaeva reached up for the horse's mane and was about to end the display by climbing onto his back when Caesar exclaimed.

'Enough. I've seen enough.' Caesar took a deep breath and brought himself under control, not allowing his discomfort to show. He stepped forward and led his horse back to the manger, patting his neck as he went. 'I'm going to have to think of a role for you, young man. Something to keep you busy, and I promised your father I would keep you safe. Run along now and wait for me back in Commius' office.'

Scaeva nodded and turned to leave the stables when Caesar added, 'Did you slip something from your pocket into your mouth back then?'

'Mint,' replied Scaeva with a cheeky grin. Then he ran off across the empty parade ground.

'Confident little sod isn't he,' remarked Sabinus.

'He certainly is,' replied Caesar. 'I'm beginning to think beyond installing Mandubracius as our proxy in Britannia.'

Caesar was privately nurturing the fantasy that Cordelia would rule, and that last night's dream had promised the fulfilment of the prophecies of world domination for them and their progeny, in alignment with the prophecies made at the foaling of Genitor. However, he shunned those thoughts as wishful thinking, a general tendency of mankind, not to be given in to by men of his ambition. 'All being well, he will be succeeded by his son, and I'm thinking we have an opportunity to give the boy a proper Roman education before we send him home.'

'What, here in Samarobriva?' questioned Sabinus. 'If we're handing him back once we've dealt with the Britons, there's not enough time, even if we had a team of *grammarians* in the garrison.'

'I'm going to send him to Rome.' Caesar had made his mind up. 'I will send him to live with Pompeius and my daughter Julia. Pompeius can have him tutored at home initially. He seems to have a flair for languages and once he has a grasp of Latin, he can be sent to school.'

Sabinus raised his eyebrows. 'As a princeling from the mystical island of Britannia, I assumed you would want to parade him in the triumph the senate is bound to award you on your return to Rome.'

'The boy is barely ten years old. He needs to be taken into the bosom of Rome, not paraded through the streets like a wild animal to be jeered and gawped at.'

'But what about Mandubracius?' enquired Sabinus. 'Won't he be expecting his son to be returned once he's kept his side of the bargain?'

'I don't care what that barbarian expects. As long as I have Scaeva he will have to keep Rome sweet. Caesar will leave for his province in two days and Scaeva will accompany him until we pass the Alpes. Then I will need someone reliable to deliver him to the house of Pompeius once we have arrived at Mutina. Sabinus, who in the garrison do you think would be most suited to this task?'

'I can think of a few. Many have family back in Rome and would welcome the opportunity of furlough, if only for a few days. However, escorting the sprog of a barbarian and delivering him into the presence of Pompeius is another thing altogether.'

'I will of course dictate a letter of introduction. I will also be writing to Pompeius explaining my intentions. I have been thinking about that too; if he is to be educated in Rome, he needs a proper Roman family name so I will adopt him myself. It is fitting that a son of mine rules the tribes of Britannia. He will be known as Gaius Julius Caesar Scaevanus, and for an additional cognomen, Philippus would be most appropriate, don't you think?'

'From the Greek, meaning lover of horses,' confirmed Sabinus.

'Indeed,' replied Caesar. 'The letter can be delivered with the boy. Do you have anyone in mind?'

Sabinus considered for a moment. 'I think Gaius Arpineius is your man. I know him well. He's from a solid family of equites.'

Caesar thought better of it. 'No, it's such a long return journey. It will be months before he returns, and I think Arpineius would be more useful here. I was thinking along the lines of one of the military tribunes. Typically, they only serve a year or two before returning home to prepare for a career in the senate. Laberius Durus acquitted himself well at the Sabis, and again while deputising for Labienus in Britannia. I'll send him home with the boy.'

While Scaeva's future under a new identity was being planned in the stable across the other side of the *principia,* he sat waiting in Commius' anteroom, elbows on knees, chin in hands, watching the orderly working methodically through his scrolls and tablets. The soreness of his back reminded him of the mystery of the true meaning of the runes and caused him to ponder on what the future had in store.

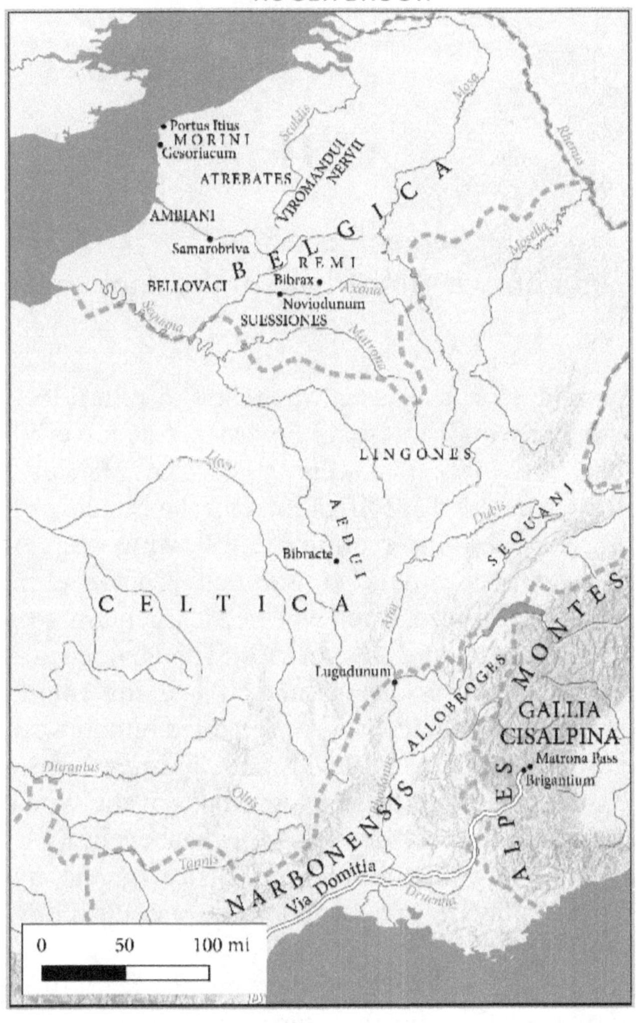

Gallia Transalpina 55 BC

XXII

September 55 BC
Samarobriva, in the land of the Ambiani

Two days later, Caesar was ready to return to Italy for the winter to attend his assizes as governor of the province of Gallia Cisalpina. He left his generals with detailed specifications for the building of the invasion fleet he would require the following year. After giving last-minute orders to Sabinus, Caesar climbed aboard his customised, four-wheeled carpentum to join Faberius and his team of secretaries. The covered wagon Caesar used for transporting himself and his entourage between his army and his province enabled him to work on his correspondence during the arduous journey across the Alps. Extra cushioning and heavy drapes at the windows for comfort, and elbow supports on the benches for his secretaries to take dictation more easily on the move. Caesar would dictate several letters at once to allow his scribes to keep up.

A sharp command to the driver and the team of eight mules took their first shuffled steps, breaking into a steady trot by the time they passed through the back gate of the *castrum* and into the open countryside. In the following carriage, Scaeva, still deep in thought, sat and peered across the flat marshes at nothing more than the early morning mist rising from the river, as Lugh rose comfortingly above the horizon ahead. Unlike his travelling companions who reclined against their backrests, Scaeva propped himself forward, elbows on knees and chin in hands, unable to endure the pain across his back that a more relaxed pose would entail. He shared his carriage with four men; one was a Roman soldier and the other three were dressed in matching white tunics. They were enjoying a ribald conversation in their own language. The three in tunics all had the swarthy complexion and jet-black hair of the soldier, but their skin was smoother and darker. A different tribe, perhaps? Although Scaeva did not understand a word they were saying, two names, unmistakably Generali, and Cordelia, littered their conversation. The soldier broke off his conversation with the others and addressed him, attempting the same Gallic-Brythonic dialect used by Commius.

'So, you are Philippus, my name is Durus,' said the soldier slowly, taking care to pronounce his words.

Scaeva, suddenly disturbed from his thoughts, responded a shade indignantly. 'I am not Philippus, my name is Scaeva.'

'Of course,' said Durus, 'Gaius Julius Caesar Scaevanus Philippus to be precise. The General told me all about you. I am to escort you to the house of Pompeius the Great in Rome, where you are to receive a good Roman education before returning to Britannia.' The look of shock on the boy's face told Durus this was all news to him. 'Didn't the General inform you?'

'I've not seen Julius these past two days, he's been busy. I've been with Commius, and he's been telling me about his adventures in Prydain and how he saved Julius by bringing Queen Cordelia and his own tribe to his aid.'

'I am sure he has,' nodded Durus knowingly, before continuing. 'The General has also asked me to prepare you. There will be no one in the household of Pompeius who speaks or understands your language, so during the journey, I am to teach you as much as you can learn. So let us begin, repeat after me. *Salve, mi nomen Philippus.*'

'*Salve, mi nomen Philippus,*' repeated Scaeva obediently, but his mind was racing. Who is Pompeius the Great? Is he greater than Julius? If Julius is a king of his tribe of warriors, does that make Pompeius the Great the King of Kings in Rome? Although his flight from Prydain had suppressed his immediate concerns regarding Cassivellaunus, he was still fearful of the meaning of the other prophecies regarding the rest of his family; but this revelation presented a new and terrifying possibility.

'Very good. *Salve, mi nomen Durus,*' said the soldier.

The following evening, Caesar's convoy came to a halt. His carriage was preceded by five hundred of Labienus' cavalry, escorting them through the recently conquered Belgic lands of the Bellovaci and the Suessiones. The escort would be required until they entered the territory of the Gauls and the Aedui tribe, who had been on friendly terms with Rome for generations. His cavalry commander reported the funeral procession of Diviciacus, the old king of the Suessiones, had that morning left the fortress of Noviodunum and was proceeding towards them, blocking the road ahead.

It was just two campaigning seasons ago when Caesar, during his advance through the lands of the Belgae, had failed to take that fortress by storm, so he built a camp and laid siege to the citadel. On seeing the size of his siege towers and the speed with which the Romans bridged the moat, the defenders sent envoys asking to be allowed to surrender. The party of envoys had been headed by their new king, Galba. Caesar had taken many of the leading men of the tribe as hostages, including two of Galba's own sons, both of whom had since been returned to him.

Not wishing to sow dissent in a tribe so recently conquered; by disrupting their sacred procession, Caesar ordered his cavalry commander to move his troops to the side of the road in a show of respect. The drivers were given similar instructions to pull over to the side, and all the occupants of both carriages were ordered to disembark and stand in silence. As the procession passed by, led by the druids of the local priesthood, Caesar caught Galba's eye and a nod of recognition and respect passed between the two men. Then the corpulent corpse of the dead king carried shoulder high on a pallet by eight stout tribesmen came into sight, and unsolicited thoughts came into Caesar's mind. Try as he may, he simply could not banish them until he saw them through to a conclusion in his mind's eye.

Now that Diviciacus was dead, the dream that had haunted him for days took on a new reality. There was now nothing left outside of his control to prevent him from taking Cordelia back to Rome, marrying her, and siring a dynasty that would rule the world in fulfilment of the prophecy.

There was the detail of subjugating the tribes in Britannia to Roman rule so that Cordelia could legally obtain the *jus Latii* necessary to allow *conubium* with a non-Roman. After that, divorcing his wife, Calpurnia, on his return to Rome would be a simple matter of announcing it and returning her dowry. Caesar had married Calpurnia, his third wife, during the year of his consulship. She was a humble woman who proved to be a faithful and virtuous wife who also tolerated his affairs; an attribute which had suited him well.

So, what would his future hold with Cordelia? The possibilities were too vast to contemplate further. Finally, he cleared his mind of all thoughts of what, in reality, was just a fantasy, the like of which men like Caesar did not indulge.

For Scaeva, the procession was simply a sad reminder that he could not take part in his own grandfather's sacred funeral rites.

After spending the night at the camp Caesar had built for the siege of Noviodunum, the route to the Alpine pass left the undeviating gravelled highway along which Celtic oppida was often sited. The ancient ways were laid along solstice lines calculated by the druids in the days when Rome was a mere trading post at a crossroads on a primitive salt route. The convoy turned south through the territory of the Lingones, who had remained neutral during Caesar's conquest of Gaul.

The boredom of the featureless landscape was eased by the lively language lessons that Scaeva was enjoying, now that the other three men had joined in—what had become a game. The men, whose names Scaeva learnt, were Ramiro, Lorenzo, and Gomez.

'Salve, mi nomen Ramiro.'
'Salve, mi nomen Lorenzo.'

'Salve, mi nomen Gomez.'

These were the personal slaves of Julius and had been his faithful servants ever since Caesar's campaigns in Hispania. Durus had realised quite early on in their journey that a one-to-one dialogue was becoming tedious, and the trio had happily joined in with the lessons. The game was for Scaeva to ask a simple question to Durus in his Brythonic dialect of the Gallic language Durus was familiar with. Durus would do his best to translate the question into Latin for the slaves to answer, in Latin. Then Durus would repeat their answers back to Scaeva in the best Brythonic he could manage. The exercise would be validated; thus, Scaeva would repeat his question trying to remember the Latin phrase Durus had used, and the slaves each had to remember the answer in the halting Brythonic that Durus had used. After a few rounds of this, with varying degrees of success, it occurred to Scaeva to ask an innocent question, the answer to which had been troubling him ever since he had learned the purpose of his journey.

'Is Pompeius the Great, King of Rome?'

For some reason, Durus found this question comical. *'Numquid Pompeio Magno, a Romulo rex fuit?'* he asked the slaves through chuckles, shoulders bouncing with merriment. The three Spaniards chuckled too, but only because Durus found it so funny. They just looked at each other, smiled back at Durus, and shrugged.

'There are no kings in Rome, Philippus,' explained Durus, who was now over his fit of giggles. 'Although Pompeius might like to think of himself as one. There haven't been kings in Rome for over four hundred years.'

Durus considered, just for a moment, trying to explain their system of government, but immediately thought better of it. Thoughts of Rome, where he would discharge his duty to Caesar before returning home to Cingulum, made him realise he was at a crossroads in his life. Caesar had made it plain that Durus had completed the obligations of his military tribuneship with distinction and would now be free to climb the *cursus honorum* and enjoy a career in politics. However, he would also be included in Caesar's plans for a second invasion of Britannia, should Durus decide to extend his military career. He would be the first of his family to join the senatorial classes, something that he knew would make his father immensely proud, but he felt deep inside that Britannia was unfinished business. The tribulations he suffered during the crossing had all been for nothing, just a few head of hostages, and what had he seen of that mystical land at the very edge of the known world? Storm clouds, pebbles and less than a mile of rain-sodden turf. There had to be more than that. What's another year? He would still be young enough to become a *plebian* aedile before his thirty-seventh birthday as a steppingstone to praetor.

'No, Philippus,' said Durus softly, bringing the game to an end for that day. 'No kings in Rome'.

* * *

After nine days of good roads and fine autumn weather, they reached the territory of the Aedui and approached their capital, the oppidum of Bibracte. The hill on which it stood came into view a full day's journey away, rising out of the forests of the plateau they were traversing. On the border with the Lingones, Caesar's Roman cavalry returned to winter in Belgae and a detachment of loyal Aeduan horsemen took over as escort. Scaeva and his travelling companions had played the question-and-answer game most days, but only for as long as it remained an engaging pastime and didn't become a chore. Most of the time between his brief but frequent conversations with Durus, was spent gazing at the slowly changing landscape as they passed through the trading villages of the Aedui, protected by warrior garrisons who simply waved the convoy on its way.

They skirted the more mountainous lands to the east, gradually ascending to an undulating plateau. Between games, Ramiro, Lorenzo, and Gomez spoke amongst themselves in their own language or slept. Durus and Scaeva learned about each other's past during the language practice, and Durus had related his life as a ten-year-old in his father's vineyards in Picenum, while Scaeva contrasted it with his own experiences. Inevitably, Durus was interested to know why he was sent to Caesar as a hostage. Scaeva told him the story of the feast, the discovery of his dead grandfather and brother, and his consequent journey to Samarobriva; but he skipped any mention of Epona or the prophecies, the evidence of which had been causing him less discomfort day by day.

As they began the slow ascent to the citadel, the forests gave way to cultivated fields of recently harvested corn, then nearer the fort, funeral pyres, and rows of well-kept tombs. Although still quite a distance away at the summit, sections of the stone wall defences came into view. Instead of taking a gentler course gradually crossing the contours, the incline of the road steepened as it headed straight for the gates through a low col where a fast-running stream danced down the hill in the soft autumn afternoon sunlight.

The hardy mules struggled to keep their footing on the gravel, but they stuck to their task under the urging of the driver. Soon they passed through the ditched ramparts topped by huge stone walls, the like of which Scaeva had never seen in his life. Timber beams, fixed together with long iron nails and faced with stone blocks. On the other side of the gates, the incline softened considerably, but the road continued to a second set of stone-walled defences through which the Aedui escort was already trotting and exchanging cheerful greetings with the guards atop the walls.

The smell that greeted them as they passed into the noisy buzzing interior reminded Scaeva of Samarobriva, for there must have been a tannery somewhere in the vicinity. Similar too were the smoke and noise from the smelters, ironmongers, and bronze-workers, at their forges and benches in open-fronted stone-walled workshops that lined the main street. Wagons were being loaded and unloaded by gangs of burly porters, some of whom paused from their labours to gawp at Caesar's carriage. They trundled along the main street of crushed stone and gravel until the workshops and familiar thatched roundhouse dwellings of the artisans were left behind. They entered a shady grove of trees where the main street was split by a low, slender, oval-shaped parapet, hollowed out inside in the shape of two perfectly formed arcs. Made of smooth polished stone, the shape reminded Scaeva of the solstice diagrams the druids had shown him at school that summer.

He was still pondering the strange object when the convoy came to a halt in a wide-open space surrounded by the most magnificent buildings Scaeva had ever seen. The largest was a two-storey edifice, made of white stone that ran along one side of the square. There were steps up to two rows of colonnades that supported a red-tiled roof that formed a covered patio to the front. Aeduan citizens, immaculately dressed in garments only the richest of his home tribe would have been able to afford, went about their business amongst the smaller public buildings that surrounded the square. A face appeared at the open doorway of the carriage; it was Faberius.

'Come on you three, out. Caesar needs a change of clothes before he meets with the Vergobret.'

'What's a Vergobret?' asked Durus as the Spanish slaves hurried out of the doorway on the other side.

'Chief magistrate. He's got a meeting with him and his council of nobles. He needs to know if the Sequani have been behaving themselves. As for you and the sprog, you've got a couple of hours to kill before you need to be back here. Then you'll get fed and shown to your quarters for the night.'

The Aedui had a long, but not unbroken, history as an ally of Rome. Their relationship had been put under strain less than a decade before when Rome stood aside while they were defeated in battle by their rivals, the Sequani, with help from powerful Germanic tribes from across the Rhine. More recently, the migration of the Helvetii, westwards from the Alps, had threatened their territory, but Caesar, in his first campaign in Gaul, had pushed them back. He also defeated the powerful German king, Ariovistus, who was still claiming dominion over the Aedui. Despite that, there remained factions amongst the Aedui nobility that resented any Roman intervention.

Scaeva got out of the carriage and stretched. The forum in which he stood appeared to be the centre of the plateau, although the ground ahead of them still rose on either side of the main street lined with shop fronts. To the right stood the residential area of the nobility, and the hill was covered with the red-tiled roofs of Roman-style townhouses. To the left, the ground sloped back down into a gulley where the dancing stream he saw on the way in flowed out through the battlements that bridged it. Ahead of them was a peak, clearly the highest point of the oppidum, and beyond it, the main street continued its ascent to a temple in the distance. However much Scaeva would have liked to explore the buildings around the forum and beyond, there was something about the remote temple that beckoned him.

'Would you come with me Durus? To that temple up there,' pleaded Scaeva, pointing to the distant object.

'I've no interest in a Gallic temple, but I could do with the walk. We've been cooped up for days,' and he stretched, kneading the small of his back with his knuckles to ease his stiffness.

Scaeva set off up the hill and past the open shop fronts where slaves called out to passers-by attempting to attract trade from the city dwellers. Aeduan nobility rubbed shoulders with artisans, workmen, and native tribesmen. Scaeva was familiar with the stalls selling produce from local fields and orchards, as well as game and spoils from the hunters. He was even accustomed to the richer products from looms far beyond the shores of Prydain that were imported through the riverside docks of his hometown. Fine clothes and linens from Rome and exotic fabrics from even further afield. But Durus had to explain to him the purpose of the dyes and perfumes on sale for the toilette of the wealthier ladies. Diverse products such as pigments for wall decorations and Eastern spices were amongst the items that gave him an early glimpse of the world he was destined to discover.

As the main street levelled off and left the bustling commercial district behind, it followed the contours around the small hill on which the temple stood, where a narrow track led straight up to it. As he approached, it seemed to grow in size. He stood at the open doorway and looked up at the twin stone towers looming above him. The stone walls appeared to be much older than the blocks in the city wall and just inside the doorway, fixed to the walls, were boards covered with small squares of lead. Curse tablets. Scaeva picked a few of them off their nails, unfolded them, and furtively studied the inscriptions before carefully putting them back, even though he couldn't read them. His eyes took time to adjust to the darkness as he stepped across the threshold.

The interior was quite small, and the single room was lined with wood panelling. Just then, the afternoon sun came out from behind a cloud and shone through a window in the stone towers above and behind him. Lit up on the back wall of the temple, behind a stone altar, was a shrine. An almost life-sized triptych of wooden figures carved in relief inside three tall, hinged frames. Those on either side depicted horses in a wooded setting. The one in the middle was of a female figure mounted on a horse, unmistakably Epona. Relieved to find a friendly face from home, Scaeva studied the carved image. Disappointingly, whoever the artist was, he had certainly never met her in person. In the cool darkness of the temple, Scaeva closed his eyes and was back in the woods by the one-tree pasture. Someone called his name, but it wasn't Ebracus; he was dead. And it wasn't even his name.

'Philippus, come on up here, I want to show you something.' It was Durus, who had climbed to the highest point of the oppidum.

Scaeva broke from his thoughts and stepped outside. The view back down the hill made him catch his breath. The panorama over the roofs of the residential area in the foreground took in the forum and basilica, then beyond the woods to the plumes of smoke wafting in the breeze across the workshops by the entrance gate. But Durus was pointing in the opposite direction. Scaeva set off towards him across the springy turf between the temple and Durus' vantage point. The summit where he stood was surrounded by an ancient ditch and abandoned earthworks. Standing beside Durus and following the line of his finger into the distance beyond the citadel, the furthest horizon was marked by a jagged white hem.

'What is that?'

'That, dear Philippus is the Alpes. And beyond the Alpes, Italy, and Rome.'

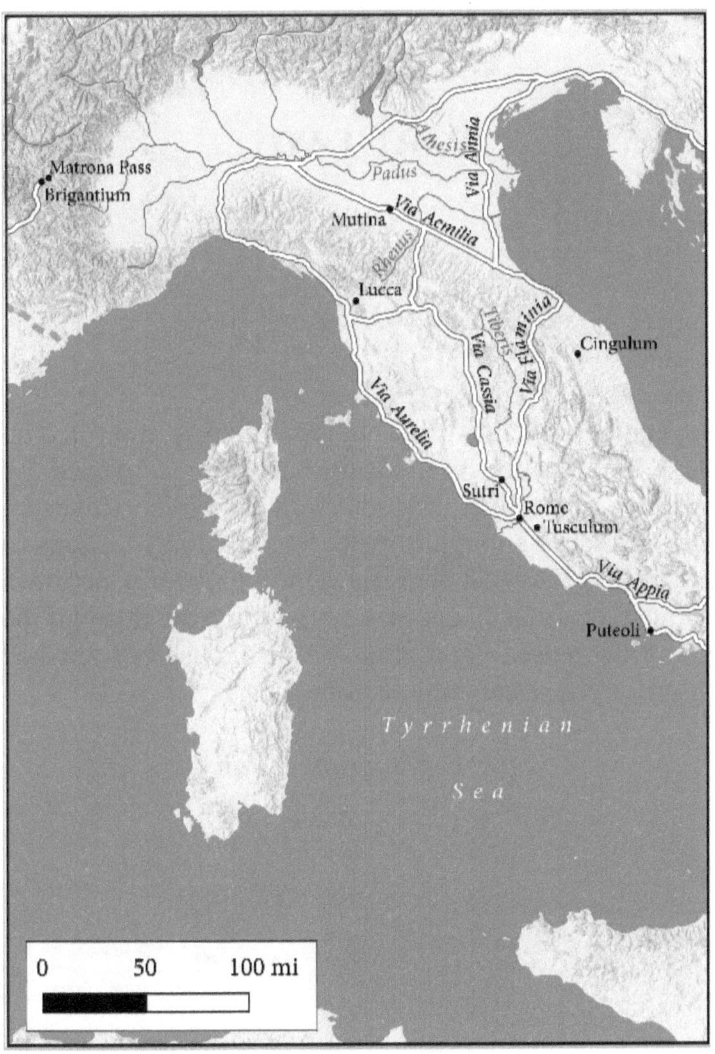

Matrona Pass
Brigantium
Athesis
Via Annia
Padus
Mutina
Via Aemilia
Rhenus
Lucca
Tiberis
Via Cassia
Via Flaminia
Cingulum
Via Aurelia
Sutri
Rome
Tusculum
Via Appia
Puteoli
Tyrrhenian
Sea
0   50   100 mi

PART TWO

ROME

'They have paved the roads, cut through hills, and filled up valleys, so that the merchandise may be conveyed by carriage from the ports. The sewers, arched over with hewn stones, are large enough in parts for actual hay wagons to pass through, while so plentiful is the supply of water from the aqueducts, that rivers may be said to flow through the city and the sewers, and almost every house is furnished with water pipes and copious fountains.'

Strabo; Geography, V.iii

XXIII

October 55 BC
Rome
The Domus Rostrata. House of Pompeius
Magnus

'Twenty days of public thanksgiving? Twenty fucking days!'

'Do keep your voice down Crassus,' said Pompeius. 'Julia is entertaining her family in the *peristylium,* and you know how voices can carry. How do you think I feel? The senate only granted a ten-day *supplicatio* when I defeated Mithridates. And what will Caesar bring home for the glory of Rome by comparison? Nothing more than a handful of slaves.'

Caesar's dispatches from Samarobriva were carried to Rome via the private courier service run by his agent, Gaius Oppius. The news that the mythical land at the edge of the known world had been conquered by their own Julius Caesar had generated euphoria amongst the public. This had not been lost on the senate. Consequently, they voted to mark the news with an announcement calculated to meet with public expectations.

'Cato opposed the motion in the senate, of course,' said Crassus. 'But these days, the senate is more in fear of the *pleb*s than they are of him.'

'Do you suppose Cato will stir up trouble at the elections of the *curule* aediles?'

'I think not,' replied Pompeius with an air of confidence. 'The election of praetors was made peacefully, and Cato offered no violence in retaliation for last year. Furthermore, we allowed his brother-in-law, Domitius, a clear run at consul in this year's elections. We have nothing to fear from that with Claudius Pulcher as second consul; my eldest son Gnaeus was married to Pulcher's youngest daughter only last month, so we may rely on him to counter any mischief that Domitius may wish to cause us. And besides, we've postponed the elections of the aediles long enough for tempers to cool.'

Pompeius and Crassus, the two consuls, were holding a final meeting in private at Pompeius's new *domus* ahead of Crassus' preparations to take up governorship of Syria, and his planned war against the Parthians.

The consular elections of the previous year had been deliberately delayed, allowing Pompeius and Crassus time to announce their candidacy in the wake of their meeting with Caesar that spring at Lucca, the southernmost town in his province. All but Lucius Domitius Ahenobarbus had shied away from challenging them. On the morning of the vote, supporters of Pompeius ambushed Domitius' party on their way to the voting pens. Cato and several others were injured in the attack, and the torchbearer of the party was killed. Furthermore, Pompeius had blocked Cato's bid for praetorship by dissolving the voting assembly, alleging that he had heard a peal of thunder, an inauspicious omen.

'Well, I hope you are right,' said Crassus. 'I will be leaving for Syria in November to take over the province from Gabinus, so I will not have time to get involved. As the only consul present in Rome, it will be upon you to preside. And here's another thing, do not forget about that business with Gabinus. A lot of people are truly angry about the restoration of Auletes, particularly Cato's faction, for the sibylline books forbade it. They take that kind of thing very seriously. So seriously that it was not safe for Gabinus to remain in Rome after word got around about his meeting with Rabirius.'

Their conversation was interrupted by a knock on the door of Pompeius's *tablinum*. It was Demetrios, his janitor, who was bearing the sealed leather cylinder given to him by Durus.

'Please excuse the intrusion, Magnus. You have visitors: a military tribune and a boy. They have borne this message from Caesar.'

While the consul read the contents of the container handed to him by his servant, Scaeva and Durus were left kicking their heels in the magnificent *vestibulum* of the Domus Rostrata.

Since Scaeva's first sight, in Bibracte, of Roman architecture, countryside villas, and public buildings, examples had appeared more frequently after they passed through Lugudunon, the fortress of the god Lugh. Before leaving that ancient oppidum, Faberius had bought him clothing suitable for the freezing temperatures they would endure as they travelled through the mountain passes ahead of them. They continued their journey southwards along the valley of the Rhodanus, crossing into the Roman province of Narbonensis, before turning towards the rising sun and the white Alpine peaks, first glimpsed from the highest point within the capital of the Aedui six days earlier. By the time they reached Brigantium and the final ascent along the gritted stone slabs of the Via Domita to the Matrona Pass, Scaeva had become accustomed to the wild, high mountain terrain that surrounded him. That last climb entailed the entire party leaving their carriages in freezing temperatures and tackling the incline alongside the mules to reach a mountainous plateau, a world away from the flat horizons of his tribal homeland. His onward journey through northern Italy, and his daily conversations with Durus, incrementally expanded his knowledge of the Latin world and offered him an insight into what was to come; but would it prepare him for the sights and sounds of Republican Rome?

At Mutina, Caesar had taken the time to give him a short tour of the city, described by Cicero as *Mutina splendidissima,* and tasked Faberius to have Scaeva's hair styled, and kit him out with clothing befitting a boy of his age and family connections. Durus had taken the opportunity to pack away his military garb. He now sported the angusticlavia, a white tunic with a thin purple stripe dropping from each shoulder, under a short toga. This was the recognised apparel for a citizen of equestrian status; as he told Scaeva, who was reluctant to dispense with his trousers, even though he'd drawn disapproving looks from the citizens of Mutina. But he welcomed his new woollen cloak and fine white cotton tunica. It was belted and a little longer than the one he was used to, with a red border denoting his noble free-born status. It came with a broad purple edged toga and tunic, with two matching broad purple stripes for formal occasions that he hoped would not occur too frequently.

Even more pleasing was the gold-plated locket Caesar had given him to wear on a gold chain around his neck. It was engraved with the head of a horse and contained a small solid gold icon resembling a phallus. The *bulla* was given to all male Roman children to give them luck and ward off evil spirits. Sadly, this meant relinquishing the torc his father had given him, but Caesar promised he would hold it in safekeeping for the next time they met, when he promised he would return it.

On the morning of their departure from Mutina, Caesar had introduced them to his nephew, Quintus Pedius, who would share their carpentum the remainder of the journey. Pedius was the son of Caesar's eldest sister and had been a general in Caesar's campaign against the Belgae at Bibrax two years earlier. Having already held the senatorial rank of quaestor, and on hearing that the elections for the *curule* aediles—the next step up in the *cursus honorum*—had just been announced, he had thrown his hat into the ring and was in Mutina to obtain his uncle's blessing and backing for his campaign. He now needed to return to Rome to prepare for the elections that were only three weeks away. Caesar had briefed him on why the young Briton was being sent to Rome, and Pedius was duly respectful of his status, not only that of a foreign prince but also as a newly adopted member of the gens Julia. With the introductions completed, Caesar handed Durus the leather cylinder containing the letter to Pompeius and sent the trio on the final leg of their journey along the Via Cassia, while Caesar himself stayed behind to attend to his duties as governor of the province.

Eight days later, they reached the point where the Via Cassia joined the ancient Flaminian Way and crossed the

Tiber in the valley below the heights of the Collis Hortorum. Pedius, who had spent years as a *legate* of Caesar in Gallia and spoke the common language of the Gauls more fluently than Durus, told Scaeva their journey would soon be coming to an end, and he would point out landmarks as they came within view. As the banks of the Tiber veered away westwards and with the Hill of Gardens now behind them, the open expanse of the Campus Martius spread before them below the Capitoline Hill. Scaeva stood at the open doorway of their carpentum, holding tightly to the sides, to get a better view of their approach and gasped at the sight of the twin peaks of the most ancient hill in Rome, each topped by an awesome temple overlooking the Servian Wall. The wall breasted the heights before dipping into the col between the Capitolium and the Quirinal Hill, that now rose above them. Durus stood dutifully at the other doorway as the carriage slowed up the incline to the col and came to a halt outside the city gates.

'Stay here,' ordered Durus, as he stepped down from the carriage to approach the gate. Scaeva obediently sat back inside, breathless at the thought of what would be revealed to him once inside the city walls.

Pedius bade him farewell and asked to be remembered to his cousin Julia, then he followed the tribune up to the gates. Pedius had already explained that because of the congested state of the narrow streets, no carriages or wagons were allowed into the city during daylight hours. Scaeva was in a state of excitement, anticipating walking the streets of Rome at the end of his epic journey. But he was to be disappointed. After what seemed like an eternity, Durus returned with a porter pushing an empty handcart.

As the porter began loading Durus' baggage from the carriage, Durus shared with Scaeva the information he had received at the gatehouse.

'The consul has no official business in the capital today and is at his new residence outside the city. The porter will show us the way.'

Scaeva could not disguise his dismay. Ever since Durus had revealed Caesar's plans for him, the excitement of the journey as an adventure had buoyed his spirits through the long hours in the jolting carriage. He had hardly given a thought to what would become of him when he reached his destination. The practicalities of what his life would be like were too far beyond his comprehension even to contemplate.

He pulled his new cloak tight around his shoulders and trudged back down the slope, following Durus and the porter. At the bottom of the hill, the porter turned off the main track and passed the open entrance of a long straight paved walkway, adorned with sculptures and statues on pedestals, that led out into the grassy void. It had a red-tiled roof supported by fluted columns. At the far end, near the middle of the Campus, was a raised stone table Scaeva recognised as an altar. They continued along a main road through a wealthy district of suburban villas that spread up the lower slopes of the Capitolium until the street opened out at the corner of a wide colonnaded square surrounding a temple. Another four ancient structures, outside the square, stood in a row facing it. Most had the now familiar stone steps leading up to various arrangements of columns topped with a decorated triangular pediment, but one was circular and contained a gigantic marble statue of a goddess. Behind these, a huge edifice was being erected.

When completed, it would dwarf the row of ancient temples before it.

'What is being built here?' Durus asked the porter,

'When it is finished it will be known as the Curia of Pompeius Magnus,' he replied, with a touch of pride in his voice. 'Magnus' theatre was opened this year. You will see it when we turn the corner.'

'Durus, what is a curia?' asked Scaeva, who had picked up the gist of what the porter said but still lacked the vocabulary.

'It's a big house where people can meet. Important people.'

'And a theatre, what is that?'

Durus paused. 'I'll have to think about that. You don't have them in Britannia.'

They followed the porter to the end of the site and turned the corner. Behind the curia, a vast rectangular colonnaded garden was under construction. At the far end, the magnificent structure of the theatre dominated the landscape. Neither Scaeva nor even Durus had seen anything made by man of that magnitude before and the first sight of it took their breath away.

'We are nearly there now,' puffed the porter, calling over his shoulder, and beginning to flag. 'Pompeius' new residence is just beyond the theatre.'

Durus was busying himself studying the inscriptions on the marble plinths of the *rostrum* along the back wall of the *vestibulum*, while Scaeva was staring down the wide tree-lined boulevard that led from the *domus* back towards Pompeius's theatre. He had counted twelve guards standing to attention in front of the house, six on either side of the steps that led up to the *vestibulum*. All of them shouldered a bundle of rods with an axe head showing between them, bound with a red thong, but they had made no move to challenge the visitors as they approached the house. The porter had unloaded Durus' belongings at the top of the steps and returned the way they had come.

Now that he had arrived at his final destination, Scaeva had been casting his mind back over the more memorable moments of his journey. Anything to blot out the uncertainty of the immediate future. At the far end of the boulevard, a body of men appeared bearing a *lectica*; Scaeva recalled seeing these during his time in Mutina with Caesar. At that moment, his attention was taken by a clamour of childish voices coming from the interior of the house. The door from the *vestibulum* suddenly opened and out came a young woman and two children, richly dressed in the Roman style. The girl, Scaeva guessed, was a few years older than him, the boy perhaps a year younger. But the woman, who appeared to be pregnant, had the face of what Scaeva imagined being that of Branwen, whose beauty was lauded by the bards in his homeland. As the trio entered the *vestibulum* and encountered the unexpected stranger, their happy conversation came to an abrupt halt. There was a look of surprise on the faces of the children, but the woman smiled, a smile that made the young boy's heart leap.

She simply said, 'Hello, can I help you?'

Scaeva opened his mouth to answer, but no words came out. He had understood the simple Latin phrase but was so flustered he blurted the first words that came to him. *'Salve, mi nomen Philippus.'*

'Not another Philippus,' groaned the boy in jest. The girl gave him an admonishing look, and at that moment, Durus, who had escaped their attention altogether, spoke up from behind them, taking them all by surprise.

'Please excuse the boy, he is not well-practised in Latin. Allow me to introduce myself. I am Quintus Laberius Durus, military tribune recently with the Tenth Legion in Britannia. I'm here to deliver a letter to the consul.'

'Britannia!' exclaimed the boy. 'With great uncle Julius?'

'So you must be, let me guess,' Durus paused for effect, 'Octavius?' The boy nodded and beamed. Turning to the girl and stooping to her height, Durus continued. 'And you must be?'

'Octavia,' she said breathlessly, looking into the deep brown eyes of the handsome soldier who, unknowingly, had just swept the young girl off her feet.

Julia and the children had a myriad of questions to ask the two new arrivals. Julia longed for news of her father. Octavius wanted to know all about the battles against the mythical Britons. All of Rome was agog, still celebrating and giving thanks for Caesar's great victory over a previously unknown people. Octavia was just desperate to know if Durus was married or betrothed. But those questions would have to wait.

'Has anyone attended to you?' asked Julia.

'Yes,' said Durus, 'the janitor who came to the door took the letter. He told us to wait here for a reply.'

'That awful man Demetrios! Ever since Gnaeus granted him his freedom, he takes advantage of my dear husband's good nature. He knows that Gnaeus never looks to the bad in people. He should have realised you had travelled a great distance and brought you into the *atrium* and offered some refreshment. When was the last time you ate?'

Scaeva could only pick up a few of Julia's words spoken at true conversational speed, but that didn't matter. The sound of her voice caressed his ears more softly than the most tuneful bards and harpers back home.

'Breakfast this morning, before leaving Sutri,' replied Durus. 'But we took some lunch with us.'

'Then you must both stay for dinner,' said Julia, aiming another devastating smile at the shy young boy.

'Can we stay too?' pleaded Octavius. 'I want to find out about the Britons and their war chariots.'

'No Octavius,' said Julia gently. 'Look, your stepfather's *lectica* has arrived. Your mother is expecting you both home before the streets darken.'

'Oh please, please Julia, can we stay?' implored Octavia, suddenly blushing at the thought of the soldier guessing her reason for wanting to. Julia looked down at the two young, expectant faces before her.

'All right, I'll ask Demetrios to send the *lectica* back with a message. You can travel home in mine later.'

Octavius was thrilled. Not only could he listen to the stories the soldier had to tell, but he would be out after dark, travelling home by torchlight. What fun he would have, teasing his sister about the evil demons lurking in the shadows.

Turning again to Scaeva, Julia asked, 'So, Philippus, where are you from?'

'*A me Britannia*, no, no, sorry, sorry, *ego EX Britannia*,' Scaeva corrected himself and blushed.

'By Jupiter, he's a Briton!' declared Octavius. 'Just wait 'till I tell my friends at school!'

'He's very sweet,' said Julia to Durus. Then she added mischievously. 'Have you brought him home as your slave?'

Octavia was old enough not to miss the connotation of Julia's question and was horrified at the thought.

'No, not at all,' replied Durus, glossing over the innuendo. He was pondering whether it was his place to explain Caesar's intentions for the boy when the janitor returned and ushered them through to the *atrium*.

Meanwhile, the consuls had been discussing the contents of Caesar's letter to Pompeius. It was carefully worded not to add any more detail of his expedition to Britannia, or future plans in that direction, than had already been revealed in his earlier missive from Samarobriva. It simply explained the treaty he had struck with Mandubracus and requested Pompeius to take care of his ten-year-old son and school him in preparation for his return to Britannia, as a client king under the patronage of Rome.

'So what does this mean?' said Pompeius, staring at the letter in his hand. 'Does Caesar plan to return to Britannia next year and join forces with this King Mandubracius?' He turned to Crassus with an exaggerated shrug of his shoulders. 'And how long is his barbarian sprog expected to remain here in Rome, as my guest? What am I to do with him?'

'Typical of Caesar, if you ask me,' said Crassus. 'He's keeping his options open. Why don't you hand the boy over to that chap Auletes dumped on you? What was his name, the one that tutored his daughter?'

'Ah yes,' exclaimed Pompeius, clapping his hands together. 'Philostratos. I've been struggling to find him something suitable to attend to. I tried putting him in charge of the household over Demetrios, but the two of them clash dreadfully. It will be years before I need his services for my own child, so the task of educating this young princeling should suit him admirably.' Crassus smiled inwardly at the ability of his co-consul to view the boy as a barbarian one moment, and a princeling the next.

'And to introduce him into the ways of governance here in Rome,' Crassus added tartly. 'Why don't you take him with you to witness the elections of the *curule* aediles? Then he can see you in action, presiding over proceedings.' The sourness of Crassus' comment was lost on Pompeius, who was now on a roll of positivity following his earlier exasperation.

'Excellent idea Crassus. I will summon Philostratos and tell him he has but two *nundinae* to give the boy a grounding in Latin. He taught Cleopatra nine languages, including, so they say, the barbaric tongues of cave dwellers in Africa, so I'm sure he will rise to the challenge. I will bid Demetrios bring him here urgently and show our guests into the *atrium*.'

The two consuls and the elderly Greek scholar were waiting when Julia and the children bustled in from the *vestibulum* with the two strangers in tow. Durus was a country boy at heart despite the desire of his parents for him to aspire to a career in the senate. Before joining the military, he had only visited Rome occasionally, and although a trusted confidant of Julius Caesar, his sinews stiffened as he stood before the two most powerful men in the known world. He had prepared himself for a dutiful encounter with Pompeius Magnus, but the brooding presence of Marcus Licinius Crassus, the richest, and possibly the meanest man in Rome, made him swallow hard.

'And which one of you is Quintus Laberius Durus?' declared Pompeius, playfully addressing the assembled family members and strangers alike, partly to amuse the children but also to put the young tribune at ease.

'Magnus,' nodded Durus, presenting himself.

Scaeva was aghast. Caesar had briefed him on his relationship with Pompeius, so Scaeva knew he was the husband of Caesar's daughter Julia. But now that he had met them both, the thought of that ageing blob of lard doing *that*, to the adorable creature he had just fallen hopelessly in love with, filled him with loathing.

'Laberius, yes, I have heard the family name,' said Pompeius, stroking his chin. 'The Equestrians in Lanuvium, near my villa in the Alban Hills, perhaps?'

'No, Magnus. My family is from Cingulum.'

'Ah, Cingulum, a district of Picenum. A fellow from my homeland,' said the consul. 'Perhaps you are related to the writer of mimes, Decimus Laberius?'

'I was teased at school because I shared the name, but we are not related Magnus,' replied Durus, appreciating the efforts that the great man was expending to make him feel welcome.

Turning to address Scaeva, Pompeius continued, 'So you must be …' the consul paused to check the name written in the letter that he still held between his pudgy fingers, '… Gaius Julius Caesar Scaevanus Philippus; the son of the King of Britannia!' Pompeius ended his announcement with a flourish that brought gasps of amazement from Julia and the children. Julia also experienced a pang of guilt, wondering if the boy had understood her earlier remark to Durus. 'It is Caesar's wish that the boy receives a proper education and learns our ways of government before returning home to claim his birthright and rule Britannia as a friend and ally of Rome.'

Crassus cut across the clamour that greeted Pompeius' announcement.

'My business with you, Magnus, is concluded,' he interjected brusquely. 'I will take my leave.'

'Will you not stay to eat with us, Licinius?' asked Julia, sweetly. 'I have told Demetrius to prepare places for our guests.'

'Thank you, Julia, but I have other matters to attend to. I leave for Syria in three days.' Crassus was never one to make small talk and was in no mood to hear any more discussion of Caesar's heroics. Demetrius held open the door and Crassus swept outside to the *vestibulum* where the twelve guards that Scaeva had counted earlier were now arranged in single file. Through the open door, Scaeva watched them depart in a formal procession along the wide boulevard, with the consul striding out in their wake.

As the janitor closed the door, Scaeva turned to face the room and panicked to find that, with Durus having already been greeted and Crassus now departed, he was the centre of everyone's attention. Surprisingly, it was the older man who stepped forward to address him, and even more surprising, to the whole assembly, that he spoke perfect Gallic,

'Good evening, young man. My name is Philostratos. Do you speak the language of the Gauls?'

'I know it well enough,' replied Scaeva, greatly relieved that his sparse knowledge of Latin would not immediately be put to the test.

'I had hoped so. I am to tutor you in the language of Rome until you are ready to go to school and be with other boys of your age.' Then, in recognition of the gasps of surprise amongst the small assembly, reverting to Latin, he addressed the room. 'During my tenure as chief librarian at Alexandria, tens of thousands of written works passed through my hands. Some of them, mainly found on ships from Massalia, were written in the language of the Gauls in the Greek lettering introduced by the founders of that city. It was incumbent upon me to learn all languages, and by chance, some slaves set to work in the library were also from Gaul, a porter and a copyist. Hence, I have attained good working knowledge. Their vocabulary is not extensive, but as Diodorus Siculus writes, they often converse in riddles and use one word when they mean another.' The smiles and noises of approval continued, encouraging him to warm to his theme and further demonstrate his learning. 'The same author goes on to say that although the Gauls often extol themselves and depreciate all others, they are not without cleverness; whereas the inhabitants of Britannia,' he paused briefly to smile at Scaeva, 'according to Pytheas, who sailed to those parts, were simple in their habits and far removed from the cunning of modern men.'

'And you had the works of Siculus at your library?' presumed Pompeius.

'Of course, Magnus, but I also had the honour of being in his company while he was in Egypt studying our customs ...'

It was just as well that Scaeva soon lost the gist of what the old man was saying. He was too engrossed in the grandeur of his surroundings to notice the patronising smile from his new mentor. The mosaic floors, the richly illustrated tapestries, the marble statues, and the pond in the middle of the floor. The reason for which he simply concluded, was to collect rainwater, because the room had no roof. Pompeius politely allowed Philostratos to conclude his anecdote before leading the group from the *atrium* into the family *triclinium*, where slaves were hastily laying out extra dinner places under the chaotic directions of Demetrios. As Scaeva settled himself on his tummy between the reclining figures of Durus and Philostratos, he suddenly realised for the first time since the fateful night of the great feast, he felt happy and calm.

During their journey, Durus had coached Scaeva in various aspects of life in Rome, and with dining, as with many other things, the advice was to observe and do as the Romans do. Scaeva copied everything the young boy opposite did, choosing from the same dishes and using the same utensils to eat with, although lacking in dexterity. The boy saw plainly what Scaeva was doing and embraced the idea that the noble young savage was happy to learn from him. Scaeva found the dishes chosen by Octavius delicious, and the wine, being well watered, was far more palatable than the few sips he had tried of the undiluted product preferred amongst the tribal community of the Trinovantes.

There was only one topic of conversation, the story of the invasion. Durus kept his eager audience enthralled with his tale of the sea crossing, the battle on the beachhead, the storm that drove back the fleet of Labienus and the final engagement in which the chariots of the Britons had been put to flight. Most enthralled of all, but trying not to show it, was Octavia. She was yearning for someone to ask him about himself, so she might gain some insight into his life. Something she could use to build her fantasies around; but no one did, and it was not appropriate for her to ask. Durus had been briefed by Caesar before leaving Mutina, not to make any mention of Cordelia, or the ambush in the wheatfield, and Durus was quite happy to keep things simple. Most of the questions had been directed at him, even those that required an answer from Scaeva.

Only Julia spoke to Scaeva directly. 'Tell me Philippus, you have a Greek name. How did you come by it?'

It was a simple question. He understood it and wanted to respond immediately and impress her by using the Latin he had learned on the journey. With prompting from Durus, he conveyed to Julia that her father had adopted him into the family Julii Caesares and given him the additional cognomen of Philippus in recognition of his affinity with horses; granted to him by the Celtic goddess Epona. Julia and the children were wide-eyed in amazement.

'This gets better and better,' shouted Octavius to his sister.

Delighted and encouraged by the response around the table to this revelation about Epona, Scaeva related his encounter with Caesar's cloven-hoofed horse in the stables at Samarobriva. In his excitement, he frequently resorted to his own language, requiring both Durus and Philostratos to act as translators. Julia was open-mouthed in awe at the conclusion of the story.

'So you have made friends with Toes!' she exclaimed to the astonishment of all present. She went on to explain. 'Toes was the pet name I gave to my father's horse when he was foaled. He was born with his hooves split, like a deer. It was seen as a good omen. I was just a young girl at the time. I loved him dearly, but as he grew, he would not abide anyone to approach him too closely except my father.'

No one thought to translate Julia's response for Scaeva's benefit, but he didn't care. Settled between the comforting figures of his travelling companion and his kindly new mentor, and gazing into the smiling eyes of Julia, Scaeva felt a depth of happiness he had never before experienced. Of the children on the couch opposite, the girl was a little shy but pleasant enough and her younger brother, with his sticking-out ears, reminded him gently, but not too sadly, of his dear brother Ebracus. Even the obese, but jovial Pompeius appeared tolerable enough and Julia seemed not to mind her undeserving husband at all.

That night, as he lay on his soft mattress, staring up at the decorated ceiling of his bedroom, he failed to notice there was no longer any soreness in his back. The *cubiculum* he shared with his new mentor was lit by the soft glow of an oil lamp on a table in the corner, and the only sound was the heavy, even breathing of the old man in the cot against the wall opposite. After his epic journey, and the doubts and fears of what he might find at its end, his pain and anxiety had been replaced by relief. He had finally arrived, and all was well. As sheer tiredness took him, he closed his eyes and hoped to dream of Julia.

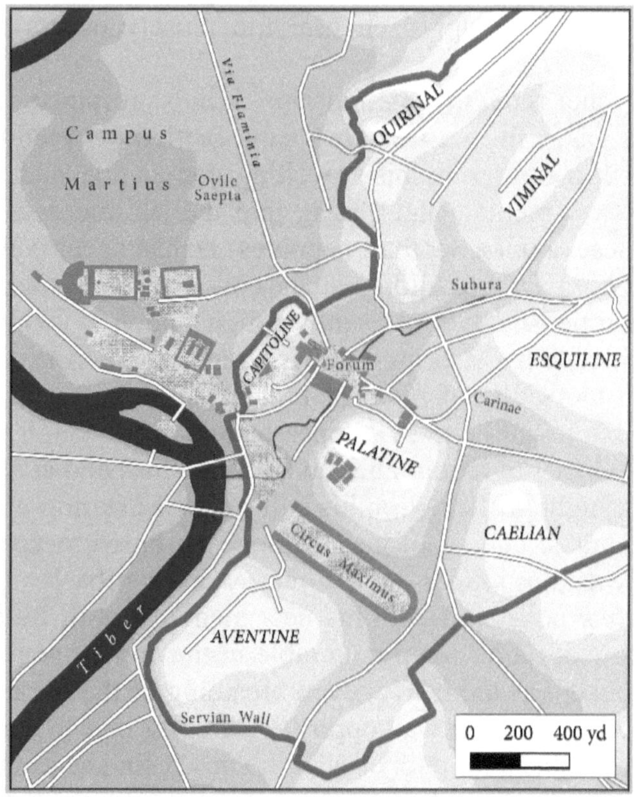

The Seven Hills of Rome and the Field of Mars 55 BC

XXIV

October 55 BC
Rome

The following morning, he bade farewell to Durus and hoped they would meet again one day back in Britannia. It occurred to Durus in a moment of fantasy that if he returned to Britannia the following year with Caesar and installed Mandubracius as a client king for Rome; then, at some future time, when he had made a name for himself in politics and perhaps become governor of the province of Britannia, that Scaeva might have returned as king by then.

Scaeva's sadness at the departure of Durus was softened by the relationship that had developed with Philostratos. They rarely spent time outside of each other's company. The elderly Greek scholar had introduced him to the rest of the household of the Domus Rostrata who, except for Demetrios, were all slaves owned by Pompeius. Although it was becoming the fashion for the super-rich to flaunt their wealth by having a separate slave to perform each household task, Pompeius and Julia, in keeping with their distaste for ostentation, kept a more modest number of kitchen staff, gardeners, and other servants besides their personal attendants. Much to Scaeva's enjoyment, Octavius had been a more frequent visitor. He would call by after school, ostensibly to visit Julia, who was often found in the *atrium* at her loom at that time of day, so he always sought the company of her brother by adoption; the enigmatic barbarian princeling, who boasted the indulgence of a Celtic Goddess.

The only incident that gave Scaeva cause for alarm was when Philostratos took him to visit the public baths. The closest bath house was in the district of Pallacinae. Scaeva had passed through it with Durus on the day they had arrived outside the gates of Rome. This time, Philostratos turned off the main road, skirting the newer opulent suburban villas of the Roman elite. Soon the streets got narrower and the buildings older. Small groups of young, and not so young, women assembled in twos and threes on street corners. Some of them called out to Philostratos using colloquialisms that Scaeva didn't understand. The old Greek ignored them and hurried on, leaving the women in fits of giggles.

When they arrived at the baths, Philostratos paid the minimal entrance fee and led Scaeva through the *apodyterium* into a cubicle to undress. Scaeva peeled off his tunic, just as the *capsarius* came in with a pile of towels. The attendant let out a gasp of horror.

Although the hideous scarring of the runes across his back no longer pained him, the sight of them was still shocking. Ever since he had embarked upon his journey to Rome, there had been no reason to expose his torso. Since his arrival at the house of Pompeius, he had not been reminded of the scars by pain or discomfort. So it didn't occur to him that going to the baths would reveal the secret he had kept about the bloody prophecies and the deeper reason for having to leave his homeland.

Philostratos' attention was caught by the reaction of the slave. He grabbed Scaeva by the shoulders and spun him around, so the boy's back was towards the light from the high window. He was more than shocked. Philostratos stared at the runes in disbelief.

His first words were directed at the slave attendant. 'Get out! Get out and guard the door, let no one else in.' The slave needed no second bidding and left immediately, slamming the door shut behind him.

'Where did you get these? Who did this to you?' demanded the Greek, his voice trembling.

Scaeva was so taken aback that it took a moment for him to realise what Philostratos was referring to. 'I don't know what they mean, honest I don't,' cried the boy, who was startled by his mentor's sudden alarm. 'Only the top line. It is why I had to leave Britannia.'

'These are prophecies. I recognise the runes from my travels in the East. Is this the work of your druids?'

Scaeva could think of no other credible explanation to give other than the truth. 'I did a bad thing. I killed someone. I didn't mean it. He was hurting my brother.'

'And this was your punishment?'

'Yes. I killed the nephew of Cassivellaunus. He swore an oath of revenge, but the druids took me to the vate. They see that justice is done. The vate summoned the spirits and the spirits foretold my future.'

'So, these prophecies are about your future?' said Philostratos, whose tone was now more sympathetic.

'They said I would die when I came face to face with the King of Kings, and that meant Cassivellaunus. He murdered my grandfather, so my father gave me to Caesar for my safety. The other prophecies are about other people. I don't know who they are, by Taranis I do not.'

'Keep still boy, let me see,' said the elderly Greek, squinting at the symbols and prodding Scaeva's back with his bony finger. 'Each row begins with an arrowhead pointing to the right. That denotes a prophecy about the future. Each arrowhead has a shaft, the longer the shaft, the further into the future it foretells, but the runes that follow? I have seen their like before, but I would need books I left behind in the library at Alexandria to decipher their meaning.'

Scaeva could feel his mentor's finger tracing left to right across his back, moving higher and higher.

'Yes, I can see in the topmost row, there is a reference to kings. Yes, it could mean King of Kings, but there is another symbol I recognise; death. As you have confessed, it must be your own death.' Then the old scholar took a sharp intake of breath, and with alarm creeping back into his voice, continued. 'But the symbol of death is in each of the other rows!'

The incident at the Balneae Pallacinae had put Philostratos in a quandary. Should he warn Pompeius of the deathly prophecies seared into the flesh of his young charge? Especially as he shared Crassus' misgivings about the likelihood of violence at the forthcoming elections. But the prophecies had been made and could not be evaded indefinitely. A sobering fact he imparted to the boy, and after much deliberation, he decided to keep Scaeva's dark secret. Scaeva told him the runes would fade and disappear once they had been fulfilled. A revelation that Philostratos took with a degree of scepticism; but when they returned to their private quarters, he made a copy of the symbols and secreted the copy amongst his personal possessions.

Two *nundinae* later and Pompeius proved as good as his word. The consul had been delighted, not only with Scaeva's aptitude for Latin, but also with the way Julia and her family had taken to him. He now considered the boy sufficiently civilised to include him in his entourage while presiding over the elections of the *curule* aediles. Consequently, Pompeius always referred to him by the more civilised name of Philip, which Scaeva was content to answer to.

On the morning of the elections, the household was roused well before dawn and Scaeva stood and shivered on the steps of the *vestibulum*. Several paces ahead of him was a single column of twelve *lictors*; *fasces* and axe heads shouldered, and ahead of them, lining the boulevard, was a party of torchbearers. Behind him, Pompeius' retinue of assistants, secretaries, and personal slaves was assembled, awaiting the appearance of the consul. In due course, Pompeius, resplendent in his purple-edged *toga praetexta* made of the finest imported Egyptian cotton, took his place in the space between Scaeva and the *lictors*. He barked a sharp command to the primus *lictor* immediately ahead of him, and the procession moved off at a business-like pace along the boulevard.

They passed the great curved *cavea* of the theatre. The sculptures around the base, depicting the nations that Pompeius had defeated, appeared to come alive in the flickering torchlight. On they hurried through the quiet, darkened streets where the only light was from candles glowing between the columns of a few isolated temples.

They reached the flat void of the Circus Flaminius and Scaeva was glad of his cloak flapping tightly around him in the wind from across the Tiber. Early signs of life were heard from the riverbank ahead; sounds of barges being unloaded, and barrows of fresh produce being wheeled across the cobbled quayside into the vegetable market. Before long, they were entering the city through the Porta Carmentalis. The torch bearers led the column along the Vicus Iugarius towards the city centre. Artisans opening their shops on the ground floor of red-brick *insulae*, and setting out their stalls along the street, paused in their labours to acknowledge the progress of the consul.

By the time they emerged into the forum, by the steps and marble columns of the Temple of Saturn, the day had dawned, bright and chilly, with clouds scudding across the sky on a fresh breeze. Throngs of citizens awaited the calling of the auspices from the *auguraculum*, a consecrated space set high above the forum on the Arx, the northern summit of the Capitolium.

Pompeius had previously taken the trouble to explain to Scaeva, with the help of Philostratos, the role of the augur in Roman elections. It was his function to determine the will of the gods from the flights and songs of birds. He would first mark out with a wand, a division in the heavens within which he intended to make his observations. He would then watch for the flights of eagles or vultures in that division and listen for the sounds of a raven or crow. If the auspices were unfavourable, according to the accepted conventions, the business of the day was brought abruptly to an end. Scaeva found it strangely comforting to learn that the gods of the Romans spoke to their augurs by the same method that his own gods spoke to the druids back home. Empowering even, to know exactly what birds to look for or to listen to. This was something he would, no doubt, tease Caspar with on his return to Prydain.

Crowds parted as the consular procession continued past the Rostra in the open, stepped circle of the Comitium and up onto the steps of the senate-house, the Curia Hostilia. Pompeius turned to face the augur high upon his vantage point and gave the signal to begin. The augur raised his wand to the skies. The watching crowds fell silent as the distant figure performed his ritual observances.

Everyone had their faces upturned towards the *auguraculum*. Everyone except one of a group of boys that had been playing on the platform of the Rostra. They had been mimicking the procession of the consul and his *lictor*s but had now paused their game and one of them, with red hair, was looking down at Scaeva. Scaeva stared back up at him and met his gaze until a shrill cry was heard from high upon the Arx.

No inauspicious omens had been observed, and the elections were to proceed. A shout of approval issued forth from the assembled citizens of the four urban tribes of the city of Rome, and the crowds made their way up the steep rise of the Clivus Argentarius—the street leading from the forum to the Campus Martius via the Porta Fontinalis in the Servian wall. They would join the even bigger crowds from the thirty-one rural tribes assembling around the voting pens outside the city gates.

The senate had previously reviewed the list of candidates and narrowed it down to just six, from which the voters would select the final two. They would become magistrates in charge of property and provisions in the city, and most importantly, the games.

Back in the forum, the doors to the senate-house opened and the candidates and attendant functionaries filed out to join the end of the consular procession to the ancient altar of Mars in the Campus Martius, from where the elections would be administered. Pompeius had to order his lictors to clear a way through the crowded incline, which they did with liberal use of their ceremonial rods.

Once through the city gates and with the wind from across the distant Tiber stinging his face, Scaeva suddenly recognised where he was. This was the gate at which he, Durus, and Pedius had arrived outside the city, seemingly a lifetime ago. As the cortège re-traced Scaeva's steps down from the col, he felt dampness in the wind as the clouds above the Campus darkened. This time, instead of passing by the entrance to the covered walkway, as he had done with Durus and the porter, Scaeva followed Pompeius and his *lictor*s along it. The consular procession progressed along the mosaic floor and garlanded monuments of the Porticus Aemilia, while crowds of country dwellers on the outside flocked to peer at the consul from between the columns and statues. Scaeva couldn't help feeling their eyes were on him as he trailed in Pompeius' footsteps. Most of this population had travelled many miles to cast their vote and take the opportunity to stare at the First Man in Rome.

The tribes were regional groupings for the purposes of taxation and military recruitment, nothing to do with kinship. Their collective mood was of grim anxiety. The auspices, taken at dawn, were valid for a single day only, and because the day was so late in the year, they feared the voting might not be concluded before sunset.

When the *lictors* reached the altar at the end of the porticus, they fanned out in a semi-circle around it, facing the populace. Pompeius ascended the steps to the altar and opened proceedings with a brief prayer to Vesta, Goddess of the Hearth and Fire, whose sacred flames were believed to be indispensable to the preservation and continuity of the Roman State. Three of his attendants joined him, producing a shawl to cover the top of his head, an amphora of undiluted wine, and his ivory *curule* chair which was set behind him. The trio then rejoined the group behind Scacva, watching from the cover of the porticus.

With his left arm across his chest and right arm outstretched to the side, fingers closed, palm to the ground, a hush came over the crowd.

'Be well, revered Vesta, Goddess of the Flame.
May you look favourably upon our assembly.'

Then, he stooped to grasp the neck of the amphorae in front of him, straightened, and ceremoniously tilted it, spilling its entire contents onto the steps below him.

'May this finest Falernian wine find favour with you.'

Pompeius ended the brief incantation by putting the tips of the fingers of his right hand to his lips, and blew a kiss to the ground before him, as the liquid soaked away.

Another of his attendants brought him a scroll, from which he announced the names of the six candidates, one of whom, to Scaeva's complete surprise, was Quintus Pedius. Although Pedius had discussed his candidacy with Durus during the final leg of their journey, and Pompeius had spoken to Scaeva about the procedures for the forthcoming election, he hadn't understood enough to link the two. Before voting commenced, the candidates had their final opportunity to address the voters. One-by-one, they took their place beside the seated consul and addressed the crowd, straining to make their voices heard above the wind. Scaeva was already getting bored. He could neither hear, nor understand what was being said. His ears pricked up when it was the turn of Pedius to speak. A faint ripple of applause and a few shouts of approval greeted him, but quickly died away.

When the last candidate had spoken, Pompeius stood and dispelled the crowds from around the altar with the traditional cry of, '*Discedite Quirites*.' That was the signal for the citizens to form their separate tribal groups in the open voting pens that filled the space from the vicinity of the altar to the Flaminian Way. Scaeva had taken them to be animal enclosures when he had first sighted them from his carpentum.

Lots had been cast for the prize known as the *principium;* the first tribe to cast their vote. It was prized because the result of their vote was announced before the other tribes cast their own. It often set a precedent for the rest of the tribal assembly to follow. The winner of that lottery was the urban tribe of Suburana, the district of Rome from where Caesar himself hailed. This was the tribe with the highest population due to the number of high-rise *insulae* packed closely together in the region.

Now that the speeches were over and the act of voting was about to begin, Scaeva ran up the steps of the altar to get a better view of proceedings over the heads of the *lictor*s. The citizens of the Suburana had assembled in their thousands and been counted into their enclosure. They were now exiting the voting pens, in single file, along a narrow-raised gangplank, towards a platform where groups of election officials were seated above several rows of tall wicker baskets.

Pompeius noticed Scaeva at his shoulder and suddenly remembered why he had included him in his entourage.

'Philip! Yes, you need to see this.' He put his arm around the boy's shoulder and mimed the actions with his other hand. 'This is how the voting happens. Each citizen is handed a wax tablet, just large enough for him to write the name of his preferred candidate. He then drops it into the voting urn. When the urn is full, the custodes, the guardians of the urns, take them to the *diribitores*, the tellers, and the votes are counted.'

Together, they watched the first few citizens exercise their right, then, having discharged his obligation to instruct the young prince, the consul retired to the large tent that had been erected behind the altar. Once inside, he swept aside the curtain to his private quarters to enjoy a late breakfast with the closest of his coterie. Scaeva was left amongst the underlings of the party, who were lounging in the tented antechamber, helping themselves to the food laid out by Pompeius' slaves.

He soon got bored with eavesdropping on the gossipy conversations and ventured outside in search of Pedius, with whom he would have liked to renew his friendship. By now, many voting urns had been forwarded to the tellers, and officials were hurrying the citizens of the Suburana along the gangplank with a genuine sense of urgency. By late morning, the sky was overcast, and a steady drizzle dampened the mood of the assembly even further. The *diribitores* were working most diligently and not long after the final vote was cast, the result was hurried to Pompeius' tent. When the result of the Suburana vote was announced by the consul, Pedius, who had reappeared with the other candidates in front of the altar, was the clear winner. Being Caesar's nephew, he was identified as Caesar's preferred candidate and a favourite of the *populares*. Scaeva, who was again taking a keen interest in the proceedings, clapped his hands in excitement on hearing the result. Pedius thought privately that his uncle had little need to bribe members of his home constituency. He thought it more likely money had changed hands to fix the lottery for the *principium* in his favour, ensuring his supporters got to influence proceedings.

Now the voting began in earnest as every other tribe of the assembly had been counted into their pens and their members were already trickling out along the planks to cast their votes. Scaeva had lost sight of Pedius amongst the crowds, and as the rain intensified, he returned through the line of *lictor*s to the cover of the tented antechamber. As more and more citizens cast their votes, crowds began to form around the platforms of the *diribitores* to get an early indication of which candidates were proving most popular amongst the other tribes. There was a rumour that the vote of the Suburana had failed to influence the other tribes, and several of them had candidates favoured by the *optimates*, leading the vote count. Wagers were being laid on the outcome of the election, based on a mounting conviction that the two new *curule* aediles would both be on the *optimates* side of Rome's political divide. Under the darkening sky, supporters of the *optimates* got more anxious that the *solis occasus*, the hour of sunset, would be called from the steps of the senate-house, cancelling the proceedings and robbing them of their victory. After the temporary excitement of Pedius winning the first vote, Scaeva had slunk back to the antechamber to stay out of the rain; rivulets of water were snaking along the ground inside.

He was picking at the food left on the breakfast table when his ears detected a faint rumbling of thunder above the noise of the rain drumming on the roof of the tent; but then there was such a commotion outside he thought he may have been mistaken. He stepped outside, braving the weather to find out what was going on. From between the stout backs of the *lictors*, he saw crowds of angry voters approaching the altar. Supporters of the *populares* had heard the thunder and, led by Pedius himself, were calling out the consul to declare it an inauspicious omen. The *optimates* amongst the assembly denied it and tried to prevent their rivals from making their protest. On hearing the disturbance outside, Pompeius left his inner sanctum and ascended the steps of the altar, into the teeth of the wind and driving rain. Amid the rising tumult, one thought dominated his mind. Having robbed Cato of his chance of a praetorship the previous year by spuriously declaring he had heard a peal of thunder, he dare not deny the *optimates* again, even though there were grounds for doing so. He spread his arms wide and appealed for calm over the heads of the *lictors*, who were now hard-pressed to keep the crowd at bay. A shout went up that someone had drawn a knife. The struggle intensified until a blade flashed and one of the lictors spun around, clutching his neck, blood spurting from between his fingers. He collapsed onto the steps of the altar, his lifeblood pumping across the hem of the consul's toga.

Pompeius looked down at his blood-stained clothing in a state of horror. He raised his arms in a posture of helplessness, then turned to the members of his shocked entourage.

'Stop gawping and somebody help me, you imbeciles!'

Scaeva, who was the closest, stepped forward and carefully lifted the edge of the blood-soaked toga away from Pompeius' still-white tunic. The other servants fussed around unwinding the soiled garment from the personage of the consul before dumping the yards of cloth into Scaeva's arms. As Pompeius was ushered back down the steps and into the shelter of the tent, he shouted over his shoulder.

'Philip, take that back to the *domus* and bring me clean clothes. Run boy. Quick as you can.'

Scaeva glanced back along the covered porticus that led from the city gate to the altar. It was blocked by crowds following the *lictor*s who had arrested the assailant and were bearing their fallen comrade back to the city. His sense of direction told him that if he set off southwards across the expanse of the Campus, once past the row of trees, visible through the mist in the mid-distance, he would, no doubt, arrive before the unmissable bulk of the new theatre. From there, simply follow the paved exterior to the boulevard that led to the *domus*. It would surely be much quicker than trying to retrace the steps the procession had taken that morning. His mind made up, Scaeva set off at a sprint across the sodden turf into the teeth of a gale. Long, wet grass, and heavy ground hampered his progress. The bloodied and saturated toga frequently caught the wind and acted like a sail, holding him back. He paused to look behind him. The porticus and the tents were a fair way distant, but infuriatingly, the row of trees he was heading for appeared little closer. He lowered his head against the wind and carried on, squelching through the marshy ground until he realised, to his consternation, the trees were no longer visible. The mist rolled down around him from the Mons Janiculum across the Tiber. He glanced all around, and a frisson of panic ran through his body; there was not a single object or shape to be seen in any direction.

He realised with a sinking feeling in the pit of his stomach that he had changed direction several times as he picked his way through what had become a bog. Now, he stood ankle-deep in mud, he had no idea of which way to turn. At least the rain had abated, and the wind was stilled. At that moment, he heard voices. Yes, there they were again. He lifted his feet one-by-one out of the clinging mud, leaving one of his sandals behind, and made his way towards the sounds until the heavy ground gave way to a flag-stoned pavement.

There were people just ahead of him coming out from under the vaulted archways of a building after sheltering from the storm; some of them giving his dishevelled appearance disparaging looks. Scaeva lifted his gaze above the alcoves. The massive height of the Theatre of Pompeius Magnus, topped by a colonnaded gallery, towered above him. Above that, built atop a huge buttress at the mid-point of the auditorium, the Temple of Venus Victrix was still shrouded in swirling mist. He offered a silent prayer to the goddess, kicked off his other sandal, and sprinted through the puddles of the wide-open terrace surrounding the theatre. Along the boulevard he ran and didn't stop until he arrived panting, on the magnificent *vestibulum* of the Domus Rostrata.

There he paused to catch his breath and push his plastered hair off his forehead before attracting the attention of the Janitor, with liberal use of the heavy iron ring of the ornate, lion-headed brass door knocker. The curses of Demetrios echoed loudly as he came through the *atrium* to answer the door. He clearly was not expecting visitors, with Pompeius attending the elections and not expected home until late. As soon as the door was opened, Scaeva, who had no time to lose, pushed past the startled servant and into the *atrium*. He was met by Julia, who stared at the rain-sodden figure in abject horror. It was not the sight of Scaeva that horrified her, but the blood-stained toga belonging to her husband that he carried.

Putting her hands to her cheeks, eyes wide open, she shouted the word 'No' in a long piercing agonised scream that echoed around the *atrium* and brought all the household running to the scene. Her whole body shook. Her shoulders heaved. She sank to her knees and dropped her arms to her sides, hugging her swollen tummy. A dark patch appeared in her lap and spread downwards, showing a deep red through her white cotton *stola*. Julia looked imploringly at the young boy, slowly shaking her head and wailing. She fainted and toppled over on her side, unconscious. Golden tresses splaying in waves across the mosaic floor. Her attendant ladies, with the help of Demetrios, carried the limp body of his beloved Julia to her room, leaving a dark pool of blood by the pure white marble *impluvium*, and ugly red smears across the floor. Scaeva threw the bloodied toga of Pompeius to the ground and ran to his *cubiculum*. Hurling himself face down upon his mattress, his body trembling, he sobbed uncontrollably.

XXV

November 55 BC
Rome

Scaeva's intense relief when Julia regained consciousness had been tempered by the order from her physician that she must have complete rest and no visitors. There was to be peace and quietness throughout the house, which meant that Scaeva and Philostratos had to leave. Pompeius had cancelled all forthcoming engagements and had spent each day and night since that fateful day of the election, ensconced with his wife in her private quarters. He had declared that, for the sake of everyone, it would be better for Philip and his tutor to move to the house his father had built on the Carinae in the year he became consul. Scaeva had been distraught, believing he had caused Julia's collapse, but he also blamed Pompeius for not considering the consequences of his wife seeing his blood-stained clothing, especially as elections in Rome were becoming increasingly violent affairs.

However, Pompeius had been at pains to explain to him that no blame should be apportioned, and that Philip would have fewer distractions from his studies.

He went on to say. 'My father's house on the Carinae would be most suitable for you to prepare for your studies.

When the time comes, you will be closer to the school of Orbilius. Furthermore, there is an extensive library there. The books my father took from Asculum, when he defeated the rebels during the civil war, are all there at the Carinae. The senate was displeased that he failed to share the booty, but they waited until he died before prosecuting me for it. So, you might at least gain some use from them.'

The Carinae was an exclusive neighbourhood of Rome, amongst the foothills of the western spur of the Esquiline Hill. The *domus* of Lucius Marcius Philippus was also located there, so the boy would be much closer to Octavius, who had taken to him at that first meeting and was keen to seek his company on subsequent visits. On the day of their departure from the Domus Rostrata, Scaeva's sadness at leaving Julia blotted out all thoughts for his future. Not being allowed to say goodbye and not knowing when he would even see her again caused him a pain in his heart, the like of which he had never before experienced. Knowing that her last vision of him was one of such horror made it even worse. Could she ever forgive him for giving her the shock that caused her to lose her unborn child? Would he ever forget the sight of her limp body being carried across the *atrium,* leaving a trail of blood across the mosaic floor?

Pompeius was right. The only way for Scaeva to drive those terrible thoughts and sights from his mind and its eye was to throw himself into his lessons. He convinced himself that if he studied hard and did well at school in Rome, he would put Caspar in his place on his return to Prydain.

Scaeva and Philostratos made an odd couple, bound together from opposite ends of the known world. The old

Greek with his wealth of learning, and the young Briton, with everything to learn. Because they both had a working knowledge of the language that was spoken in various dialects from the Alpes to Oceanus Britannicus, there was a common base from which to build. Despite his advanced age and great learning, Philostratos was eager to absorb anything Scaeva could tell him about the 'dreamers' that his gallic library slaves in Alexandria had often referred to. Beyond the episode of the prophecies, Scaeva, who now wished he had paid more attention during his schooling with the druids, wasn't able to add much to what his mentor was already aware of. He could not throw any light on the burning questions in the mind of the Greek scholar. But Philostratos did not expect to learn anything from the boy that could explain the meaning of the prophecies. More intriguing were the reasons for the similarity between the symbols he had first seen east of Judea, and the runes deployed by the dreamers of Britannia.

Prior to Scaeva's arrival at the Domus Rostrata, Philostratos had spent much of his abundant spare time scouring the archives in the *Tabularium* for items of particular personal interest. Once he had been charged with the boy's education, he abandoned his private interest in the archives of the city and set about obtaining the books necessary to prepare the boy for formal schooling. He made an inventory for himself, cataloguing the contents of the library, looted from Asculum during the social wars, now at the house of the late Gnaeus Pompeius Strabo. But it bore nothing of interest to himself, nor anything of use to his pupil. Consequently, much of their time together was spent in sniffing distance of the fish market, scouring the bookshops along the Argiletum. Philostratos was eventually informed by a shop owner that the type of volume he was looking for— works of the great Greek poets, dramatists, and philosophers—was more likely to be found in the private libraries of wealthy Roman citizens. The frustration of Philostratos' fruitless search turned to barely contained anger as he turned and stomped away. He trudged back amongst the scaffolding and boarded-up marble columns of Paullus' renovations of the Basilica Aemilia, still muttering to himself in several languages as he emerged between wooden shopfronts into the weak winter sunlight of the forum.

'Wait for me, I can't understand what you're saying,' wailed Scaeva, tugging at his elbow and preventing him from bumping into a woman engaged in selecting fabrics from a stall.

'I know all about the wealthy Roman citizens and their books,' said the old man angrily. 'Aemilius Paullus looted the royal library of Macedonia over one hundred years ago. His sons brought it back to Rome but what has happened to the books? Before that, during their wars with Carthage, Marcellus sacked and looted Syracuse, killing most of the inhabitants, including Archimedes, who must have been approaching his eightieth year. Those worthless creatures emptied the library and took away the books, the cream of Greek literature. Where are they now?'

'But wasn't that all a long time ago?' said Scaeva, not really understanding. 'And who was Archimedes?'

'And still it goes on,' he complained, ignoring Scaeva's question and bustling on past the shop fronts, not caring whose path he crossed, drawing affronted looks and the odd ripe comment from the citizens of the city. 'More recently, that monster Sulla, after he had captured Athens, he carried away the library of Apellicon of Teos and brought it here to Rome. I've seen the shabby copies of Aristotle and Theophrastus, available in the bookstores. Full of errors they are. Then there was Lucullus, he looted the library of Mithridates at Pontus. I've heard he brought it back to his villa at Tusculum where his son now drools over it, showing it off to his indifferent and unknowing high-born friends, no doubt.'

'Couldn't you write a letter to him and ask permission to visit?' said Scaeva in all innocence, but still proud to demonstrate that he understood what a letter was and what it was for.

The old man's bushy eyebrows shot up at the boy's sudden and uncharacteristic display of precociousness.

'I couldn't bring myself to touch them, stained with the blood of so many innocents. The books in my library at Alexandria were all obtained by honest and peaceful means.' Philostratos blushed lightly at the knowledge of how the original manuscripts of the plays of Aeschylus, Euripides, and Sophocles had been obtained, then continued quickly. 'And besides, I have no one in Rome to vouch for me, now that Pompeius is not to be disturbed.'

'But has Pompeius had any visitors that might remember you?' asked Scaeva, gaining confidence as his questions were no longer being dismissed.

Philostratos stopped, turned, and glared down at the boy. 'And why should any of Pompeius' visitors remember me?'

Scaeva's bubble of confidence burst in an instant. The old Greek hurried on, heading out of the forum until he suddenly stopped again, under the newly restored arch of Fabianus, and thought for a moment.

'Come to think of it, you might be right. Memory is a remarkable thing. I can remember things from half a lifetime ago as if they occurred only recently, but sometimes I struggle to remember recent events. Pompeius held a *convivium* in honour of Auletes the first evening we arrived in Rome. Cicero, an ex-consul was there with a friend of his whose name I do not recall, but I do recall overhearing him mentioning Cicero's garden and library. It was while we were walking through the *peristylium*. Cicero and his friend were engaged in a hushed conversation that I was particularly interested in. More so than the conversation I was having with someone else. Yes, it's all coming back now.'

The odd couple hurried through the archway and out of the forum, passing behind the headquarters of the *Pontifex Maximus*, then swiftly along the Via Sacre and its luxurious shopping emporiums, to the now-familiar route home. The old man's pace slackened past the temple of Jupiter the Sustainer at the foot of the Palatine, but Scaeva, still feeling chastened, was careful to remain in his wake. Then came the long ascent of the Clivus Pullius to the neighbourhood of the wealthiest and most influential families of Rome, where they both felt out of place, despite having a house full of servants to attend them. Philostratos had been struggling the last part of the way and was quite out of breath by the time they reached the *vestibulum*. It was south-facing and offered a fine view along the valley between the Palatine and Caelian Hills. The distant sound of a large gathering floated on a light breeze. Then a great roar built up to a crescendo that barrelled up the valley towards them. It emanated from a packed crowd in the

Circus Maximus, of which the upper tiers of one end were visible in the distance.

Scaeva gave his mentor a questioning look.

'The *Ludi Circenses*,' puffed the old Greek between breaths. 'A form of entertainment for which I have not the least taste. The games have no novelty, no variety, nothing, in short, that anyone would want to see twice. I am astonished that so many thousands of grown men should be possessed again and again with a childish passion to look at galloping horses pulling slaves standing in chariots.' The old man was clearly in a mood to complain about the habits of the Romans. His earlier diatribe condemning the looting of libraries had now transmuted into a denouncement of their leisure activities, but the mention of horses and chariots as entertainment intrigued the young Briton,

'What sort of games are they?'

Ignoring the question, Philostratos warmed to his theme. 'If indeed these men were attracted by the swiftness of the horses or the skill of the slaves, we could account for such passions. But it is a scrap of cloth they favour, a scrap of cloth that captivates them.'

'A scrap of cloth? I don't understand.'

'Neither do I,' replied Philostratos, mistakenly thinking that Scaeva knew what he was talking about. 'And what is even more unfathomable is that if during the running, the racers were to exchange colours, their supporters would change sides, and instantly abandon the very drivers and horses whom they were just before recognising from afar, and loudly cheering by name. And that,' concluded the Greek, just as the janitor came to open the front door, 'is the level of favour, of weighty influence, that one cheap tunic has with not only the vulgar herd who are more worthless than the tunics they wear but with certain people of gravitas!'

Philostratos, having recovered his breath, brushed past the janitor and scuttled across the *atrium* to the dusty *tablinum* of Strabo, where he kept his writing implements. He was still muttering while he selected a sheet of papyrus from a drawer in the writing desk and lifted the brass, split-nibbed pen from its holder on a matching brass inkwell.

'When I observe such men so insatiably fond of an entertainment that is so silly, so low, so uninteresting, and so common, I congratulate myself that I am insensible to these dubious pleasures and am glad to devote my time, which others throw away upon the idlest employment, to literature.'

And with that, Philostratos began to pen a letter to Marcus Tullius Cicero, reminding him of their meeting at the house of Pompeius Magnus. He made sure to mention his previous employment, that of chief librarian at the Great Library of Alexandria—a detail Philostratos considered would prove irresistible to the senator—and requested permission to examine his library with an option to borrow volumes of interest.

XXVI

May 54 BC
Rome

Cicero had received the letter from Philostratos with a great deal of excitement, seeing it as a second opportunity to cultivate a relationship with so great a scholar after having met him briefly the previous year. He had even written to his friend Lucullus asking for high-quality copies from his library at Tusculum of any volumes the scholarly Greek had requested that Cicero did not already own. Consequently, with a full set of texts at his disposal, and having had the benefit of, and the desire to utilise, the expert tutelage of one of the most learned men of his age, Scaeva was well prepared for his first day.

The credentials of the new boy at school were impressive. The old Greek *paedagogus* who had escorted him on his first day was said to be the tutor of the King of Egypt's daughter. Not everyone believed that. Another claim was that he was the son of a king of Britannia, sent to Rome by none other than Julius Caesar, who had adopted him into the familia Julii Caesares. Even fewer believed that one, and no one at all believed he was protected by a Celtic horse goddess, even though the Matrona had introduced him to the class as Julius Philippus, and the boys knew enough Greek to understand what his cognomen meant.

Had Octavius not befriended two other boys below his station, and consequently lost credibility amongst his classmates, his claims about the connections of the new pupil would have been readily accepted. Octavius had told the other boys in his class about the boy from Britannia, who was living at the house of the consul. He had met him several times when visiting his mother's cousin Julia, who was now pregnant again, after suffering a miscarriage the previous year. He had also told them that the boy would be joining the class as soon as he could converse in Latin and read from Homer. And he had told them that when he did, he would join his gang, comprising just the two other new boys, Vipsanius, and Horatius, and that the rest of the class, led by his imperious cousin Lucius Pinarius, had better watch out.

After giving a final comforting smile, the Matrona turned and left the room, leaving Scaeva standing next to Orbilius facing his new classmates. The blank, challenging stares of Pinarius and his gang of devotees, lackeys, and toadies, were in stark contrast to the other three boys. The beaming smile of Octavius, the awestruck expression of Horatius, and a rather questioning look on the face of Vipsanius.

'Let Julius Philippus demonstrate his knowledge of Hesiod,' declared Orbilius, stepping towards a bookshelf and returning with a volume. This was his method of assessing the competence of new boys. He placed it on the lectern that stood on a small dais at the front of the class, opened it on a particular page and stepped aside, motioning for Scaeva to step up and read the selected text. 'Are you familiar with the Wedding of Ceyx?' he asked matter-of-factly.

'I am sir,' replied Scaeva, whose state of high anxiety evaporated the moment the *grammarian* spoke the title.

The Wedding of Ceyx was one of Philostratos' favourite poems to teach. It contained many riddles that he fondly remembered explaining to Cleopatra and was one of the first works he had taught Scaeva. Scaeva had learned the Greek and Latin alphabets side by side and was equally proficient, for his age, at reading both. He traced his index finger along the Greek text and pronounced the words slowly but confidently. The hostile expressions of Pinarius and his gang— which had been replaced by smirks when the new boy had been called to the lectern—were now overtaken by expressions of disbelief. Scaeva continued steadily until Orbilius raised his hand, signalling him to stop.

He turned to the class and said, 'Here we have a paradox. Having satisfied their hunger at the wedding feast, and then gone on to gather, roast, and eat acorns, why did Heracles declare the guests were devouring the mothers of their mothers?' Three rows of blank faces made up a disappointing response. 'Will no one answer? Then I shall hint at the correct answer: what infant, at birth, devours its parents?'

Pinarius' hand shot up. 'Sir, the infant is fire.'

'Precisely! And the parent is of course, wood. So now perhaps, Pinarius, you can also tell us how the riddle of the fire pertains to the riddle of the acorns?' Pinarius' hand returned sheepishly to his lap. Orbilius turned to face the lectern. 'And you, Julius Philippus? You clearly have an understanding of Hesiod.'

'The guests at the banquet were Pelasgians, sir,' answered Scaeva hesitantly.

'Go on,' replied Orbilius, 'you are on the right track.'

'The Greeks regarded the Pelasgians as the first men. It was believed they were hewn from oak trees. Roasting acorns in a fire and eating them could be seen as devouring their grandmothers, sir.'

'Excellent!' beamed the *grammarian*. 'You have indeed been well-schooled. Take your place in the front row, next to Horatius.'

Orbilius liked to arrange the pupils in his class with the younger or newest boys at the front, where he could monitor them more closely, and the older boys in the rows behind. When Octavius had joined the class, there were no more spaces on the front benches, so his new companions were all required to shuffle back one row. Not that he had found his new classmates companionable, being the youngest by nearly two years. This meant that when Horatius and Vipsanius came to join the class, they were both as delighted to be seated next to Octavius, as he was to be with boys nearer his own age. Now, the long-awaited new boy had arrived, and the three gave him warm welcoming smiles as he took his place on the front bench, directly in front of Pinarius. For the rest of the day, Scaeva sensed the beady eyes of the young patrician just behind him, burning with resentment.

When the school day was over, discipline was maintained until all the boys had left the building. First to leave by the door at the back of the classroom were the older boys on the back benches, followed in single file by the rest of the class, with the youngest being the last to leave. As the youngsters filed past Aphrodisius in his customary position, seeing the boys safely off the premises, Horatius' father was waiting for them in his usual place across the road. He was standing outside the barber's shop, passing the time of day with the *tonsor*, who was keeping an eye out for likely customers. Seeing his son and his friends emerge from the schoolhouse, he bid his companion a scant goodbye and strode across the street to meet the boys.

Pointing to Scaeva, he remarked, 'So you must be the wild boy from Britannia Octavius has been telling us about.' His eyes lit up at the gilt locket on the gold chain around his neck. 'Nice *bulla*, I'll wager I could make a *denarius* or three in commission for something as valuable as that.'

'It was a gift from Caesar, sir,' replied Scaeva.

'Ooh, it talks,' jibed the auctioneer, whose jocular manner whilst conducting business at his office in the forum proved popular with the bidders. 'And so polite too! No need for sir, call me Felix, everyone else does,' and turning to Horatius with a wink, 'except you, my son.'

Horatius beamed back at his father.

'Now gather round boys. I've got a real treat for you. I've got five tickets for the first day of the *Ludi Apollinares*, three rows back, right on the turning post.'

Scaeva joined the other boys in their cries of excitement, not knowing what he had been invited to. He understood the Games of Apollo but didn't get the reference to a turning post.

They all thanked Felix, who replied, 'Don't thank me boys, they are company tickets. It was just my turn to have them.' Then, Octavius, Vipsanius, and Scaeva headed for home towards the Carinae, while Horatio and his father departed in the opposite direction.

'Are these games of Apollo anything to do with chariot racing at the Circus Maximus?' asked Scaeva.

'You bet they are,' answered Octavius, still in a state of excitement. 'There's loads of other stuff going on too, bear hunts, gladiator games, but not the ones where anyone gets killed. Boring stuff like plays as well. Felix is a massive fan of the Reds, so we are too, aren't we, Vipsanius?'

'Up the Reds,' cried Vipsanius, giving a vigorous clenched fist salute.

The scornful words of his mentor, Philostratos, came to mind and Scaeva considered declining the invitation. But the thought of war machines racing each other in front of a vast cheering crowd was a spectacle that excited him. Just then, a group of older boys stepped out in front of them from an alleyway beside a taberna. They formed a line of four across the pavement. Scaeva recognised them from amongst the boys that had sat behind him in the classroom. The two in the middle parted and Pinarius stepped out from behind them. Now standing in front of his gang, he was quite small for his age but being three years older than his cousin was still taller and stronger.

He blocked Octavius' path, pointed at Scaeva and sneered at his younger cousin. 'Well, big ears, so much for your blue-faced savage! This imposter is nothing but a trained parrot. And as for living in the house of last year's consul, I'd wager Pompeius Magnus has never set eyes on him.'

'Then you'd lose your bet.' Vipsanius pushed himself between the two cousins and stood face-to-face with Pinarius. The handsome Roman nose and deep-set brow of the *pleb* inches away from the pointed beak and high brow of the patrician. Although the same age as Octavius, Vipsanius matched Pinarius in stature. 'I can bear witness to the fact that Julius Philippus is known to Pompeius Magnus. I saw it with my own eyes on the day of the election last year; the one where one of the consul's *lictor*s was killed.'

'What did you see?' demanded Pinarius, his spine stiffening.

'I was playing on the Rostra and watched the consul's procession through the forum. I saw Julius Philippus, he was directly behind Magnus, leading his attendants.'

Pinarius hesitated for a moment while formulating a challenge to the statement, and then one of his gang members, the tallest, stepped in and took his place, staring down at Vipsanius. It was not fear of a dangerous adversary that made the younger boy grimace, but the sight of the boils on his cheeks and forehead, and the smell of his breath. Gnaeus Domitius Ahenobarbus was the oldest boy in the class, but far from the brightest. He had long been in awe of the imperious persona of the youngest member of the most ancient family in Rome and felt honoured to be permitted to act as his minder.

'Who gives a toss about Magnus, you *pleb*,' snarled Domitius. 'My father is consul now and that's what counts.'

At that moment, Scaeva took a hand and stepped forward, shoulder-to-shoulder with Vipsanius. He looked Pinarius in the eye and said calmly, 'If you have a grievance of me, tell me to my face. Your eyes have been sending daggers into my back all morning.'

'I will tell you my grievance,' replied the patrician, echoing Scaeva's moderate tones, but emphasizing his superior pronunciation. 'You have no place here in Rome other than the Cloaca. I don't care where you are from, you are just like the two other *pleb*s that recently infested our place of learning. Just look at that cheap bauble you wear around your neck, you can purchase them anywhere.' He then lifted his own ornament, a lustrous yellow metallic shape resembling a tripod, worn smooth with age and strung on a soft leather lace around his neck. 'This is the sign of a pure Roman. This is older than anything else in Rome. It has been in my family since before the kings, even before Hercules came amongst us.'

'You shouldn't be wearing that before your toga day,' chimed Octavius, stepping forward between his friends. 'You should wear your *bulla* like the rest of us until you come of age.'

Domitius turned on Octavius and pushed him heavily in the chest. 'Shut your mouth big ears. You don't tell a Pinarii what to do.'

Vipsanius, whose anger had been coming to the boil, shoved Domitius while hooking his foot around his ankle, sending him flat on his back. Pinarius swung a punch that Vipsanius parried, Scaeva then leapt onto Pinarius' back, pinning his arms by his sides and the other three older boys in the gang piled into the fray. Vipsanius fought back like a wild animal, kicking out and throwing punches in all directions while Octavius sat on Domitius, trying to restrain him on the pavement. Scaeva and Pinarius rolled over into the street, each struggling to get a hold of the other. The violent disturbance brought citizens out of the *tabernae,* but no one intervened to prevent the three older boys from overcoming the valiant Vipsanius. Nor did they stop Domitius, using his superior size and strength to turn the tables on Octavius, until a voice they all recognised called upon them to cease before the younger boys took too much punishment. The voice was that of Aphrodisius. He may have been a slave, but he was the eyes and ears of their *grammarian*.

'Stop this now, all of you, or do you want to answer to Orbilius tomorrow?' The three released Vipsanius from their holds on him. He was bleeding from the mouth and nose, but so were two of his adversaries. Domitius, who had been twisting Octavius' arm up his back, let him go, and Scaeva and Pinarius rose from the dust in the street, still glaring at each other. It was to Pinarius that Aphrodisius directed his next question. 'I may be a slave, but do you think I am as deaf as the busts of the poets in the corridor? I heard you planning to waylay these young boys as you left the schoolhouse. So, if questioned by Orbilius as to who was responsible, I will have to tell him the truth. But go now and I will say nothing.'

'When my father, the consul, hears of this,' rasped Domitius, 'he will have you flogged.'

Aphrodisius bore the threat unflinchingly as Pinarius spat a final warning at Scaeva. 'You haven't seen the last of this, you savage,' before leading his bloodied band away, around a corner and out of sight.

'Now you three, get home quickly,' ordered Aphrodisius before turning and hurrying away in the direction from which he had come.

'I really enjoyed that,' declared Vipsanius with a bloody grin. 'I've been wanting to punch those fuckers for weeks.'

Scaeva, who was thinking, not for the first time since he had first met Octavius, of his dear brother Ebracus, simply smiled.

'Felix called you the wild boy from Britannia. Orbilius refers to you as Julius Philippus. Philippus is Greek for horse lover, and you have the image of a horse engraved on your *bulla*. Shall we call you wild horse?' joked Vipsanius.

'I'll answer to Julius Philippus in the classroom. Pompeius prefers to call me Philip, but to my friends I am Scaeva.'

'I think wild horse is a more fitting cognomen for you, Vipsanius,' interjected Octavius. 'That would be something like agrios hippos in Greek.'

'That's no good. If I'm to have a cognomen, it has to be just one word.'

'Then why not shorten it to one word, Agrippa?' suggested Scaeva.

'Agrippa,' repeated Vipsanius. 'Yes, I like it.'

XXVII

6th July 54 BC
Rome

The mid-summer sun beat down on the heads of the crowds as they poured out of their red-brick *insulae* in Suburra and made their way along the wide boulevard between the Palatine and Caelian Hills, towards the Circus Maximus. Scaeva had pleaded with Philostratos to allow him to join his school friends at the races. His mentor only relented when Scaeva argued the chariot races that took place at the Circus were an integral part of the Games of Apollo; and that his exposure to Roman culture, as desired by Caesar in his letter to Pompeius, should include the festivities, as well as academic studies.

Consequently, Scaeva found himself jostling amongst the noisy throng in the boulevard, alongside Octavius, Agrippa and Horatius, under the watchful eye of Felix. Almost everyone, both men, and women, wore garlands in their hair in colours according to the faction they supported. Felix bought one each for the boys from one of the many street vendors that lined the route, to go with the red sash made for them by his wife, worn across their tunics. In the houses on the hills to either side of them, whole families feasted on the forecourts of their homes, as was the custom. Not so with the *domus* that faced onto the boulevard. The doors were locked shut, but the *tabernae* on either side of them spread trestle tables across the entrances to display faction-related merchandise; from coloured ribbons to curse tablets. In between were the wide-open doors of *popinae,* where men were drinking and gambling at dice tables in the shadows of the cool interiors. Many of these establishments offered street food, and hungry customers crowded around the marble-topped counters that lined the frontages. The aroma of the wine and ale mingled with the smells of cooking and made a heady mixture in the simmering heat. The constant chanting of the rival factions surrounding him was a world away from the incantations of the druids back home, but every bit as mesmerising, against the background of the buzz from within the Circus as they drew near.

A gaunt figure sat cross-legged on a sack between two trestle tables, gesticulating to the crowds as they passed. He suddenly caught Scaeva's eye and cried out to him.

'Beware the Primus, Beware the Primus!'

'Take no notice of him,' said Felix in a knowing tone, tapping the side of his nose with his forefinger as they passed the old man by. 'You'll see plenty more the like of him along the way. It's his way of telling you not to back the favourite in the first race. Stop and talk to him and he'll probably try to flog you a few tips. I see his kind every day in the forum, beware this, beware that, they kid you they can tell your future, but on race days they just make a few *sesterces* on the side.'

'He might not have meant the first race,' ventured Horatius. 'He could have been referring to the race offering the biggest purse.'

'Good point, my son, well made,' replied Felix. 'In fact, I have it from informed sources that the biggest purse of the day will go to the third string of the Reds. They've got this new apprentice, Ramirez. I've watched him in practice. He handles a *quadriga* better than veterans like Lanfranco, and I have inside information ...' and again he tapped the side of his nose, lowering his voice and looking secretively from side-to-side, '... that he will have Raffingora and Vorvados as his inside pairing in the big race of the day. Those two greys hug the *spina* like a barnacle on a boat's bottom and they can take the turning posts in the blink of an eye. I've heard that the plan is for him to take an early lead and set a strong pace for Lanfranco to take up the running on the last lap. But if Ramirez gets to the front on the inside, I'll wager no one will catch him.'

The elevated timber stands at the curved end of the Circus Maximus loomed before them over the heads of the chanting race fans, but the banter between the factions was good-natured.

Scaeva asked Felix, 'The colours everyone is wearing, do they denote different tribes or families?'

'That's a good question, young man, to which the answer is most definitely no. The four colours themselves were originally intended to signify the four seasons of the year.'

'So what season is Red?'

Felix thought for a moment. 'To be honest, I really don't know. Never given it a thought.'

'Then why do you support the Red faction?'

'Because my father did. Simple as that. He used to bring me here when I was just a boy. He even named me after one of the Red's greatest charioteers. It was tragic what happened to him.'

'What did happen to him?' asked Scaeva.

'Died in a shipwreck, he did. Right in front of my own eyes, here at the Circus. It was when I was about fifteen years of age. He was overtaking the leader on the final lap when the wheels clashed and came off. The other driver survived, but Felix was pulled from his chariot by the reins wrapped around his waist. He carried a knife tucked into his boot, like all the other drivers, but he couldn't cut himself free in time. He was trampled by the other teams in the home straight. The whole of Rome turned out for his funeral in the Campus Martius. Not just the Reds, but the Blues, Greens, and the Whites, too.'

'You must have been really upset,' Scaeva tried to sympathise despite not understanding Felix's use of slang for when chariots crashed.

'I was, but not as much as an old school friend of mine. He threw himself on the funeral pyre.'

Although Felix didn't give the nudge or wink that usually accompanied one of his comical stories, Scaeva wasn't sure if he was joking or not.

The crowd thickened as they approached the Circus and formed jostling queues at the iron gates where Felix showed the slave his five tickets to gain entry. The entire building at street level comprised *tabernae* and *popinae,* with narrow entrances in between giving access to wooden flights of steps leading up to the tiers of benches at the curved end of the vast stadium. When they emerged from the cool shadows into the bright sunlight at the top of the flights, Scaeva gasped at the scene before him. The sand-covered track below him ran straight as an arrow into the distance, divided down the middle by a low, solid wooden spine between two stone pillars. At the far end, a row of high gates was visible through the shimmering heat haze. Across the other side of the track, behind the stadium, people were crowding into every vantage point between the villas dotting the lower slopes of the Palatine Hill. The patios and verandas of the villas were full of garlanded families feasting and celebrating the games.

Scaeva took in the vast panorama. A similar spectacle was playing out across the gentler contours of the Aventine behind him. Above him, linen sunshades, the size of ship's sails, had been drawn across horizontal booms by pulleys. The shades continued all around the high banked ticketed seating that topped the *tabernae*. The colours of the factions were evenly spread amongst spectators there; but lining the long straights, packed tightly in the space between the backs of the *tabernae* and the trackside, the difference was stark. It was clear, on the Palatine side, that the Blue faction favoured the end nearest the gates and the Greens congregated closer to Scaeva's viewpoint. On the Aventine side, the Reds were closest to him, and the Whites faced across from the Blues at the far end of the track.

'Come on up here Scaeva, the parade is about to start.' It was Horatius calling him.

During the few moments he had spent taking in his spectacular surroundings, the others had taken their seats on the benches five rows back from the rail. He turned and sprinted up the steps of the aisle to join his friends, gratefully accepting a cushion offered by a slave, before taking his place next to Octavius in the last space on the bench by the stairway. Just as he took his seat, a fanfare sounded, and a great cheer emitted from the crowd.

Having made its way from the Capitoline Hill through the city, the *pompa circensis,* the procession that preceded the races, arrived at the gates of the Circus Maximus. Cheers rolled down the straight as it passed by the spectators at the far end; first, amongst the supporters of the Whites, then the Reds, and then, past the spectators around Scaeva and his friends, who stood and politely applauded. At the head of the procession, in a gilded biga drawn by two white stallions, was the urban *praetor* who staged not just the races, but all the festivities of the *Ludi Apollinares*. He was followed by the sons of Roman Equestrians nearing manhood and of an age to take part in the ceremony. They rode on horseback whilst the youth of the lower born, destined to serve in the infantry, went on foot behind them, waving back at the cheering spectators and clearly enjoying their moment. Then came the leather helmeted charioteers wearing the colours of their faction sewn into short tunics padded at the shoulder. They were riding in conventional chariots. The most experienced in each faction drove horses four abreast in a *quadriga,* the more popular of them acknowledging the wild applause from their supporters. The reserve drivers followed in two-horse *bigae*, while the apprentices rode behind on unyoked horses.

'Look, there at the back, that's Ramirez,' shouted Felix, pointing excitedly.

Scaeva turned his attention to the rear of the mounted charioteers of the Reds and picked out the confident young man, whose long, jet-black hair emerged from the confines of his tight-fitting helmet and fanned out across the back of his neck. He had the same swarthy look about him as the three slaves of Caesar, who had accompanied him on part of his long journey. The horses were remarkable too; it wasn't just the ribbons in the colour of their faction braided into the hair of their manes and tails. They were sleek and slender of leg, a different breed to the animals at home who pulled the heavy ploughs and carried two-man war chariots into battle.

After the charioteers came all the other contestants taking their part in the games, the athletes, and wrestlers, all naked except for white loincloths. Behind the athletes came musicians and dancers. The musicians played their short flutes and strummed at the strings of their ivory lyres. The dancers brandished their short spears. They wore bronze helmets, adorned with plumes and crests, and red tunics belted with bronze ties from which hung swords. Each division of dancers, men, youths, and boys followed the actions of their captain's rapid warlike movements in unison. Out of all these spectacles worthy of applause and appreciation, the crowd reserved the most clamour for what came next. It came as an enormous surprise to Scaeva, not only because it was so unexpected, following on from the sobriety of what had gone before, but because he recognised the significance of it from his lessons in Greek culture from Philostratos.

Following the glorious costumes and precise synchronised movements of the military dancers came an unruly host; some dressed in shaggy tunics and mantles of flowers, others impersonating satyrs wearing nothing but girdles and goatskins over their otherwise naked bodies. They bore hideous masks with bristling hair. They skipped and jumped energetically, mocking and mimicking the serious movements of the armed dancers that preceded them, invoking howls of amusement from the packed crowds of spectators. Scaeva recognised their antics from an illustration in one of his books depicting a dance performed by the chorus of some ancient Greek dramas that was in keeping with the sexually rampant, insolent, and rather cowardly nature of the satyrs.

Yet more musicians followed, playing flutes and lyres, then came the priests and censer carriers bearing ornate vessels of silver and gold that oscillated on chains. Burning incense wafted up in the hot air, filling yet another of the young Briton's saturated senses. Finally, the most awe-inspiring spectacle of all. At the end of the procession, carried high on the shoulders of men came images of the mighty gods of Rome. Some of them Scaeva recognised from the statues he had seen adorning their temples. Jupiter, Juno, Minerva, and Neptune, but there were so many others. Not just the twelve that Philostratos had taught him were recognised by the Greeks, but many, many more. gods and demi-gods, nymphs, muses and graces, all of them, like his own Epona, in human form.

The wild cheering and applause from the massed audience, both inside the stadium and outside on the hillsides, continued until the last of the god-like images had completed its circuit of the course, and disappeared through the gates. A hush then fell on the crowd as sacrificial oxen were led into the far end of the stadium, but it was too far away for Scaeva to see the details. Priests purified the beasts with water before they were killed by their assistants. Pieces were cut from the carcasses and burnt on altars, and wine was poured over them by other ceremonial officials. The altars and the remains of the creatures were dragged away, and a hum of expectation replaced the silence.

The first race, Felix explained, was not a competitive affair, but was run in accordance with the custom of the Greeks in the long-distant past. It involved the same configuration of runners as took part in the opening procession; a mixture of four and two-horse chariots, as well as solo riders on horseback. In Rome these days, it served the purpose of allowing the horses to limber up their muscles to prepare for the serious business of the afternoon. On the sound of another fanfare, the entire racing contingent of each faction, man and beast, came through the open starting gates and cantered a complete circuit, acknowledging the support or ignoring the insults as they passed each concentration of spectators. The spectators, too, took this opportunity to limber up their voices. Chants and songs of support for their own factions, and ribald ditties, aimed at their opponents, filled the air.

With the preliminaries over, a buzz of excitement, quite unlike anything that had gone before, arose from the packed enclosures. The track slaves, equipped with rakes and water sprinklers, prepared the surface ready for the first competitive race of the day. Octavius, who was sharing a program with Scaeva, explained that the first six races were heats, each comprising four teams of two-horse chariots, two from one faction against two from another, and the winners of each heat would compete in a six-chariot final later in the day.

Yet another fanfare announced the first of the *bigae* heats. The last of the hollow notes rolled across the city followed by a pregnant silence; then came the sound of the spring-loaded starting gates, and the biggest roar of the day greeted the four pairs of horses that leapt out of the stalls.

Scaeva viewed them head-on from his position closer to the far end of the track where it curved round one hundred and eighty degrees. It was difficult to tell who was leading, but just a few moments later they were halfway down the straight, and the Blue team was ahead. The only rule in the heats is that the riders steer a straight course until they reach the turning post at the far end of the *spina* on the first circuit.

The Blue driver, first to the end of the straight, directly beneath Scaeva's vantage point, cracked his whip to the right of his horses' blue-ribboned heads and sent them careering off to the left into the bend, taking the ground of the two Green teams on his inside. With his feet braced against the inside of his flimsy wicker wood chariot, the driver threw his weight to the left. The reins of both horses were tied around his waist, and the chariot skidded sideways to the right, scribing an arc in the sand around the curved end of the stadium. Both the Green drivers had to take a big pull on their reins as they went into the hairpin bend and the second blue driver, holding his mounts up at the rear, was clear to take the bend unimpeded. As the lead Blue driver straightened up against the *spina* for the return trip down the track, the Green faction supporters launched a fusillade of curse tablets, most of the small squares of lead falling short of their target. The field raced back again towards Scaeva on the second lap and the Blue driver was still ahead, skilfully blocking all attempts of the Greens to go past. He kept up this tactic until his brave horses tired, then first one, then the other of the Green drivers passed him on the home straight of the fifth of the seven laps. The field headed out on the last lap. The early leader had dropped back to last place, and it was the second Blue driver, who had been conserving his horses, that swooped up the outside, overtaking both Green drivers, whose teams were flagging. He then attempted the same tactic at the final bend as his teammate had executed at the first, but now, the track was churned up. A wheel of the flimsy chariot hit a rut and overturned as it skidded sideways, hurling the driver to the ground. Fortunately for him, the upturned chariot acted like an anchor in the sand and slowed the horses enough to be arrested by the trackside slaves.

The disconsolate driver was helped to his feet and freed from the reins tied around his waist. He suffered nothing worse than a few bruises and the verbal abuse from the supporters of the Green faction, whose jeers turned to cheers as their own two drivers galloped down the home straight to victory. Even though his adopted team, the Reds, were not involved, Scaeva found the drama of the race the most exciting spectacle he had ever witnessed. Next up were the Reds versus the Whites. This race lacked the thrills of the first, and although the Whites comfortably took first and second places, Scaeva was hooked. In between heats, while the track slaves worked their way along the course with their rakes and water sprinklers, presentations of Idumean palm fronds were made to the winning drivers as a symbol of their victory.

Octavius used these intermissions to explain some of the finer points of the races. For instance, the four colours of the factions originally meant the four seasons of the year, which Scaeva already knew from Felix, but like Felix, Octavius didn't know which was which. The seven laps of the track that constituted each race represented the seven planets in the sky, and the strange object mounted on a high platform at each end of the *spina* just behind the turning posts were the lap counters. Seven horn-shaped bronze counters, each with a large bronze egg fashioned at the wider end, were fixed along a metal spar on pivots at short regular intervals and were held in a vertical position by a taut string. As each lap was completed, the string was released and the weight of the egg shape at the top swung the counter upside down on the spar, so that the drivers, and spectators, could keep track of how many laps remained. Scaeva asked the significance of the egg shapes and had to accept that Octavius didn't know the answer to that either.

At the end of the heats, only Lanfranco of the Reds had qualified for the final. Felix and his four young charges had stood on their benches screaming themselves hoarse, as he swung around the final bend below them and sped away, down the final straight to victory. It was at that moment when it occurred to Scaeva that back on the Carinae, Philostratos would most probably be grumbling to himself at the nonsense of it all.

After the excitement of the heats, the next item on the program was the foot races and wrestling bouts. Scaeva found little interest in these, save for the wrestlers, who brought back to mind that terrible night at the feast, sparking the chain of events that ultimately brought him to Rome. Those contestants in their loincloths would have been pulverised by any of the tribesmen who pitched their strength against each other on that fateful night. To banish thoughts of what had happened to him next, Scaeva focused his attention on the spectators around him. He wondered at the number of women accompanying the menfolk or even attending in little groups by themselves. It seemed they attracted the attention of men whose reason for being at the games was not limited to an interest in the races. Then he noticed, sitting on the benches facing him from across the track, one young woman whom he thought had been staring at him earlier. He nudged Octavius with his elbow.

'Don't look now, but there is a girl on the benches opposite, seated about six in from the end of the row. Let me see, six, seven, eight rows back. I think she's staring at me. Or perhaps at you?'

Ignoring the request not to look straight away, Octavius peered across the track, scanning the distant faces opposite in the place Scaeva had described.

'Yes, that's my sister, Octavia. Oh bother, I expect now that she's seen us together, she will expect me to have asked a favour of you.'

'But she doesn't even know me. I've never met her,' protested Scaeva.

'Oh yes you have,' replied Octavius. 'Do you remember the day you arrived at the house of Pompeius Magnus?'

Scaeva nodded.

'Well, my sister and I had been visiting Julia on that day, and as we were leaving, we met you and a young soldier in the *vestibulum*.'

How could Scaeva forget the moment he first met Julia? He had recalled it so often that her image was burnt into the back of his eyes. But although he now knew Octavius as a schoolmate; of his sister, he could remember not one thing.

'Yes of course, how could I forget that occasion? But I don't recall speaking with Octavia.'

'That's because she was smitten with that chap who was with you, and paid attention to nothing else all evening throughout dinner.'

'But why does she require a favour of me?'

'She wants you to send him a letter,' then seeing the blank, but questioning look on Scaeva's face, continued. 'Let me start from the beginning. I told you she was smitten by him, didn't I' It was a statement, not a question.

Scaeva nodded in confirmation. 'Yes, his name was Durus.'

'Well, she remembered from the conversation around the table that Durus said he came from Cingulum, so she wrote to him there, and was more than delighted to receive a reply from him. They exchanged letters throughout the winter months, and she learned he intended to return to Caesar's army in Gallia in the spring, to make preparations for a second invasion of Britannia. Little did she know that our stepfather, Philippus, had been arranging a match for her, and as soon as he returned to Rome from his pro-consular duties, she was wedded to Gaius Claudius Marcellus. That's him, sitting next to her.'

Scaeva glanced up and identified the middle-aged nobleman sitting next to her, deep in conversation with a colleague seated on his other side.

'Philippus forbade her to continue her correspondence with Durus, who was by this time on his way to join Caesar. So, she secretly handed her letters to Oppius to be included with the rest of the dispatches for Caesar and his staff. Unfortunately, Philippus found out about it and threatened Oppius to hand over any letters she gave him, and any addressed to her that came through his hands.'

'That's all very sad,' said Scaeva, 'but what has it to do with me?'

'I'm just getting to that. She remembers you, of course, and she knows I see you at school. She also knows that you are the only person in Rome who knows Durus and might have reason to write a letter to him using Oppius' courier service.'

'But what does she want me to tell him?'

'No, you don't have to write anything. If you agree to it, she will smuggle a letter to me. I can pass it on to you at school, then you can address it to Durus in your own hand and take it to Oppius. She will say in her letter to send replies back to you.'

The pair of them had been hunched forward, elbows on knees and heads close together in their hushed conversation. Scaeva straightened, stretched his back and glanced across to Octavia, who had been watching them intently. He gave her a wan smile and a little wave of the hand.

The wrestlers and athletes left the arena to polite applause, and a buzz of renewed excitement ran through the packed stands. The chariot racing resumed with the main event, a purse of forty thousand *sesterces* to the winning driver. Scaeva peered through the heat haze at the distant end of the track. Three *quadrigas* from each faction, driven by a first-team driver, a reserve, and an apprentice from each racing team, took their place at the starting gates. Like the flash of light that always precedes the thunderous voice of Taranis, the god of storms and chariot wheels, Scaeva saw the gates open a split second before he heard the loud crack of the springs. A dense cloud of dust and sand rose behind each of the rapidly advancing teams of horses until the clouds merged and the entire field of twelve squeezed to the right of the *spina* and thundered down the straight towards him. Wheels clashed and whips became entangled in the melee of drivers seeking an early lead. Scaeva could not distinguish the colours until they were halfway up that first straight; there was not a Red to be seen in the leading group. By the time the leaders had reached him on the first lap, two Greens, a Blue, and a White shared the lead in a line of four. They took the first turning post in a wide arc, no one daring to employ the tactics of the Blues in the first heat of the *bigae*. Just behind the leaders, but hugging the inside was the distinctive figure of Ramirez, black hair flowing from underneath his leather-bound helmet. He leaned to the left and spun his inside greys, Raffingora and Vorvados, tightest of all around the turning posts, then two cracks of his whip stung the flanks of his outside pairing. Their instant response pulled his chariot out of the bend, drawing him level on the inside of the leading four down the back straight. When he repeated his tight turn at the *metae* nearest the gates, he swept through on the inside to take the lead, starting out on the second lap.

As Ramirez's red-ribboned team led the field into the next turn, Felix was leaping up and down on his bench, waving his betting voucher in the air, and yelling. 'I told you so, I told you so, just look at him go, they won't catch him now!'

Ramirez increased his lead at every turn, but by the fifth lap, it was clear his pursuers were making up ground down the long straights. When they made the bottom turn into the penultimate lap, Ramirez still led, but only just. His tactics had taken their toll on his horses. Four teams, the top drivers of each faction, swept past him, led by Lanfranco of the Reds. As the new leaders swung into the bend, directly below his viewpoint, Felix stared in disbelief. He didn't know whether to laugh or cry. His beloved Reds were in the lead with a lap and a half to go, but he had done his money on the apprentice who was dropping back down the field.

On the final circuit, Lanfranco was being challenged for the lead by both the Blue and the Green drivers, all three locked together, clashing wheels, pounding hooves, and cracking whips. The entire crowd was on their feet, including Felix—who had momentarily forgotten his lost bet—and all four boys, screaming for the Reds. Suddenly, a hand brushed against the back of Scaeva's neck and the next moment, his necklace was ripped away and flung high into the air across the track, landing in the sand just below the lap counter. It was Pinarius. He stood in the aisle just long enough for Scaeva to realise what he'd done, then he darted back up the stairway and disappeared into the ranks of cheering racegoers. Scaeva had just a split second to decide. Whether to give chase to Pinarius and dispense instant retribution or risk his life retrieving the precious *bulla* he'd been given by Caesar, in exchange for his own, before it was trampled into the ground. The three leading chariots were racing towards him, neck-and-neck halfway down the straight. In an instant, he calculated that if he took the steps four at a time, it would take him just three strides to mount the rail overlooking the edge of the track on one foot and launch himself into the arena, with enough time to dash across the sand, retrieve his chain, and leap for the edge of the platform below the lap counter. Pinarius could wait.

Three strides later he was in mid-air and realising he had miscalculated just how high above the surface he was. He landed in the centre of the track with such force he couldn't keep his feet and went sprawling into the scorching sand. He could feel the vibration of the pounding hooves almost upon him. Frantically, with sand filling his mouth and stinging his eyes, he lurched to his feet and half ran, half lunged for the *bulla*. In one sweeping movement, he dipped to grab it with one hand and sprung up again to reach for the top edge of the platform with the other. He felt the hot breath of Lanfranco's inside horse and heard the curses of the driver speeding by, as he caught hold of the decorated fillet that formed the platform's edge and hauled himself clear. The carved wooden fillet was as ancient as the track and creaked under the strain of his weight. Scaeva gripped the chain of his *bulla* between his teeth and reached for the iron spar, supporting the lap markers, just in time before the splintering fillet gave way. As he grabbed the spar and heaved himself up, one end of it broke loose and swung out across the track like the boom of a sailboat, with Scaeva dangling from one arm beneath. He looked on in terror as Vorvados and Raffingora, still hugging the *spina*, followed by the other back markers, raced towards him. At that moment, the iron spar came away from its fastening, dropping him under the thundering hooves of the greys.

Octavia, who saw Scaeva leap from the rails opposite before disappearing from view under the dislodged lap counter, feared the worst as the spectators on that side gasped in horror. She wondered what it was she had done that caused the gods to dash her last hopes of saying goodbye to the man she loved.

XXVIII

18th July 54 BC
South coast of Britannia, in the land of the Cantiaci

M. Tullius Cicero
From
Q. Tullius Cicero

Most dear Brother, my first words must be of apology for the abruptness of my most recent letter. My excuse is that I was hastening to complete it before embarkation to Britannia, and it therefore lacked the usual expressions of the warmth I feel for you and our boys. I eagerly await your reply, penned, as you always do, with brotherly candour.

I shall now attempt to reply to your letter dated the third of June, in which you so poetically request from me the colours of Britannia, in order to paint it with your own brush.

My fears of the ocean crossing proved unfounded. After setting sail from Portus Itius at sunset with a light breeze behind us, the wind dropped around midnight. Dawn broke the next morning with the surface as calm as Our Sea on a windless summer's day, but a strong current had taken us beyond Caesar's favoured landing point. When the current changed, the soldiers rowed magnificently to bring us ashore, unopposed by natives. We heard later from prisoners that, although large numbers had assembled to oppose us, the sheer size of Caesar's invasion fleet caused them to vanish into the interior. I don't mind telling you, my dear brother, how my heart was pounding with excitement as I waded through the surf to stand in that mythical place at last.

By mid-day, the entire fleet had come ashore. We learned, again from prisoners, that the native army had mustered away from the shore on higher ground. Caesar selected ten cohorts, two from each of his five legions, to build the camp and guard the ships. This was so that each legion could claim the honour of participating in the battles to come. Do you see, dear brother, why he keeps the love and respect of his men? Three hundred cavalry were kept back to support the guard and the rest of us rode and marched through the night to confront the barbarians. When morning came, I had my first view of the Britons and their famed chariots. They had taken positions on the far side of a river on higher ground, but our fearless cavalry easily put them to flight. The Britons had retreated to their stronghold atop a thickly wooded hill, but the veterans of the Seventh made short work of driving them out. The place had natural defences but was nothing like the oppida of the Gauls or the Belgae.

As you well know from previous letters, Caesar took great pleasure in my arrival at Blandeno, since it renewed the memory of his affection for you, and he has favoured me increasingly ever since. So much so that the following morning he selected me from amongst his *legati* to lead a force of infantry and cavalry to pursue the enemy. I was in sight of them when I was recalled by a messenger from Caesar. Despatch riders had brought news to him from the camp that a great storm in the night had damaged and cast ashore a great many ships. On returning to the coast to assess the damage, he ordered the recall of the entire army back to the camp.

The upshot of this setback is that for these past ten days, not having the required skills to take part in the effort to make repairs, I have had the leisure to compile my own assessment of this strange country; an activity that has been disparaged by my comrades to the extent that I have been taking my meals alone in my private quarters. I have also made progress on my new work entitled Erigona; I mentioned it to you in my letter dated the tenth. Based on the Greek story of Erigone, I have drawn my inspiration from the jokes the soldiers are making about the Britons. The only reason they water their wine is that they believe it to be poisoned! My Erigona is a Briton who introduces wine, unwatered, to his tribe, and when they suffer the effects of drunkenness, they mistake it for a fatal illness and stone him to death. I will keep you abreast of its progress. While I think of it, could I impose upon you to send me some of your own verses? As you may have concluded from the subject matter of my current work, I am running dry of inspiration.

But now, for this place and its people. The people, it seems, have an oral tradition. Writing is almost unknown here amongst the population. The countryside undulates gently and is wooded, mostly with oak, and there are many homesteads, similar to those of the Gauls, but here, the cattle are more numerous. They use coinage, minted both locally and on the continent, which denotes a high level of trade. In appearance, the Britons are much like the Gauls in size, and they also leave their top lip unshaven, but they also have mystical markings tattooed across their foreheads and the warriors daub their bodies in a blue colouring. I am certain that Caesar will also write to you with his own account.

But there are still more themes from my pen that may heighten your keen sense of intrigue. You may have wondered why this letter was delivered to you personally by the hand of Hippodamus. As I am sure you are aware, anything of a sensitive nature should not be transported through the usual channels, or even pass through the hands of Oppius. You may also have been wondering why, having confided that this island has neither silver nor booty, did Caesar amass a force of five legions and two thousand cavalry in over eight hundred ships in order to return? I may have discovered the true reason from a tribune who was here the year before. I cannot give details, or put anything in writing, even though I entrust this letter to Hippodamus, but you must promise to breathe no word of it to anyone. I will tell you the complete story, as told to me when next we meet. What I can say is that I am minded to make my next work a Greek romance, along the lines of Ninus, the conquering hero, founder of Nineveh, and his love for Semiramis, whom I shall make in my poem a rescued queen of a land he conquers, but Ninus is forced to abandon her and return a year later. I have not decided yet on whether it ends in tragedy or happiness. We shall see.

On the subject of romance, the tribune, whose name I dare not mention, has confided in me that whilst in Rome during the winter he met with Octavia, great-niece of

Caesar, and was quite taken with her, but too shy to make his feelings known. He was delighted to receive word from her, and they have been exchanging letters, even though she has since been betrothed to Marcellus, but her communications stopped some months ago. If you have any news of her, my young tribune friend would be most grateful to hear it.

For myself, there are countless things in regard to which I miss you and our boys daily in every possible way.

Quintus Tullius Cicero stood on the soft sand of the beach, near the water's edge on the shores of Britannia, and handed a sealed leather pouch containing his letter to his freedman, Hippodamus. He offered a silent prayer to Mercurius and bid Hippodamus a swift, safe journey as he waded into the surf to board the narrow pinnace bound for Portus Itius.

During the lull in proceedings, while Caesar's ships were being repaired on the beach and fortifications built around them, Cicero had filled his hours writing letters, plays and poems. He had also cultivated the friendship of a young military tribune who had served with Caesar in Britannia the previous year. Durus had confided to Cicero the story of Caesar's meeting with Cordelia, Queen of the Cantiaci, and because Cicero's brother, Marcus, was ever keen for titbits of gossip, particularly where Caesar was involved, this was a story he was desperate to convey to his brother, back in Rome. The letter had been difficult to write because Caesar's *legati* had been sworn to secrecy regarding his liaisons with the British queen to prevent word of it from reaching Rome, and the ears of his wife and family. Hence, Cicero's adoption of a device, hinting by means of the plot of a poem he said he was writing, to whet his brother's appetite without committing anything more explicit to parchment.

Cicero had joined the army of Caesar, primarily to further the prospects of both himself and his brother. Marcus had urged him to nurture a close relationship with the man who had been consul just five years previously and who was now in the process of adding great wealth and military imperium to his already considerable political achievements.

In addition to this, Cicero was in the precarious position of not being able to face the embarrassment of returning to Rome without the funds to clear his debts. Despite the paucity of expectations of finding riches in Britannia, a share of the spoils generated by Caesar's conquests would, he calculated, enable him to return to Rome with ample means. As he stood and watched the narrow craft being rowed out to sea, his thoughts raced ahead to the destination of his letter, and the likely scene at the house of his brother Marcus, who was looking after his son during his absence. How he missed them all.

'Cicero, stop dreaming of home and get your arse up to the command tent.' Cicero's brief reverie was rudely interrupted by Quintus Atrius, who had been placed in command of the guard, and also the fleet, now safely hauled up the beach. 'There's been a development, and the General needs all officers present for a briefing.'

After taking the refreshing breezes at the seashore, Cicero returned with Atrius through the busy camp in the midsummer heat. Unlike the dry heat of his homeland, the humidity of a British summer had caused the tunic he wore under his *cuirass* to become soaked in sweat. Even when he reached the shade of Caesar's command tent, there was no respite; the air was stale. Inside the tent, a row of perspiring Roman officers faced two Britons who had just arrived holding aloft a white fleece. Commius, dressed in his native garb, stepped out from amongst the Roman contingent and greeted both men with a kiss on the mouth, then stood by them and faced the Romans, as if the two strangers had arrived by his invitation. Although he was known to them both, on this occasion he was as surprised as anyone else at their arrival, but as ever, he deliberately put his diplomatic services at everyone's disposal should they be required. Caesar had also met with both men the previous summer, Lugotorix, he remembered well, for it was he who had made the final surrender on behalf of the tribes of Cantium. He had overseen the treasury of the old king and controlled the mint from his own stronghold of Durobrivae in the northern part of his territory. He had also taken a solemn oath of allegiance to Cordelia just prior to Caesar's hurried departure. The other one, whose hair was tied back like the tail of a horse, was familiar, but Caesar could neither place him nor remember his name.

It was Lugotorix who made the opening introduction. 'My name is Lugotorix of the Cantiaci. My friend here is Gestorix of the Trinovantes.' Gestorix, out of the corner of his eye, caught Caesar's nod of recognition. Lugotorix continued, 'We both have good reason to welcome the Romans back to Prydain. I am the envoy of Queen Cordelia, who is presently in hiding after being overthrown by her kinfolk since your departure.'

'And I am the envoy of Mandubracus, King of the Trinovantes,' said Gestorix, meeting every eye in the room. He stepped forward onto the marble paving slabs laid in the centre of the tent. 'I am here to warn you that the tribes of the Cantiaci, who unseated the queen, have sought assistance from the Cassi to the north of the Tamasa. You now face the combined numbers of the southern tribes of Prydain under the leadership of Cassivellaunus.' Turning to face Caesar, he added, 'I am here to keep my part of the bargain, General. Do you have the boy with you?'

Caesar considered for a moment and gave a curt reply, 'I will discuss these matters privately with you both.' Then, turning to his *legati*, dismissed them, including Commius, who was only slightly dispirited that his services were not required.

'What was that all about?' said Cicero to Atrius as they left the stifling heat of the tent and gulped fresh air into their lungs. 'I have not been in Britannia long enough to pick up their language, but did one of them mention Cordelia?'

'For a start, they were speaking in the common language of the Gauls,' replied Atrius tartly. 'The gist of it was that those two jokers want to do some kind of deal with the General. And a word of advice: if you want to keep the General's favour, don't go asking questions about Cordelia.'

A swift sign from Caesar and one of his slaves fetched his *curule* chair and placed it carefully in the centre of the paved marble floor. He would conduct the interview seated, as befitted a Roman governor. His personal bodyguard, who was not included in the general dismissal, stood behind him with a drawn sword, a detail that made

Gestorix, who had surrendered his own sword on entry to the camp, feel a mite uncomfortable.

Caesar began with no preamble; his first question aimed at Lugotorix. 'I heard Cordelia was with child. Has she delivered?'

'Not to my knowledge,' replied Lugotorix, avoiding eye contact.

'What do you mean by that?'

'I mean that on the occasion of my most recent meeting with her, she was close to her term.'

'And how long ago were you last with her?'

'It was before the most recent new moon, General.'

'And you've had no word since?' said Caesar, patience wearing thin.

'Very few people know of her location, and I must be careful the spies of Taximagulus do not follow my movements,' said the nobleman, raising his chin a little in response to Caesar's increasing annoyance.

'And where exactly is her location?' asked Caesar in a calmer voice, detecting the rising hackles of the Briton standing before him, and aware that he would require his cooperation to find her.

'There is an abandoned oppidum this side of the Tamasa, halfway between the marshes of the estuary and the crossing at the Island of Thorns. No one has lived there for generations. She abides there with her handmaidens, her bodyguard and a handful of devotees.' Then he added with a hint of rhetoric. 'Am I to understand from the tone of your enquiry that you are aware of the prophecies concerning the child?'

Caesar felt a flush to his cheeks that he hoped would be taken as a reaction to the humidity of the tent. How could he forget the prophecy Commius had brought to him the previous year in Samarobriva? The prophecy that confirmed the announcement Marcus Cicero had made in Caesar's dream the night before. That the child, Caesar's son, would create a dynasty that would rule all the world from Rome, and would last for a thousand years. He paused momentarily while his brain searched for a disarming reply.

'I am aware only of the death of her husband, Diviciacus. I encountered his funeral procession on my return to my provinces last year, and I wish only to offer my condolences.' Caesar could lie convincingly, especially if he had a half-truth to cover it.

'Then you will first need to remove Cassivellaunus,' said Gestorix, who was eager to turn the conversation around to his own cause. 'He has come south of the river with the Bibroci, the Ancalites, the Segontiaci and the Cenimagni, to command their forces against you, in aid of Taximagulus. His own tribe, the Cassi, dare not leave their homelands to the north unprotected because they are still at war with the Trinovantes. The bulk of his army sits on the north bank of the Tamasa at the Island of Thorns, where he has defended the fording point with rows of sharpened stakes under the surface.'

'Interesting. How do you know this?'

'Because I was there last summer when the barrier was being constructed. Commius will vouch for me. I know there are gaps between the stakes to allow his own armies to cross unimpeded. I can guide your soldiers to the right places, at the right time to enter the water when it is shallow, and Mandubracus will be ready to join the attack on my signal. There you have it. The plan for our side of the bargain. So, I will say again, do you have the boy with you?'

The boy, of course, Gestorix would want the boy. The boy whose name Caesar could not recall because Pompeius always referred to him as Philip in his letters from Rome.

'The boy is safe and well in Rome. I have been kept abreast of his development and by all accounts, his education is progressing well.'

'In Rome? That was not what we agreed. When will he be returned to us?' responded Gestorix, taking a step forward in anger. At his sudden movement, Caesar's bodyguard leapt around from behind his chair and levelled his *gladius* at the throat of Gestorix, who backed away until the guard casually resumed his position. All the while, Caesar remained unmoved from his pose, sitting upright on the backless chair, forearms on the rests, one foot tucked under the seat with the other slightly extended ahead of him.

'I am aware of what we agreed. The treaty signed by Mandubracius states that on the defeat of Cassivellaunus, Mandubracius and his son after him shall rule Britannia as a client of Rome. That cannot be achieved unless one of them, at least, has been sufficiently schooled.'

'When will he be returned to us?' repeated Gestorix, chastened but still defiant.

'In Rome, boys complete their elementary education between the ages of fourteen and sixteen years.'

'I could be dead by then,' gasped Gestorix. 'I might never see the boy again.'

'When I have dealt with Cassivellaunus,' said Caesar evenly, 'I give you my word; you may travel with me when

I return to my province, and I will arrange accommodation for you in Rome.'

Gestorix grudgingly accepted Caesar's offer with a curt nod. With Scaeva in Rome and battles still to be won, he had no other choice.

Caesar continued, 'As soon as I am satisfied that my fleet is secure and appropriate fortifications have been made to my camp here, I shall continue with my offensive. Once Cassivellaunus has retreated across the Tamasa, you will both return to me. Lugotorix, you will lead me to Cordelia,'

'You have my word, Caesar.'

Turning to Gestorix, Caesar said, 'And you my friend, will lead the way through the river defences of Cassivellaunus, and may your gods protect you.'

The briefing was over, and the two men turned and left the tent. Caesar rose from his seat and followed them outside into a warm summer breeze. Gestorix was about to mount his horse, but Caesar quietly took him aside.

'I was touched by your attachment to the boy, especially as he is not your own son.'

'I had a son once. I had to abandon him when I came to Britannia and joined cause with the Trinovantes. Mandubracus' wife died giving him his second son. His grief was such that he could not bear the sight of the child and left it to me to give the infant a name, so I named him after the boy I lost. I've tried to be a father to him ever since. Are you a father, General?'

'Indeed I am,' replied Caesar. 'I have a daughter, and you may be comforted to know that I sent your boy to live with her in Rome, so be assured he is in good hands. She is with child, and I am expecting news of the birth with every packet from Portus Itius.'

Across the open square of the *principia*, a cohort of soldiers of the Tenth legion had just been dismissed after completing their vigorous morning training session. The *aquilifer*, Marcus Cassius Scaeva, undid his chinstrap, removed his helmet, and wiped the sweat from his forehead before taking a much-needed draught of water from his canteen. While he gulped it down, he allowed his half-closed eyes to rest on his Eagle standard, proudly displayed outside the command tent. Just then, two men left the tent, followed by the general. Scaeva assumed they were Britons, but then recognised the man now with his back to him, in conversation with the general, was not a Briton. His hair was tied back in an unusual fashion. It was the same man he had confronted a year ago outside the gates of the *castrum* at Gesoriacum. That man had reminded him of the father he had last seen when he was just six years old, being bound and led away towards the river by the tribal elders to face the justice of the gods. He had never understood the crime his father had committed, and no one ever spoke his name again, but Scaeva had never forgotten it. It was Gestorix.

XXIX

18th July 54 BC
Rome

The voices came to Scaeva from deep within his consciousness and gradually rose to the surface, until it was as if someone was sitting on his bed beside him, talking to him; but when he opened his eyes, he was alone in a darkened room. He knew instinctively that the room was the *cubiculum* he shared with his mentor in the Domus Rostrata. The voices were coming from outside in the *atrium*. A moment later, the curtain across the entrance to his room was pulled back, and there stood his beloved Julia, with the sunlight from the open roof behind her forming a hazy auburn halo around her head. He sat straight up.

'You are awake,' she cried. 'We have all been so worried about you since your terrible accident.' She ran to his bedside and hugged him. Her scent, the softness of her skin against his cheek and the warmth of her body made his head swim. She sat on the side of his bed and clasped his hands between hers. 'When they brought you back from the Circus and told us what happened, I insisted to Gnaeus that I was now well enough to have you and Philostratos back as house guests so I could care for you.'

'I do not remember what happened,' said Scaeva.

'Octavius said you suddenly leapt from your seat and jumped into the arena in the middle of a race.'

The scene came back to him in an instant. 'My *bulla*, my *bulla*,' cried Scaeva in alarm. He wrenched his hand away from Julia's palm and clutched at his neck. It was gone.

'Don't worry,' said Julia softly, 'a slave picked it up. They found it in the sand next to you when they carried you from the track. The chain must have broken when you fell under the hooves of the horses. It is safe here in this small cabinet at your bedside.' The image of Pinarius sprang into his mind. Standing beside him, gloating, before dashing away up the steps; but Julia was still talking. 'It was a miracle you were not killed, but your friend Epona explained you live under her protection, so although you were bruised and you took blows to your head which rendered you senseless until now, no bones were broken, and you were not seriously harmed.'

'Epona? You've seen her?' asked Scaeva incredulously. 'Is she here?'

'No, but it was she who brought you home, borne on the back of her mare. She said she could not stay but promised she would continue to watch over you.' Scaeva's mind reeled at this disclosure. It was too much to take in. 'Come now, you look so tired. Let me help you lie down.' Julia settled him down in his bed once more and no sooner had his head touched the pillow, than someone else was at his bedside.

It was Philostratos. 'Are you awake? You cried out. Something about your *bulla* and Epona, but the rest was garbled. I couldn't understand.'

Scaeva was instantly wide awake, but in a state of confusion. 'Julia was here just now. I was talking to Julia. She has been looking after me.'

Sadness filled the old man's expression. 'It is true. Julia has been by your side every day since you were brought home from the Circus, but you have remained senseless until just now. I am so sorry to tell you that Julia died, two *nundinae* ago, during childbirth. She produced a son for Magnus, but the infant did not survive the day.'

Scaeva stared open-mouthed in disbelief at his mentor. How could it be? But the shock of the revelation was dwarfed by Philostratos' next terrible disclosure.

'Knowing how much she meant to you, I came to you and turned you over in your bed to check the scars on your back. The bottom-most row of runes has disappeared. The first prophecy has been fulfilled.'

XXX

19th July 54 BC
Durovernon, in the land of the Cantiaci

Just one day after Quintus Cicero handed a letter to his courier on the shores of Britannia for delivery to his brother in Rome, he and Durus stood again inside the fortress of Durovernon; now a smoking ruin. He surveyed the desolate scene around them. The Britons had been forced to abandon their stronghold because of the determined assault of the Seventh legion on the day following Caesar's return. But when the Romans were recalled to their camp to repair their storm-damaged fleet, the natives had returned; not to take up the defensive position they had held previously, but to strip their city of anything of use to the Romans. They had emptied their grain stores, driven away their cattle, cleared their shops of food and supplies, and set fire to the empty buildings. Cicero kicked heedlessly at the supporting leg of a burnt-out grain store and had to jump clear, as a corner of the fire-ravaged structure crumpled in a cloud of ash and blackened beams.

Durus, who had confided not only his own secrets to Cicero earlier, but those of Caesar also, chided him.

'Your brother in Rome would be disappointed to hear that you were killed in Britannia, not by a chariot-driving, spear-throwing native, but by a collapsed barn.'

'My dear brother would be inconsolable if anything at all untoward happened to me whilst I was here. But you are right, after the day we have just had, it would indeed be ironic if a stupid accident were to re-unite me with my ancestors in the underworld.'

For a moment, both men reflected on the hazardous journey they had survived since leaving their coastal camp at dawn that morning. The Britons had not re-grouped to block the progress of Caesar's army column but had deployed their cavalry and chariots in sudden sporadic raids from their hiding places in the wooded areas along the route. The Romans had suffered the worst of their casualties by pursuing their tormentors into the woods and being ambushed by superior numbers. Cicero had been relieved to find the fortress itself undefended, but the once-proud capital of the Cantiaci, under King Llyr, fourth son of Lugios, was now a burned-out empty shell; not because of the invading Romans, but on the orders of Cassivellaunus, King of the Cassi, Brehin of the tribes of southern Prydain.

Not far beyond the abandoned stronghold, along the dry, dusty highway that led to the fording point of the Tamasa at the Island of Thorns, a long column of refugees and heavily laden ox-drawn carts were heading for safety in the land of the Cassi. Better to live under the protection of Cassivellaunus, King of Kings, than suffer under the Romans, who had put all of Gaul under their cruel subjugation and were still thirsting for blood and conquest.

Their painfully slow progress was being watched by Nennius and his nephew Androgeus. With them were a group of warlords and nobles of the tribes that had sworn allegiance to the Cassi.

It was Aculia of the Segontiaci who was first to voice his concern. 'This is madness. The Romans will cut us to pieces if they catch us out in the open like this. We should have returned to Durovernon and re-enforced it when we had the chance.'

'No,' replied Nennius firmly. 'My brother has made his decision. He was appointed unanimously to oversee our resistance to the Romans, and he has been in private audience with the high priests of the druids to secure the guidance of the gods.' Nennius paused and met the eyes of all around him. There were only nods of endorsement, so he continued. 'We have all observed how the Romans, if presented with a target, will simply knock it down with their engines and overcome it. It matters not whether we are in our strongest citadel or in open battle. In battle, Cassivellaunus is the wisest and the greatest among us all. He has a plan, and it will succeed if we all keep our nerve and play our part.'

There followed more nods of approval and Carantus of the Bibrocti, Cassivellaunus' most loyal and vocal advocate, offered his support.

'He is right. We must stretch the Romans' supply chain from the coast to the banks of the Tamasa where they will be stopped by the traps we have laid, and by the forces the Cassi have assembled on the far bank. We can delay his pursuit of our people by harrying his column with our chariots, then pick them off if they dare follow us into the forest, where they cannot make their formations.'

It was the turn of Nennius to nod his approval. 'Our spies inform us that Caesar has left only half the number to defend their camp and their vessels, as came with him last year, so Taximagulus will drive them back into the sea, as he did a year ago.'

Androgeus knew the truth and jibed, 'Provided Cordelia and the Atrabates stay out of it this time.'

'Cordelia is dead, or as good as,' retorted Segovax. He was still angry at his own failure to deal with the queen when he had the chance.

Nennius glared at Androgeus for his impudence but ignored the barb. 'And Cassivellaunus has warned the puny elders of the Atrabates that we have a land border with them, and if they know what is best, they won't interfere again.'

Androgeus was about to continue his argument with Segovax, which began on the night of the great feast and had rankled ever since, but the last remark from Nennius caused something deep inside him to snap.

'Fine words, uncle, but they are not your words. They are the words of your brother. He is the true warrior. He is the one that avenged the death of my father, while you,' he fixed Nennius with a hateful stare, 'you were more content when you were breaking bread with his killer.'

Nennius flushed but was saved from making a reply when a messenger galloped up to them.

'Lord Nennius, I have news from Durovernon. The Romans are making their camp there, and small groups of them are at work on the outside ramparts, repairing the palisades. Should we attack?'

Nennius, stung by his nephew's brutal denunciation—especially in front of his subordinate commanders—needed to prove his courage.

He replied decisively. 'Take us to them. I will lead the attack.'

Nennius and his entourage kicked their mounts into a gallop and followed the messenger back to join his raiding party. It was Cassivellaunus who devised the tactics of the Britons. He understood the Romans would be at their most vulnerable whilst on the move, so it made sense to lead them deep into the interior, and adopt a scorched earth policy, denying them not just food supplies, but anything that may be of use. Instead of confronting them in a pitched battle, he deployed his armies in groups that shadowed the progress of the Romans and sporadically launched raiding parties of a hundred charioteers and mounted warriors against the long flanks of Caesar's baggage train.

Whilst he had no qualms about razing to the ground anything in their path through the territory of the Cantiaci, he was determined to halt their progress at the crossing point of the great dark river that bordered his homeland. The pointed stakes driven into the riverbed defended the banks for a mile on either side of the ford. Made with timber from the consecrated arboretum at the sacred Island of Thorns, they would mark the end of the line for the Roman advance.

The heat of the day had dissipated in the proximity of the woodland surrounding the hillfort, and the late evening sunlight still sparkled from behind the broad-leafed canopy that swayed gently above them, betraying a light breeze in the treetops. Gaius Crastinus of the Tenth supervised his century, replacing fire-damaged timbers around the gateposts at the bottom of the hill in front of the encampment. His senior officer, Quintus Laberius Durus, squeezed himself out through the small gap in the gates, one of which had just been repaired by the working party.

'Status report, Crastinus? The general wants everything wrapped up before nightfall.' Durus peered up at the sky and added, 'I reckon we have less than an hour.'

'Remember the night comes later here than in Gallia,' said the centurion. 'So I think we should be ready before the *buccina* sounds the first watch.'

Both men were veterans of the previous year's expedition and knew each other well.

'I'll take your word for that, my friend,' replied the tribune.

'You don't have to,' said Crastinus. 'The prefect back at the *castrum* brought a *clepsydra* in his baggage and he's proved it.'

Durus shrugged and looked up at the sky again. 'I don't remember the sun shining long enough last year to tell night from day. It just poured with rain most of the time. I'm not sure what's worse, the wind and rain last year, or the heat this time around.'

'Why don't you stop moaning about the weather, for fuck's sake? What's your new friend like? You know, the one who sits around writing poetry all day long. Seems like a bit of a wanker to me. What's he doing here?'

'He's Cicero's brother. Remember Cicero? Consul way back. He's the one famous for exposing that conspiracy to overthrow the Republic. It was all going on while I was still at school.'

'I don't take any notice of politics back in Rome,' replied Crastinus. 'Never even been there. So that's who he is, but what's he doing here? He doesn't seem like much of a soldier to me.'

'He's spent most of his career in the senate and was at pains to tell me that during his three years as *propraetor* in Asia, he rejected the opportunity to line his own pockets to finance a run at the consulship. So this is his first military posting, unless you count a few months on the staff of Pompeius Magnus in Sicily, organising the grain supply.'

The grizzled centurion rolled his eyes. 'So I was right. He's a real wanker.'

Durus, who was quite fond of Cicero, changed the subject. 'So, no sign of the natives then?'

'Quiet as the grave,' replied Crastinus, looking around at the perimeter of the forest. 'The sentries haven't reported so much as a scuttling rat. That's what they are, aren't they? Rats, scuttling out of their hiding places and throwing their pathetic weapons, then scuttling back again before we can get a decent shot at them. We won't be seeing them again today, not now that we've repaired the damage to the fort.'

As if on cue, simultaneous shouts went up from the sentries posted as lookouts in the woods. One of them came crashing out through the undergrowth and was about to shout another warning when a javelin took him between the shoulder blades and came out of his chest by a full arm's length. The soldier dropped to his knees, still open-mouthed. His momentum and the blow from behind would have landed him flat on his face, but for the spear, the tip of which propped him up, and left him on both knees in a grotesque pose with his head lolling over his chest. Time stood still for a few seconds with just the pounding of hooves filling the air before a wave of Britons on horseback broke from the cover of the forest less than two hundred paces away. Leading the charge and screaming the war cry of the Cassi like never before, rode Nennius, stripped to the waist, hair stiffened with goose fat and combed straight back in spikes, torso and face a mass of blue swirls. He had selected his target. It had to be one of the two Romans wearing crested helmets. These were surely the officers. One of them could even be Caesar himself. He would prove his courage today or die in the attempt.

Within moments, the hoofbeats were drowned by the war cries of the natives in hellish discord with the wailing sound of the *cornu* coming from inside the camp, calling the legionnaires to arms. Crastinus and Durus, who had naturally drifted away from the rankers and auxiliaries while privately discussing the merits of Caesar's newest *legate*, sprinted back to where the men were scrambling to retrieve the weapons they had laid down. But the Britons were upon them before they could make a defensive formation.

In the melee, the Britons jumped down from their mounts to make better use of their round shields and long swords in hand-to-hand combat. Nennius, having bloodied his sword on a soldier he had leapt upon from the back of his horse, jumped nimbly to his feet, unencumbered as the Romans were with their body armour, and found himself face-to-face with his quarry. He was wild with excitement, but Durus remained cool. His training and experience served him well. Armed only with his *gladius,* Durus circled his adversary to his left, away from the arm that would swing the Briton's blood-covered weapon. When the strike came, Durus saw it coming and parried the blow with his *gladius,* then stepped closer to chop downwards over the top of the round shield onto the unprotected head of the Briton. Nennius ducked under his shield as the blow came with such force that the Roman's weapon became embedded in it. Durus struggled to free his sword and clenched Nennius with his left hand under the Briton's sword arm, preventing him from wielding it to any effect. Their legs became entangled, and they toppled to the ground, rolling over and over in a deadly embrace.

The jolting enabled Durus to wrench his blade free. The weapon was short enough for him to draw it back and stab it into the side of his adversary. He staggered to his feet and was about to deliver the final blow when he felt a shuddering impact to his back and an explosion in his chest. A chariot rushed up from behind him. The naked, empty-handed spearman leapt down and hoisted the stricken nobleman onto the chariot's platform and the driver sped them away to safety.

Durus looked down and was simply incredulous at the pointed bulge in his chest under his chain mail shirt. A fine spray of blood was escaping through the metal links and dispersing into the evening air. While he was looking down, the ground beneath his feet tilted upwards. The trees ahead of him passed over his head until the hard earth hit him full in the face and shot dust particles into his open, staring eyes. Warm blood filled his mouth and dribbled into the brown earth, turning it a deep red. It tasted like seawater. He began to panic because he suddenly found himself out of his depth in the surf as a child on a beach by the Mare Superum. His feet could no longer touch the bottom and he felt himself sinking, down and down, before blackness consumed the last of his senses.

The following day, it was with sadness that Caesar noted in his journal that the military tribune, Quintus Laberius Durus, was killed in action. Some months earlier he had been surprised, and also mildly amused, to find that his great-niece, who he hadn't seen since she was eleven years of age, had been corresponding with a young member of his staff through the communication channel operated by his agent in Rome. Having at first teased his young officer about the relationship, he had given his blessing for Durus to send his replies by the same means. Durus had told him of the unhappy match that her stepfather had made for her, but neither of them knew the reason she stopped writing. Durus was buried where he fell, in an unmarked grave. The young military tribune would be commemorated only by a single line in Caesar's commentaries on his Gallic War.

On that same day, the body of Nennius, the pacifist, was being carried across the Tamasa to his homeland for a hero's burial. Although nowhere near as fearsome a warrior as his father Heli, or his brothers, he had died from wounds received in battle. Heli had died an old man in his bed, Ludd had been murdered in front of his children, and Cassivellaunus would be remembered for being forced to pay tribute to the Romans. The Bards would soon be at work with their harps and lyres, composing the story of Nennius, who slew many Roman invaders including the brutal Titus Labienus, Julius Caesar's second in command, then fought hand-to-hand with none other than Caesar himself, succumbing only when being touched by the tip of the craven Roman's poisoned sword.

The day after, Caesar would record an attempt by the Britons to repeat the tactic they had employed the previous year, the ambush of a foraging party. This time, the Romans were ready for the attack. Casca, the veteran legionnaire of the Seventh, and sole survivor of the catastrophe the year before, had recovered enough to give Caesar a full account of the tactics the Britons had employed. This time, the foraging cohorts were quickly reinforced by an entire legion close behind them, and the Britons were put to flight, losing great numbers. After that reverse, Cassivellaunus withdrew the surviving fighting men of the Cantiaci from their homelands to swell the numbers of the Cassi on the far side of the Tamasa. Casca retired and was granted land to farm in a veterans' colony in Narbonensis.

* * *

True to his word, having heard from his informants that the army of Cassivellaunus had retreated and re-grouped across the Tamasa, Lugotorix awaited the arrival of Caesar at the deserted stronghold of Durobrivae. He stood alone in the open gateway as Caesar approached on foot at the head of his army, resplendent in his scarlet sash of imperium, knotted at the hip and looped across the front of a polished *cuirass* that glinted in the sun.

'Welcome to my hometown General,' said the Briton, squinting as the sunlight from over his shoulder reflected off the Roman's shining silver armour. 'I'd offer you some refreshment, but there is not a crumb to be had in the citadel.'

'Not to worry, my friend, we have brought our own,' replied Caesar casually, turning to the armed column and baggage train following behind him. 'And what of the mint and the contents of your treasury?'

'All gone,' said the Briton with a shrug. 'Cassivellaunus confiscated every item of value in the treasury and emptied the mint of coinage, even though the Cassi have no use for it. They still barter sheep for cattle and dogs for horses.'

Caesar pursed his lips in mild frustration. He had built up hopes that the treasury at Durobrivae might have offered some low-hanging fruit on his return to Britannia, but it was now somewhat further out of reach. He hid his disappointment by changing the subject.

'Where is your accomplice?'

'Gestorix? He abides across the Tamasa at a small homestead amongst the Trinovantes. He knows the way through the river marshes at low tide due north of here, so he can come and go as he pleases, but it is no place for an army to attempt a crossing. The river here at Durobrivae is fordable, and it will be safe enough to stay here the night before moving on.'

'My scouts had already verified this fortress was recently abandoned. How far to the fording point of the Tamasa?'

'The nearest is two days' march from here. A man can walk across when the tide is low.'

'And what news of Cordelia?'

Lugotorix had his answer to that question ready-made in his mind. 'While those loyal to Taximagulus have been on the move to cross the Tamasa, it has been too much of a risk for me to go near. But when you make camp at the end of your march tomorrow it will be safe for me to take you to her then. I have a site in mind for you that lies within an hour's ride from her hiding place.'

Caesar's impatience for confirmation that Cordelia had given birth to a son was increasing. He had his suspicions that the nobleman was withholding information but could not fathom a motive. Lugotorix had proved himself to be a man of honour and a loyal servant to the queen. Perhaps Cordelia had charged him with bringing Caesar into her presence in ignorance so that she could make the announcement in her own way. Caesar would have his answer in a little over twenty-four hours, so there was little point in further interrogation. He nodded his acceptance of the situation, and the two men stood aside as the legions and the baggage train tramped and trundled through the gateway. Some were ordered to the palisades to mount the last watch of the day, while others were detailed by their *optiones* into their billets for the night.

The night was warm and still. Caesar shifted uncomfortably on his cot beneath the blackened, thatched roof of an empty roundhouse that retained the pungent aroma of smoked hams. His nakedness was no remedy for the humidity which intensified the further his army ventured inland. His thoughts switched from his forthcoming reunion with Cordelia to the news he was expecting from Pompeius back in Rome, announcing the birth of his grandchild. He tried to banish all thoughts from his mind and get some sleep. He would need to be fresh and alert for the military challenge ahead, but thoughts of crossing the Tamasa only increased his agitation. Where was Gestorix? What had he been doing? Lugotorix had only said he comes and goes as he pleases, but what did that mean?

When Caesar woke the following morning, his cot was damp with perspiration, but his first feeling was that of relief. Relief that he had been asleep, but for how long? All he knew was that he had been dreaming. Disturbing dreams about Cordelia, Julia, and their newborn infants. It was Gestorix who led him to them through the mist, crossing a river along a marshy causeway at low tide. He saw them both, standing together on the opposite bank, as if from behind a veil that obscured their identity. Each of them held a child in swaddling, but neither of them answered when he spoke to them.

The day passed without incident, other than the usual occasional minor difficulties encountered by an army on the move. After crossing the river at Durobrivae, the long straight highway that spanned the chalk downs in the northern stretches of the territory of the Cantiaci was wide enough to allow the long column of legionnaires and auxiliaries to march six abreast. Behind them, the teams of oxen drawing the heavy artillery and the wagons that made up the baggage train made good progress. Bringing up the rear was the cavalry, the tails of the horses swishing at the flies in the mid-summer heat.

The entire column was over three miles long and the men were in good heart. Of hostile natives, there was no sign; just abandoned homesteads, ash-filled fire pits, and empty sheep pens. Occasionally, the Romans passed by fields of wheat that had been hastily harvested, leaving small islands of uncut grain, eagerly gathered by teams of auxiliaries. At the head of the column, preceding the first cohort of the Seventh Legion, marched Caesar, Lugotorix and Commius, all leading their horses. The uneasy silence that existed between the former two men was broken by the latter, who grumbled intermittently about having to walk when he had a perfectly good horse available. Caesar was content to chide his ambassador and remind him it set a good example for his men to march with them. At least it saved him from attempting conversation with the Briton; he could not think of a single subject of discussion with him that didn't involve Cordelia.

With three hours of daylight remaining, they reached the site Lugotorix had in mind for the camp. He knew it had to be many times larger than the one the Romans had constructed on the coast the previous year. After a brief discussion with Caesar's chief *metatore*, the central point of the *castrum* was determined for the headquarters and a *groma* was hammered into the hard ground. The *gromatici* spread out the cross-pieces from which hung several plumb lines. Teams of legionnaires peeled away from their marching formations to join the subordinate *metatores* with their ten-foot measuring rods, and set about flagging the boundaries of the camp, and digging the ditch and agger that would surround it.

Caesar, after seeing the construction of the *castrum* was underway, turned to Lugotorix.

'We leave now, while we have a good two hours of daylight.'

Lugotorix nodded resignedly and, minutes later, four mounted men in single file crossed the northern boundary of the camp and headed towards Cordelia's hiding place on the banks of the great dark river. The noble Briton led the way, followed by Caesar and Commius, who had broken the news to him about Cordelia's condition, and the prophecy attached to it the year before. Caesar's personal bodyguard, eyes, and ears alert for any sign of danger, completed the quartet. For the first half hour, they followed bridleways in and out of broad-leafed woodlands, across open pastures, and past overgrown hamlets that had been uninhabited for a generation or more. Then the bridleway petered out into a trackless forest where even the birdsong diminished until the only sound was of a large river flowing nearby.

Turning to Caesar, Lugotorix said, 'This is where we dismount.'

A low horizontal bough from a spreading oak provided a perfect hitching rail for their horses. Just beyond the oak was a steep bank, which Lugotorix ascended on all fours in such an accomplished manner that it fuelled Caesar's suspicions he had visited this place more frequently than he admitted. Caesar and the others followed with not quite the level of agility displayed by the Briton. The top of the bank was rounded and was clearly the outer rampart of a sizable defensive complex. Lugotorix slithered on his heels and buttocks down into the ditch on the other side, which was as deep as the outer rampart had been high. A second ditch, even deeper and wider than the first, but not as steep, was easier to negotiate. Caesar walked upright into the trough at the bottom that was littered with broken bits of pottery and other rubble, but the slope up the other side was a tangle of undergrowth. Lugotorix went some twenty paces along the bottom of the ditch as if searching for a way through the brambles. Then he withdrew his long sword to push the vegetation aside, making a clearway up the side of the ditch to the bottom of an ancient log palisade, overgrown with creepers. Ushering the three visitors up the slope, he soon joined them and used his sword again to draw the creepers aside to uncover the entrance to a small tunnel.

First in was Caesar, followed by his bodyguard, then Commius, and finally Lugotorix, who drew the creepers back across the entrance behind him. Despite the long spell of dry warm weather, the tunnel was cold and damp, and the four men emerged on the other side with hands and knees caked in stinking mud. Caesar absolutely hated it, especially as he was about to be reunited with the queen, a meeting he had been contemplating with an increasing sense of anticipation for some time. He looked around helplessly for something to wipe his hands on, then knelt and rubbed his palms on the long grass. He glared up at Lugotorix, who returned his look with an impassive expression devoid of sympathy. It troubled the Roman that although he could read most men, he found this British nobleman impenetrable.

Caesar got to his feet and surveyed the scene; there was surprisingly little in the way of trees or vegetation in the interior. The ground rose a little to the left but dropped gradually away from in front of them, down to the banks of what Caesar assumed was the Tamasa, the great dark river of the Britons, sparkling in the late afternoon sunlight on its journey to an uncharted sea. Many roofless roundhouses were scattered across the landscape, bare timbers standing out starkly against the brightness of the sky. Roofless except one, which was clearly in need of repair. A thin veil of smoke escaped from the gaps in the thatch.

Commius was the first to speak. 'What is this place, and what happened to it?' He did not direct the question at anyone, but Lugotorix was the only one among them who could make a reply.

'It was originally the fortress of the ancient kings of the Cantiaci. Llyr was the last one to abide here, but he abandoned it many years ago and created a new seat at Durovernon.' The questioning looks on two faces invited him to elaborate; the third face, that of the bodyguard, had remained disinterested in the conversation, but watchful, so the Briton continued. 'Llyr had married Etain, the widow of his eldest brother King Madawc, and incidentally, the mother of Imanuentus. She had expected her son to ascend the throne on Madawc's death, but the boy was judged to be too young, and the crown passed to the other of Llyr's older brothers, Blad. The story goes Etain poisoned Blad, and on his deathbed, he put a curse on Etain and her household, here on the banks of the Tamasa. Etain was found dead in her bed three days later, and Llyr took fright and left, taking his entire court with him. He soon remarried and had three daughters. The youngest of them was Cordelia.'

Caesar's mind was racing. 'So why did she come here, knowing that the place was cursed?'

'She reasoned it would be the last place Taximagulus would search for her, and she was right. Although both I and Brennus, her bodyguard, argued against it. She is headstrong and overruled us. If Digueillus was here, she might have listened to him.'

'And who is Digueillus? I have heard of that name,' said Caesar, who—because of the Briton's last remark—was suffering a mounting feeling of unease.

It was Commius who stepped in with the answer. 'Digueillus was the queen's chief advisor. He sought assistance from the Trinovantes when her in-laws attempted to abduct her last year. Imanuentus refused to get involved and Digueillus hasn't been seen or heard of since.'

'Yes, I remember now,' Caesar nodded as the memory of his first encounter with the young beauty came flooding back. 'She did mention it to me.' Then impatience and anxiety got the better of him. He turned on Lugotorix and demanded, 'Where is she?'

Without waiting for an answer, he pushed past the startled Briton and marched determinedly towards the smoking roundhouse halfway down the slope towards the river. As he approached, a tall figure emerged from the hut and stood waiting by the entrance. Caesar recognised him immediately as Brennus, captain of the queen's bodyguard, who had led the Atrebatian cavalry to his aid the previous year. From inside the hut came the cries of a baby.

The face of Brennus was a white mask of grief. He spoke only two words by way of a greeting. 'She's inside.'

Caesar pushed past him and ducked under the eaves of the thatch, and in that dreadful moment, he cared not a jot about his appearance. The interior was lit with candles and the still-smoking embers from a grate in the middle of the room. On a dais opposite the entrance, two women in white robes knelt either side of a figure laid out in a cot. A bassinet, from which came the cries of an infant, was on the floor in front of the raised platform. Caesar covered the distance from the entrance to the dais in four strides and knelt next to the body of the queen. Her attendants took a pace back, out of reverence for the child's father. Cordelia's eyes were closed. Her hair, carefully parted in the front and made into plaits that wound around the sides of her head. She was as peaceful and radiant as he remembered her in the moments he had spent watching her sleeping after their first lovemaking. The only difference now was she was not breathing.

Before Caesar could form a question of why, when, or how, Brennus appeared at the doorway.

'Why don't you attend to your daughter Caesar?' mocked the captain bitterly. 'Pick her up. Hand her to the nurse.'

'Daughter?' gasped Caesar incredulously. 'The prophecy foretold of a son.'

'But this place is cursed,' replied Brennus. 'I tried to warn her, but she wouldn't listen. When she delivered a girl, she blamed herself for defying the curse. Then when she heard of your return to these shores, she convinced herself you would hold her responsible for breaking the prophecy and shun her. She wanted to take her own life. I had kept her safe from herself until yesterday. Then our scouts told of your imminent approach. She had kept about herself a potion, given to her a year ago by her priestess. She was to consume the powders if ever she was taken into the custody of her sisters. This morning, she secretly took the potion.'

At that moment, Lugotorix, who had been waiting respectfully at the entrance with the other two men, came into the room, took in the tragic scene and dropped to his knees in despair. He prostrated himself on the floor and was wracked with huge sobs of unrestrained grief. After a few moments, he recovered sufficiently to seek forgiveness for his behaviour.

Between shuddering sobs, he implored Caesar. 'I didn't know she meant herself harm. I swear it. I knew she had delivered a girl-child, but on my oath, I swear that on the last occasion I saw her, she forbade me to divulge it to you. She made me swear an oath that I should lead you to her without knowing, so she could explain her actions and beg your forgiveness.'

Caesar said nothing. What was there left to say? He leant across the body of the woman who, no doubt, had shared his most secret of dreams. He kissed her tenderly on her forehead and sought a last waft of sweet aroma from her hair. Then he rose and stepped down off the dais, bent over the bassinet, and paused to untie his red neckerchief and wipe the last of the mud from his hands, before lifting the fussing infant in its swaddling onto his shoulder. He gently comforted her and planted a delicate kiss on her tear-stained cheek before handing the helpless bundle to the nearest of the nurses. Then he turned and left the room to face the setting sun.

The last half mile of bridleway was traversed by starlight before the lights of the newly completed *castrum* came into view. As Caesar dismounted outside the *praetorium*, his quaestor hurried out of the communications tent waving a leather cylinder.

'This came for you shortly after you left this evening, General. It is from Pompeius Magnus. I thought you would want to read it immediately on your return.'

'Thank you Antistius, tell Faberius I am cancelling this evening's briefing with the *legati*. We shall reconvene in the morning.'

A groom took his horse, and without so much as a glance at the three men who had accompanied him that evening, he retired immediately to his private quarters. His servants had laid out his customary supper of bread and olive oil, to be washed down with the contents of two small amphorae, one containing water, the other, a strong white Falernian.

Caesar sat at his desk, placed the leather cylinder carefully on its end next to the amphorae, and rubbed his eyes hard. He tipped half the contents of the Falernian into a beaker and only half his normal measure of water. He took two deep sips, and with the beaker held between his hands, rested himself forwards, elbows on knees and head hanging loose. He wanted so much to sob as Lugotorix had done, but nothing came. He desperately wanted to empty out the grief he felt so deep inside before reading the news of his long-awaited grandchild. He stared wide-eyed at the flickering candles and felt not the merest prick of a tear. Leaning back into his folding canvass chair, he took a deep sigh and reached for the cylinder. For a moment he twisted it around and back in his fingers, making the candlelight reflect off the waxen Lion's head imprint from Pompeius' personal seal ring, before breaking the wax with his thumbnail and easing off the cap. He forced a smile to his lips to improve his mood before drawing out the single scroll, then his false smile vanished, and he raised his eyebrows in surprise at how short it was.

Letters from Pompeius with news from home were usually of considerable length, updating Caesar on all the latest political manoeuvrings, besides any family events. The scroll took only a second to unfurl. Caesar held it to the candlelight in both hands and began to read. The ink was smudged as if with droplets of water.

'I cannot bear for you to read the words I must write. I cannot bear to write them, but write them I must. My dearest wife, your dearest daughter, our dearest sweet Julia, light of both our lives, is dead. She died after bearing me a son who did not survive the day. I brought the finest physicians in Rome to her side, but none could stem the flow of blood. I was with her constantly, through it all, as her young life ebbed away. She spoke only of her love for her family and begged our forgiveness at the sadness she would cause by leaving us too soon ...'

There was more, but he let his hands fall to his lap and, without his bidding, salty tears welled up in his eyes and overflowed onto the page, joining those of the man who, until recently, had been his son-in-law. He was alone and there was no one to witness, so he allowed his tears to run freely until he wiped them away with the back of his hand. When his vision became less blurred, he continued to read,

'... I have lost a beloved wife and son, you, a beloved daughter and a grandson. What a man he would have been, Caesar, with your blood mixed with mine coursing through his veins. What further glory might he have won for Rome? But it is the loss of Julia that grieves me the most. I have two fine sons already, and a daughter, in whom I may seek some consolation, but you, my dear friend, have lost your only daughter ...'

Again, Caesar paused, this time to contemplate the fact that unbeknown to Pompeius, he had handed over a newborn daughter to the care of a nurse, not two hours beforehand, intending never to lay eyes on her again. He also reflected on the loss of Cordelia, but she was never truly his anyway. She, like Julia, was gone and there was nothing to be done about it, but with Julia gone, there was no longer a family link to bind Pompeius to him; a worrying situation that threatened the existence of the Triumvirate agreement between themselves and Crassus. It was the foundation of their power base. However, he had another female relative of marriageable age that might repair the potential damage, his great-niece Octavia. It was the tribune, Durus, who had confided in him that Octavia was unhappy with the match her stepfather, Philippus, had arranged for her. Not caring for whatever remained of Pompeius' closing commiserations, Caesar held a corner of the parchment above the lighted candle until it caught fire. Then watched the contortions of the flame as the burnt edge worked its way down the page towards the tips of his fingers. He resolved to write to Octavia, urging her to divorce Marcellus so she would be free to marry Pompeius.

XXXI

29th July 54 BC
The banks of the Tamasa, at the Island of Thorns

The long, hot dry spell had come abruptly to an end. Marcus Cassius Scaeva stood in the pouring rain, grateful for the lion-fur cape that covered his shoulders. He cut a fearful figure with the snarling head of the animal strapped to his helmet, Eagle standard by his side and eight cohorts of the Tenth Legion in full battle formation behind him. Ahead, through the early morning mist, flowed the Tamasa; the tidal waterway that separated the Cantiaci, permeated as they were with Belgic culture and influence, from the Cassi, the last of the pure Celtic tribes in southeastern Prydain. The surface of that great dark river was tormented by the pounding raindrops into a rage of spits and spurts. Lining the bank opposite were wooden spikes set at an angle with their sharpened tips protruding an arms-length above the water. A second row beneath the surface ran parallel to it. Beyond the bank were the Cassi hoards, with their numbers boosted by subordinate tribes and what remained of the warriors of the Cantiaci, who had attempted to delay the progress of the Romans through their homeland. The deafening roar of their combined ululations rose above the sounds of the wind and rain but was wasted on the veterans of the Tenth and the Seventh legions. They had heard it all before and stood unmoved, a steadfast example to the other troops, new to Britannia, who also stood in line awaiting the signal to attack.

When the legions had first been sighted coming out of the mist on the south bank, the Britons had rushed to the water's edge to hurl their weapons against the invaders, but the Romans had stopped short, just out of range. Now only the occasional slinger tried his luck, only to see their missile fall short, or ping harmlessly off the row of rectangular curved shields, behind which the Romans stood. As the natives jeered and gesticulated on the far bank, Marcus heard the rumblings of heavy artillery being drawn up on carts behind the ranks. He knew what was coming next. The metallic clicking of the ballistae as the bowstrings were ratcheted back. Then the command to fire, followed by the twang, thud, and whoosh of the feathered bolts. The missiles shot through the air and across the water. Volley after volley causing havoc amongst the Cassi, who had not experienced the devastation they wreaked on the southern coast of Prydain the year before.

Gestorix, who had previously spent time in Camulodunon making plans with Mandubracus, had taken his well-trodden route across the marshes and re-joined Caesar at the head of his column on the final day's march to the Tamasa. The following day, he identified the place where the gaps had been left to accommodate the retreat of the Britons and had instructed the centurions on the construction of the defences and how they should be breached. Scaeva and his century, along with every other century in all five legions, had spent that day practising tactics for the assault on dry land replicas.

Now the moment had come as the river level ebbed to its lowest point. The legions were aligned under the direction of Gestorix, with a gap between the formations that corresponded with the narrow gap between the shorter stakes in the centre of the riverbed beneath the surface. On the far bank was a similar gap in the defences, hidden by a second row of stakes, set just a chariot's width in front of it.

The last of the Ballistae volleys whistled overhead, and Gestorix led Caesar's cavalry through the gap between the rows of troops. He paused and blew three mighty blasts on a conch shell, a signal to Mandubracus and the Trinovantes, who were waiting hidden in the shelter of the woods that adjoined the riverbank, downstream of the army of Cassivellaunus. Scaeva looked around at the sound of the conch and saw, less than a hundred paces away, the man he had last seen talking with the General before leaving the coastal camp. The same man he had confronted the year before at the gates of the *castrum* at Gesoriacum. The man he now recognised as his father. Gestorix kicked his mount forward into the ford, followed by the column of Roman cavalry riding eight abreast.

On seeing the movement on the opposite bank, the Britons, in their tens of thousands, who had retreated out of range of the deadly artillery fire, rushed forward in a rage. Horsemen and the nobility in their war machines led the charge, followed by screaming half-naked warriors, men and women, brandishing their weapons. A thousand Cassi chariots came once more into the range of two hundred wagon-mounted ballistae. The charioteers plunged, axle-deep, into the saturated ground churned up earlier by the retreating tribesmen. Many of them were now sitting targets for the Roman artillery.

Gestorix emerged on the far bank, followed by the first ranks of cavalry who had passed through the gaps left for the retreat of the Cantiaci. Simultaneously, the *cornu* sounded the attack and the legions, headed by Scaeva—who was desperate to keep Gestorix in sight—charged into the river. He laid his shield against the row of submerged spikes to act as a bridge, as he had done in practise. But instead of waiting for the rest of his century to cross before retrieving it, he crossed the barrier himself and waded chest-deep through the turbulent water. On reaching the towering, spiked barricade defending the far bank, the giant aquilifer hurled his Eagle standard over it. Then, he reached up with both hands, grabbed two of the pointed stakes above his head, lifted himself out of the water and scrambled across. He didn't wait for his comrades, who worked in groups of three, to help each other over the menacing obstacle.

Cassivellaunus and his coterie of lieutenants and advisors watched aghast from his vantage point. The charioteers that should have swept the enemy from the riverbank were stranded in the mud and were being picked off by the devastatingly accurate spear-throwing machines of the invaders. His horsemen had been engaged and bested by disciplined Roman cavalry, and his wild-eyed infantry was breaking against formidable rows of locked shields and spears that emerged—as if by some terrifying magic—from behind the giant defensive spikes he had assembled along the bank the previous year. The druids had assured him this was the most perfect place to assemble his defences. The ancient solar pathway, protected by the gods, on which the major citadels had been sited, crossed the river at this point, the sacred Island of Thorns.

But this meant nothing to Mandubracus, who had only abided the druid doctrine under sufferance while his pious but ruthless father had been alive. Leading waves of Trinovantian cavalry out from the cover of the woods, he was now in full view of his sworn enemy, cutting down the unguarded flanks of the Cassi warriors.

The foot-soldiers of Cassivellaunus were being pushed back by the formidable, unbreakable advance of the Legions, as row after row crossed the river to bolster their numbers. In the melee, the leading group of Roman cavalry, including Gestorix, were in the thick of the fighting and were the first to be relieved by the Trinovantian re-enforcements.

Amongst the shining helmets of the Romans and the spiked hair of the Cassi, Mandubracus picked out the unique head of Gestorix just as he was unseated. Scaeva too, who had never lost sight of his father amongst the tumult of the encounter, saw him go down. He had left his standard driven into the mud on the riverbank. Armed with his *gladius* and a shield retrieved from a fallen warrior, he fought his way through the mud and the blood to find Gestorix and Mandubracus fighting back-to-back, surrounded by a mob of Cassi tribesmen. With an almighty war cry from his homeland, Scaeva set about the enemy. Gestorix, suddenly distracted by the familiar cry, turned his head just as the tip of the flashing blade of his nearest assailant took away both eyes and the bridge of his nose.

The stricken warrior dropped to his knees, pressing his palms into the empty sockets to stem the gush of blood. Mandubracus, too late to save his old comrade, turned and cut down the assailant with a single blow, while Scaeva's sudden and terrifying intervention scattered the rest of their adversaries.

Much to the surprise of Mandubracus, the burly legionnaire knelt, cradled Gestorix in his arms and sobbed.

'Father, it is I, your son Scaeva. You are safe now.'

He unknotted his scarlet neckerchief and clasped it to the gash across his father's face; the blood darkening the colour of the cloth. Although spoken in their native language, the meaning was not lost on Mandubracus. Gestorix felt for the face of his son. The son he hadn't seen for longer than he could remember, and now, tragically, he would never see again. Hesitantly, he touched Scaeva's pockmarked cheek and rough stubble. His trembling fingers explored the ears, nose and chin of the legionnaire, detecting his son's tears.

Scaeva recovered his composure enough to ask, 'Do you remember, a year ago at the gates of the *castrum* at Gesoriacum, you enquired the whereabouts of Commius, and were turned away by the guards?'

Gestorix nodded faintly.

'I was there. I was one of the guards. I stood and watched you walk away, all the way to the top of the hill. You turned and waved. Tell me you remember.'

Gestorix nodded again. 'Yes, I remember,' but try as he may, he could not conjure up a vision of his son's face.

By now the Cassi and their allies had left the field. Cassivellaunus had accepted the situation and signalled a retreat, saving what was left of his soldiers and chariots to defend his own fortress. Despite the belief of the druids, he could not hold the Romans at the Tamasa but would make a last stand at his stronghold, deep in the woods far to the North. Ceasar, riding the special horse he had reared from a foal, flanked by Commius and his most senior *legati,* crossed the river to congratulate his brave soldiers and centurions and accept their acclamations. On noticing the tribesmen of the Trinovantes assembled some short distance away, displaying none of the jubilation he might have expected at the routing of their sworn enemy, he rode across to them. As he approached the brightly clad warriors in their chequered and striped garb, they parted with an air of solemnity to allow him to pass through. He turned and signalled to Commius and his *legati* to wait where they were. Suddenly realising he was the only man on horseback, he dismounted out of respect and continued on foot to where Mandubracus stood, next to the stricken Gestorix who lay in the arms of the *aquilifer* of the Tenth Legion.

It was the young King of the Trinovantes who greeted him with his customary scowl.

'Behold, Caesar, a son has been returned to his father. The Trinovantes have spilt their blood in keeping my part of our bargain. When do you intend to complete your part and return my son to me?'

With the house of Pompeius in such turmoil since the death of Julia, and the education of the young Briton hardly a matter of priority, that was a question Caesar could not possibly answer. At least the boy was alive and well, whereas Caesar had relinquished one daughter and learnt of the death of the other in the past forty-eight hours. The death of Cordelia had robbed him of the future he once glimpsed in a dream, and the loss of Pompeius as a family member threatened his real-life ambitions.

Mandubracus would have to remain patient for an answer to his question.

EPILOGUE

It would be many more days of marching as the army of Rome snaked its way northwards, further and further away from the river, before finally arriving at the stronghold of the Cassi. The soldiers grew tired of it. Caesar's cavalry was curtailed in their efforts to plunder and devastate the country far and wide by the chariots that Cassivellaunus had deployed to cover his retreat. Consequently, they remained close to the column and contented themselves with such burning and pillage as could be achieved under the protection of the legions.

The tribes that had once been subordinate to Cassivellaunus followed the example of the Trinovantes and came over to the Romans, promising tributes and hostages. Mandubracus, with a feeling of deep satisfaction, had guided Caesar personally through the surrounding forest to the oppidum of Cernodunon. There, the legionnaires made short work of capturing the citadel and forcing the once proud King of the Cassi to surrender himself and his tribe to their sworn enemy. Caesar then left immediately and hurried his entire army back to the coast. Mandubracus had Cassivellaunus executed as soon as the Romans were out of sight. The head of the once feared King of Kings was burned and the ashes buried in a deep pit in a secret place. This was done to prevent the dreaded prophecy from ever coming true, and to allow the heir to the kingship of the Trinovantes, and all the tribes of southeastern Prydain, to return home in safety.

The druids migrated to the north and the west, and Caspar continued his studies, far away from his old home in Camulodunon, and the nightmarish memories it held for him of his encounter with the new king.

Caesar never did recover the coinage that had been removed from the mint at Durobrivae. He wrote to Cicero from the nearest coasts of Britain dated 26th September.

'Britain done with ... hostages taken ... no booty ... a tribute, however, imposed.'

It would be many war-torn years before he returned to Rome. Would he remember the promise he made to the king of a faraway land that he was determined to forget?

Meanwhile, in Rome, Gabinius was put on trial for extortion, committed during his governorship of Syria, with particular reference to the massive bribe he received from Auletes. He was found guilty, even though Cicero had been pressured by Pompeius to speak in his defence. However, there was a public outcry when he was cleared of the charge of treason for deserting his post in Syria and marching to Egypt to re-instate the king; all in defiance of the senate and the sacred Sibylline Books. During this trial, Cicero, who knew what was good for him, said little of what he had learned that evening at the Domus Rostrata. Later that autumn, when heavy rain caused the Tiber to flood and the entire valley of the Circus Maximus was under water, the people cried out that the gods were punishing them in disapproval of Gabinius' acquittal.

The funeral of Julia brought the entire city out in mourning. Pompeius had planned to keep her ashes at his private villa in the Alban Hills, but so loved was she by the people, that they called for a public shrine containing her remains to be erected in the Campus Martius. The proposal was debated in the senate but prohibited by the consul, Lucius Domitus Ahenobarbus, a sworn enemy of both Caesar and Pompeius, and incidentally, the father of Gnaeus, a sworn enemy of Scaeva, who had taunted the Briton over Julia's death on his return to school. Popular demand prevailed, the shrine was erected, and Gnaeus Domitus Ahenobarbus was added to the growing list of people Scaeva was determined to get even with.

The list already contained the name of Lucius Pinarius, who had snatched his *bulla*—a gift from Caesar— from his neck and hurled it onto the track at the Circus Maximus. The other name on the list was another Gnaeus; Gnaeus Pompeius Magnus. Scaeva swore he would never forgive Pompeius for the death of Julia. He would make him pay somehow. Even if it took years of service to him in order to establish a position of trust from which to do him the greatest harm. The mystery of the remaining prophecies was the subject of whispered conversations with his mentor, often lasting deep into the night, with no explanation in sight. He knew he would be required to return home at some point in the future, but that would have to wait. There were scores to be settled before he left Rome.

THE END

ROGER BROOK

AUTHOR'S AFTERWORD

The germ of an idea that became this book came to me many years ago while listening to a radio phone-in program. The presenter had asked his audience to call in with a historical event they would have liked to witness. The one that caught my imagination was the resurrection of Christ. That set me thinking about what other events someone from those times might also have seen, or even been part of. My first thought was Caesar's invasion of Britain, but I didn't know exactly when it occurred. So, I did what anyone else would do, and Googled it. I discovered there were two invasions, 55 and 54 BC. So yes, it would have been possible for one lifetime to span both events, provided the person was a child at the time of Caesar's invasion and lived to a ripe old age. It then occurred to me what a great story that life would make. So, I wondered, what if a young Briton had been taken by Caesar and sent to Rome, to live through the times of all those famous people I had heard of: Pompey, Augustus, Mark Anthony and Cleopatra, right through to the biblical times of the New Testament? I turned again to the internet to see how feasible the idea was. I learned that in between Caesar's two invasions, a nobleman of the Britons had given his son, Scaeva, to Caesar as a hostage. That attested historical event was all I needed to set me off.

Then I set about researching what was written about the people of Britain before Caesar, to give me a background to the story, and also the events in Rome from 55 BC onwards for ideas of a plot going forward. I decided right from the start that the story would be true to historical facts, and told by someone not entirely fictional, from behind the scenes. One of the first hooks I found to pin the hero of my story to an actual event was the blood-stained toga of Pompeius that was carried back to his house by a 'slave,' causing Julia's collapse. Soon afterwards, I devised the five prophecies that would drive the story to its ultimate end, with Julia's death being the fulfilment of the first.

I considered the period and the momentous events it covered would be too much for a single book, so the five prophecies presented a suitable vehicle for a series of five novels. The first sequel, 'The Cuckoo of Rome,' continues the story of Scaeva; acting as a double agent between Caesar and Pompeius during the civil war that followed Caesar's crossing of the Rubicon in 49 BC. The third and fourth in the series will see Scaeva taking a hand in the siege of Alexandria and then taking sides in the war between Octavian and Mark Antony. The final book in the series will undoubtedly be called, 'The Fifth Prophecy.'

The in-depth research and the crafting of the story, weaving myth and legend together with the more factual elements, as well as adding my own inventions to fill in the gaps, has been hugely rewarding. Without a doubt, one of the most painstaking elements of research was to determine three geographical locations: the stronghold of Cassivellaunus, Caesar's crossing point on the Thames, and Pompeius' Domus Rostrata with its famed vestibule.

It is still unproven whether it was his father's old house on the Carinae, or the newer one built in the Field of Mars.

Another fascinating field of research was the backstory of the tribes of southeastern Britain prior to the arrival of Julius Caesar. Caesar himself gives us the merest hint of that by telling us Mandubracius of the Trinovantes put himself under Caesar's protection because Cassivellaunus had killed his father. There is a parallel with this story in a book entitled: 'The History of the Kings of Britain,' written by the twelfth-century historian, Geoffrey of Monmouth. He tells of a Duke Androgeus, who had a dispute with Cassivellaunus, and sent his son, named Scaeva, as a hostage to Caesar in return for his support. Many commentators have argued that Androgeus and Mandubracius were one and the same person. However, I then discovered a book entitled 'The British Chronicles,' written by David Hughes and published in 2007. In it, he gives a regnal list of the iron age high kings of Britain going back centuries before Caesar. It contains not just the list of names, but the stories behind them. In it he explains, in fine detail, exactly who Androgeus and Mandubracius were, both being descendants of Lugios, the Shining One, who lived during the 2nd century BC.

The story of his descendants accommodates the versions of both Caesar and Monmouth, and forms the backstory of my tale, conveyed to the reader by the conversations of various characters at different points in my story. The Chronicles continue into the mid-50s BC. They tell the legend of how Cordelia, daughter of King Llyr, marries Diviciacus of the Suessiones (Shakespeare's Aganippus) who restores her to the throne before returning to his homeland after a few months, leaving her with her ailing father. Cordelia is restored to the throne for a second time by the arrival of Julius Caesar. She later bears Caesar a daughter.

The story of King Lear, as told by Shakespeare, also appears in Monmouth's history, but occurring at an earlier time in another part of Britain. I have gone along with Hughes' suggestion that Caesar expunged all references to Cordelia in his commentaries and he never again believed soothsayers. The writings of Caesar, Monmouth, and Hughes provided three jigsaws of the same picture, each of them with missing and overlapping pieces that fitted in some places but not in others.

Consequently, it has been a most engaging task, sticking to Caesar's timeline, using Hughes' family structures, and throwing in episodes from Monmouth, particularly the great feast held amongst the tribes in celebration of Caesar's retreat. I like to think that my story pays homage to them all.

Having once discovered the name 'Scaeva,' I scoured the web for other references to him but found nothing other than the deeds of Marcus Cassius Scaeva, Caesar's heroic centurion. By some accounts, the standard-bearer of the Tenth Legion, the first man on the beach of Britain in 55 BC, and in action again the following year while crossing the Thames. What a coincidence that the only two men in history to bear that name were in the same place at the same time. There had to be a story there, hence the invention of Gestorix and the inclusion of the prologue.

My primary inspiration for writing a historical novel was the series of books set during the French Revolution, written by Dennis Wheatley. The first title was, 'The

Launching of Roger Brook,' whence comes both the title of this book and my chosen Nome de Plume. Roger Brook was the daring, handsome, resourceful double agent of William Pitt during the Napoleonic wars. A fitting role for Scaeva to play during the forthcoming civil wars in the Roman republic.

The idea of Scaeva being espoused by the horse goddess Epona is to support the decision of Caesar in awarding him the cognomen of Philippus, meaning lover of horses in Greek. Pompeius was known to have a freedman named Philip. It is also useful for Scaeva to have a goddess at hand to help him out of scrapes and keep him alive long enough to fulfil his destiny.

ACKNOWLEDGEMENTS

The Roman Invasion of Britain: Graham Webster

CAESAR The Conquest of Gaul: Translated by S.A. Handford

A New Topographical Dictionary of Ancient Rome: L. Richardson jr.

The Ancient Paths: Graham Robb

The History of the Kings of Britain: Geoffrey of Monmouth

The British Chronicles: David Hughes

The Project Gutenberg eBook of Letters of Marcus Tullius Cicero: Translated by E.S. Shuckenberg

JSTOR digital library

THE LAUNCHING OF SCAEVA

Glossary of republican terminology, place names, and characters mentioned in the text

Lucius **Accius**   Roman playwright and poet, born 170 BC, whose favourite subjects were the legends of the Trojan war.

adventus   A ceremony held to celebrate the arrival at a city of a dignitary. In imperial times, this included the Roman emperor. The city would be decorated for the occasion and a public procession would come out of the city to ritually escort them into the town. Speeches in their honour would be made, followed by a festival and games.

aedile   An elected office of the Roman Republic. They were responsible for the maintenance of public buildings and regulating public festivals. There were two pairs of aediles elected each year; two *plebian* aediles open to men of *plebian* rank, and two *curule* aediles open to both *plebian*s and patricians. The office of *aedile* was held by young men intending to follow the *cursus honorum* to high political office. *Plebian* aediles were elected by the *Plebian* Council under the presidency of a *plebian* tribune. *Curule* aediles were elected by the Tribal Assembly under the presidency of a consul. Aediles were elected in July and took office on the first day in January.

Agamemnon   From Greek mythology, Agamemnon was the husband of Clytemnestra and commanded the united Greek armed forces in the Trojan War. He is also one of the main characters in a trilogy of tragedies by Aeschylus.

agger   see *castrum*

agmen formate   The command for legionnaires to form a square.

Alban Eilir   The druidic festival of the spring equinox.

Alban Hills   Located 12 miles south-east of Rome, the area was used by the wealthy to build their country villas as a retreat from the heat and crowds of Rome.

amphora (pl. amphorae)   Ceramic pot of a standard shape but varying in size. Used for storage and transportation of wet and dry goods, but mostly for wine.

Ancalites   Minor tribe of southeastern Britain mentioned only in the writings of Julius Caesar.

Antipater   Governor of Idumaea under Hyrcanus II. Antipater insinuated himself into a position of influence and became a client of Pompeius Magnus when he conquered Judea in the name of Rome in 63 BC. He was the father of Herod the Great.

Apennines   A series of mountain ranges bordered by narrow coastlands that form the backbone of the Italian peninsular.

apodyterium   The main entrance room of public baths containing cubicles or shelves where citizens could store clothing and other belongings while bathing.

aquilifer   A soldier bearing the eagle standard of a legion. Losing this standard was a terrible disgrace and the position of *aquilifer* was accordingly one of prestige. He was ranked below a centurion and above the *optiones*.

architecti   Legionary engineers from an officer class of troops known as immunes since they were excused from regular duties. They requisitioned and directed regular soldiers as required to build marching camps at the end of each day whilst on the move.

Argiletum   A street that passed through the district of Suburra to enter the forum between the Comitium and the Basilica Aemilia. It was the street of many booksellers.

Ariovistus   The leader of the Suebi and other allied Germanic tribes. Took part in wars in Gaul against the Aedui who were friendly towards Rome. They settled in Gallic territory until they were defeated by Caesar in 58 BC and driven back across the Rhine.

Armorica   The part of Gaul between the Seine and the Loire that includes the Brittany peninsula.

Aryanrot   of the Cassi. Sister of Vellaunus and mother of Hirelglas.

***as* (pl. *assēs*)**   Large cast bronze Roman coin worth one tenth of a silver *denarius*. Fractions were also produced, including *quincunx* (5/12), *triens* (1/3) and *uncia* (1/12).

Asculum   The first Italian city to rise against Rome in 90 BC in a war between the Roman Republic and several of its autonomous allies demanding Roman citizenship.

Atia Balba Secunda   Niece of Caesar via the youngest of his two older sisters. Atia married Gaius Octavius and was the mother of Octavia Minor and Gaius Octavius (b.63 BC) who became the Emperor Augustus. She was an exceptionally religious and moral woman. The same year her husband died

(59 BC) she remarried to Lucius Marcius Philippus (consul 56 BC).

Atrebates   Belgic Iron Age tribe, an offshoot of which migrated to Britain in the first century BC and settled in Hampshire. Joined with other Belgic tribes in opposition to Caesar and were defeated at the battle of the Sabis 57 BC. After the battle, Caesar nominated one of their tribesmen, Commius, as their king.

atrium   see *domus*.

auguraculum   A roofless temple on the Arx of the Capitoline Hill from which Roman priests observed the flights of birds in order to predict the future.

Aurgania   of the Cassi. Sister of Vellaunus and mother of Caradoc.

Axona   The river Aisne in northeastern France. King Galba of the Suessiones led a Belgic alliance and attacked Caesar's camp there in 57 BC. His army was repelled and suffered serious losses when they disengaged and retreated.

Balnaea Pallacinae   Public bath house in the Roman district of Pallacinae.

Basilica   A building functioning as a meeting hall. Typically designed with a rectangular base and a central nave flanked by two or more aisles divided by columns and covered by a roof at two levels. These buildings often formed the sides of a city's forum and were fronted by a row of shops.

Basilica Aemilia   Basilica built on the northern side of the forum in 179 BC by Marcus Fulvius Nobilior replacing a preexisting building. Initially known as the Basilica Fulvia, it was completed by his colleague Marcus Aemilius Lepidus and frequently restored by members of the Aemelian gens. In 55 BC, a new edifice was started by Lucius Aemilius Lepidus Paullus, using the foundations and many of the original columns. On completion, it was known as the Basilica Paulli.

Basilica Semprona   Basilica built on the southern side of the forum in 169 BC by Tiberius Sempronius Gracchus.

Bellovaci   Belgic tribe defeated by Caesar in 57 BC.

Beltane   Celtic festival held halfway between the spring equinox and the summer solstice.

Berenice IV Epiphaneia   Ruled Egypt jointly with her mother, Cleopatra Tryphaena, during the exile of her father Ptolemy XII Auletes from 58 to 55 BC. Tryphaena died of unknown causes in 57 BC, leaving Berenice as sole ruler until overthrown by a Roman army in 55 BC led by Aulus Gabinius who restored her father as king in Alexandria. Auletes executed Berenice as punishment for usurping his throne.

Bibrax   An oppidum near the Axona river occupied by a tribe friendly to the Romans. It was besieged by a coalition of Belgic tribes until rescued by Caesar in 57 BC.

Bibroci   Minor tribe of southeastern Britain mentioned only in the writings of Julius Caesar.

biga (pl. *bigae*)   Two-horse racing chariot.

Blad   Second of the sons of Lugios by his third wife, Gwen. When his elder brother Madawc the Brehin died, Blad took the throne of the Trinovantes ahead of Madawc's sons, who were not of age. He was murdered, poisoned by their mother, Etain.

Blandeno   Unknown location mentioned in a letter from Marcus to Quintus Cicero dated 3rd June 54 BC. Marcus had received letters posted from Blandeno from both Caesar and Quintus, despatched at the same time. Caesar's letter was, apparently, full of pleasantries about the arrival of Quintus and the renewed memory of his affection for Marcus.

braccae   Woollen trousers worn by the Gauls and Britons. The Romans considered anything encircling the legs be to a sign of ill health and effeminacy.

Brehin   The Iron-Age high kings of Celtic Britain were called Brehins. The Brehin was the overlord of all the British tribal chiefs and/or British regional kings. The first Brehin was reckoned by medieval historians to have been the ancient heroic legendary figure Brutus. His story is told by medieval writer Geoffrey of Monmouth in his book 'Historia Regnum Britanniae'.

Brigantium   Present day Briançon. The first village in Gallia after crossing the Alps along the Via Domita.

Brutus of Troy   According to legend, was a descendant of Trojan hero Aneas, son of the Greek goddess Aphrodite. Brutus was the leader of a colony of Trojan descendants who settled in Britain circa 1100 BC.

buccina   The *buccina* was like the *cornu*, except it had a slightly smaller bore and a more flared bell opening at the end. The *buccina* was used to signal changes of watch during the night, wake-up calls, and for announcing mealtimes.

bulla A neck chain and round pouch containing an amulet to protect against evil spirits, given to Roman boys before manhood. The amulets were usually phallic symbols. The materials used depended upon the wealth of the family, a cloth or leather pouch and lead amulet for the less well-off, and gilt or solid gold for the upper classes. Roman boys wore a *bulla* until they came of age and wore the toga virilis (toga of manhood) . The *bulla* would be put into the care of the parental household deity.

Caelian Hill A fashionable residential district of Rome.

calculator A teacher of arithmetic in Roman schools. Instructed children in using an abacus and, according to Horatius (the famous Roman poet who was taught by Orbilius), favoured tablets of thin black wax for the use of the pupils.

caliga (**pl.** ***caligae***) Heavy-soled hobnailed military sandal-boots worn as standard issue by Roman legionary soldiers.

calix Shallow, bowl-shaped, wide-brimmed drinking vessel with a stemmed base and vertical handles on either side. Often lavishly decorated or engraved.

Campus Martius Field of Mars. The open expanse of ground bounded by the Servian Wall to the east and the river Tiber to the west. Dedicated to the god Mars after the last Etruscan king was exiled, it was used for military training and political gatherings. Several temples were built over the centuries and in the early first century BC, blocks of *insulae* and private villas encroached outside the city walls. In 55 BC, Pompeius Magnus built the first permanent theatre in Rome.

Camulodunon The stronghold of Camulus, the god of war. The Citadel occupied by the Trinovantes in the early to mid-first century BC. It became the Roman town of Camulodunum on the site of present-day Colchester.

Cantiaci   Iron age tribe occupying the area of Kent in the southeastern corner of Britain. Caesar mentions four kings who held power in this region at the time of his invasions, Taximagulus, Segovax, Cingetorix and Carvillus. Their capital was Durovernon.

Cantium   The territory of the Cantiaci. Present day Kent.

Capitoline Hill   The geographical and ceremonial centre of Rome at the western end of the forum. Its twin peaks were the site of the earliest temples built during the time of the kings.

Capitolium   The Capitoline Hill. The word Capitolium first meant the Temple of Jupiter Optimus Maximus, but was used later for the entire hill.

capsarius   Attendant at a public bathhouse, usually a public or privately owned slave. The *capsarius* took charge of the clothes and belongings of bathers.

Carinae   Meaning, Keels. Exclusive neighbourhood of Rome at the foot of the Esquiline Hill. Favoured by the senatorial classes. Gets its name from a row of small hills and valleys, that, from a certain viewpoint resemble upturned boats.

carnyx (pl. carnyces)   Wind instrument of the Iron Age Celts. A type of bronze trumpet with an elongated S shape of significant height, often made with an open-mouthed animal's head at the bell end. Used in warfare to incite troops into battle and intimidate opponents.

Cassi   Iron Age tribe of Celts I have assumed to be the tribe of Heli and Vellaunus, occupying an area of twenty by thirty miles bounded by the north bank of the Thames. Archaeologist Graham Webster suggests that the lack of coinage finds in this area showed it was occupied by a tribe which resisted any entry by migrants into their lands; presumably the kingdom of Cassivellaunus.

castrum **(pl. *castra*)**   Roman military camp. The layout of these fortresses was of the same overall design and differed only in size depending on the number of legions it catered for. From a permanent military base to a marching camp erected at the end of each day, they were all constructed with a rectangular ditch (*fossa*) and bank (*agger*) topped with a timber palisade of stakes. There were gates halfway along each side linked by the Via Principalis, which crossed the Via Praetoria, linking the main gate (Porta Praetoria) to the back gate (Porta Decumena). An open square in the centre of the camp where the two streets crossed was known as the *Principia,* which was used as a parade ground and was the site for the camp headquarters (*Praetorium*). During the summer campaigning season, the legionnaires slept in tents. In the winter, they built wooden barracks.

Marcus Porcius **Cato**   An influential conservative senator. Effective orator and follower of stoicism, he adopted an austere lifestyle and was noted for his incorruptibility and scrupulous honesty.

cavea   The curved seating sections of Greek or Roman theatres and amphitheatres.

Cenimagni   Minor tribe of southeastern Britain mentioned only in the writings of Julius Caesar.

Cernodunon Meaning the stronghold of Cernunnos, the god of wild animals, is the name I have attributed to the stronghold of Cassivellaunus. The exact location of the fortification remains a mystery. There are only a few known iron age camps in the area north of the Thames indicated by the Archaeologist Graham Webster to be the territory of Cassivellaunus, and none of them would appear to be large enough. In 1932 Sir Mortimer Wheeler excavated Devil's Dyke, a large first century BC entrenchment near Wheathampstead in Hertfordshire. A plaque was placed in a wall at the entrance saying it was probably the site attacked by Caesar in 54 BC, but no archaeological evidence of military activity was found.

Cingulum Town in the region of Picenum. Comments from Caesar and Cicero indicate that the town was built or rebuilt by Titus Labienus, senior *legate* of Caesar in Gaul.

Cisalpine Gaul Roman province bounded by the Alps in the north and west, the Adriatic Sea in the east, and the Rubicon River in the south. Cisalpine means 'on this side of the Alps', as opposed to **Transalpine Gaul,** meaning 'on the far side of the Alps'. Caesar was given governorship of both provinces at the end of his consulship in 59 BC.

clepsydra A water clock. It measured time by the regulated flow of a quantity of water into or out of a vessel.

Cloaca Maxima A sewer built in Rome to drain local marshes and remove waste from the city. It ran across the forum, covered by planks, and into the Tiber, but was later taken underground.

Clytemnestra From Greek mythology, Clytemnestra was the wife of Agamemnon, who commanded the united Greek armed forces in the Trojan War. Also, the title of a play by the Roman playwright Accius, that was staged at the opening of Pompey's theatre in 55 BC.

Coit Andred   Large area of west Kent and east Sussex, thickly forested and sparsely inhabited. A territory unclaimed by any tribe.

col   The lowest point of a ridge or saddle between two peaks, typically providing a pass from one side of a mountain to another.

Collis Hortorum   A hill to the north of Rome where it became fashionable for wealthy citizens to create lavish terraced gardens.

Comana   A city in the historical region of Cappadocia in present day Turkey.

comfrey, poultice of   A potent herbal remedy for curing cuts and bruises.

Comitium   The original open-air public meeting place of Rome, situated in the northwest corner of the forum, in front of the senate house.

consul   Either of the two highest ranking posts in Rome after the fall of the kings; effectively heads of state. Consuls were nominated by the senate and elected by the Centuriate Assembly (a committee of citizens). They held office for one year, and each consul had the power of veto over the other's decisions. They each had a personal escort of twelve *lictor*s. When their term of office expired, consuls generally were appointed to serve as governors of provinces.

conubium   The right, sometimes given to non-Romans, of contracting a Roman marriage.

convivium   An informal banquet for invited friends and family.

cornu   A large brass horn used as a military and ceremonial instrument. Formed in the shape of the letter G, it had a crossbar brace that supported the weight of the instrument on the player's shoulder.

cresset   A metal cup or basket, often mounted to or suspended from a pole containing oil, pitch or something flammable. They are burned as a light or a beacon.

cubiculum   see *domus*.

cuirass   Body armour comprising breastplate and backplate fastened together.

Curia Hostilia   The senate house in Rome situated on the north side of the Comitium.

cursus honorum   The sequential order of public offices held by aspiring politicians, designed for men of senatorial rank. Each office had a minimum age for election, there were also minimum intervals between holding successive offices. Prior to entry, a young man was expected to serve in the military. The posts were: quaestor; minimum age thirty, aedile: thirty-six, praetor: thirty-nine, and consul at age forty-two.

curule **aedile**   see aedile.

curule **chair**   A chair of high office traditionally made of or veneered with ivory. It had curved legs, low arms and no back, forming a wide X shape. It could be folded and was easily transportable.

decimation A form of Roman military discipline in which every tenth man in a group was executed by members of his cohort. It was used to punish large groups guilty of offences such as cowardice, mutiny, desertion or insubordination.

denarius Standard Roman silver coin originally worth ten *assēs* but revalued to sixteen *assēs* due to the reduction in weight of an *as.*

Diodorus Siculus Contemporary Greek historian who researched and wrote, between 60 and 30 BC, a forty-volume history of the world. Arranged in three parts, it covered the mythical history of the Trojan war, the death of Alexander the Great, and the contemporary period up to 60 BC.

diribitores Officers who distributed voting ballots to citizens during an assembly. They played an important role in ensuring fair and accurate voting during these assemblies.

Diviciacus King of the Belgic tribe of the Suessiones. Described by Caesar as having been the most powerful king in Gaul, controlling a large part not only of Belgic country but also of Britannia. His existence is evidenced by bronze coinage. In the legend of King Lear, as told by twelfth-century historian Geoffrey of Monmouth, Lear's daughter, Cordelia, was married to the king of the Franks; purported by David Hughes in his British Chronicles to be Diviciacus.

Divico Leader of the Helvetian tribe of the Tigurini. Defeated a Roman army in 107 BC at the battle of Burdigala, killing the consul, Lucius Cassius Longinus. In 58 BC, he attempted to negotiate safe passage for his tribe through the Roman region of

Provence. The request was denied by Caesar out of revenge for a relative killed at Burdigala.

Lucius **Domitius** Ahenobarbus   Father of Gnaeus Domitius Ahenobarbus. A friend of Cato and an enemy of Caesar. In the consular elections for 55 BC, he was a candidate, but was forcibly driven away from the voting arena, leaving Pompeius and Crassus to be elected. He was not impeded the following year and became consul for 54 BC alongside Appius Claudius Pulcher, a relative of Pompeius.

domus   A type of town house occupied by the upper classes or wealthy freedmen. The *domus* included multiple rooms, indoor courtyards and gardens. The *vestibulum* (entrance hall), usually set between shopfronts facing the street, led into a large central hall, the *atrium* which was the focal point of the building and contained a statue of, or an altar to the household gods. In the centre of the *atrium* floor was a sunken *impluvium* that caught rainwater from an opening in the roof. Rooms opening onto the *atrium* were cubicula (sing. *cubiculum*) (bedrooms), a *triclinium* (dining room) and *tablinum*, the office of the householder, usually set between the *atrium* and the *peristylium* (garden).

Domus Rostrata   The home of Pompeius Magnus, said by Cicero to have a *vestibulum* decorated with *rostrum*, the ramming beaks of ships captured by Pompeius in his campaign against the pirates. The location of this building is assumed by many to have been the one built by his father on the Carinae. However, it is likely this building, described by Plutarch as 'simple and modest', would have been destroyed by the great fire of 64 AD. The Domus Rostrata of Pompeius Magnus was occupied long after that date by the Gordians in the third century AD. The only other possible location is the house Pompeius built near his theatre in the Campus Martius on his return to

Rome after his campaign against the Mediterranean pirates in 67 BC. It was said by Plutarch to be 'more splendid than the one he had before, but not large enough to excite envy'.

Dun Bury   Iron age hill fort site at Danbury near Chelmsford in Essex, the territory of the Trinovantes.

Durobrivae   Sited on the river Medway at present day Rochester, it was the second largest oppidum in Cantium after Durovernon. Likely to have been a centre of administration.

Durovernon   Capital of the Cantiaci. Thought to be Bigbury Camp, an iron age hillfort near present day Canterbury.

englyn (pl. englynion)   A style of ancient Welsh poetry that used emotive language to animate and propel the verses.

Ephesus   Ancient Greek city on the coast of Ionia, in present day Turkey. Site of the Temple of Artemis, one of the Seven Wonders of the World. It became a subject of the Roman Republic in 129 BC.

Esquiline Hill   A fashionable residential district of Rome.

Etain   The second wife and widow of Madawc the Brehin. Her sons, Manan (Imanuentus) and Malin were minors when their father died, so Madawc's brother, Blad took the throne and Etain married Madawc's younger brother, Llyr. Etain plotted Blad's murder, but she died soon afterwards.

fasces lictoriae   Ceremonial axes bound with bundles of rods that symbolised power and authority. Tradition and protocol demanded they were carried by officials called *lictor*s in procession before a magistrate. The number of *lictor*s required depended on the rank. Twelve *lictor*s for a consul and lesser numbers for praetors, *curule* aediles and quaestors.

Flaminian Way   Constructed in 220 BC, the road from Rome to Ariminum (Rimini) on the Adriatic coast.

fossa   see *castrum*

Gallia   The Roman name for the area of western Europe encompassing present day France, Belgium and neighbouring countries inhabited by Celtic tribes.

garum   A fermented fish sauce used as a condiment, popular in the Roman world.

gens Julia   One of the most ancient patrician families in Rome. The first of the family to attain consulship was Gaius Julius Iulus in 489 BC. They claimed descent from the Greek goddess Aphrodite, worshipped in Rome as Venus.

Gesoriacum   A coastal town of the Morini tribe on the site of present-day Boulogne-sur-Mer. Likely departure point of Caesar's expedition in 55 BC.

gladius   A short-bladed sword used by the Romans. It was more effective in close combat with opponents armed with heavier swords with longer blades.

Gonerila   The eldest of the legendary King Llyr's three daughters. Shakespear has her commit suicide in the final act of his play. In my version of the legend, she takes as a second husband, Taximagulus, the father of Segovax, both of whom are mentioned by Caesar as Kings of Cantium.

grammarian   A teacher responsible for the second stage in the traditional Roman education system after a boy had learned his basic Greek and Latin. They taught the works of the ancient Greek poets either at the home of their students or at their own schools.

greaves   Pairs of metal leg armour protecting the shins. In Roman defensive formations, a greave was sometimes worn on the left leg only, which was more exposed under the shield.

groma   A Roman surveying instrument operated by a ***gromatici***. It comprised a vertical staff with horizontal cross pieces mounted at right angles on a bracket. Each cross piece had a plumb line hanging vertically at each end. It was used to survey straight lines and right angles, thence squares and rectangles.

gustatio   The first course of a dinner in ancient Rome intended to stimulate the appetite.

Hesiod   Poet of ancient Greece, a contemporary of Homer. A major source of Greek mythology.

hirst   A small woodland settlement.

Homer   Poet of ancient Greece who lived in the eighth century BC. Famous for his epic poems about the Trojan war.

horseheal   A plant native to Asia famous for its therapeutic and medicinal properties.

John **Hyrcanus** II   Jewish High Priest for much of the first century BC. Appointed King of Judea 67 BC on the death of his mother, the queen, but swiftly challenged by his brother causing a civil war. Restored to the throne by the intervention of Pompeius Magnus in 63 BC.

Idumean palm   The Roman province of Idumea (present day Israel) was famous for its fine palms. The palm fronds were given to chariot drivers as signs of victory.

Illyricum   A Roman province along the east coast of the Adriatic Sea and its inland mountains. An area covered by many of the present-day Balkan states.

impluvium   see *domus*.

insulae   Blocks of tenement buildings providing affordable housing for the poorer classes of Rome. They were constructed of red brick, covered with concrete, and were often five or more stories high. A water supply and cooking facilities were provided in communal courtyards. The street level characteristically housed artisan workshops and commercial establishments.

Julia Major   Eldest of Caesar's two older sisters. She was the mother of Quintus Pedius and grandmother of Lucius Pinarius. Together with their cousin, Gaius Octavius (the grandson of Julia Minor), they were named as Caesar's heirs in his will.

Julii Caesares   The most illustrious family of the gens Julia.

jus Latii   Certain rights and privileges amounting to qualified citizenship of a person who was not a Roman citizen. Essentially, the right to legal intermarriage (*conubium*).

kalends   The first day of the month signifying a new lunar phase. Romans reckoned the days backwards from three named dates in the month. *Kalends* was always the first day; nones, the seventh day of the long months (March, May, July and October) but on the fifth day of other months; and ides the fifteenth day of the long months, but the thirteenth day of the others. Therefore, the seventh day before the *kalends* of September means 23rd August. Although by 55 BC, January and February had been added to the Roman calendar, August was originally the sixth month and known as Sextilis, it had 29 days. In 8 BC it was re-named August to honour the title of the first Roman Emperor.

tribunus **laticlavius**   A 'broad-striped-tribune' was one of six military tribunes in a legion. Usually, a young man around the age of twenty that belonged to a wealthy family. Or they were friends of the *legate* they served under. They did not need previous military experience, and it was common to return to Rome to run for a quaestorship after two or three years as a tribune. The position was the first step on the *cursus honorum.*

lectica   A portable couch with a leather roof supported by four corner posts. It stood on four feet with detachable poles on each side so it may be carried on the shoulders of up to eight slaves. Curtains at the side were provided for the privacy of the occupant. Wealthy Romans kept certain strong handsome slaves to act as their *lecticarii* and dressed them in smart liveries.

legate (**pl.** *legati*)   Officer who acted as a deputy general to governors of provinces conquered by Rome in the 2nd and 1st centuries BC. Julius Caesar started the practice of appointing legates to command legions in the army.

Leno   One of the stock characters in Roman comedy. The pimp or slave dealer. Although the activities of the character are portrayed as highly immoral, the leno always acts legally and is always paid for his services.

Publius Cornelius **Lentulus** Spinther   Received the backing of Caesar and Pompeius to become consul in 57 BC. He moved successfully in the senate to have Cicero recalled from exile and have his property returned to him. As proconsul, he became governor of Cilicia (to which the island of Cyprus had been added). He secured for himself instructions from the senate to intervene in the Egyptian dynastic struggle, but stopped after a Sibylline oracle prohibited the use of an army.

lictor   A Roman civil servant who was an attendant and bodyguard to a magistrate. They carried *fasces*—a bundle of rods surrounding an axe—which symbolised power to carry out capital punishment.

Llyr   Youngest of the three sons of Lugios by his third wife, Gwen. Emerged as King of the Cantiaci after territorial disputes with his half-brother Heli. He married Etain, widow of his brother Madawc the Brehin, and adopted their two sons, Manan (Imanuentus) and Malin. A curse was put on his citadel when his other brother, Blad was murdered by Etain. Etain died three days later, so he moved his court to Durovernon. He remarried and had three daughters who took precedence over his stepsons. He married off his youngest daughter, Cordelia, to Diviciacus, a powerful king in Gaul, and gave equal shares of his kingdom to his two elder daughters, Gonerila and Rigontia. As he grew older, his power was reduced by his daughters and their husbands until he went to Gaul to reconcile with Cordelia. He returned to Britain supported by the army of Diviciacus and was restored to the throne. He executed the husbands of his daughters, and Diviciacus returned to Gaul. His two eldest daughters remarried local warlords and continued their campaign against him. He died in reduced circumstances three months before the arrival of Caesar, leaving Cordelia on the throne of the Cantiaci.

GLOSSARY

Ludi Apollinares A festival of games, chariot races, plays and sacrifices in honour of the Greek god Apollo. They were held annually at the Circus Maximus between the 6th and 13th of July. First organised in 212 BC.

Ludi Circenses Games presented in the circus. The earliest games were horse races in the Circus Flaminius. The term also referred to chariot racing at the Circus Maximus.

ludus grammaticus A school for boys at their second level of education.

Lugudunon A Gallic settlement and oppidum on the river Rhone in the Roman province of Narbonensis. Site of present-day Lyon.

Lugh Celtic god of light and the sun.

Lugios 'The Shining One' Legendary King of the Britons, also known as Locrine. He created British colonies on the continent and joined the Gauls and the Germans in the Cimbrian wars against Rome, 113 to 101 BC, sometimes known as the second Celtic storm. On return to Britain, he was killed in a civil war against his ex-wife Gwen, mother of Madawc, Blad and Llyr.

Luna of the Trinovantes. Daughter of Madawc the Brehin. Became Queen of the Trinovantes after her uncle Blad was poisoned. Married her cousin Ludd to unite the Trinovantes and the Cassi. She and her husband were murdered by her half-brother, Manan (Imanuentus). She had two sons, Androgeus and Tenvantius.

Madawc Eldest of the sons of Lugios by his third wife, Gwen. Emerged as the Brehin after territorial disputes with his half-brother, Heli, on the death of their father. He had a daughter,

Luna, by his first wife, and died while his sons, Manan (Imanuentus) and Malin, by his second wife Etain, were still minors.

Malachite   An opaque, green-banded mineral referred to in ancient Rome as 'the Peacock stone', sacred to the goddess Juno. It came to Rome via Egyptian mines in the Sinai Peninsula.

Malin   Son of Madawc by his second wife, Etain. Murdered by his brother Manan.

Manan   see Imanuentus

Mare Superum   The upper sea, the northern section of the present-day Adriatic.

Gaius **Marius**   Roman general and statesman. Brought in reforms to the military recruitment process that enabled him to defeat an alliance of Celtic tribes that ended the Cimbrian wars in 101 BC. He was consul seven times and was married to Julia, the paternal aunt of Julius Caesar.

Massalia   A Greek colony founded circa 600 BC in the western Mediterranean. Site of present-day Marseille.

Matrona Pass   The lowest of the principal crossings of the main range of the Alps between Italy and Gaul. Route of the Via Domitia.

medicus   A military physician. During the period of the Republic, they mainly treated wealthy officers in the army. Common soldiers had to purchase medical treatment from local civilian practitioners or receive first aid and other remedies from fellow soldiers.

Mercurius   Roman equivalent to Hermes, the Greek messenger of the gods.

metae   The three cone shaped posts along the *spina* of the Circus. One at each end acted as turning posts, a third was placed in the middle.

metatores   A military surveyor, responsible for laying out fortifications.

Miles Gloriosus   A stock character of Roman comedies, a vain, lustful and stupid soldier.

milites gregarii   The non-specialist regular soldiers that made of the bulk of a legion.

mons veneris   In females, the pubic mound.

Morini   A Belgic coastal tribe of the present-day Pas de Calais region. Caesar fought an indecisive campaign against them in 56 BC, but they sent envoys the following year while he was preparing his expedition to Britain.

Mutina   Present day Modena. Capital of the Roman province of Cisalpine Gaul, where Caesar performed his administrative duties during the winter months of his governorship.

Nervii   One of the most powerful Belgic tribes in northern Gaul. They were almost annihilated by Caesar at the battle of the Sabis in 57 BC.

Noviodunum   Oppidum of the Suessiones that was besieged by Caesar in 57 BC. The site of present-day Pommiers.

Noviomagus   Capital of the Atrebates in Britain. Near present day Chichester.

nundinae   The cycle of market days of the Roman calendar separated by an inclusive nine days. The earliest Roman calendars had 38 such cycles running for 304 days from March to December preceding an unorganised expanse of about 50 winter days.

Oceanus Britannicus   To the Roman Republic, it was the sea at the edge of the known world. With massive tides and strong currents accompanied by variable winds, it presented a formidable challenge to the Romans, who were used to the Mediterranean, where tides are hardly perceptible.

Gaius **Oppius**   A close friend of Caesar who managed his private affairs during his absence from Rome. He organised a relay of letter carriers for communication between Caesar in Gaul and Rome, which was also used by Marcus Cicero to correspond with his brother, Quintus, while with Caesar was in Britain.

optimates   Meaning 'the best ones' and *populares* meaning 'supporters of the people' are the labels applied to politicians, political groups, traditions, strategies or ideologies during the late Roman Republic. The *optimates* were the supporters of the continued authority of the senate.

optio **(pl. *optiones*)**   from the Latin 'to choose', was an executive officer chosen by a centurion to be his second-in-command.

Our Sea   In Latin *Mare Nostrum*. The name the Romans gave to the Mediterranean Sea.

Ovile   Meaning 'sheep fold' in Latin. This was an enclosed are of the Campus Martius used for voting. The name came from its resemblance to sheep pens. Sometimes referred to as the *Saepta* meaning 'enclosure'.

paedagogus   usually a slave or freedman who taught Greek to the young sons of citizens and would sometimes accompany a child to school and be in charge of their appearance and behaviour.

Pallacinae   A district in Rome, mentioned only in the works of Cicero, thought to be near the northeast end of the Circus Flaminius.

Pallatine Hill   The hill on the south side of the forum and one of the most ancient parts of the city. During the Republican period (c. 509-44 BC) many affluent Romans built their residences there.

Lucius Aemilius Lepidus **Paullus**   Roman politician and friend of Cicero who, as aedile in 55 BC, rebuilt the Basilica Aemilia. It became known as the Basilica Paulii.

peristylium   see *domus*.

Lucius Marcius **Philippus**   A politician who claimed descent from Alexander the Great. He had two children, a daughter, Marcia and a son, also named Lucius Marcellus Philippus. His second marriage was to Caesar's recently widowed niece, Atia Balba, mother of Octavia and Octavius. He was consul in 56 BC.

Picenum   A northern region of Italy on the coast of the Adriatic. Birthplace of Pompeius Strabo and his son Pompeius Magnus.

pilum (pl. *pila*)   A javelin with wooden pegs that held the iron head to the shaft. On impact, the pegs would break and render the weapon unusable to an enemy. It was used by the Roman army at a distance of 15 to 30 metres immediately before engagement in close combat.

Pillars of Hercules   In antiquity, the phrase was used for the promontories that flank the entrance to the straights of Gibraltar. The northern peak is the Rock of Gibraltar. The identity of the corresponding North African peak has never been established.

Pindar   Greek poet of the 5th century BC. Better known by his reputation than his writings in the late Republican period, but was later imitated and popularised by Quintus **Horatius** Flaccus..

plebian (*pleb*)   Free Roman citizens who were not members of the patrician, senatorial or equestrian classes.

plebian **aedile**   see aedile.

pompa circensis   The procession that preceded the official games held in the circus as part of religious festivals and other occasions.

Pontifex Maximus   The highest office in the state religion in ancient Rome. A distinctly religious position under the early Roman Republic, but gradually became more politicised. Members of the office were elected for life. Caesar was elected *Pontifex Maximus* in 63 BC.

popina (pl. *popinae*)   A type of wine bar frequented by the lower classes and slaves. They were simply furnished and provided food, drink, sex and gambling.

populares   see *optimates*

porticus   A covered colonnade, usually with an enclosed back wall and one or more parallel rows of columns, but occasionally open and entirely columnar.

Portus Itius   Caesar twice used the term *ad Portum Itium* to describe the embarkation of troops for his invasion of Britain in 54 BC. The site is likely to have been north of his departure point the previous year but the exact location remains unconfirmed. *Itium* literally means 'That's it' in Latin, so *Portus Itius* could be translated as 'Journey's end,' or equally 'Journey's beginning'

praetor   A senior magistrate one step below the consul who was attended by six *lictor*s. In the late Republican period, there were eight elected each year. These included the **praetor urbanus**, who could not leave the city for more than ten days at a time and was given appropriate duties in Rome. He superintended the *Ludi Apollinares*. See *cursus honorum*.

praetorium   see *castrum*.

primus pilus   (First Spear) The senior centurion of the first cohort in a Roman legion.

principia   see *castrum*.

principium   Decided by lots, the name given to first tribe to vote in a tribal assembly. It was believed that the order of the lot was chosen by the gods, and thus, that the result of the first tribe to vote was approved by the gods.

Propontis   Present day Sea of Marmara, a small inland sea linking the Black Sea to the Aegean.

propraetor   A former *praetor* in Rome whose term in office after one year was prolonged as a governor of a province.

pteruges   A skirt made of strips of leather, worn dependent from the waists of Roman and Greek *cuirasses* of warriors and soldiers, defending the hips and thighs.

Appius Claudius **Pulcher**   see Lucius **Domitius** Ahenobarbus.

Puteoli   Present day Pozzuoli, a harbour city on the north side of the Gulf of Naples.

quadriga   A chariot drawn by four horses, favoured for chariot racing.

quaestor   During the period of the Republic, quaestors were elected officials who supervised the state treasury and conducted audits. This could be expanded in the military to encompass leadership and command. See *cursus honorum.*

quincunx   A bronze Roman coin worth five twelfths of an as. It was produced only during the Second Punic War 218 to 204 BC.

Quirinal Hill   Northern-most of the seven hills of Rome

Gaius **Rabirius** Postumus   A Roman Banker.

Rhenus   The river Rhine, a barrier between the Germanic tribes and Gaul.

Rhodanus   The river Rhône, a major channel for trade and communication between the Mediterranean and central Gaul.

Rigontia   The second of the legendary King Llyr's three daughters. Shakespear has her poisoned by her elder sister in the final act of his play. In my version of the legend, she takes as a second husband Carvillus the father of Cingetorix, both of whom are mentioned by Caesar as Kings of Cantium.

Quintus **Roscius** Gallus   A renown Roman comic actor who was once defended by Cicero in a lawsuit.

The ***Rostra***   A speaker's platform built within the circle of the *comitium*. It derives its name from the six *rostrum* mounted to its side. The *rostrum* were captured following the victory which ended the Latin War in the Battle of Antium in 338 BC.

rostra (pl. *rostrum*)   The ramming beaks of a warship that extended from the keel at the bow.

Publius Sulpicius **Rufus**   Roman general under Caesar in 55 BC. He was entrusted with holding the harbour at Gesoriacum against any clans of the Morini that had not sent envoys.

Sabis   Present day river Selle in northern France. Site of a battle in 57BC where Caesar defeated a union of four Belgic tribes.

salt route   Ancient trading route where salt was brought inland from Ostia at the mouth of the Tiber river.

Saône   A river in eastern France that joins the Rhône at Lyon.

Sappho   Female Greek poet from 6th century BC. Her poetry was written to be sung while accompanied by music.

satyr   In Greek mythology, a satyr was a male nature spirit with a permanent exaggerated erection. It stood upright and had the mane, ears, rear legs and tail of a horse.

scutum   A large rectangular semi-cylindrical shield carried by Roman soldiers in the first century BC.

seer   see vate.

Segontiaci   Minor tribe of southeastern Britain mentioned only in the writings of Julius Caesar.

Septimus   The seventh (month of the year). Initially, the Romans had ten months in the year beginning with March. January and February were added later but the old names remained until the fifth and six months were renamed after Julius Caesar and Augustus.

Sequani   A Gallic tribe dwelling in the upper river basin of the Saône river in the Jura mountains. Before the arrival of Caesar, they joined with Germanic tribes to defeat their rivals, the Aedui.

Servian Wall   The city walls of Republican Rome constructed in the early 4th century BC.

sesterce **(pl. sesterces)**   Silver Roman coin worth ¼ of a *dinarius*.

shipwreck   Roman slang word for a crash at the chariot races.

Silphium   A plant used in antiquity as a perfume, aphrodisiac, medicine and contraceptive. Now extinct.

spina The central barrier that ran down the centre of the Circus Maximus in Rome. It featured ornate columns, statues and commemorative obelisks. There was a turning post at each end.

stola A long dress that reached down to the feet that was worn over a tunic. Worn by respectable women throughout Roman history.

Gnaeus Pompeius **Strabo** Father of Gnaeus Pompeius Magnus. Served as consul in 89 BC. Known for his avarice and cruelty.

Suburra A vast and populous neighbourhood of Rome. Home to an urban underclass who lived in miserable conditions. Caesar lived there in the *domus* of his family until he was made *Pontifex Maximus* in 63 BC. The Suburra had grown up around the property many years before his birth.

Suessiones Belgic tribe that dwelt in the present-day Aisne and Oise regions of France. Besieged and conquered by Caesar in 57 BC.

Lucius Cornelius **Sulla** Felix Roman general and statesman. He won the first large-scale civil war in Roman history and became the first man of the Republic to seize power by force. Died 78 BC.

summo canis Top dog

supplicatio A thanksgiving when a great military victory had been gained. It was usually decreed as soon as official intelligence of the victory had been received by a letter from the general in command. The number of days during which it was to last was proportioned to the importance of the victory.

Sutri   A town 30 miles north of Rome.

***taberna* (pl. *tabernae*)**   A type of shop or stall, usually a single room for the sale of goods including food and drink, or services. They were often incorporated into domestic dwellings on the ground floor flanking the main entrance to a *domus*, but with one side open to the street.

Tabernae Novae   A row of shops lining the front of the Basilica Aemilia, opening onto the north side of the forum.

tablinum   see *domus*.

Tabularium   The official records office of Rome, housing the offices of many city officials. It stood at the western end of the forum at the foot of the Capitoline Hill, below the Temple of Jupiter Optimus Maximus.

Taranis   The Celtic god of thunder. Often depicted as a bearded figure with a thunderbolt in one hand and a wheel in the other.

Tarentum   A field once used for ancient games and later kept for equestrian exercise at the western edge of the Campus Martius.

Tigurini   A clan of the tribe of the Helvetii that dwelt in the present-day Swiss canton of Vaud. They took part in the Cimbrian wars against Rome 113-101 BC. The migration of the Helvetii across the territories of Gallic tribes friendly to Rome prompted Caesar's expedition into Gaul in 58 BC.

Titus Tatius   According to the Roman foundation myth, he was the King of the Sabines and joint ruler of the Kingdom of Rome for several years.

toga day   17th of March each year was the day when all boys turning fifteen in the preceding year took part in a ceremony in the forum, the festival of Liberalia. This signified their coming of age and allowed them to don the toga of manhood, which was totally white. They also gave up their *bulla*, a neck-pendant containing a charm, to their household gods.

toga praetexta   A white toga with a broad purple stripe on its border, worn over a tunic with two broad vertical purple stripes. It was the costume of *curule* magistrates (consuls, praetors and *curule* aediles) in their official functions. Also worn by freeborn boys before they came of age. It represented their protection by law from sexual predation and immoral or immodest influence.

tonsor   A barber. They could be mobile, working in the street, or from a fixed location known as a *tonstrinae.*

torc   A thick neck ring, open at the front, made from either a single piece or strands of metal, twisted together. Celtic torcs were usually made of gold and identified the wearer as a person of high rank.

Transalpine Gaul   see Cisalpine Gaul.

Treeno (slang)   Member of the Trinovantes tribe.

tribune   The title of various elected officials. The two most important were the tribunes of the *pleb*s, who could act as a check on the authority of the senate, and military tribunes, who commanded sections of a Roman legion.

triclinium   A formal dining couch for reclining at mealtimes, extending round three sides of a table, and usually in three parts. see *domus.*

triens   Roman coin worth five twelfths of an *as*.

Trinovantes   One of the Celtic tribes of pre-Roman Britain. Their territory was present day Suffolk and Essex. Their capital was Camulodunon, present day Colchester. Caesar described them as about the strongest tribe in Southeast Britain.

Tyrian Purple   A reddish-purple natural dye. The name refers to Tyre in Lebanon, an early Phoenician metropolis. It is secreted by predatory sea snails. Extracting the dye involved tens of thousands of snails and substantial labour, and as a result, the dye was highly valued.

uncia   Roman coin worth one twelfths of an *as*.

urban praetor   see ***praetor***.

Vate   One of three classes of Celtic priesthood, the other two being the druids and the bards. The vates were the prophets and performed human sacrifices under the authority of the druids. In pagan Rome, the vates lived on the Hill of the Vates i.e. the Vatican.

Veneti   A Gallic tribe dwelling in Armorica, in the northern part of the Brittany peninsular. A powerful seafaring people, defeated by Caesar's fleet in 56 BC.

Venus Victrix   The gens Julia claimed descent from Aphrodite/Venus, and that was important to their political ambitions. Recognising the significance of a connection with a popular deity, Gnaeus Pompeius Magnus dedicated a temple to Venus Victrix ('Bringer of Victory') built on the top of the *cavea* of his Theatre in 55 BC.

vestibulum   see *domus*.

Gaius **Verres**   Roman magistrate, notorious for his misgovernment of Sicily. Successfully prosecuted by Cicero, despite engaging Hortensius to defend himself in 70 BC.

Via Cassia   An important Roman road branching north-east from the Via Flaminia (Flaminian Way) near Rome.

Via Praetoria   see *castrum*.

Via Principalis   see *castrum*.

Via Sacra   The main street of ancient Rome. Leading from the top of the Capitoline Hill through the forum. It was part of the traditional route of the Roman Triumph that began on the outskirts of the city.

Viridovix   He assumed the command of a Gallic army and was defeated by Caesar's *legate* Quintus Titurius Sabinus in 56 BC.

wattle   A fabrication of poles interwoven with slender branches and reeds to form a wall or fence.

Way of Lugh   An ancient road oriented on the summer solstice connecting the British ports of Noviomagus (Chichester) with Durobrivae (Rochester).

Wedding of Ceyx   An ancient Greek poem attributed to Hesiod. It was popular for the witticisms and riddles uttered at the wedding banquet, at which Heracles was a guest.

DRAMATIS PERSONAE

Marcus Vipsanius **AGRIPPA**   Born of humble *plebian* origin whose father gained Roman Citizenship.   Schoolfriend of Octavius and Horatius.

ANDROGEUS   of the Cassi. Son of Ludd, brother of Tenvantius, nephew of Vellaunus and Nennius.

Gaius **ANTISTIUS** Vetus   Served with Caesar in Britain as quaestor (senior lieutenant) 55 BC. Previously a tribune in Rome 56 BC.

Marcus **ANTONIUS**   Fled to Greece to escape debt in 58 BC. Joined Aulus Gabinius in Syria as a cavalry commander 57 BC. Participated in the restoration of Auletes to the throne of Egypt 55 BC.

Quintus **ATRIUS**   Roman officer with Caesar in Britain. Commanded the guard of the beached fleet in 54 BC.

AULETES   King Ptolemey XII of Egypt. Father of Cleopatra. Known as Auletes (the flautist). Restored to the throne of Egypt by the army of Gabinius 55 BC.

BODELIC   of the Cantiaci. The marsh guide.

BRENNUS   of the Cantiaci. Captain of the bodyguard of Queen Cordelia.

Gaius Julius **CAESAR**   Statesman, general and governor of both Cisalpine and Transalpine Gaul. Member of the Triumvirate with Crassus and Pompeius. Consul 59 BC.

CARADOC of the Cassi. Son of Aurgania, nephew of Vellaunus and Nennius.

CARANTUS of the Bibrocti. Tribal leader and supporter of Cassivellaunus.

CARVILLUS of the Cantiaci. Brother of Taximagulus, father of Cingetorix and husband of Gonerila.

CASCA Roman soldier of the 7th Legion.

CASPAR Student of the druid priesthood amongst the Trinovantes.

CASSIVELLAUNUS See Vellaunus.

Marcus Tullius **CICERO** Roman statesman, lawyer, scholar and philosopher. Consul 63 BC. Brother of Quintus, friend of Hortensius.

Quintus Tullius **CICERO** *Legate* of Caesar in Britain 54 BC. Brother of Marcus.

CINGETORIX of the Cantiaci. Son of Carvillus and cousin of Segovax.

CLEOPATRA Daughter of Auletes.

COMMIUS King of the Atrebates. Trusted ambassador of Caesar.

CORDELIA Queen of the Cantiaci. Daughter of Llyr, sister of Gonerila and Rigontia.

Marcus Licinius **CRASSUS**   Roman general and statesman. Member of the Triumvirate with Caesar and Pompeius. Richest man in Rome. Consul 70 and 55 BC.

Gaius **CRASTINUS**   *Primus Pilus* Centurion of the 10th Legion. Served in Britain under Caesar.

DEMETRIOS   of Gadara. Freedman of Pompeius. Janitor at the Domus Rostrata.

DIANANN   Daughter of the forest goddess, Flidais, and priestess of the druids. Protectress of Cordelia.

DIGUEILLUS   Chief advisor to Queen Cordelia.

Lucius Marcius Philippus (**DROOPYPUS**)   Son of Lucius Marcius Philippus (consul 56 BC), brother of Marcia, step brother to Octavius and Octavia.

Quintus Laberius **DURUS**   Military tribune of the 10th Legion. Served with Caesar in Britain in 55 and 54 BC.

DWYNRID   Priest of the druids. Brother of Eneid.

EBRACUS   of the Trinovantes. Elder brother of Scaeva.

EPONA   Celtic goddess of horses.

FABERIUS   private secretary to Caesar.

FELIX   Father of Horatius. Auctioneer in the forum and supporter of the Red Faction.

FLIDAIS   Celtic goddess of the Coit Andred forest.

Aulus **GABINIUS**   Roman politician and general. Governor of Syria and supporter of Pompeius. Reinstated Auletes to the throne of Egypt. Consul 58 BC.

GALBA   King of the Suessiones. Commander-in-chief of a Belgic alliance against Caesar in 57 BC.

GESTORIX   of the Trinovantes. Military Commander. Friend of Mandubracus and uncle to Scaeva.

GNAEUS Pompeius Magnus   See Pompeius.

HELI   Eldest of the sons of Lugios by his first wife Moru. Emerged as King of the Cassi after territorial disputes with his half-brothers: Madawc (who became the Brehin), Blad and Llyr, on the death of their father. Heli had three sons, Ludd, Vellaunus and Nennius, plus two daughters, Aryanrot and Aurgania.

HIRELGLASS   of the Cassi. Son of Aryanrot, nephew of Vellaunus and Nennius.

Quintus **HORATIUS** Flaccus   Schoolfriend of Octavius and Vipsanius (Agrippa). Known in the English-speaking world as Horace, the leading Roman lyric poet during the time of Augustus (also known as Octavian).

Quintus **HORTENSIUS** Hortalus   Roman lawyer, orator and statesman. Friend and professional opponent of Cicero. Consul 69 BC.

IMMANUENTUS (Manan)   Son of Madawc the Brehin by his second wife, Etain. Adopted by Llyr when his widowed mother remarried. Killed his brother, Malin, before murdering his cousin Ludd, and his wife, Luna (Immanuentus' half-sister) in Camulodunon to claim his right to the throne of the Trinovantes. Father of Mandubracus.

JULIA   Daughter of Caesar, wife of Pompeius.

JULIA (Minor)   Youngest of Caesar's two older sisters. Grandmother of Octavia and Octavius.

Titus Atius **LABIENUS**   Born in Cingulum near Picenum. Senior *legate* of Caesar during his campaigns in Gaul. He was left in full command of the legions during Caesar's winter returns to his province. He was a skilled cavalry commander.

LOLLIA   Wife of Aulus Gabinius.

LUDD   of the Cassi   Eldest son of Heli. Ludd married his cousin Luna, daughter of Madawc the Brehin, on the death of her uncle Blad to unite the Cassi with the Trinovantes against tribes and mercenaries migrating to Britain from Belgica and Gaul. He fortified the citadel of Camulodunon and was murdered by Manan (Imanuentus), who was Luna's half-brother. Ludd had two sons, Androgeus and Tenvantius.

LUGOTORIX   of the Cantiaci. Nobleman, loyal to Cordelia.

MAGNUS   See Pompeius.

MANDUBRACUS   of the Trinovantes. Son of Immanuentus.

MARCIA   Daughter of Lucius Marcius Philippus, Husband of Hortensius, sister of Droopypus, stepsister of Octavius and Octavia.

MARCUS   See Marcus Cassius SCAEVA or Marcus Vipsanius AGRIPPA.

NENNIUS   of the Cassi. Son of Heli, brother of Ludd and Vellaunus.

OCTAVIA   Sister of Octavius.

Gaius **OCTAVIUS** Thurinus   Grandson of Caesar's youngest sister, Julia (Minor) Great-nephew of Caesar. Brother of Octavia and schoolfriend of Horatius and Vipsanius.

Lucius **ORBILIUS** Pupillus   *Grammarian* who taught in Rome. A strict disciplinarian.

Quintus **PEDIUS**   Son of Caesar's eldest sister. Served with Caesar in Gaul 58-56 BC before returning to Rome to run for office.

PERRUS   Agent of Commius in Gaul. Colleague of Teuto.

PHILIP   See SCAEVA of the Trinovantes.

Julius **PHILIPPUS**   See SCAEVA of the Trinovantes.

PHILIPPUS   See DROOPYPUS.

PHILOSTRATOS   Head librarian at the Great Library of Alexandria and tutor to Cleopatra.

Lucius **PINARIUS** Scarpus   Grandson of Caesar's eldest sister, Julia (Major). Great-nephew of Caesar. Second cousin and rival gang leader of Octavius at school.

Gnaeus **POMPEIUS** Magnus   Roman general and statesman. Member of the Triumvirate with Caesar and Crassus. Married to Caesar's daughter Julia. Consul 70 and 55 BC.

Lucius **RACILIUS**   *Legate* of Caesar in Britain 55 BC. Previously tribune in Rome 56 BC.

Quintus Titurius **SABINUS**   *Legate* of Caesar during his Gallic wars.

SCAEVA   of the Trinovantes. Brother of Ebracus. Adopted by Caesar and given the name Gaius Julius Caesar Scaevanus Philippus (lover of horses). Abbreviated by Pompeius to **Philip.**

Marcus Cassius **SCAEVA**   *Aquilifer* (eagle standard bearer) of the 10th Legion.

SEGOVAX   of the Cantiaci. Son of Taximagulus and cousin of Cingetorix.

Titus **SILLIUS**   *Legate* of Caesar in Britain in 55 BC. Taken prisoner with Velanius by the Veneti the previous winter.

TAXIMAGULUS   of the Cantiaci. Brother of Carvillus, father of Segovax and husband of Rigontia.

TENVANTIUS   of the Cassi. Son of Ludd, brother of Androgeus, nephew of Vellaunus and Nennius.

Atia Balba **(TERTIA)**   Third daughter of Julia (Minor) and aunt of Octavia and Octavius.

TEUTO   Agent of Commius in Gaul. Colleague of Perrus.

Quintus **VELANIUS**   *Legate* of Caesar in Britain in 55 BC. Taken prisoner with Sillius by the Veneti the previous winter.

VELLAUNUS of the Cassi. Son of Heli, brother of Ludd, Nennius, Aryanrot and Aurgania.

Marcus **VIPSANIUS** Agrippa   See Marcus Vipsanius AGRIPPA.

www.ingramcontent.com/pod-product-compliance
Lightning Source LLC
Chambersburg PA
CBHW031435160726
47994CB00005B/1735